Hannah Kingsley was a fina Young Writers Award. In ad special edition, sprayed-edges produced custom editions for Penguin Random House, Bonnier Books and many more.

Hannah lives in Wiltshire with her husband and Billy, their three-legged cat. *Soul Hate* is inspired by her frustration at the romanticisation of 'fate', when she believes that choosing who you love is far more romantic than destiny.

- instagram.com/HannahKingsleyAuthor
- tiktok.com/@HannahKingsleyAuthor

SOUL HATE

HANNAH KINGSLEY

One More Chapter
a division of HarperCollins*Publishers* Ltd
1 London Bridge Street
London SE1 9GF
www.harpercollins.co.uk

HarperCollins*Publishers*
Macken House, 39/40 Mayor Street Upper,
Dublin 1, D01 C9W8
This paperback edition 2025
1
First published in Great Britain in ebook format
by HarperCollins*Publishers* 2025

Copyright © Hannah Kingsley 2025
Hannah Kingsley asserts the moral right to be identified
as the author of this work

A catalogue record of this book is available from the British Library
ISBN: 978-0-00-870752-1

This novel is entirely a work of fiction. The names, characters and incidents portrayed in it are the work of the author's imagination. Any resemblance to actual persons, living or dead, events or localities is entirely coincidental.

Printed and bound in the UK using 100% Renewable Electricity
by CPI Group (UK) Ltd
All rights reserved. No part of this publication may be reproduced, stored in a retrieval system, or transmitted, in any form or by any means, electronic, mechanical, photocopying, recording or otherwise, without the prior permission of the publishers.

To Alex,
In a world where soulmates are forged, not found, I am forever glad we chose each other.

PROLOGUE

At the dawn of humanity there was a couple in love.

Aldo and Chiara. Young, beautiful, and utterly enamoured with each other. Their love was known across the land. Their devotion unmatched and unparalleled, a marvel for many to witness.

In fact, they loved each other so much, they proclaimed that no feeling nor command in the world or heavens could compare to this. They boasted proudly how Fate could do nothing to tear them apart and they forswore the emotion of Hate entirely, for how could any power or emotion ever equal the love they had for one another.

Father Fate heard their boastful words, and was angered by their rudeness and rebellion. So he sent his daughter, Sister Hate, to teach them a lesson.

On the first night, Sister Hate came to them, and set them a challenge. She whispered to Aldo, that he must show his devotion to Fate and earn her father's forgiveness. He must kill Chiara's beloved brother. To aid him, Sister Hate filled

Aldo with such burning rage, he was blinded to almost everything. Except his love for Chiara. Aldo resisted the hatred, and by the next day he still had not done as Fate had asked.

The following night, Sister Hate returned, instructing Chiara that to earn Fate's forgiveness she must prove her dedication to him. She must kill Aldo's mother. Chiara was filled with a fire that pained her every muscle, that tore her insides apart. But with Aldo by her side and his love as her armour, she made it to the next day and did not do as Fate asked.

On the third night, Sister Hate returned for a final time. Her father was so enraged by the couple's defiance, she laid bare the most devastating command of all. *Kill their son*, or else every person in the world will feel the torment that consumes them. *Kill their one and only child*, or Father Fate will bring his burning rage upon the whole of humanity and ensure his commands are never disobeyed again. Once more, Sister Hate filled them both with a fire so untenable and agonising, with urges so violent and brutal to help them in their task.

But Aldo and Chiara were selfish with their love. Their pride was so wilful, their defiance so strong, they refused again to complete the task Fate had set for them. As the clock struck midnight, their infant child remained alive.

Father Fate was enraged that anyone dare defy his will, and sent out his daughter to do his bidding once more. He bound the most extreme, violent loathing to each living human soul, and every soul that would come after them. He bound the people to each other in a blanket of hatred. To punish Aldo and Chiara, they were the first pairing to be consumed by Sister Hate's dark, violent loathing. They beat each other to death in the home they had made. Soon people turned against those they had once loved, violence and darkness consuming humanity for a whole day.

Sister Love watched her father's command, and wept for the loathing that was enveloping the world. Horrified to see a world so out of balance, she petitioned her father to bring her will down upon the earth to match her sister's, to provide hope and light as an antidote to the violence and darkness. Father Fate agreed, and for the final time, brought down a blanket of love to match her sister's. He bound every human soul to two others. The first, an ideal, perfect romantic partner to travel with through life. A love so pure and a joy so rich, a gift sent from Fate to be thankful for. A Soulmate. The second, a vile archnemesis to fill their world with blistering fire and immeasurable agony, a person Fate demanded be killed to show duty and devotion. A Soulhate.

Father Fate has used these bonds ever since to convey his will, to remind his people of their duty towards him and his great work. Defying him comes with great consequences, not just for us but for the world as a whole. That hasn't stopped people trying.

But Fate always has the last laugh.

CHAPTER I

I'm Renza Di Maineri, and Fate is a sick, twisted god.

I don't think he likes me much, either.

Fate's mocking sniggers lurk faintly in my ears as my gaze locks on the cardinal's empty seat. Tall creamy columns proudly flank the gaping absence. Wrapped with exquisite gold and silver filagree, they drip with vivid hues and rainbow flecks cast down by the spectacular stained-glass ceiling of the High Chamber. The breathlessly beautiful glass dome glows with an ethereal majesty, filling this circular chamber with rivers of coloured light from every corner of creation. Yet my eyes don't stay skyward for long, falling back to the cardinal's vacant seat. The twisted dark wood bleeds crimson as the late sunshine rushes through the arched stained window behind it. A spotlight to showcase its emptiness.

No note. No warning. Cardinal Bellandi left our city without a word two days ago. No one knows why, or when he'll return.

It's beyond irresponsible. He's an Electi, one of the seven elected officials that govern our free city of Halice. Free in that our city earned its independence almost three centuries ago from the sprawling empire of the Holy States. As an Electi, it's both our privilege and responsibility to guide Halice from one greatness to the next—but he didn't deign to inform us he was running off. He couldn't even muster the decency to send a proxy. Everyone else is here. Every other dark wooden seat is filled by their representative. Heck, even the audience is filled with all the usual faces, their muttering a low, ever-present hum at the back of my mind.

I press my lips together, holding back the indignation bubbling in my chest. This is the first time I've put a bill before the High Chamber without my father as co-author. This bill is mine alone, and I've worked hard to bring my fellow Electi to my side. This isn't the first time I've lost a vote of course, but to lose like this? It makes the bite so much sharper.

I refuse to give my opponents the satisfaction of seeing me sweat. Instead, I shift my weight in my chair, brushing off the immaculate silk of my blue tunic. The decorative pins running along the top of my sleeves twinkle with the movement.

"This motion is about enrichment, about peace, about prosperity." I rip my eyes away from the empty seat and towards my father's impassioned speech. He supports my motion, though others think it's really his in disguise. At least we both know the truth of it.

The tall, circular chamber is beginning to darken thanks to the lateness of today's session. The creamy stone columns and intricately carved walls are pooled with shadows, sliced with rippling prismatic light gushing through the ornate stained-glass dome above their heads. Pillars of yellow, pink and blue strike through the encroaching shadows; the lazy dust dancing in their path transformed into flickering, glittering art.

All those beams gather into a single white stream, falling on the circular stage in the centre of our seven chairs. That's where my father, Tomas Di Maineri, stands, his dark hair and time-lined face cast in a thousand bold flecks of light.

"The value of the Garden is always returned a thousand-fold. It has always been, and will always be, a valuable investment," Father continues, moving without falter around the mosaicked central stage. He takes care to meet the gaze of each of our fellow Electi, cobalt fire in his eyes and passion championed on his tongue. A master in command of his work.

Electi Jacopo Patricelli watches with lips thinned and eyes pinched. He's been Father's main opposition in this chamber for years. And today marks him as one of mine.

His chair sits in front of my favourite window; yellow and patterned with climbing flowers. It floods his fair face and receding blond hair with a buttery warmth—which does nothing to soften his disdain. He doesn't study our colleagues' faces for hints; he doesn't take notes or murmur arguments under his breath. His unnerving patience turns my stomach. How confident is he that this vote will fall in a split?

If we lose this vote on a technicality I swear to Fate's Fury, Bellandi will have me to answer to.

"That is why investing in the Garden is the only real way to truly preserve the greatness of Halice through the ages. To embolden opportunity. To empassion beauty. To empower innovation." Father presses a hand to his heart, sincerity soaked into his words. "Esteemed Members of the High Chamber, I do not deny that Member Patricelli has many informed opinions. The extra finances would indeed make our City Guard stronger. But stronger for what? Safer from whom? We are at peace. Our neighbours are our allies. Will that continue if we signal we are readying for war? Will we not appear as aggressors? History remembers the horrors of the sword with scorn. Yet, the accomplishments of the mind last forever."

Father looks around at the sway votes one last time before smiling, head held high.

"Esteemed Members, I relinquish the floor."

Father returns to his seat, flashing me a quick wink as he goes. I nod slyly, eyes skipping to Member Yaleni's face. Marble is more forgiving than their expression. Each angle of their features is tinted a vivid green thanks to the window behind. My stomach rolls under my ribs.

I've worked at Yaleni tirelessly the past four weeks. Yaleni's election-winning votes came mostly from the farming and rural regions in the land around our city, meaning the distribution of tax to either the Guard or the Garden is a persuadable issue for them. I'm still not certain on how they'll cast their vote. Jacopo Patricelli has also undertaken his fair share of political manoeuvring; I feel certain Member Gattore is on his side. Jacopo's face creases, the corner of his mouth twitching upwards. The tinge of smugness in his movements sends a surge of doubt up my spine.

Jacopo surveys our colleagues.

"Any more comments on this bill?" His deep voice rolls around the quiet chamber.

No one stands to claim the floor.

"In which case, we shall vote."

I open the small panel in the arm of my seat, running my fingers over a number of coloured stones, indicating how my seat will cast their vote. Jacopo clears his throat. It's his turn to lead the vote. In the event of a split, he decides the outcome.

"In the matter of redistributing the unexpected additional funds gained from the glass tax this year, you may cast your votes as follows. For the movement presented by myself, Member Jacopo Patricelli, to allocate the extra funds to our military, cast red. For the movement presented by Member Renza Di Maineri, to allocate the extra funds to the Garden, cast blue."

I close my fingers around the blue stone, glancing to see my father confidently doing the same. My heart leaps to throb in my throat. This is my bill, my first solo-authored bill. How it lands will set a tone for my future proposals and how I'm viewed in here—whether I'm just my father's lacky or an independent voice to consider. The next few seconds determine everything. I look across to Member Yaleni. Their face is unmoving as they select their stone, keeping it close to their palm.

"Cast!"

All at once, six coloured stones fly onto the circular

white stage. My heart jumps, catching a flash of blue coming from Yaleni's hand as it leaps into the centre of our circle.

I've done it. I've swayed them!

Yet the high sours when my gaze darts across the stones. My heart sinks. I close my eyes, slipping back in my seat. Disappointment curls like a bitter aftertaste at the back of my tongue. Three blue, three red. Electi Morteselli had switched.

The grin on Patricelli's face says it all.

Every session of the High Chamber is open to the public, anyone is allowed to attend. It's the law. The spectator seats erupt with chatter. Surprise. Upset. Some angry, some thrilled. Their voices bounce off the domed ceiling ringing around the tall columns and decorated walls.

"The votes are cast. A split," announces Member Morteselli, sitting back in his seat currently strewn in a veil of violet light. I clench a fist, my teeth on the verge of shattering. If looks could blister, there would be a smoking pile of embers where that damned empty chair stands. Curse Bellandi and whatever he's doing! Patricelli sits back with a triumphant grin, turning pointedly to my father.

"NOT QUITE!"

A deep voice rolls across the circular chamber, drowning out everything else. Voices still. Questions rise as heads turn in unison.

The arched High Chamber doors hang open, swaying slightly. The setting sun frames the newcomer's inky silhouette in amber and gold as they march across the brightly tiled floor. He strides down the aisle, through the rows of spectators until he reaches the gate. The City Guard swoop forwards, preventing him from getting any further.

As the newcomer moves towards our chairs, colours ripple around him like a diamond personified. His ebony hair flutters with each tilt of his head, that chiselled jaw set with determination as he waves a letter in his hand.

"I bring a message from Cardinal Bellandi. I'm to be his proxy." It takes me a minute longer than it should to place that face and that deep, rich voice. The years apart have changed him so much. A smile creeps up around the corners of my mouth.

"Too late! The vote is cast and called," snaps Patricelli getting to his feet.

"But not yet ratified," I disagree, with a steady voice and unwavering gaze. "Section thirty-five of the Absence Bill, written into law five years after our founding, states that any Electi may vote only once, but may cast that vote at any point before the voting is ratified. Not called. Ratified. Which has not yet happened."

My heart gallops. My pulse thunders in my fingertips.

Patricelli narrow his eyes.

"He's a proxy, not Electi."

"Amendment two to that bill, written into law thirteen years after founding, states that a legal proxy must be treated with the full respect and consideration given to an Electi during their time acting as proxy. Would you like me to list the last three times this amendment was enacted, because one was by yourself but three months ago?" I refuse to back down. At twenty-one, I might be the youngest Electi ever elected, but I know the law. Bluster can't intimidate the mountains, so neither will it me. "Proxy or not, so long as he has written confirmation adorned with the cardinal's seal, he may cast for Cardinal Bellandi."

"Which I do!" Our hero's voice is deep and rich like listening to crushed velvet. Has he always sounded like that? Or is my memory failing me? Patricelli marches over to the gate, snatching the rolled letter out of our mystery hero's hand. He slips it open, face falling in a single moment.

I hold my breath, waiting for Patricelli to speak. To disallow a legal representative to cast in the High Chamber is treason. We may constantly disagree on policy, but everyone in this room knows Patricelli would never commit treason. Like my father and I, his motives come from a desire to serve this city.

We simply disagree on how.

Patricelli sighs, nodding at the guard. They part and the newcomer walks onto the floor. I meet his familiar green eyes and my heart skips a beat. I fervently fight the urge to clear my throat; the emerald seems to pierce right into my soul.

"How do you cast, signore...?" Electi Gattore trails off in question.

"Rizaro. I'm Nouis Rizaro, from the Holy States. I have been instructed to cast in favour of the Di Maineri motion."

Chatter erupts from the spectator seats. The crimson light of the window enshrines Nouis as he sits in the cardinal's seat. Nouis looks for the compartment with the stones, fingers running over the twisted wood for an opening. He looks up, catching my eye with those startlingly sharp ones. I slyly tap the right arm of my chair, where my panel holding the stones is still open.

Humour rolls across that face, mischief sparkling in his gaze. He mouths his thanks before holding up a blue stone, tossing it into the centre of the room.

"The votes are cast. The Di Maineri motion is called." Jacopo spits the words from between clenched teeth. Relief and pure, giddy joy bubbles up in my stomach. Patricelli and his loyalists march away, ending the session in a hump. They retreat through the giant arched doors and into the sunset.

Victory is ours. Victory is mine.

CHAPTER 2

"I'm going to find Giulia," I tell Father as we stride out of the High Chamber, descending the grand steps with a bouncing gait. Each step is intricately carved and painted, reaching with rippling technicolour patterns to the open square below. Tall buildings of creamy stone and carved columns surround the square, separated by a maze of busy streets. The High Summer heat is slowly slipping away, the cool shadows slowly leaving their nooks and crannies to stretch across the cobbled stone.

I don't fight the smile stretching across my lips.

Today was a victory for the future. I'm ready to find my sister and celebrate! Good food, wine and a rare but glorious chance to relax—just for one evening, of course. Maybe we'll even grab the girls and go out dancing.

Over my shoulder, Father is backlit by the magnificent stained-glass dome at the top of the High Chamber building. The setting sun slashes the vibrant colours with streaks of amber and vermillion. Cooling shadows wind down the tall, gilded columns and stretch across the bright steps.

At the base of the steps Jacopo marches away, his staunch supporters at his heels and tunic flailing with his frustrated gestures.

"You would've thought after twenty years in service, he'd get used to losing," I chuckle.

"It's always hard to lose a vote that narrowly. Particularly by that kind of margin," Father says graciously. "If my twenty years of opposition with the man has taught me anything, it's that he'll come back swinging on the next bill."

Father and Jacopo had clashed on most issues since they'd both won their respective elections over twenty years ago. Neither wasted an opportunity to try and change this city for the better. The problem was a serious disagreement on what needed changing the most. They often put opposing bills before the High Chamber, meaning only one would pass and the other would fail.

The two had become rather famous for their opposition throughout Halice, the rivalry of Maineri and Patricelli. At first it had managed to stay on the polite side of civil. But then the Patricelli family decided to snub my mother's funeral, and that blatant disrespect cemented the strong opposition between the two camps of supporters.

"We'll be ready. But for today, we won," I remind him. Father grins widely, his blue eyes meet mine. Eyes that mirror my own, not only in colour, but also glinting with victory.

"Yes, go find your sister." He claps his hands, orange tunic shining in the movement. "And bring Michelle with you—this is an occasion for all the family!"

The stifling High Summer heat is beginning to fade. Its hot, sticky fingers trace my hairline, weaving my brown waves with thin threads of perspiration. The ends of my low ponytail trail over my shoulder. I brush back the dark strands wriggling under the lazy efforts of a lacklustre breeze.

Movement drags my gaze over my father's shoulder. A wide grin splits across my face. Our last-minute hero hurries out of the High Chamber, his dark hair gleaming crimson in the fiery sunset. He flashes a cheeky smile when he realises he's finally caught my attention. With shoulders back and one easy hand in his pocket, he quickly descends the few steps to my position.

"Nouis, my boy," my father greets with joyful warmth soaking his words. He wraps Nouis in a brief hug. Nouis laughs, patting my father on the back.

"Well, well, if it isn't the proxy with perfect timing," I chuckle as Nouis turns to face me. He laughs, dimples forming in his cheeks as he rakes a hand through his hair.

"Ah that!" Nouis says with good humour. "Sorry about the theatrics. I rode all day without rest to get here in time. I was afraid I'd be too late."

"Don't apologise, it might have been one of the most spectacular entrances ever seen in that chamber—and as for drama? It's politics. The two walk hand in hand," I snort. "Besides, you just made history. You're the first non-Halician to ever cast a vote in our High Chamber."

"I'll consider it my highest honour," he grins. I step forwards, wrapping this man in a hug.

Fate's Mercy, he's changed. How has it been five years already? We saw each other almost every summer as children, when his uncle came for business to the city. The Rizaro family run the most prominent bank in the Holy States. My family, the Di Maineri, run the biggest and only bank of our success, influence and size outside the Holy States. Naturally the two businesses overlapped.

But he and his uncle hadn't been back in over eight years, and now the gangly teenager from my memories has vanished. In his place is a tall, muscled, charming man. When did that happen?

Still, it begs the question, what is he doing in Halice? Why come all this way from his home in Kavas, the Capital of the Holy States, just to cast a vote—particularly one he had no vested interest in?

I release him, stepping back to tuck a stray, lazy curl behind my ear.

"Giulia didn't tell us you were coming," I say, letting the real question leak through my words. My sister is a brilliant woman and in charge of the family bank. She would've mentioned if Nouis had asked for a meeting.

"Ah, that'll be because she doesn't know. I'm here for other business I'm afraid," Nouis answers with a chuckle. "Still, I was hoping we could all catch up. It's been far too long."

"Absolutely. You must join us for dinner," my father invites, giving him a back-pat. "We were just saying it's a family affair."

"I would be delighted. But first I'll go change," Nouis

laughs. "Wash all the travelling off me and be more presentable."

This is what he looks like after days and days of travelling? Fate really did right by him.

"Where are you staying while you're here?" I ask.

"I'm booked in at the Occasus."

"Forget the hotel, you must stay with us," Father invites brightly.

"I'd hate to impose—"

"Nonsense, Nouis," I laugh, cutting him off. "We have more than enough room and we have so much to catch up on."

"Yes, it appears we do, *Electi*," Nouis teases softly, a sparkle in his eyes as he gives me a small smile. My throat tightens and I chuckle in a vain attempt to relieve it.

"Right, I'll see you two later. Nouis, just head to ours and we'll sort everything out for you," Father says, giving me a parting side squeeze before walking away. "Renza, remember to invite Michelle."

"Will do," I promise. As if I'd ever forget one of my closest friends. I watch my father walk towards our waiting carriage.

"Thank you for your help in there," Nouis says, giving me a friendly shoulder nudge. "I could have been scrambling in that seat for ages looking for the Voting Stones." Fate's Fury, his voice is so soothing and deep. Listening to him speak is like getting into a warmed bed at the end of a long, cold day.

"Of course," I answer, slowly heading for the Garden. "What are friends for?" He walks with me, two of his long strides matching three of mine.

"Still, you have my thanks all the same."

"How long has it been? Eight years?"

"I was last in this city when I was fifteen. So yes, eight years sounds about right," Nouis agrees, shaking his head ruefully. "Though I have met your cousins on occasion."

"Don't hold them against me," I say, only half joking. The Di Maineri banking family was spread far and wide—and held many strong characters.

"Never," laughs Nouis softly. "I merely meant that I've heard a few stories about you over the years. You're an Electi now, winning people's hearts and minds."

"Guilty," I snort. "Hard work but it's worth it."

"Perhaps we can spend some time discussing it, and the last eight years?"

"Of course, that's why you're staying with us." I grin up at him. "So we can all catch up."

"But perhaps the two of us can go out to eat?" He stops suddenly in the street, lowering his voice so only I can hear. "Just you and I, to really catch up. Without needing to filter ourselves for others. Some stories really shouldn't be shared with your father ... and I'm guess you have a few of those yourself."

"Whatever do you mean, signore?" I gasp in mock horror, "I'm a well-behaved young lady."

"I would never cast any other aspersion, signora!" Nouis cackles, giving me a wink as he leans closer. The air between us grows unexpectedly thick, fizzing with something that makes my throat go dry.

My heart sputters at the intense look in those remarkable

green eyes. He cracks a crooked smile, like an unapologetic kid caught with his hand in the cookie jar. He takes a slow step closer, the sunset making his warm complexion glow.

"So, dinner?" he asks again. Suddenly, I'm not sure whether it's just as friends or something more. My thoughts scramble as I mull the argument over.

I shouldn't. He might be a family friend but he is also, technically, a competitor. Financially and politically—he's clearly involved with Cardinal Bellandi somehow. What if we don't work out? What about our friendship? His home is in the Holy States, how could things ever work? *He's Nouis.* I can't decide if that works for him or against him.

"Nouis, I'm not—" I begin but Nouis holds up a hand to cut me off.

"Look, it's just dinner. Two friends reacquainting themselves."

I bite my lip, indecision rolling around my gut. But it stills and solidifies as I meet those gorgeous green eyes. My pulse throbs in my throat as my cheeks warm. My tongue moves of its own accord before I can really consider the words.

"Tomorrow. Eight. I'll pick the place." Nouis grins, the corner of his mouth curling in victory before he could smother it.

"As friends," I say pointedly. Nouis nods, holding up his hands.

"Friends, you got it."

"Now if you'll excuse me," I continue before I can change my mind, "I have to find my sister and tell her you've arrived."

"Of course. I look forward to seeing her again. See you soon, Renza." He inclines his head towards me, stepping backwards before turning to leave with a new bounce in his step.

A high buzzes through my veins as I take off through the streets of Halice. Shadowy curtains and spotlights of amber climb over the tall creamy buildings and busy, winding roads. Citizens wave, smile or simply nod in acknowledgement. Children laugh and call out their hellos. I smile and wave back to each and every one. If only the thrill of victory could be bottled. It's addictive.

The air is limp, all its energy has drained away. The day's heat is baked into the stone of the buildings and radiates from every surface. The painted street columns are slowly being lit to combat the encroaching night. Brilliant murals decorate walls and art pours from every corner, even the cobbled roads beneath me are cut in decorative patterns, all of it leading to one place, and every step closer just gets grander and more beautiful.

I round the last corner and there it stands. The Garden.

Spilling out of the vibrant walled community are wondrous sounds, smells and sights. The telltale signs of the genius held within that can't possibly be held back by something so ordinary as stone and mortar. A huge bang erupts behind those massive walls, and fluttering black smoke pours over the thick brickwork, tickling my nose and sticking to the back of my throat.

No one blinks. No one gasps or even flinches.

It's simply expected of the genius held within.

I take a deep breath as I pass under the giant gates. Every

time I set foot here, a wave of amazement rushes over me just as it did as a child.

The Garden. A community of the most talented minds in the world, each with their own city-funded workshop. Artists, musicians, engineers, designers—the truly exceptional brought together.

This is my favourite place in the whole of Halice. Step through the gate and a person walks on ground that will change the world.

I walk down the familiar wobbly path. Vibrant grass and bursting blue flowers cover the giant courtyard, large, sweet blossom trees throw out rivers of frolicking peachy petals. The painted walls that create this community are also homes, alternating haphazardly between two and three stories tall, with the ground floor of these terraced homes all converted into large, open workshops.

Today, doors and windows are thrown wide in a weak battle with the heat. A violin's sweet tune strokes my ear, mingling with the arrhythmic banging of an engineer next door. On a luscious grassy lawn, two writers argue over prose. Sitting in the branches of a blossom tree, an artisan sketches something into a pad of paper, his fingertips blackened with charcoal.

I stop walking, confronted by a massive contraption that looks half slingshot, half trombone, blocking the path ahead. A familiar pair of long, dark legs stick out from under it. Smoke from a recent explosion lingers in the air around this device, staining my tongue and stinging my eyes.

"Well, well, Serra Stacano," I chuckle as my ex-lover

wriggles out from under the device. "Should've known you'd be the one disturbing the peace."

Serra blesses me with one of her wild grins, pulling the goggles from her eyes to rest them in the dark halo of tight curls on her head. Her skin is the majesty of midnight, and those eyes are the darkest, purest stars I've ever seen.

Why did we break up again? Seeing the engineer caught in the grips of discovery, that undiluted enthusiasm plastered to her face—it brings back every reason I fell in love with her, even sweaty and splattered with grime.

"I'm so close!" Serra explains excitedly, hopping up. "It's almost there. Soon I'll be able to fire the explosions into the sky."

I hand her one of her discarded towels. She wipes her face, sweat shining like a badge of honour as she looks at her project like it's the sun walking.

"Why?" I can't help it. One of the many reasons I'd never be an artisan or engineer: a painful failing of imagination.

"So we can see them!" Her eyes shine as she throws the towel back down. "Explosions are incredible to watch but everyone is always running away, and they destroy everything around them. But if we launch them into the sky, we can relax and enjoy. Nothing to destroy up there."

"Except birds."

"Nasty creatures," Serra retorts.

I snigger, patting her back. "I look forward to the show." I start down the path again, giving her explosion machine a wide berth.

"Yours'll be the first invite," she calls.

"I expect no less!"

She winks before getting back to her contraption. I shake my head before dragging my eyes back to my journey.

I pass a familiar workshop adorned with mint green paint and brilliant yellow flowers. Mother's. Or it used to be. Mother brought us here every day. This was my childhood, wrapped up in discovery. My love for the arts and sciences took root at the knees of the masters.

Bittersweet strings tug at the edges of my heart as images flash past. Little Giulia and I played on the patio while mother worked. My sister passed out on the sofa as I read my books. Evenings where Father would come to get us after Mother forgot the time. He'd always looked at her with so much love, amusement in his eyes even at the late hour.

Now it's home to my mother's best friend, Uncle Ruggie. My step falters slightly as I catch sight of him leaning over his forge, the flames lining the familiar ridges of his face with yellow and orange. The jeweller seems to feel my eyes, turning his head up. He flashes me a smile, and a shallow wave. His grey hair is thick with sweat, that sticks like a second skin on his face, but missing is the old spark of life in his eyes that used to be ever-present as he worked.

I hope one day he'll get it back.

I draw closer a few paces, giving the flames a wide birth.

"Evening, Renza," Uncle Ruggie chuckles, wiping his brow, "Good day?"

"Pretty good thanks," I answer before turning my eyes to the portrait of his daughter, Fausta. I rarely pass this memorial without stopping to think about my friend. The protected portrait is surrounded by planters bursting with colourful flowers. That's what she would've wanted. Living flowers were far more fitting to celebrate her life, nothing dead that could wither away and be forgotten. My gut twists with the memory of her brutalised Soulhate lying still in the mud, lifeless eyes staring endlessly up at the pouring rain.

After a minute more I bid Uncle Ruggie goodbye and continue down the path. I finally come to the workshop I'm actually looking for. Nestled in a corner, the small butter-coloured home could easily be missed. Peaceful and quiet. I walk across the small stone patio, through the wide arched doors and into the open space.

Giulia sits by the window, the stream of vermillion light flooding across the bank documents in front of her. Golden hair falls around her face like waves of spun candlelight. Her enviable porcelain features are pulled in concentration, a pen poised between her slender fingers. Those blue eyes are twinned with my own—a copy of our father's.

A few paces from my sister is her girlfriend, the current occupier of this workshop. A tall, skinny woman with tight, dark curls bundled on top of her head and blue paint smeared across her narrow nose. Michelle's dark eyes are thinned in concentration, shoulders pinched as she carefully wields a paintbrush against a canvas board.

I cross the wooden floors quietly, standing behind the artist as she works. This depiction of Giulia is going to be phenomenal when it's finished. Michelle's work is so expressive, every emotion poured into paint. Her total adoration for my sister is evident in each brushstroke.

Michelle's head springs up, giving me a toothy grin.

"So, did you win?" she asks.

"We won," I answer. She throws her hands up in celebration.

"Yes!"

"Of course, you did," chuckles Giulia without looking up. "I never doubted you."

"Thank you, lovely, even if you're lying through your teeth." I scoff softly, throwing myself into a chair opposite her. The furrowed concentration doesn't leave her brow as a beat passes. "Everything okay here?"

"I'm sure it's nothing." She waves it off, setting down her pen and gesturing to a letter lying open to one side. "Though on another note, Cousin Eliseo is asking for more money for another investment."

"Urgh." I wrinkle my nose and cast my eyes over the irritatingly familiar scrawl. "How ridiculous is this one?"

"I've already written back to his brother instead, to let him know about the request." Giulia shakes her head. "There's no way someone as sensible as Marino knew what Eliseo was asking." I snort at the utterly mad scheme Eliseo details in his letter, chucking it to one side.

"Probably because Eliseo already asked Marino and was soundly rejected." I smirk.

"Enough bank talk. Today was a win for Renza and a win for the Garden. This deserves a celebration!" Michelle excitedly throws down her paint palette and tosses her paintbrush into some water. "We need drinks. I have a bottle here somewhere."

"Great but just the one. We're going out for dinner," I say as Giulia starts sorting the massive pile of banking files and documents to put them away. "Father's handling the details. You're invited too, Michelle, in case that wasn't clear."

I look over my shoulder to see Michelle rattling through her wooden cupboards. Her head pokes out from behind a cupboard door, flashing me a grin and a thumbs up.

"So, how did the session go?" Giulia asks. "Smooth sailing?"

"Hardly," I scoff as Michelle reappears with a bottle and glasses, starting to pour generously before sliding the drinks around the table. "Cardinal Bellandi didn't bother to turn up."

"No!" Giulia gapes, doing the mental maths before quickly adding, "Did Bellandi nominate a proxy?"

I nod, sipping my drink.

"He did, but the proxy didn't turn up until after the votes were cast and called. Thankfully the proxy got there before it was ratified. At the last minute, he charged into the chambers with the papers held high and saved the vote."

"Wow." Michelle sits down next to my sister, pecking the side of her head with a kiss. "Dramatic much."

"Tell me about it."

"Oh well," shrugs Michelle. "All's well that ends well, right?"

"Speaking of dramatic, has Serra lost a finger yet?" asks Giulia.

"Not from what I saw." I frown, turning to Michelle. "Do you get why she wants to launch an explosion into the sky?"

"Engineers are a law unto themselves." Michelle shakes her head. "Art doesn't involve risking life and limb. At least mine doesn't." Giulia links her fingers around her girlfriend's hand and lifts it up, giving it a quick kiss.

"A fact I'm thankful for every day."

An explosion punctuates Giulia's words. The drinks ripple. The plants shudder. A flicker of worry passes between Giulia and me. In tandem we lean out of our seats to see another flurry of black smoke rise into the sky. I get up, crossing to the door quickly.

"Serra?" I yell down the street. "You alive?"

A beat passes.

"All good!" her muted voice comes back. Shaking my head, I cover my eyes, unable to stop the nervous smile breaking across my features.

Giulia snorts, a spark filling her blue eyes as she watches me.

"You know ... she might be free tomorrow night," she starts, slyly.

"Well, I'm not. I have dinner plans," I explain quickly. It's not a real date, just two old friends catching up ... alone ... right?

"With who?" demands Michelle immediately, setting down her drink. Giulia bolts forwards in her seat, the banking now completely forgotten. I smile, sipping on my wine to hold the suspense a moment longer.

"Bellandi's proxy of course. Nouis Rizaro."

"Nouis is back?" Giulia grins, eyes going wide with delight. "What's he doing in Halice?"

"Business, I think. We'll have to ask him at dinner; he's coming tonight," I dismiss with a wave.

"Who's Nouis?" Michelle asks eagerly.

"An old family friend," Giulia quickly explains. "We used to spend our summers together. So he finally asked you out, huh? When you said dinner plans you really meant date."

"What do you mean 'finally'?" Michelle pushes, head leaning on her hand as she settles into the gossip.

"It's not like that. He's asked to go out as friends," I shoot back at Giulia.

"Nouis always had a crush on Renza, ever since we were little. It was so sweet but also really painfully obvious," Giulia chuckles. "And don't be silly, Renza, of course it's a date."

"It's not like that," I insist, leaning back in my seat.

"Oh my gosh, from when you were both little? Like, as in first sight?" gasps Michelle excitedly. "What if he's your Soulmate? They say that if two people meet when they're really young that sometimes it can be tricky to tell."

I wrinkle my nose in disgust. The memory of how Fausta had transformed when meeting her Fated hovers like a bad taste in my mouth.

Everyone has their Fated. Two other people that Fate has linked you with for life. The first, a Soulmate, a partner perfectly designed by the gods to be your one true love. The second, a Soulhate, that one person destined to be your most loathed enemy. It's a fact of life. We all have our Fated; our Soulmate and our Soulhate. Meeting them, however, is a matter of chance. It's uncommon but it happens, one in ten, or so the saying goes.

A Fated Bond can never be broken. Once discovered, it's for life—however long or brief. Thousands of people have tried to break with their Fated over the centuries. History books brim with sweeping brutal tragedies around such a hopeless quest.

And yet, seeing how Fausta changed upon meeting her Soulhate, I could see the path towards that desperation.

Fausta had been one of the sweetest, most caring people I'd ever met. When we were kids she was forever nursing animals back to health or stopping to help when people were upset. She spent all of her free time volunteering with various charities and had just begun training to be a nurse.

But then she met her Soulhate. In an instant I watched this sweet, gentle woman turn into a vicious, bloodthirsty animal. Clawing at a woman she'd just met at a bar—she didn't even know her name yet—Fausta started spitting words calling for her death. That Fate-inflicted loathing, an unfathomable urge to kill a complete stranger, had transformed her into a totally different person.

Fausta and her Soulhate decided to follow tradition and duel at dawn, to settle it once and for all as the Church taught us. A fight to the death. And as per tradition, the duel was held privately for "the sake of public decency". Both sides of the fight were allowed two spectators. Fausta asked her father, Uncle Ruggie, to spectate, and then she asked me. One of my closest friends was potentially marching to her death. How could I refuse?

A holy servant was required to be present to sanction it. On learning I'd be attending, Cardinal Bellandi offered to be there personally as moral support for all involved—despite it being a little beneath his position.

So I watched the sweet girl I'd grown up with, the girl that saved baby birds and helped every single kid that scraped their knee, as she tried to slaughter this stranger. The two fought with daggers as rain poured from the sky. There was no skill. It was gruesome and brutal. It was just wild lashing and unrestrained loathing.

I wanted to stop it. To save Fausta. To end the senseless violence of it all. We all did, but we weren't allowed. Then the other woman stopped moving and the cardinal declared her dead. But Fausta's injuries were ghastly. She limped home, and died two days later, consumed by grief at what she'd done.

Uncle Ruggie hasn't been the same since, and truthfully, I don't think I have either.

The idea of Fate controlling something so visceral and important makes me physically uncomfortable. And while a Soulmate is vastly different from the raw fury and loathing of a Soulhate, the Soulmates I've seen have rarely been as easy or romantic as the Church screams at us they should be. They seem to be dramatic, twisted and designed for Fate's entertainment, rather than actually matching us with the right people. Yet...

I was instantly attracted to Nouis when I saw him again. Maybe, it was just because he's handsome, or perhaps it was his confidence. Or maybe because he swooped in like a hero and saved my first solo bill?

I shake my head, shifting towards my seat.

"I don't ... I don't think so," I say the words out loud, to myself more than anything. I furrow my brow. "I mean, he's—objectively—attractive for sure. But nothing ... Fated."

I forced the last word out past the lump in my throat.

"Besides," I continue, "it's just dinner between old friends. Nothing more."

"Nothing more, right. He's just '*objectively attractive*'." Giulia mocks my words with a snort, "Don't kid yourself, Renza, this is a date."

Michelle's face stretches to a cheeky grin. "When was the last time you even went on a date?"

"I see people," I argue.

"One-night flings are not dating." Giulia counters without missing a beat. I poke my tongue out at her.

"Not all of us can be in nauseatingly happy, committed relationships at the ripe old age of twenty," I jab back with a teasing grin. "I'm enjoying my life."

"So Nouis, he was Bellandi's proxy?" Michelle's face crinkles, questions brewing in her eyes. "How does he know Bellandi?"

"I'm guessing through the Church? I mean, Nouis's aunt is the Holy Mother," I offer, mind spiriting away to Giulia's comment and that victorious smile on Nouis's face. Did he think it was a date?

Giulia narrows her eyes at me for a long moment. She sighs.

"Go on, out with it," she commands. I give her a sour look, to which she only raises her eyebrows.

"What's wrong. You're all…" Giulia waves a hand at me like that was enough description. I shrug.

"You really think it's a date?" I say in response.

"Yeah," Giulia and Michelle answer at the same time. I bite my lip.

"What if I ruin our friendship? He lives in Kavas; I live

here. How could things work? He is the heir to our biggest banking rival on this continent; he's technically our competition. He's—"

"He's also one of your oldest friends," Guila says softly, "and he'd never do anything to make you uncomfortable. Besides, you've said yes to dinner, which should tell you something about how you feel about him."

Michelle holds out her glass for the two of us. "Well then, here's to a great day."

I tap my glass to hers and Giulia's, smiling.

"And hopefully a great night too."

CHAPTER 3

The rainbow leaks through the stained window behind the bishop. His black and white robe flails with each exaggerated gesture as he preaches from his pulpit in the Grand Temple.

"Father Fate guides all our actions. Father Fate dictates life's every opportunity at His divine discretion." Spittle flies from his lips, showering the first row with a multicolour spray. The bishop prattles on, his ridiculous hat wobbling like it might fall off.

I close my eyes, head dropping down to pinch the bridge of my nose. My hair acts as a dark curtain as it obscures my boredom from the congregation. A yawn lurks at the back of my mouth.

Halice is technically a city of free religion, a law that was established early on after we gained our freedom from the Holy States. It's this way in many of the Independent States. But with Father Fate taking such an active part in the lives of so many, and the long history of entanglement with the Holy

States, it isn't surprising that the Holy Faith is still the dominant religion of the continent.

But from what I understand, the demands of the Holy Faith are a lot more relaxed here in the Independent States than in the Holy States. For the citizens of Halice, church attendance is not compulsory, but a free choice. Yet many still regularly attend the weekly service held at the Grand Temple, either out of obligation to Father Fate or for the sake of appearances if nothing else.

I should not have drunk that much last night. A headache buzzes at the back of my skull. Noises are sharper. Lights are harsher. Every second ticking by is like sandpaper scraping at a new layer of my brain. I jump, my father suddenly leaning closer.

"Recovering from last night, Renza?" Amusement hides in Father's deep voice. I try to suppress the smirk, eyes flickering up to the pulpit again. Given the amount I drank at the dancehall last night, and the fact I crawled into bed only three hours before we got up to come here, I think I'm handling things wonderfully.

"You know me." I shift on the unforgiving wooden pew, covering my mouth with my hand. "Work hard, play harder. It was worth it."

I turn to look at my father. My smirk begins to infect my father's face.

"Father Fate blessed us with his two divine daughters. Sister Love and Sister Hate!" shouts the bishop, making every half-asleep member of the congregation flinch. Our eyes leap back to the preacher as he slams his fist on the polished stone podium. "The two most divine and powerful of human emotions. The Sisters follow their father's command and bless each of us with our Fated. Our Soulmate and our Soulhate. Those whose lives are woven with our own, those who bring to us the most divine purity of feeling in the world—"

I keep my voice low, trying not to wrinkle my nose as the bench creaks under me. "Still no Cardinal Bellandi? This guy is—"

"Enthusiastic?" The same displeasure ripples from Father's words. "The cardinal has been called back to the Holy States, and is residing in their Capital of Kavas. By personal invitation of the Holy Mother herself."

The Holy Mother is the head of the Holy Faith, the one true interpreter of the gods' will on earth. That fact also makes her the de facto ruler of the sprawling and powerful Holy States Empire. All cardinals across the continent look to the Holy Mother for spiritual guidance and instruction.

"Fate's Fury." I rub my brow to hide my grimace, eyes turning up to the high painted ceiling. "For long?"

"Doubt it. Word would've spread by now."

A moment of silence passes. Restlessness grows, like the memory of an itch running all over my body. I tap my foot to the floor, searching for a distraction.

"I'll give the cardinal this," I whisper to Father, "he gives a blessedly short sermon. While he's away we should look to capitalise in the High Chamber—"

"I'm already on it. Why do you think your sister is sitting with Electi Morteselli?"

I throw a sly look over my shoulder. My scan instead catches on Nouis, given he's only two rows back. His dark hair and angular features are soaked forest green thanks to the window he sits under. He cracks a wicked grin and dares to wink my way. My stomach ripples with warmth. My breath catches in my throat as my pulse races faster. I answer with a flirty smile. My eyes jump a few rows down, skipping past the bright glass depictions and the creamy stone.

My sister's blonde hair gleams blue and pink under another colourful window. As Father said, Giulia sits with Electi Morteselli, leaning in close to whisper in his ear. The golden sister indeed.

I turn back around, a smirk painted on my lips.

"What's the plan?" I whisper.

"If you'd gotten here sooner, perhaps you'd know."

"Don't play that game if you're not prepared to lose," I retort without losing a beat.

A low chuckle radiates from my father's chest. He covers it with a quick cough. After a minute or two of continued preaching, I lean closer.

"We should push—"

"The new trade agreement with Nimal," Father interrupts me. Our eyes meet, agreement sparking between us.

"Excellent." Cardinal Bellandi has always been an obstacle when building stronger trade relations that weren't with the Holy States. Without him, we have a real chance of pushing it through.

"What's more," Father continues, "before church, I struck a deal with Patricelli for how the first year of taxes from it will be spent."

"Do tell."

"We're going to refurbish the housing near the port. The quality is so low, people get sick all the time. Cleaner, better housing will lead to a healthier, happier people and workforce."

"Which is good for Patricelli," I mutter mostly to myself. "They own most of the businesses that move in and out of that port."

"Hence his agreement. He actually invited us over this afternoon to hammer out details."

"Us?"

"Me. But I'm inviting you, assuming you're in?"

Father learnt to ask the hard way. The first time I actively voted against Father, he lost. Father never held it against me. Though losing stung, he claimed it was a balm to know he'd raised a daughter with the strength to act on her own convictions.

That didn't stop the rest of the city seeing it as just an isolated act of youthful rebellion. After all, I'm an extension of my father, of course.

That attitude has followed me from the first day I set foot in the High Chamber like a curse. I got some nasty comments from rivals in my election season, and the whispers never really stopped.

I'm not a yes-man. I don't follow blindly where my father walks. But when I'm in the room, all they really see is him. My father casts a long shadow and it's difficult to find a way free.

"I agree," I assure Father. With Patricelli, Father and I united on a bill? We could really get this through quickly.

"Excellent. Patricelli's cooperation should make this easy."

"Hopefully," I mutter, thinking about the practicality. The

other Electi will want specifics, particularly around the housing and the costs of the project, "I'll line up an architect for housing plans. I'll start work this afternoon."

The bishop slams his hands together. The sharp snapping radiates like lightning over the semi-conscious congregation.

"And now, may we all go in the grace of Fate!" announces the bishop, lifting both hands to the sky.

"Grace of Fate," the congregation choruses. Chatter fills the temple as people file out. The groaning of the wooden pews punctuates the rising voices as the bishop sprints down the aisle to wish everyone goodbye at the door.

I run a hand up my arm, spinning around. My skin is marching with invisible ants.

My father turns to look at me, eyes wide and relieved. "Fate's Mercy, let's hope Bellandi is back before next week."

I snigger and stand, smoothing out my purple satin tunic. My eye catches on the Patricellis in the opposite pew. It'll be impossible to avoid them now. They stood at the same time as us.

They're dressed head to toe in expensive red fabric, fair faces strewn multicolour with streaks of sunshine pouring into the holy space. Their bejewelled shoes clap over the polished tiles as we all ease into the aisle.

"Jacopo," my father's face creases with manufactured warmth. "What time should we come by yours this afternoon, to discuss details?"

"Any time after midday." Jacopo's gaze flickers to me with a tenseness. "We weren't expecting you at service today, Signora Renza."

"Why? I come most weeks," I ask pleasantly.

Jacopo shrugs, a slither of humour warming his tight words. "I thought you'd be celebrating, as is your ... ah ... pattern, after your win yesterday."

"You know me too well, signore." I fabricate an easy, warm laugh. "I woke early, and felt attendance today would be important. Though I'll admit, my head doesn't thank me."

Jacopo cracks a sly smile.

"The joys of youth. Speaking of which, my son will be joining us this afternoon."

"Your son?" My father's response is instantaneous. My heart skips a beat, teeth clamping together. I shake it off, focusing on Jacopo's response.

"Yes, he's arriving home this morning. He's finished his work in Chalgos."

Chalgos, the floating city. I've seen so many depictions in books, I can't help but envy anyone who's had the chance to go there. Formed around a lone mountain protruding from the ocean, the population expanded beyond the capacity of the island. Having no other choice and its position generally protected from any real storm hazards, the population built floating buildings and latched them to the mountain. That idea only spread further and further, and now the majority of the bustling city floats. Before winning its independence, Chalgos was half mine, half prison for the Holy States. Now it's the busiest trading port on the continent, a place known for exceptionally muddy waters around what was legal and illegal trade.

So Patricelli's son has spent time in Chalgos? Doing what, I wonder.

A shadow of doubt flashes over Jacopo's face. "He

should've arrived before the service today, but alas, he was delayed."

"Fantastic news of his return," my father lies brilliantly.

"Yes, it's wonderful to have him home. Do excuse us. We should go meet Idris."

That name.

All the hairs on my arms rise as if a monster lurks behind me.

"We'll expect you at midday, Signore Tomas." Patricelli nods his head towards Father then me. "Signora Renza."

Patricelli and his wife walk down the aisle without another word. I put a hand on the wooden pew, watching them retreat across the blue and white chequered floor. My pulse is jumping. Pins and needles ripple across my toes like they're being nipped at by an imaginary frost.

Idris Patricelli. Jacopo's famed one and only heir is finally returning from his extensive studies abroad.

Only *thinking* the name has me clenching my fingers to keep them still.

Father and I begin to follow the Patricellis, allowing the space between us to grow with each shallow step. We're thinking the same thing.

This changes everything.

Jacopo's not stupid. If his son is coming home, that means he's already working on a plan to make him an Electi. But who would he target? When an Electi wins their seat, it's theirs until they abdicate, die or a vote of no confidence is called. Should the other Electi vote that their colleague is no longer fit for the High Chamber, they are forced to abdicate their seat.

Jacopo wouldn't abdicate his seat for his son. Not when anyone can run for Electi. There's a slim chance, but it's still there that someone completely unknown would snap up the seat in the election.

Meaning Jacopo's going after another seat. He'll either get them to abdicate or call a vote. It's probably not Gatorre's seat. Gatorre won his election by securing the support of the City Guard—and Jacopo hugely supports any bills giving them more money and resources. The two of them are thick as thieves.

Maybe Morteselli? The man is old, and won his election over five decades ago. Perhaps Jacopo knows he wants to step down? Or perhaps he would go after Bellandi or Yaleni? He wouldn't try coming after Father or me ... would he? My stomach churned at the thought.

"We need to seal the Nimal deal tomorrow. No later. We need to discover what Jacopo is planning," I barely utter the words. Father nods, dark hair glinting as he rakes a hand through it.

"I think it's time to introduce myself to Idris Patricelli, see if the rumours about him are true. If he's half as competent as his father, he's worth our concern."

"It certainly makes things more interesting," I agree, clutching at silver linings. Our short strides bring us just paces from the huge arched doors, out into the bright city square. "But competence and experience are wildly different things. I have both in spades, and rapport with every member of the Electi. He's a stranger."

As we arrive at the exit, that crawling sensation over my

skin increases. I look around me, desperately searching for whatever is causing this discomfort.

"He's a powerful stranger looking to cut his teeth. Which makes him dangerous." Father's face creases, lips thinning. He looks at me confused.

"Are you alright?"

"Yeah," I almost bite back. "Why?"

"You're ... bouncing? On edge?" he offers, eyes running up and down as if calculating. "You seem ... not yourself."

"It's just the hangover," I dismiss, turning around. It has to be.

"Are you sure? If you want to go home and rest, I can handle Gattore and Jacopo."

"Don't be ridiculous." I roll my eyes at him, pulling the ends of my low ponytail over my shoulder to keep my hands busy.

A lazy breeze wipes its cool fingers across my nose. I squint against the over-enthusiastic attention of the sun as we reach the front of the line, and turn to the bishop. I take his hands warmly in mine.

"Bishop Adar, fantastic service. I've never felt closer to the gods." I give his fingers a friendly squeeze. "But I'm afraid I must dash. I do hope you'll be able to cover for the cardinal again—should business take him away."

A brilliant smile fills the bishop's round face.

"Always a pleasure to serve, and a delight to see you, Signora Di Maineri. May Fate bless your steps."

"Thank you, and yours, bishop."

I turn around, hopping hurriedly down the first few steps

of the Grand Temple. The bells begin to ring, their tune familiarly arrhythmic as they mark the hour. Blue skies toss golden light over every inch of the great square as I search through the crowd for Electi Gattore's familiar face. Sunshine bounces off the pale stone masonry, spotlighting the bright public murals and the vivid clothes worn by the prestigious congregation.

I stop dead, the task evaporating from my mind. Dread hits me like a fog. I spin on the spot, eyes darting through the crowd.

"Running away so soon?" Nouis seems to materialise beside me. I don't look at him, keeping my gaze on the bustling crowd. My breath comes quickly. My fingers won't keep still, each pulse of my heart echoing in my ears.

"Renza?" asks Nouis concerned.

"Sorry. I have ... work. We'll talk ... later?" I offer, continuing down a step into the crowd. What work again? I can't remember.

Nouis walks with me.

"You don't look ... Are you okay? Can I help?" Nouis asks warily. "Who are you looking for?"

"I don't know," I sigh, spinning around again. I can feel it. I know it. I just can't find it.

Whatever *it* even is.

"Renza?"

"Something's wrong," I whisper. The admission sends a frost through my chest.

"What?" The words are sharp, all sense of mischief dropped from Nouis's voice. He steps closer, his handsome face etched with concern.

"I don't know. I just ... know!" I raise both hands to my

hair, spinning around again. My gaze cuts through the crowd of people, some of which are beginning to give me a side eye. Nouis puts a hand on my back to try and get my attention.

"Okay, then let's leave?" he offers. "I can give you a lift home?"

My ears are ringing with thunder. My fingers spark with discomfort, itching to dig into something, to feel something warm and sticky running over my palms.

At the base of the steps, I spy Jacopo Patricelli and his wife. They're talking with two young men. One takes me a second to recognise as Alfieri Barone. The other is a fair-haired stranger.

The world slows. Every inch of my skin feels like it's splitting and peeling. Revulsion wraps a stranglehold around my throat, dragging me closer. My tongue is coated in bile and bitterness.

I take three steps forwards, ringing consuming my mind, my head suddenly turned to wool. My feet move on their own.

"Renza? Renza!" Nouis tries to get my attention in alarm, taking my arm.

That stranger's face comes into view. His sharp jaw. Glowing creamy skin. Golden hazel eyes snap to mine.

The world goes red.

A brutal scream erupts from my throat and I barrel into my enemy at full speed. I slam him to the ground, smashing his disgusting head against the solid stone. I punch his face, again and again. A satisfying warmth ripples up my arm as my knuckles connect with his jaw, his blood coating my fingers like a soothing balm.

His hands launch forwards, crashing into my face, jarring my chin up and shooting pain through my spine. His backhand goes across my face, sharp stinging ripping across my cheeks.

I shriek as I fall off him. He reaches for me again with both hands, this time aiming for my throat. I knee him in the crotch as hard as I can, watching him buckle and brace himself on the floor. I swipe, my nails going for his eyes. Instead I catch his chiselled cheekbones, carving four gashes. I lunge for him, wrapping my fingers around his throat and clenching tight.

Die! Die! Die!

"Renza! Renza!"

Strong arms wrap around my waist, hauling me away. My bloodthirsty roar rolls between my teeth as I thrash out against the restraints. My nemesis is held back too—the scum. Jacopo and two others grip his arms so tightly their knuckles are white. Blood oozes from his nose, the four gashes on his cheeks leak and crimson drips from his jaw to mar the creamy stone below.

I writhe, fire coursing through my veins. I must destroy him. I *need* to destroy him. Nothing in this world matters more.

Nouis swears behind me, and I realise it's him holding me back. That traitor. My father and sister race through the crowd towards us.

"Renza," shouts my father jumping in front of me, using all his strength to help Nouis hold me back. "Renza, enough! Get her out of here!"

My sister nods, helping Nouis and a member of the City Guard wrestle me back.

"I'll kill him!" I rail against their grip, teeth gritted. The disgust so sharp it curdles in my brain. "I'll rip him apart!"

My sister's slap rockets across my face like dunking me in ice. Gasping, floundering in shock, I stare at her. My heart throbs in my ears and my cheek stings in memory of her touch.

"No, you won't," Giulia snaps at me, her perfect face torn with stern anger. My breath is racing and hot as I stare into her eyes. "That's Idris Patricelli."

No.

My gaze snaps back to my enemy. Five men are kneeling on him, pressing him flat against the floor in an effort to restrain him. A snarl is etched across his features. Utter hatred pours from his hazel eyes.

Everything blisters. Acid burns my tongue.

"Giulia, get her gone. Now!" shouts my father, walking towards the Patricellis. Giulia steps in front of me, face serious, voice sharp.

"Eyes on me, Renza, eyes on me," she barks. Her hands go to my face, forcing me to obey. Nouis pulls me back. I stumble and gasp for breath.

The entire world has shifted under my feet. Only one coherent thought stands out from the torrent of rage, disgust and horror running rampant through my body.

I've found my Soulhate.

CHAPTER 4

I march through the milky columns of my family home. Masterpieces of colour sprawl from every wall, floor, and ceiling, the beautiful paintings a lingering remnant of my mother's touch.

It does nothing to soothe me now.

My heart won't slow; its pace would put a racehorse to shame. Bruises blossom over my knuckles and chin like poisonous flowers, dripping pain into my veins with each sharp movement. My stomach aches. Each breath falls short. My shoes snap against the mosaic floor as I stalk into the living room. I cross to the full-height gothic windows, glaring out at the dancing fountains and sunshine gushing over our manicured garden.

Two people follow me. Nouis and my sister. Giulia sits down on the sofa without saying a word. Nouis pours a shallow glass of wine from the bottle sitting on the sideboard, and crosses to me. He gives me a warm smile, holding out the drink.

"Here." He pushes the glass into my clenched fingers. I take it, unable to meet his eyes.

"Are you hurt?" I manage to mutter.

"Only my pride," he says conspiratorially, leaning on the wall next to me. "You're deceptively strong."

"I'm sorry."

He winks at me, a coy smile flirting with his lips.

"Don't be. I like strong," he whispers, far too low for Giulia to hear. My stomach fizzes with warmth, and my throat goes dry. I shake my head, rubbing my eyes.

"I can't believe he's my Soulhate."

"Everyone has one."

"Have you ever met your Fated?" I ask, now only daring to meet his green gaze. He shrugs, shaking his head.

"I don't think so, but I know some who have. There's no shame in it."

Sure, Nouis. There's absolutely no shame in a barbaric public brawl. Nothing to be embarrassed about, not my feral screaming or unhinged violence.

Fausta's sweet, freckled face contorted with wild rage springs to mind. The blood smeared over her broken nose during her duel. Her visceral, violent transformation into a complete stranger.

Fausta's duel was at sunrise. The sky was stained crimson as rain fell in fat, heavy droplets, as if the city herself already knew what was coming. They slashed at each other without remorse or composure, their blades wet and dripping scarlet. The pain of their injuries was utterly inconsequential next to their loathing. They were consumed, until one lay unblinking and staring up at the weeping sky.

Repressing the bile swelling in my throat, I drink deeply from my wine and desperately pray it'll wash this foul feeling away.

Why did it have to be me?

Why, of all people, did it have to be him?

I spin around, leaning back against the glass. Sunshine strokes the back of my neck, radiating through my dark hair like it's baking the memories of my vile brawl into my skull.

My Soulhate is Idris Patricelli.

As if I needed any more proof that the gods are twisted and sadistic.

"You don't think I'll have to..." I swallow, unable to finish that thought as the memory clogs my throat. Giulia looks up, brow pinching.

"What? Duel at dawn?" She sniffs in disdain. "Bit brutal, don't you think?"

Brutal? Understatement of the century.

"The Church's teachings are clear," Nouis counters in disbelief. "Fate has spoken. One of you must kill the other."

"Rubbish. Fate made a decision and there's no changing it, but Renza still has a choice. So does Idris." Giulia disagrees. "No one else can make it for them, not even Fate."

"But everyone knows that defying Father Fate will bring about his revenge," Nouis says incredulously. "That one way or another, Fate will have satisfaction. If Renza doesn't bend to his decree, worse things will come for her."

Giulia shrugged, a small smile pulling at the corner of her mouth as though this amused her.

"Well, of course you believe that more hardcore superstitious stuff. Your aunt is the Holy Mother," Giulia answers as though this were nothing more than an abstract hypothetical debate, "but Renza doesn't."

Had I been asked mere hours before this, I would have emphatically agreed with Giulia. But now, with the reality looming over me like an axe ready to swing, the words fail to find footing on my tongue.

"Renza." Giulia turns her attention back to me. "You have a choice."

"Perhaps, if it'd happened in private with only a small circle of those in the know. But I attacked him in perhaps the most public way possible. Everyone will expect it," I groan.

"Who cares? We aren't everyone; we are the Di Maineri. Do you want to kill Idris Patricelli?" Guila cuts me off sharply. Like a flash, Fausta's duel replays again in my mind, but this time with me in her place. Her wild strikes are mine, her feral screaming is my own.

No. I will not be that. I refuse to be that.

"Of course not," I snap, spinning around to face Giulia, "I'm not a killer."

"Then that's what'll happen. What others want is completely irrelevant, Fate included. Besides, Father won't allow it. He'd never risk you like that." Giulia sits back, crossing her legs as if that settles things. "He'll come to an arrangement with the Patricellis."

"What about Idris? He might insist."

"He won't," Giulia sighs and looks me dead in the eyes, no humour in her face. "The Patricellis only have one son. They won't risk him either."

I nod. She's right—of course she's right.

But my heart won't slow. I set down my drink, hands

shifting to tug at my tunic and then run through my hair. Several of the thick waves have slipped from my ponytail to wriggle around my face. I pace up and down the mosaic floors, my heels clipping against the expensive tiles.

"Would you please relax?" Giulia almost groans.

"I can't relax. I have to be sharp. I have to be ready."

"For what? Idris Patricelli isn't about to jump through the windows with an axe."

I scowl, the mention of his name bringing bile to my tongue.

"Even if he did, we'd never let him get close to you," adds Nouis, uncharacteristically serious. He widens his stance, eyes cutting outside as he says the words.

I shake my head. My insides jump up and down like a tiny bird is running rampant on my ribs.

The front door opens. My head snaps around as the familiar cadence of my father's steps fill the hall outside. Giulia sits forwards as he enters the room. The air is so thick, one wrong breath could shatter everything in sight.

Father tosses his cloak over the back of the sofa, his hands resting on the wooden frame. "I spoke briefly with Jacopo. We've agreed that the ... ah ... traditional way of handling these things would be catastrophic."

"Meaning that Idris and Renza aren't going to pummel each other to death at dawn?" Giulia mocks disappointment, throwing me an I-told-you-so look. A lead blanket has lifted from my chest. I take a deep breath, collapsing into one of the armchairs. Nouis walks up behind me, patting my shoulder.

"Correct." Father slides his hands into his pockets, as that familiar gaze flickers around to me. "It helped that the Patricellis have a real loathing for the Church, but they readily agreed. No one should have to face their child's murderer, let alone every day in the High Chamber."

"The High Chamber!" I cover my eyes with both hands, the fresh reality of this horror washing over me. "How am I supposed to sit opposite that man in the High Chamber for the next few decades of my life? Let alone do my job?"

I hear Father walking closer. I drop my hands to my lap. Father's face tugs into a familiar smile, his warmth melting through me the way only a father's love can. He eases onto the coffee table opposite, leaning closer.

"Are you hurt?"

I shake my head. "Not seriously."

"Well then, I suggest you rest up and mentally prepare for tomorrow. I'll go speak with Gattore."

"I have the best rapport—"

"No, I've got this." There's no room for negotiation in his voice, as he reaches for my shoulder, giving it a reassuring squeeze. "You need to be prepared to face Idris in the High Chamber tomorrow."

"What?" I gape. "He's going to be there? After this?"

Father sighs and nods, raking a hand through his hair. "I tried to argue with Jacopo that perhaps we should wait for a few weeks or even just a few days to test the waters some more, but he refused. Much as I disagree, he has some good points. Idris is a Halician citizen with every right to be there. He wants to see the chamber, observe how it runs, learn about his father's work just as you did. Besides, we need to prove sooner rather than later that it's safe for you and him to be in the same room, particularly in that environment, before rumours get out of hand and ruin one or both of your future careers in the High Chamber. You both need to appear to be acting normally, or at least like this doesn't interfere with your ability to be an Electi."

I want to scream with frustration.

"But I'm the Electi. Idris is a citizen."

"I made that argument too. It didn't stick. So I don't care how you do it, but do whatever it takes not to kill him. So we can demonstrate to the whole of Halice that this is the right decision."

My heart clangs like the bells of the Grand Temple in my ears, disjointed and harsh. I meet his blue eyes, feeling a lump forming in my throat.

"I've never felt anything like it before," I admit. The words feel like sandpaper as they leave my tongue, barely louder than a whisper.

"I know."

"It was... I was out of my mind. The world shrank to him and that ... that ... hatred." The fragility in those words makes me want to vomit. I look down at my lap. Shame forces blood to my cheeks.

"I know. But you can't kill him."

My father leans closer, wrapping his arms around me. I let him pull me close and scrunch up my eyes. I rest my head on his shoulder and his embrace feels like it could hold the world together even when everything is falling apart.

I take a shuddery breath, gripping him close.

"How?" That question barely escapes my lips but my father hears it. He sighs, his arms tightening as if to protect me.

He can't.

"I don't know." Worry leaks through his quiet words. "But I do know it'll take every ounce of strength you have."

I squeeze my eyes shut for a moment before he releases me. He plants a kiss on the top of my head before standing, walking towards the door. He looks back and gives me a nod, bottom lip thinned in a calculated smile. That says it all.

You've got this. I believe in you.

He gave me the same look when I joined him in the High Chamber for the first time. When I first spoke publicly about a reform, and then again when I ran for and secured my election two years ago. That look … has always filled me with confidence. Knowing my father believes in me, it's like a guarantee. A wind to propel me forwards.

Now it's another gust in the storm.

I force myself to smile before he leaves.

Nouis moves behind me, making his way towards the door.

"Wait, Nouis," I say, hurrying after him. He pauses, looking back at me with a small question furrowed in his brow.

"Yes?"

"I'm sorry," I say, "for what happened, and for hitting you —I think I hit you anyway. It's all a bit of a blur, but I'm sorry all the same."

Nouis smiles. He runs his hand down my arm, sending out radiating waves of shivers as he wraps his warm fingers around mine. He gives my hand a gentle squeeze.

"Don't be sorry. I'm happy to help Renza," he says quietly, his voice taking on a deep warmth that makes my breath hitch in my throat. "Shall I consider this a raincheck for tonight?"

Tonight. Our dinner. "As friends"—a distinction I'm starting to care about less and less by the second.

"I think that'd be best," I groan.

"As far as excuses go ... this one is pretty good." He winks. "How about tomorrow night instead?"

"Perfect."

"I'll see if I can move some things."

"Thank you," I say, the words tumbling forwards but I'm glad I said them, "for ... everything today."

Nouis chuckles, leaning closer. I'm wrapped in his smell, almonds and vanilla, as he presses his soft lips to my ear, whispering only for me.

"For you?" his voice, rich and deep, sends a storm of shudders rolling across my face, "Anything."

He leaves without another word. Giulia chuckles, giving me a pointed side eye. I throw a rude hand gesture her way as I leave. My feet fly over the mosaic floor and up the grand curved staircase.

I have less than twenty-four hours to find a way to overcome a gods-sent hatred. Otherwise, I won't just let down my father, but I'll start a blood feud between the Patricelli and the Di Maineri families that could rip apart our democratic High Chamber and destroy this city.

Failure isn't an option. But neither is success, not real and lasting success anyway. This will never go away. This is a war I'll be fighting for the rest of my life.

But I'm Renza Di Maineri. I'm not afraid of a fight.

CHAPTER 5

My father has a thousand books in his study. The brightly bound leathers form a rainbow stretched across the warm wooden shelves. They contain answers to countless questions, about geography and history and art. There are endless daring tales and sweeping stories. But do you know what none of them are?

Useful!

I slam the book on religious history shut, the gilded title winking up at me in the sunlight. *The Founding of the Great Holy States* by Ezio Corsetti. Corsetti, one of the so-called greats, was truly prolific at wittering on endlessly. Not to mention his irritating melancholic ramblings about "the breaking of the continent" otherwise known as the Civil Holy War. The continent didn't break; it was a triumph for all parties!

Three hundred years ago, our entire continent was under the thumb of the Holy States—then called the Great Holy States. But when the established cardinals couldn't decide on a new Holy Ruler, the Civil Holy War broke out. On one side, the old, previously established doctrine. One where Soulmates were forced to marry, regardless of age, relation, or situation. If they were already married to other parties, they were forcibly divorced. Soulhate fights were a spectacle held in temple for all to watch. If either of the Fated parties refused or rebelled against this, they were executed.

But on the other side was a sect of cardinals lead by Holy Father Benignus, who proposed a more humanist way. He preached that it was wrong for the Church to force people's hand. That people must have the strength of faith to follow the decisions of Fate, and that the Church should help them instead of forcing and punishing those who refused.

No matter which account I read, including Corsetti's painfully biased scribblings, the war itself was a brutal, bloody affair. Thankfully, with the help of the resource-rich territories now known as the Independent States, Holy Father Benignus won the civil war. The Holy States relinquished its more violent doctrine and the Independent States got the freedom they craved.

It was a victory for the continent. Not this grief-stricken nonsense Corsetti prattled about!

I toss the tome to one side, collapsing into the soft, sweet grass in our garden. I glare up at the entwined arms of the apple tree overhead, the swelling fruit swaying side to side like rosy bubbles. The fickle shade offered by the tree sways over my face in time with the lazy breeze, and dark leaves rustle like a mocking snigger.

That's it. I need a walk.

I throw myself to my feet, stomping off. I'm blind to the

explosion of colours pouring out from the petals in our flower bed, their sweet fragrance falling unappreciated. The sweat beading my brow goes unnoticed, as does the assault of the setting sun on the bridge of my nose.

There's only the dread of tomorrow looming like a spectre.

I try to take long deep breaths as I walk over the grass, forcing myself into smooth deliberate movements. I round the corner of a manicured flower bed to a corner of our property my mother used to adore. Standing with its back to the corner hedges is a small circular pavilion. The carved columns stretch tall, connecting the bright mosaic floor with the painted arched roof. The curved stone seating faces a small pond with a tiled edge and the water is scattered with floating greenery, crushed sunlight glinting on the undulating surface.

I ease down onto the stone bench, the knot in my chest building. My fingers turn white as I grip the edge of my seat with my eyes locked on that water. So calm, so gentle. Completely unbothered by the world turning upside down around me.

Frustration coils at the back of my throat. I grab an obliging rock, and hurl it into the silky water. The splash crashes satisfyingly. Water is thrown to the sky to shake the world around it.

Panting, I'm disgusted at myself, at how good the release feels tingling in my fingertips. I need to do it again. Harder. More violently. I need—

No wait. This isn't right. The hairs on my arms stand on

end. Ghostly nails dig into the flesh between my shoulder blades.

Back straight as a poker, I climb up onto the stone bench of the pavilion. I lean forward, popping my head over the hedges that are caged by stone walls. I look down at the sunken road below to see a vile blond head.

Idris Patricelli.

He's changed his clothes, donning a lightweight, cream tunic and dark trousers. His broad shoulders are pulled back in determination, his muscled arms tense as he marches towards the front door of my home.

My breath turns to fire and my fingers ache as they cling to the pavilion column like an anchor. Every fibre of my being begs me to launch over this wall and batter his stupid face into the cobbled road.

Idris stops like someone slapped him, his posture suddenly made of marble. He turns slowly to look at me and he's so tall he barely has to turn his head upwards. His cheek is carved with four crimson gashes, the damage from my nails healing up already.

"How dare you come here?" I snarl, breath rushing uncontrollably from my lungs. "This is *my* home."

"I'm not here by accident, Maineri," snaps Idris, marching closer. "I'm here for you."

"You changed your mind? You want to fight?" Fate's Fury, with him here right now, that sounds delightful. Then the memory of Fausta hits me like a boulder and my legs almost go out from under me.

No. No, I won't do this. I won't lose myself.

"Don't be ridiculous." Idris scowls, folding his arms so tightly he hides his shaking fists.

"Then what for, for Fate's sake?" I hiss, my very blood boiling in protest. I can't seem to tear myself away from his golden hazel eyes.

"Did that blow to your head earlier slow your senses? To talk to you. Obviously." Idris shakes his head, muttering under his breath. I dig my fingers harder into the stone column, clamping my teeth together.

"Oh no, please roll your eyes. Maybe you'll find a brain back there and realise this is a stupendously horrible idea," I snap. "You couldn't give me a day? A single day to process this?"

"This can't wait. Our fathers struck a deal but I need to know how you feel about it."

"Feel about it? What a stupid question, perhaps you're the one who hit your head. I hate everything about this. But then, that shouldn't be a surprise. You are my Soulhate." I snarl the last word.

"Yes, it's all aptly named, who would've guessed it?" Sarcasm drips off Idris's words. He lets out a growl of frustration, bending over his knees to stare at the ground. "Don't look at me."

It would be so easy. I could get the drop on him while he's not watching. So easy to wrap my fingers around his—

"Don't look at me," snaps Idris again. "It'll help. It'll be easier."

Just looking at him is agonising. Yet it's at war with my every instinct to look away, to allow myself to be so vulnerable with him around. But I can't do this if I see him, this thread holding me back is fraying fast. I squeeze my eyes shut and press my head to the stone of the column. I let the ridges of stone dig into my temples for a moment before turning my back to the column. Facing away from him, unable to see him ... this is better.

"I came here," Idris continues with strained words, "because we need to take control of this."

"This doesn't feel like control," I grind out through gritted teeth. I wince as I hear his footsteps bring him closer. I dig my fingers into the stone behind me to stop launching myself at him from my hiding spot. He's on the other side of the column now, a resigned note in his words.

"We're both still breathing. I'd say we're doing rather well."

"Get to your point."

"This is our bond. *Ours*. Your father and mine can make all the deals they want, but they mean nothing if we don't care. So I have to know, do you want this deal?"

"Do you?" I fire back, not daring to open my eyes.

"Do you really think I'd be fighting this hard if I didn't want to?" Idris pauses. "I wouldn't be here if I wasn't serious about making this work."

I take a deep breath, pressing my head harder into the stonework before answering.

"I won't let Fate control me. I won't let Fate turn me into something and someone I'm not. I am not a violent killer. I don't want to kill you, not in my rational mind anyway."

Whether I said that for him or myself, I don't know.

Idris stays silent for a while, before he answers.

"I don't want to kill you either."

"So we're both committed then?"

"It appears so."

The silence lingers between the two of us for an uncomfortable stretch of time. Nouis's words come crawling back to me, slithering around my ear as they attempt to take root. Then the words spring forwards almost of their own accord.

"Idris"—I hate the way his name digs hot thorns into my tongue—"you're not worried, are you? About defying Fate's will?"

He's got to be asking himself the same questions right now, hasn't he? He's really the only one who could possibly understand what's running through my mind.

That concept makes me want to throw up before battering his skull as quickly as possible.

Idris gives a deep sigh.

"You didn't strike me as the superstitious religious type," Idris answers, with an inflection I can't start to dissect. I scowl at the accusation, spitting my retort indignantly.

"I'm not. But what about you?"

"I think those that believe Fate will take their satisfaction eventually are looking for an excuse to absolve them of the choice they're about to make. I think those with stories or anecdotes about Fate taking their vengeance are reading the situation as they want to see it. Every decision has consequences, the majority we can't foresee regardless of the choice we make. Good and bad."

"That's very ... considered," I answer.

"I've seen a lot in my time abroad," is all Idris says in response. I let out a sharp sigh.

"Great. Now unless there's something else, go away and leave me with some semblance of peace in my own home."

Idris hovers, the air thick with something else he wants to say. But whatever it is, the words don't come. Instead the fire in my blood starts to dilute, the hairs relaxing back onto my skin as the bile slides back down my throat. I slowly peel one eye open to stare at the empty spot on the road where Idris once stood. Empty.

I slide myself slowly down the column, curling up in a ball on the hard stone seat. I let my head fall back, taking three deep breaths.

This is going to be a disaster.

CHAPTER 6

Butter melts to blistering blue above our heads. The sun shoots beams of canary around the winding streets of Halice, pooling stark shadows in tight crevasses around murals and carvings as I walk.

Halice is waking up.

Fresh bread carries on a dreamy breeze. Chatter hovers around my ears. People fill the streets, winding around each other on their way to their daily calling. Some travel by long public wagons that carry people all over the city.

I need to be seen to be doing things normally. People need to see me alive and well and most importantly, not bothered by this turn of events. This public stroll to the Garden is a great way to do just that.

"Signora Di Maineri! Wait up!" calls a young voice. I pause amongst the crowd, turning as a group of young boys run over.

"Morning, signora!" says one boy excitedly. His bright

brown eyes are wide, as a toothy smile fills his freckled face. The three other boys smile at me too, one shyly waving.

"Well, good morning to you too," I smile. "Are you off to school?"

"Yes! Will you be there today? The new library is finished, and Teacher Veletor said you were going to open it!"

They must go to the New College—one of the three schools my father founded in his early days as an Electi. He founded it with family money, appointed the teachers himself and paid for most of the upkeep out of his own pocket—at least early on in their creation. Over his long career he's successfully campaigned to get most of the running costs for all the schools in Halice covered by High Chamber funding. But any upgraded equipment or buildings sometimes still require a family donation. This new library was my idea, having seen just how small the last one was. The funds are an investment in our children, and in turn in the future of Halice.

"Not today boys, I have to be at the High Chamber," I say apologetically. "But I will be there next week, when it's properly opened for you."

"We have to wait a whole week for the books?" says the boy, frowning. Fate's Mercy, he sounds like me at his age.

"If that's what your teacher says, you must listen. The teachers are very smart."

"I know," he says, bottom lip pouting forwards.

"What's your name?" I ask, hands going to my hips.

"Maso," he answers instantly, puffing out his chest.

"Well, Maso. If you promise to be good for your teachers

all week, when I see you next week, you can show me what books you want to read. Sound good?"

"Who will open it if you lose your duel?" Maso asks. My heart sinks, though I refuse to let it cross my face.

"Where did you hear about that?"

"Mum was talking about it. You and Idris Patricelli are Soulhates. You have to fight now," Maso says matter-of-factly.

"Well, we actually won't be fighting so you don't need to worry. I'll be there."

"Really?" Maso frowns, "Mum said you have to fight. You have no choice."

"Well, it's more complicated than that. You'll understand when you're a bit older." I force my tone to be light and problem free. "Now, you don't want to be late. Off you go and I'll see you all next week."

"Bye, signora!" they call in unison before racing away through the crowd. I shake my head, a fresh smile lurking around my lips.

I turn back towards the Garden, striding for the artisanal paradise.

I pass through the open gates, pushing through a curtain of cool shadows as I head down the path. Our best and brightest are up already. Some lounge outside with steaming tea between their fingers, others are setting up for the day, one or two are out for an early stroll.

That's when I see her waiting.

Emilia sits under the tree where we agreed to meet. Her long legs are pulled tight to her body, the pretty yellow dress bunching around her middle. Her dark hair is pulled on top of her head like a bird's nest and her brown skin glows in the sunshine filtering through the fluttering sage ceiling overhead.

The architect has a pencil between her fingers, her lips pursed tightly as her eyes flicker over the bundle of papers before her. My gut squirms when I spy smudges of purple around her dark eyes.

"Knock knock?" I tease, patting the tree. She jumps, head twisting up.

"Sorry, Renza!" she laughs, shoulders dropping again. "Just making some final adjustments."

"No worries. This is a lot of work, Emilia, you didn't stay up all night, did you? I only need a rough idea so I could plant a seed today at High Chamber." I slide down the tree and sit with her. The grass's clammy fingers seep through my dark trousers, the rough tree bark digging ridges into my back.

Emilia pushes the binder of papers to my lap.

"I repurposed an old project," she says matter-of-factly. "I conducted this thought experiment about two years ago: how cheaply could I build a decent abode?"

"Oh that sounds promising!" I mutter, scanning the drawings. I take one of the pages, turning it around. *Wait, that doesn't seem right? Does it?*

"I've made some modifications, given they'll be that close to the docks," she says. "I was also thinking about the space situation."

"The space situation?" I frown, turning the drawing again. *That can't be the right way up.*

"Well, the docks are one of the main employers and it's only growing by the day," Emilia reasons, "but there's only a finite amount of space for accommodation close to the docks. What we don't want is for demand to push the prices so high it's unaffordable for the workers they were designed for. So, I considered stacking them."

"Stacking?" I repeat. She nods, taking the page in my hands and turning it so the terraced houses might line up on top of each other. "The floorplan for the home is on one level, so we can stack them on top of each other. There would be stairs going up the outside, so they can reach their level of the building. On a plot where there was previously one house, there would now be four. That way, although we have the same square footage to work from, we can house more people than before."

Fate's Fury, she's talented. These look amazing—more than I could've asked for.

"Stacks. That's ... brilliant!" I laugh. "You're a genius, Emilia."

Her cheeks go red as she shrugs, reaching for the pages with her pencil again.

"It's just an idea."

"Better housing *and* more of it without sacrificing on space? You're handing me a winning vote," I tease gently. Her cheeks are flaming as she refuses to meet my eyes, but the smile fixed on her soft face is everything.

"Come on. Time for you to get some sleep, and time for me to start winning hearts and minds." I get up, offering her a hand. She stands a good head taller than me and delicately wipes her skirt down, as we head back down the path at a strolling pace.

"I hear the Library at New College is done?" I ask. It's

another one of Emilia's projects. Her genius will shape much of this city before the end of her career. She nods.

"Yes, there are a few tweaks here and there. Michelle provided some paintings for it that are still with Giles, the woodworker, to frame."

"I know Giles. His work is great. I look forward to seeing your masterpiece in person," I chuckle. Emilia nods. Uncle Ruggie stands at a table clothed in damp shadows, backlit by the crimson of his forge. Next to him is the unmistakable figure of Serra Stacano; the two are bent over a drawing. Uncle Ruggie stares at me in open shock as Serra waves me over. Uncle Ruggie wastes no time folding me into a hug, and squeezing tightly.

"What are you two concocting?" I ask, patting his back.

"Serra needs some metalwork done for her contraption. Oh it's good to see you," Uncle Ruggie chuckles, releasing me. He takes my forearms, looking into my face. "You look okay."

"Of course I am. Why wouldn't I be?"

His weathered brow puckers as if I've gone mad.

"Patricelli..." he says slowly. Oh Fate's Fury, of course. He must be thinking about Fausta again. I'm such a thoughtless idiot.

"You heard," I sigh, folding my arms.

"Are you kidding? Everyone in the city had heard before lunch even rolled around!" snorts Serra, leaning against the table, crossing one dark leg over the other. "Nothing spreads like gossip in this city, particularly around the Patricelli and Maineri."

"So, he really is your Soulhate?" asks Uncle Ruggie. I nod.

"Yes."

"And you beat him?" frowns Uncle Ruggie, well aware that my only experience with a blade was at a dinner table.

"No. No, we decided we aren't going to duel."

There's a moment of silence as shock ripples around the group. Uncle Ruggie steps back, mouth hanging open. Emilia's eyebrows shot up, nodding slowly. Serra whistles, shaking her head so her dark curls bounce from side to side.

"You disapprove?" I challenge, straightening my back.

"Of course not. It's... You do what's right for you." Uncle Ruggie nods with a tightness to his words. I know Fausta is weighing on his mind.

"Are you sure?" Serra frowns. "I mean, we're Fated for a reason."

"Are we? Or is that something the Church tells us because it sounds nice? What evidence is there? Perhaps we're Fated by random. Perhaps rather than having a plan, Fate binds us together at their whim for entertainment," I debate. "I refuse to be a killer because Fate decided he'd enjoy the drama."

"Trust you to pick a fight with a god," snorts Serra, rubbing her brow.

"Why should she kill him? He's done her no wrong," Emilia pipes up. "This is just a horrible situation."

"Exactly." I smile at her. "Who knows why we're Fated? No one; it's all guesswork. We will *never* know why we're Fated. But Idris Patricelli isn't guesswork. He's real. Fact: he's done nothing wrong. Fact: he has a family that loves him. Fact: killing him would cause that family immeasurable pain. I won't be the cause of that grief."

"You're Fated. It's inevitable," Uncle Ruggie laments

softly. "The bond will force it one way or another. Bad things come for those who refuse Fate."

"Superstitions," I rebut. "Anecdotal stories based on confirmation bias."

"Besides, if anyone can fight it, it's Renza. Even if it's just for a couple of days, surely the effort is worth it. Right?" adds Emilia. "Intention matters, even if the end result is the same."

"I just… Good luck." Uncle Ruggie surrenders, worry still glinting in his eyes as he forces a weak smile and walks away to his forge. My gut squeezes. I'll be alright. I have to be.

Serra purses her lips, but I can see the mirth twisting the edge of her mouth.

"Don't," I warn. Serra's control slips, her shoulders shuddering with humour.

"Fated with a Patricelli! Oh, even you have to admit it's funny." Serra barks with laughter.

"Serra," gasps Emilia, more scolding than shocked.

"Oh *come on*, you must see the irony here. You're always the one who says Fate doesn't decide for you. Perhaps it's your blasphemy that's sent you this." Serra's wicked grin displays her perfect pearly teeth. I scowl, looking for something handy to throw at her smug face.

"Not helping, Serra," I glower.

"Oh please," Serra chortles. "Emilia, back me up. It's funny!"

"I mean, it could be worse." Emilia detours quietly. "Would you prefer he was your Soulmate?"

"Ew!" I shudder. The only thing worse than Fate-sent hatred is a Fate-sent infatuation.

"Exactly. It could be a lot worse."

I can only imagine. What must it be like for those who find their Soulmate? The overwhelming loathing at the merest sight of Idris was like I'd lost my mind. My hands shake at the memory.

"Wait, you don't want to meet your Soulmate?" frowns Serra. "Think about the sensation of it, the purity. Imagine being loved that intensely."

"That's not always a good thing, Ser," Emilia says quietly, folding her delicate arms. "A Soulmate is a person like any other, what if they're bad? They could be violent, or a criminal. And, even if they aren't all those things, just because they supposedly love you doesn't mean they'll be good to you."

Of course Emilia would feel that way. Something cracks inside me, and my fingers itch to comfort my friend.

Emilia was born Emilio, in one of the farthest villages from Halice. When she started to recognise her truth, her father went from loving to violent. Thankfully Emilia's mother defended her, and the two ran away to Halice and have never looked back. Her parents were Soulmates. But that didn't stop her father's violence towards Emilia or her mother.

Emilia had embraced her true self long before I met her, and is one of the most impressive young women in Halice. But the scars of her father's sudden brutality still haunt her.

Fate's Mercy, I hope someone will be able to ease the fear one day. Someone just as gentle and caring as Emilia, someone who can hold her and make her feel utterly and completely safe.

"Anyone who doesn't like you is an absolute fool," I tell her softly.

"Yeah, and they'll have us to contend with," Serra promises, raising two fists like she is prepping for a fight. Emilia flashes a weak smile.

"My point still stands. The Fated aren't perfect. We still have our choices."

"Valid. But I still wonder about the experience, you know?" Serra waves off. "Either way, take this."

She pulls something off her belt and hands it to me. I look down to see a small dagger wrapped in thick brown leather with slithers of sharp metal glinting in the early morning sunshine. The wooden handle looked worn and comfortable in Serra's grip.

It would look good protruding from Patricelli's skull.

I swallow, shaking my head.

"I wouldn't know what to do with it."

"It's easy, you stick the sharp end in the bad person," Serra teases.

"I'm not a fighter. Not like that anyway." I take a step back.

"You fought yesterday—pretty well from what I hear of it," Emilia muses.

"People will stop me. Him too."

"Will they?" Emilia asks, her quiet voice a few shades darker than normal. I meet her warm, brown gaze as a long beat passes between us. She has a good point.

While Halice is no longer ruled by the Holy States, the Holy Faith still has a strong grip on many of its people. If Idris and I can't control ourselves, many will simply stand back and wait to see the outcome, believing in repercussions for themselves if they get involved.

"It's just a precaution, Renza. I'm not hoping you'll need it, and I'm not pushing you to use it. But at least you'll have it," says Serra stepping forwards, seriousness fleeting across her incredible dark eyes as she pushes the dagger into my fingers. "I need you to be safe."

We might not be together anymore but she loves me still, as I love her. Warmth ripples across my chest as I soften my words for her.

"You're not allowed to die, you understand?" Serra instructs. "We need you, Maineri. Halice needs you."

"Halice is strong enough to stand without me. But the sentiment is sweet," I chuckle, as Serra straps the dagger to my belt. "Speaking of the people, they expect me to work today and I won't be late. Goodbye, ladies."

"Remember, don't kill him," shouts Emilia.

"Unless you want to!" Serra adds. I shake my head, turning to make my way down the cobbled path, my new dagger pressed against my waist.

~

A pale caricature stares back at me from the small window of a shop. I'm standing, inspecting my reflection in a narrow alleyway outside the High Chamber, in my last moment of privacy before the pandemonium begins. My dark waves are pulled back into my signature low ponytail. My smart blue dress fits loosely, its silky hem swaying around my knees. But there are dark circles hanging under my eyes, undeniable proof of how evasive sleep was last night.

I look powerful, confident and, most importantly, like nothing has changed. Appearances are a weapon and I will wield them to my full advantage.

My fingers brush my mother's brooch, sitting in pride of place over my heart. The bejewelled blue and gold butterfly is like having her with me. I take a deep breath, dropping my hand and pulling the binder containing Emilia's drawings closer to my side.

Let's do this.

I step out onto the creamy pavement and unfiltered sun begins to bake the bridge of my nose. I'd give anything for a cool hand to wipe the beads of perspiration beginning to dampen my hairline as the sun's vicious glare bounces off the gilded columns and stained-glass.

Despite the unrelenting solar attack, the High Chamber is mesmerising. The building shines like a rainbow made solid. Every inch of its domed roof is gleaming in all the colours of creation.

I tuck the housing plans under my arms, climb the vibrant steps and cross the High Chamber's threshold. Inside the quiet chatter drops like the crowd are witnessing a catastrophe. Everyone stares, the air thick enough to shatter.

"How many of you bet I'd be dead?" I only half joke to the audience. Every High Chamber session is open to the public. Everyone is allowed to watch and contribute to the discussion if invited by an Electi to do so. So it's common for us to have spectators. The dagger on my belt feels heavier. A hot gaze falls on my face and my eyes snap to the source.

My knuckles go white as I clench my fingers together. Idris's hazel eyes blister, before cutting to the floor. My blood screams in my ears. My heart thumps hard, each beat whispering.

Kill.

Kill.

Kill.

"Don't look," hisses Jacopo, eyes narrowing and making to step between us.

I grit my teeth, forcing my eyes away from Idris. The fire in my blood drops; instead of an inferno, it's an unpleasant warmth that has me shifting on my feet. I can't get comfortable. My throat is still swollen but at least I can think. I force myself to breathe long and slow. I will separate my own thoughts from the feral violence.

"Fate's Fury, that helps," I mutter, trying to calm my thumping heart.

"This is madness," breathes Electi Morteselli, turning to my father in horror. "We can't have them both in the High Chamber. Tomas, you can't be serious about this—"

"My father supports *my* decision," I say as pointedly and politely as I can muster. "My choices are my own, Morteselli."

"You cannot both be in this chamber," Morteselli shoots back instantly.

"Why not? This is my job, and he's a citizen. We both have every right to be here," I rebut with no humour.

"This is the High Chamber, not a colosseum!" Morteselli puts his hands on his waist, narrowing his eyes. "There will be no bloodshed here."

"Then we're agreed. No one will die here today."

Morteselli stammers, somewhere between angry and appalled. "Fate is clear. If you ignore his design, then great anguish will fall upon you both. You should go outside and finish this—"

"No." Another voice rings in tandem with mine. Idris. I grit my teeth, a flare of anger flooding up my throat.

Outrage hovers on Morteselli's tongue. "One must die. It has been decreed."

"I've never been one to blindly do as I'm told." I march past the crowd of people staring, towards the seats.

"That's foolish and blasphemous. Fate has their will known—"

"My will is stronger!" My voice rings against the domed roof. The silence soaks into the air, brittle like a single whisper would echo like a thunderclap. I take a deep steadying breath, looking Morteselli dead in the eyes.

I want to scream about how my personal decisions are none of his business, that he should keep his ideas of faith to himself. But I can't, insulting him would come back to bite me in the next vote—in the plans I'm presenting today and probably for weeks to come.

Instead I continue in a level tone. "Member Morteselli, I understand your concern. However, our decision has been made and for now we are sticking to it. Please be certain that if we feel the choice was a mistake, we will change our minds. That is the beauty of choice. We can try it, for better or for worse. Now might I suggest we all take our seats and we call this session to order? I would hate to waste any more of the city's time and attention on my personal matters."

I am perfectly capable of being an Electi despite having a Soulhate.

People slip into movement. The other Members take their seats. The audience of citizens sits in the circular rows of chairs.

I keep my eyes on the seat that's been my home for the last two years. The beautiful pink and blue window glows, the colours so calming as they ripple over the dark wood of the chair.

I walk past my father, his hand gently squeezing my shoulder on the way. Our eyes meet.

"Well done," he whispers softly.

"Don't congratulate me until session end."

I slide into my chair and set my papers upon the table, shifting in the familiar seat.

Every move Idris makes feels like a blister at the edge of my vision. I'm fixated on every detail, like how he sits as close to Jacopo as the spectator seats will allow. How he's positioned right in front of my favourite yellow window. How people are muttering, looking between the two of us and spinning the gossip mill further. An uncomfortable heat writhes around my fingertips, taunting me. I force myself not to look up from my papers, willing myself to focus on anything else.

"I call today's session to open." My father opens the floor, and five choruses of "Agreed" roll around the room in a quick fashion.

Before Father can get to his feet, Morteselli bolts out of his seat and my head snaps up at the sudden motion.

"I should like to bring the first order of today's session before the High Chamber."

A rare moment of confused silence lingers in the room.

Why have none of us heard about this before now?

"Member Morteselli, please, present your order," says Jacopo, distaste evident in his words. Morteselli has held his seat for almost fifty years. Backwards, resistant to real change—a swing vote that is difficult to crack. Normally he'd be thick as thieves with Cardinal Bellandi.

"I present a new motion to the floor. As many of you know, Cardinal Bellandi was recently called to the Holy Capital of Kavas at the personal invitation of the honourable Holy Mother. He has written to me of a request that her spiritual majesty has to make of our city."

My jaw sets.

This does not sound good.

"As you know," Morteselli continues, barely pausing for breath, "the Holy States pay for the upkeep of our curates, bishops, spiritual buildings, and other holy works here in Halice. This is a great expense to the Holy States."

I hear a derivative snort from across the room. Instinctively, my head whips across and I'm hit with instant regret. Yellow light bounces off Idris's blond head and sharp jaw. I grit my teeth, every muscle in my body tense. I turn away, sucking in a deep breath, followed by another. It's like swallowing hot ashes.

"The Holy Mother," Morteselli continues without noticing, "asks that we provide a percentage of our income to go towards these ever-growing expenses. This would allow our citizens to continue to receive the best spiritual enrichment, here in our city, and lessen the burden on our ally."

"A percentage of our income?" Member Yaleni frowns.

"Yes. A percentage of the net income this city generates every year," Morteselli explains brightly, trying to garner support from the other Members. "No matter whether Halice's income goes up or down, faces famine or war, our services will be the same. The gesture would go a long way in securing our alliance with the Holy States—"

"We are already allies with the Holy States," argues Member Gattore. "Unless they intend to break that long-standing agreement now."

"How big a percentage?" My father's tone is unwelcoming, but far friendlier than the disgust that erupts from Jacopo at the same time.

"Taxes? For the Holy States?" Jacopo almost growls in outrage. It's predictable, even if his rage is uncharacteristically sharp. Fifteen years ago, half the seats in here would have been filled by some bishop or cardinal—the change is mostly thanks to Jacopo and his insistence that religion has no place in politics.

I'll easily admit it's for the better. Cardinal Bellandi and Morteselli are the last remnants of the old ways still standing, both men extremely popular with the religious groups and elite wealthy families in the city.

Morteselli holds up his hands as if to calm the room.

"The Holy Mother suggests a settlement as low as seven per cent."

"Seven per cent!" my father shouts in shock. I'm right

there with him, instantly shaking my head. There are a few more shouts of ridicule and outrage amongst the crowd.

"Settle! Settle!" comes Yaleni's voice, hand slamming on her armrest. The din of voices starts to drop, but not before Jacopo's fierce anger cuts across them all.

"Absolutely not!" He scowls at Morteselli, leaping to his feet to be the first to argue the proposal. "Halice, and all the Independent States this side of the Argenti Straight, earned its freedom from the selfish whims of the Holy States over three hundred years ago. When Church infighting almost tore the Holy Faith apart, it was the Independent Alliance that secured our freedom by blade and blood. The Holy Mother's demand is an insult to the liberty of our city!"

It's an interesting take on our history, though not necessarily wrong.

The independent cities and fiefdoms today, collectively known as the Independent States, did indeed form an alliance ... to do *nothing*. At the time we were all a part of the sprawling Holy States Empire. But we decided to leverage the whole religious mess to our advantage. It was a masterful move of international diplomacy and cooperation called the Independent Alliance. We aligned ourselves with Holy Father Benignus, but we refused to send anything for the war effort. Not a single man, blade, or grain of rice, not unless he guaranteed our independence. And it worked. Our resource-rich territories became the key to turning the tide and winning the Civil Holy War.

Jacopo's take on history might hold some questionable dramatic flair, but he also isn't that far wrong.

"It's not a demand, but a request—"

"And how long until we're paying the Holy States thirty, fifty, seventy per cent?" Jacopo interrupts. "Just to provide a spiritual service to our people? How long until we're swallowed up into the Holy States again and this High Chamber is little more than a footnote in history?"

"I, for one, agree with Member Patricelli, though perhaps not his hyperbole." I jump to my feet, signalling my demand to speak and bring some of the process back to this debate. "Halice is not a Holy State. We are not the subjects of the Holy Mother. We are a free, independent, true republic. All the wealth this city has and creates is built by the sweat of our brows and the burden of our backs. The reward that effort reaps should go back into the pocket of the people, not lining the pocket of an already rich principality who did nothing to generate it."

"Member Di Maineri, you surprise me." Morteselli scowls, turning to look at my father. "Is this really your view, Tomas?"

I slam my hand onto the arm of my chair more harshly that strictly necessary as I stare down this old man.

"Who cares? It is mine. What's more is that it shouldn't be a surprising one," I answer swiftly before my father can speak. "The Holy Mother chooses to provide these, as you call them, 'spiritual services' in Halice. She makes that choice of her own volition. Should she wish to remove them, that is also at her discretion."

Morteselli huffs, giving me a cold look as he turns to my father only to be met with the same steely blue. I stay standing, refusing to back down in the wake of his anger. In the past, Morteselli has seen us as an ally against Jacopo's purge of the Church, perhaps even playing my father by using their rivalry as bait. But not today.

"This donation—"

"This tax," counters Jacopo.

"This donation," Morteselli continues irritated, "would go towards the upkeep of the Holy Order within our own city, the connection between us and Fate. The interpretation of Fate's will amongst—"

My teeth snap shut as a bitter wave rolls over my tongue. My low laugh does nothing to rid me of the taste.

"Forgive me, Member Morteselli, but if you think bringing up Fate or his twisted wills, on today of all days, is helping your case then you've gravely misread the room."

I sit back down, hating that I can't look around to read the faces of my fellow Members. I have to make do with a smattering of "hear, hear" and the slamming of open palms on the table.

"Every person in our city benefits from the spiritual nourishment of the Church," Morteselli appeals, disapproval swelling in his eyes as they flicker around the room. "Is it not right that we support those who dedicate their life to the service of others?"

"Then let's fund the Guard, to reduce violent crimes in our city," Idris Patricelli chimes in, like acid eating away at my threadbare control. He hasn't specifically been invited to speak but he is Jacopo's son. There's no point challenging it when Jacopo will just invite him to speak anyway. "Or create a public fund to care for the sick so the poor can receive affordable treatment. The money you propose to remove from our coffers is not finished being spent here."

Wait. What?

Amongst his voice triggering my gag reflex ... something stuck. A fund for the sick? What is that? Can medicine be done differently? Jacopo hasn't mentioned anything like that before. Or is the idea all from Idris? Much as his presence is corrosive to my mind, and my stomach churns admitting this ... I'm intrigued.

"Our coffers? A bit presumptuous of you, Patricelli the younger," says my father, standing up. "You've been in this city for less than a day and already you're trying to spend its money?"

"I was born here."

"You were raised and educated in how many countries was it again?"

"My heart has always been in Halice."

"And my son's education is not the point of this conversation, Di Maineri," Jacopo snaps back.

"He's not an Electi."

"Anyone may speak during the session—"

"Why are we arguing?" Frustration raises my voice to ring around the room. I take a long deep breath, rubbing my brow and taking a minute to let the quiet settle. I don't stand to speak, now at a far more reasonable volume. "This might be the one thing the chamber majority agrees on without the need to discuss. Let's settle the vote and move on to something worth debating, as I also have a bill to put forward today."

The silence lingers. I smile, lifting my head from my hands. A smirk flirts with my lips, as I look around my fellow Electi, meeting all their eyes.

"If another Electi feels differently, then speak now. Otherwise we might as well consider the vote already cast and the proposal rejected?" I offer. I meet the gaze of Members Gattore and Yaleni.

"Excellent. Motion denied," says Father with finality. "Let's hear some other ideas."

I catch sight of my father in his seat, who gives a long encouraging nod. I swallow tightly, forcing my chin up as I get to my feet. I take my papers to the central stage.

"Esteemed Members, I put before you a new trade agreement with Nimal, our neighbours on the north-eastern border. In addition, I would like to proprose a strategy on how we would spend this new revenue, by improving housing and hygiene for those who live near the docks."

I hear Idris muttering to his father from the other side of the room. I clench my fists together, nails digging into my palm as I try to force any discomfort from the smile on my face. That dagger at my hip is calling to me, an imperceptible whisper telling me to launch across the room.

Fate's Fury, this is going to be a long session.

CHAPTER 7

Today's humidity proves once again that Fate hates me. Otherwise I wouldn't be late trying to wrangle the chaotic mess on my head into a semi-respectable ponytail for my dinner with Nouis. My bedroom door swings open and the candles jump in shock as Giulia sweeps into the room.

"Shoes!" announces Giulia throwing several pairs onto the bed. "I'd go with these gold gladiator sandals, with the thicker heels. Nouis is tall; you can get away with some added height."

"One moment." I pull the last free strand away from my face, sliding a red pin into place. Hopefully that'll be enough to lock it down for the night.

"You don't think this is too much?" I sigh, assessing my reflection in the pearl-framed mirror. "This dinner is supposed to be as friends. I made a point of saying that to him..."

But I can't deny when he's around, I feel calmer. Not to

mention how he didn't hesitate to spring into action when I needed him outside the Grand Temple. How he didn't complain, being exactly what I needed, when I needed it, without being asked.

Giulia shakes her head, grinning. "Not too much at all, but you have a stray."

She marches over, every step makes her golden hair shine, smoothed into a perfect bun at the nape of her neck. I slump forwards as she deftly starts work on my head, wishing I had a tenth of her effortless grace.

Michelle appears in my doorframe, greeting me with a wicked grin.

"Did you kill him?"

Giulia throws her girlfriend a sharp look. Michelle smirks, not at all sorry as she presses a kiss to my sister's cheek.

"What? That's what the whole city wants to know," Michelle teases, perching herself next to my vanity.

"I didn't kill anyone," I scowl, playing with the end of my sleeve.

Michelle lets out a whistle of appreciation and I'm almost able to hear her thoughts as she tries to keep them to herself. Michelle doesn't have any semblance of a poker face. Most of the time I appreciate it.

Today is not one of those days.

"But!?" I push, folding my arms. She shrugs, looking down at her feet.

"My brother met his Soulhate a few years back. At my aunt's wedding. Bludgeoned his head in right then and there, in front of the man's wife and three kids. It was like he was possessed or something."

Fate's Fury! Michelle had never told me that before. I shudder, my stomach curdles ... because I get it. Hadn't I almost done the same thing yesterday? Children were present. His family had been there.

I twist my body to face her, one hand going to the warm wood vanity.

"Your point?"

Michelle hesitates before answering, looking for the right words. She holds up her hands, as if trying to remove herself a step from the words she says next.

"Do you think it wise to tempt Fate?"

"Coming from you? Seriously? You don't even go to church!" Disbelief drains blood from my face as my jaw hangs open.

"True, I don't go to the weekly service," Michelle says. "I've never been able to find spiritual comfort sat in the pews of a temple, listening to some bishop or cardinal prattle on about scriptures I haven't read. But of course I believe in Fate. It's everywhere around us, all the time. I just prefer to worship the world around me by capturing its majesty with a brush and paint."

"Well, it's been decided now," Giulia cuts in, giving us both meaningful looks. "Now Michelle, did you bring the earrings?"

"Yeah, right here," says Michelle, pulling them from her trouser pockets. They had to be one of Uncle Ruggie's creations; the dancing dragonflies are so delicate I can't imagine another artist crafting them.

Giulia quickly pops them in for me. I study my reflection sceptically in the looking glass. The red slides gleam like a crimson crown, matching the soft vermillion organza dress Giulia had picked for me. My earrings glitter as they sweep the tips of my shoulders.

"What are you two doing tonight?" I ask them, tugging at the sleeves of my dress. I can already tell by their attire, however. Both wear gorgeous, shorter silk dresses with gleaming beaded belts.

"Dancing," Michelle answers. "There's a new drummer at the Castrum. We want to see if he's any good. Plus, they're doing a three for two deal on drinks if you arrive before ten thirty. Serra and Emilia are meeting us there."

"Renza, you look perfect!" announces Giulia, with a flourish of her hand like she's created her best work of art yet. A knock comes from my bedroom door.

My father leans on the doorframe, folding his arms and wearing a wry smile. He speaks quietly.

"Nouis has called his carriage around."

"Excellent. Let go see what he's got planned for your date," grins Giulia, grabbing Michelle's hand and darting from the room. I snort, shaking my head. Father raises one eyebrow, turning back to see me.

"I take it you're going out this evening then."

My heels clip against the wooden floor and I offer a playful shrug.

"Nouis and I are having dinner ... as friends."

"Good. You should be seen in public living your life like normal."

I don't know how to answer that. He's not wrong, and I'd be lying if I said the thought hadn't occurred to me already.

"But clearly this is more than as friends," Father adds, taking in my attire. Self-consciously I run a hand over Giulia's dress. When she wears this, it highlights her tiny waist and generous bust, the red organza fluttering like magic with each movement. She's a knockout while I'm a child playing dress up.

"I should change. My black tunic is nice—"

"Oh no, don't keep that young man waiting. He's already at the mercy of your sister," chuckles Father, eyes glinting.

"Oh please, we both know he can handle Giulia," I answer before blowing out my candles. Their warm smoke tickles my nostrils before I follow Father into the hallway. He nods slowly, something churning behind his eyes. He hesitates before he opens his mouth, locking his gaze on mine.

"Enjoy yourself this evening, but be careful, alright." The warm wood creaks under our steps as we walk down the wide hallway, lined by creamy stone walls draped in rich tapestries.

I don't blame his caution. The last few days have seen so much change, things feel like they're almost spinning out of control. But Nouis has been so wonderful. So calm and caring, taking the chaos in his stride. I owe it to myself to at least give this a chance.

"Of course," I promise as we come to the top of the staircase, and I lower a hand to the smooth wooden banister. "It's just dinner, there's no need to worry."

"I'm your father, worrying is part of the job," he says,

planting a tender kiss on the side of my head. "Have fun, and try not to break his heart."

I smile at him before turning and looking down the stairs. The mosaic floor below is arranged like a blossoming garden—one of my mother's designs. Tall columns line the edges of the hall, wrapped with metallic flowering vines which ripple with amber and canary from the many candles they hold. My sister leans against the dark banister as she faces Nouis, seeming to capture his whole attention.

My throat goes tight at the sight of the tall, dark man waiting for me at the bottom of the steps.

Nouis's gaze jumps up to me. His jaw goes slack, green eyes widening. I narrowly defeat the instinct to shuffle on my feet and tug at my dress, instead I slowly descend the steps, and give him a coy smile.

"Ah, here she is. Isn't she beautiful?" chuckles Giulia as I reach them. I'm about to give my sister a snarky reply, but don't get the chance.

"Beautiful is an understatement. You are stunning." Nouis's sparkling green eyes glint with mischief. My heart skips a beat as warm roses bloom over my cheeks. He offers me a hand, and as I wrap my fingers around his, goose bumps tingle up my arm.

"I hope Giulia hasn't been giving you too hard a time," I respond, eyes flickering to my golden sister.

"Not at all. Apparently, the plan for this evening even has her seal of approval."

"Now that is impressive," I tease.

We walk to the front door, Nouis opening it for me like

the chivalrous gentleman he is. My eyebrows jump in surprise, my gaze cutting down to the small bundle wrapped in a plain blue muslin. I stoop, identifying the contents of the strange parcel as books.

"Did you order something?" asks Nouis confused, looking back inside. No one answers, so I guess not. I pull the three books free of their wrapping to inspect them.

The Art of Mind-Stilling by Eshin Shakya, *Inner Peace* by Khoa Saanvi and *Your Relationship With Fate* by Arif Mudaris.

"They're foreign translations. Those two look like they're from Malaya." Nouis points to the first two titles. "Not sure about the other one."

"Malaya?" I ask, eyes wide. *That's all the way past the Holy States to the West.* "How do you know?"

"I've seen books like this before. When they stain their leather for books, it comes out this faded green colour, and their paper has this almost orange quality to it," Nouis says, taking one of the books and raising it to his nose. He gives it a sniff and nods, holding it out for me. "See, it still smells kind of sweet from the sap they mix into the leather stain to give it the emerald colour."

"Interesting," I mutter, deciding not to sniff the books for myself.

"No note?" Michelle reappears, taking the book from Nouis's grasp and flicking through the dusty pages. "These have to be at least a little expensive if they've come all the way from Malaya."

"Well, it's pretty clear who they're for at least," Giulia chimes in.

"That doesn't forgo the politeness of a note," I say, flicking open the first few pages, quickly scanning the foreword from Arif Mudaris. "But clearly someone wants to help me 'take control' of my relationship with Fate."

"And here I thought going to the temple helped with that," chuckles Nouis as though the concept is bizarre and unnecessary.

"There's notes scribbled in the margins. Someone's really studied this," Michelle says, showing me the stranger's scrawl. I close the book in my hands, shaking my head.

"Who would just leave books like this at the door without a word?" Giulia frowns. "It's not like they're common translations." I shrug, handing them all over to my sister.

"A question for later. Right now, we're leaving."

"Indeed. Your carriage, signora," Nouis says, wrapping his arm around mine again. He pulls me close as we step out into the night.

The warmth of his body radiates over me, chasing away any thought of a chill. I cast my head back to my sister who throws me an enthusiastic thumbs up, sharing giggles with Michelle as she shuts the front door to our home.

My head snaps back around to my date, stomach fluttering. His eyes trace my face as we stroll towards his carriage. Blood threatens to flood my cheeks, but thankfully he speaks, giving me something to focus on other than my frolicking pulse.

"Did you have a good day?" he asks as we settle into the plush carriage. I'm surrounded by luxurious, blue velvet cushioned seats. Two candles sit behind glass protectors and shower the small space in wriggling creamy gold. He eases next to me, his thigh pressing against mine and making my heartbeat crash against my ribs.

"Yes, in the end it was."

He smiles, leaning closer. All thoughts drop from my mind, those sharp features cast in golden candlelight and inky shadow.

"It isn't over yet." His deep voice sends my stomach into somersaults. He knocks on the front wall, the carriage starting off.

"How was your day?" I ask, the jostling carriage seeming to push us closer together.

"I spent it reacquainting myself with Halice. It's even more beautiful than I remembered."

Pride floods up my spine and a warm smile spills across my face.

"Where did you go?"

"Well," he says, running a finger over the back of my hand currently folded over my lap. All thoughts freeze in my head. Small sparks shoot up my arms as he makes small circles on my skin. "I went for a walk along the river. I had lunch at a lovely little cafe with live music near the Grand Temple. I handled some business. But, most importantly, I'm spending my evening with you. That's the real highlight."

Fresh memories of my childhood friend bringing me flowers and playing in the garden flood my mind's eye. Walks by the river where we threw stones in the water and the times we ran away from my mother to explore Halice together. My cheeks are on fire. I dip my head, looking at him through my lashes. "You, sir, are a charmer."

He ducks his head down, lips brushing against my ear. "I try. Particularly with you."

His gorgeous face is inches from mine, green eyes sparkling even in the dim lighting.

Friends. We're supposed to be *friends*. There is so much that won't work here, too many factors. We can't cross that threshold. We shouldn't.

"So, where are you taking me?" I ask softly, trying to break this ... this connection that seems to be taking us further and further to that point of no return.

"I hear the best restaurant in town overlooks the River Vitta. I made us a reservation."

My eyes widen, delight flooding onto my tongue.

"Pulchra Tradite?"

"It's promising that you've heard of it."

Live music, the best wine, exquisite chefs. He's really going all out.

The carriage journey doesn't take long. As we walk towards the restaurant entrance, Nouis takes my arm, pulling me close to his side and shielding me from the cool breeze peeling off the river. He shortens his stride to suit mine without making it a big deal. The confidence of his gait and the generous greeting to the server only feed my rapid pulse and stretching smile.

We walk the long hallway to the central dining room. The circular area is made of large arches of stone, with shallow balconies looking over the river. The patrons are some of the city's wealthiest, many watching as we're shown to a small, intimate table right by a balcony. Outside the swirling lanterns of purple, blue, and green slowly trickle with the onyx water, the colours mingling and dancing beneath a clear, navy sky. The gentle strokes of the evening breeze send delicious tingles up and down my body, as I sit across from my handsome date.

"We should've gone somewhere more private. Save you the gossip this will cause." Nouis's brows pinching in question as his eyes dart around the crowd.

Guilt forms a knot in my throat. I'm not really using him, but it's far more helpful if we do this in public.

"I can handle gossip. Besides you're already staying with us." I clear my throat, not quite able to meet his eye as the wine is poured. "Plus there are a hundred rumours floating around about why you're in town. What's the harm in adding one more?"

Nouis leans forwards, flashing me a wicked, intelligent smile.

"Is that your way of asking me what business I have here?"

"No, but now you've piqued my curiosity." I pick up my glass, waiting for an answer. "Are you working with Cardinal Bellandi on something?"

Nouis chuckles. "Business before pleasure?"

"I'm always both." I lean forwards, giving him my best sultry voice.

"Well, no, I'm not working with or for, or around, Cardinal Bellandi," Nouis chuckles. "He asked for a favour and I didn't see any reason why not. Besides I couldn't pass up the chance to see Electi Renza Di Maineri in action."

I laugh quietly, fixing him with a bright smile. "So how do you know him?"

"We've crossed paths a couple of times before, I think we've made small talk maybe five times?" Nouis shrugs. "But I was coming this way anyway. I'm actually here to assess some financial matters for the Holy Mother."

"That required your attention in person?" My brow pulls together. Considering the tax bill Morteselli brought before us, I'm suddenly concerned about just how expensive the Spiritual Works in this city really are.

"When the Holy Mother speaks, you listen. When she tells you to go, you go," Nouis explains wryly, before sipping his wine. "Particularly when she's your aunt."

I chuckle. "Sounds demanding."

"She has every right to be. She raised me after the accident." Nouis's lips tighten and his tone holds forced levity. "Well, both she and my uncle. The two halves of my life, the Church and the Bank."

Despite hiding it well, a familiar sadness seeps into his handsome face. It hits like a sucker punch. I reach across the table and wrap my fingers around his.

When a building collapses and the richest man in the Holy States is crushed to death, people talk. Particularly when that leaves a young boy of only twelve as his successor. The pain hovering in Nouis's eyes is all too familiar. It's lived in my reflection since my mother died. Not exactly the same ... but no less sharp. I squeeze his fingers, lowering my voice softly.

"Let's not dwell on old history." He tries to wave off the heaviness.

"Old history leaves long scars. They hurt," I say softly. He squeezes my fingers tight as the waiters set down some starters for our table.

"We both know that well enough," he agrees gently.

Nouis flashes me a smile, turning to the food. The minute the smoked fish hits my tongue I can't help but smile. The smoky salt mingles with the rich velvet of the wine like a symphony.

"So tell me, when you aren't shaping this city in your image, what do you enjoy doing?"

"Being an Electi is an all-consuming honour. I don't have much free time."

"Oh, come on, it can't be utterly consuming—you're here with me. What do you enjoy the most? You always enjoyed art and music and the theatre when we were younger. You've always been an avid supporter of the Garden."

"That's because the Garden will shape the future." I gesture with my wine, feeling a flame beginning to flicker in my belly. "Our efforts have already secured Halice as the capital of innovation and art across the continent. Here, people are free to challenge the boundaries we think we know and change the world. Not to mention—"

I cut myself off, a hand going to my face embarrassed. "Sorry, I didn't mean this to turn into a lecture."

"Not at all," Nouis answers instantly, a spark lighting in his own eyes. "Never apologise for passion. No wonder you're such a revered politician. You speak so well."

My cheeks are sure to be the same shade as our wine.

"I take it then that you don't like our Garden?"

"That would be a scandalous disservice." He shakes his

head emphatically, setting his wine glass down on the white linen tablecloth. "You know I love it, if not quite as much as you. I'm merely aware of its potential threat."

"Threat?"

"Challenging boundaries isn't always a great thing. Sometimes good can become great, but sometimes bad can also become worse."

"And what about all the beauty it's proven to bring?" I ask. "Is that not worth the potential of a little danger?"

"Hmm," Nouis leans forwards, catching my gaze and locking me in with those warm green eyes. "Sitting across from you seems to make my position clear. Beauty like yours is absolutely worth a little danger." Warmth flickers in my chest.

Nouis stands up. He sets his glass down and holds out his hand. "The next course won't be out for a while. Dance with me?" he asks.

I hesitate a moment. I look up at him and find swallowing doesn't alleviate the tightness in my throat. My palms are sweaty and my knees feel weak.

We're supposed to just be friends. But friends can dance, right?

I gently lower my hand to his. Sparks fly up my arm, my heart picking up a speedy tempo. *Fate's Fury, how does he do it? How does he make me feel like this?* A feeling that is enough to battle my sane logical arguments and my good reasons for wanting to hold back.

Nouis leads me to the small dance floor, already populated with a few other couples. He pulls me in close, his strong arm wrapping around my lower back. There are inches between us as he starts to lead. The strings' serenade is sweet and soaring, the drum is slow, steady, and dependable.

His embrace is warm, his arms are secure. I'm floating. Our gazes lock and everything inside me drops; tension slipping from muscles I didn't even know I had, my skin bursting with tiny exploding stars.

"You're a wonderful dancer," Nouis murmurs, his voice soft and inviting like a warm feather bed.

"You're not so bad either."

"Well, I'm glad you think so. You know, you never answered my question." The warmth of his breath tickles the tip of my nose. I can't think of anything except how beautiful his eyes are, and the closeness of his body to mine.

"Oh?"

"What's your favourite thing to do in your spare time?"

"Same as everyone else I suppose—"

Uncomfortable heat licks down my bones. I stop in my tracks, an itching spotlight appearing on the back of my head. Familiar, damning whispers flicker around the base of my skull.

"That bastard," I hiss. A frown mars Nouis's perfect face, before his eyes jump over to the entrance.

"Ah." That noise tells me all he needs to. Patricelli.

"I'm sure he'll leave," I scowl.

"Actually, he's heading this way."

"What?" I spin around just as Idris arrives at my side. Outrage bolts through me like being doused in acid. His lips are thinned, eyes narrowed and glued to the floor. My hands shake, my entire body coiling and hardening.

Kill.

Rip out his throat.

Quick and easy. End this, once and for all.

Nouis shifts, slipping his shoulder in front of mine as he prepares to intervene. To protect me or hold me back, I'm not sure.

"Maineri," Idris says in clipped greeting.

"Patricelli, what do you want?" I fight to keep my tone civil, though it still flirts with irritation. I turn my entire head away, glaring at the pretty floors. My muscles lessen their shaking even if I can't unclench my fists.

"On any other night, I'd just leave, given that you were here first," Idris explains. "However, tonight is my parents' anniversary. It's the first time I'm back in the city in almost a decade. I was hoping you'd agree to leave, as it's a special occasion for my family."

Change my plans? For him? Pah! Spite writhes on my tongue but I don't release it. I swallow the poison and shuffle where I stand, searching for any position where my bones aren't crawling.

I look anywhere but at Idris, and realise people are staring. Other dancers have stopped, tables have quieted. They're waiting for the violence they all see as inevitable.

I grit my teeth together, stubbornness swelling like a storm. *No. I won't let the gods control me. Not like this.*

Not ever.

"Fine," I reply sharply. "But remember this favour Patricelli, because I will collect."

I'm squeezing Nouis's hand like a vice. I drop it, unable to look anywhere but the door as I leap for it, flying past the tables. My breath is fast. My lungs ache. My pulse feels like lightning under my skin.

I push past the staff until I'm outside. My rushing breath begins to slow as the cool air pulls all the disgust from it, dragging that toxic sensation from my body.

I double over with relief, reaching for a tall stone column to steady myself. Its coolness sucks any remaining venom from my fingers, washing the memory of Patricelli far away.

Footsteps approach behind me and I turn to see Nouis. His smile is careful, like he's waiting for the influence of Patricelli to leave my mind.

"You ... okay?"

I nod, rubbing my eyes. Shame crawls up my tongue. "I'm so sorry," I groan. "I didn't... I shouldn't..."

A lump forms in my throat and my fingers itch to do something, anything. I pace back and forth, taking several deep breaths. This is going to be the rest of my life. Anywhere I go, I'm going to have to dance around Idris Patricelli. This hatred, this loathing can come anytime, any place. It'll be with me forever. I was a fool to think he'd only be in the High Chamber.

Nouis takes my hand, and my head jumps up.

"Come on." He tugs softly, pulling me towards the river. We leave the cobbled road and start down the worn path to the riverbank. The gravel crunches with each step, as we drift further and further away from the street. His warm fingers are woven through mine.

"Where are we going?" I enquire.

"Just follow me and you'll see." The moonlight sprays his eyes with a sheen of silver, as the world folds us in varying shades of navy. A smile creeps over my face as I follow him towards the giggling water. Above us, the sapphire sky bleeds into the river and lanterns of pink, green, and blue twirl lazily along their path. A stray breeze mingles with the overhanging willow trees, making each trail of leaves sway and dance.

"Better?" he asks, fingers still linked through mine as we stroll. The music from the restaurant floats out of the arched windows and balcony. The strings are so sweet, serenading the stars and the stream.

"Thank you for understanding," I whisper. "I'm still ... learning to deal with it."

"I'm sure you will."

My eyes lock with his. Nouis's angular face is outlined in moonlight. That jaw is sharp enough to cut glass.

"What makes you so sure?"

"I know you," says Nouis softly, stepping closer to me. "You love this city, and this city loves you. Killing Idris Patricelli would cement a war between the Maineri and the Patricelli that could tear Halice apart. You'd never let that happen."

A rush of relief floods through me. The intensity of it shocks me, rushing from my shoulders to my toes and pushing a gasp from my lips.

"Everyone thinks I'm mad. That a bloody, violent end is inevitable," I admit, searching his face as if the answer would appear there. "I can't help wondering if they're right."

Nouis seems to consider that for a moment.

"Maybe it will come to that. Maybe it won't. But if it

happens ... I don't think it'll be a slip in your control. You're much too strong for that."

I can't fight the smile itching itself onto my face.

Nouis takes my other hand and we stand almost chest to chest. His eyes sparkle with lantern light, his lips pulling into a crooked smile.

Friends.

We're friends. This can't work. We live in two different places and we think differently. What if this doesn't work and we lose each other permanently?

"No matter your choice, you'll have my support ... should you need it."

Friends. We're friends. Only friends.

He leans closer but stops, his lips barely an inch from mine. His cologne of almonds and vanilla mingles with the fresh night air. "Renza, I would like to kiss you."

Forget being friends. I push up on my toes, closing the distance between our lips. Sparks flurry up and down my spine. His mouth is soft, tender with each gentle movement. His arms circle around me, pulling me close so every line of my body is pressed against him. So secure, so strong. One of my hands snakes up to tangle amongst his dark hair, the stubble on his jaw brushing against mine.

His lips are patient, savouring and exploring. Like he refuses to rush a single moment he has with me. Eventually he breaks the kiss, both of us now breathing a little raggedly. My lips are red from the scratch of his stubble, but the sensation is glorious. Neither of us says anything, smiling at each other, soaking in the euphoria of the moment.

Standing here under the moonlight, safely wrapped in his

arms, I can't help but think: this is perfect. "Come on," says Nouis pulling himself away. "I think Giulia and Michelle said they were going out dancing. If we hurry we can catch them up."

And just like that, I let Nouis whisk me away for a night of drinking and dancing on the town.

CHAPTER 8

Fate's Fury, why won't this heat give? My skin is all but melting off. The carriage comes to a stop but Father doesn't look up from the letter he's penning across his lap.

Giulia wastes no time, jumping out of the carriage and wafting her face with the fresh air.

"Oh, I forgot Terzo is getting married today," Giulia says pointing at the decorations outside the church. I lean out of the open door to see them, an eyebrow rising higher. The eccentric sculptor is marrying the daughter of a wealthy merchant, and as per his usual style, these decorations are fabulous and opulent. Of course, for such a prominent Soulmate wedding, the Grand Temple would be used.

"I'll have to write with our congratulations," I muse, turning back to my father. He's reviewing his letter, deaf to our conversation.

"Father, we're here," I remind him. He nods absently.

"One moment, it's about the school opening the library," mutters Father, blowing on the ink.

"Yeah, Emilia and Serra said they were going to be working down at the school this morning. I hope that doesn't spell trouble for the opening," I frown.

"Not from what Teacher Veletor says here. They just want to confirm we'll be there and let us know that they're excited for the opening."

"Well then, as it's not urgent the ink can dry during the service," I say, pulling the letter from his hands and setting it on the seat next to him. He nods at me with a short chuckle.

"You're right of course, my dear."

I snort before I step out of the carriage to join Giulia, beads of sweat dampening my hairline and skin glistening in the heat. Giulia continues in vain to waft the air around her neck for some relief, as her cutting blue eyes search through the brightly coloured crowd.

Around us the congregation is slowly slipping up the steps towards the Grand Temple for our weekly spiritual lecture. Sunshine blasts off the pale stone and bright windows in a vicious glare, challenging anyone to enter.

I turn away from the malicious sunshine as Father steps out of the carriage, checking around him. It's obvious who he's searching for. Irritation flares in my stomach.

"For goodness' sake, if I didn't murder him in the High Chamber, I'm not going to murder him now." I scowl, spinning on my heels and marching up the stairs towards the Grand Temple.

"Renza!"

That deep voice halts my steps. Nouis's dark hair gleams like polished obsidian in the relentless sunshine as he confidently hurries across the steps towards me. His smart green tunic compliments his eyes. A smile stretches across my face as he stops in front of me.

"Hi." I grin as he takes one of my hands in his.

"Can I steal you for a bit?"

"I really should go inside—"

"We'll be quick." He winks, giving me a gentle tug. I look behind me to see Giulia chuckling to herself as my father shakes his head in amusement.

"Where are we going?" I ask, following him away from the Grand Temple.

"Trust me." His hand in mine sends a shiver down my spine. I can't pry the girlish grin off my lips as we sprint across the courtyard.

"Trust you? My, my, that sounds like trouble." I lean into him. His wicked grin answers me. He pulls me around the corner of a building, his strong arm wrapping around my waist as his lips slip down to hover over mine.

"Trouble?" he murmurs softly. "I think you like that."

"Maybe I do." I wrap my fingers around his tunic. My pulse hammers in my ears, every inch of me craving his warm confidence. Everything has been so unbalanced since meeting Patricelli last week. Like I've been teetering on the edge of a cliff. But with Nouis I don't feel like I'm on the edge. He's safe, I *know* him, and right now I need that more than ever.

The bells start to ring, the Grand Temple's attempt to

hurry the stragglers. I sigh, pulling away to create some space between us.

"Come on. We'll be late for service—"

Nouis moans, leaning back against the wall.

"Let's skip it," he suggests, a glint entering his eyes.

"Skip it?" I mock horror. "What would your aunt say?"

"Oh, don't bring her into it," Nouis half groans, half chuckles. "One sermon won't blemish our souls. I want to spend time with you."

"We've spent time together almost every day since you've been in Halice," I answer.

"Yes, stolen moments and secret whispers at your home, in between your meetings and family dinners. Don't get me wrong, I love every second with your family, and with you," he whispers, "but I want more than that. I want to take you out and spoil you properly."

"I'm a busy woman."

"Believe me, I get that. It's part of what makes you so damn attractive," Nouis groans as though he knows this well but can't help himself. "But I want another date. A *real* date."

"Well, then ask me out again properly," I tease.

"That's what I'm trying to do, if it wasn't obvious." Nouis sighs in mock exasperation. "Besides, it looks like we're too late now."

I spin to see the huge black and white chequered doors of the Grand Temple being pulled shut. The beginnings of the first hymn start swirling out of the stained windows and tall spires. "Not quite, if we're quick we can slip in through the side door." I grin, easing out of his arms.

"Fine. I can deny you nothing, Maineri. We'd better be

quick then." He chuckles, grabbing my hand as we hurry together back into the square, the sunshine lighting up his face like a beacon. My heart swells, the edges pushing against my ribs.

SLAM!

A vicious blast whips towards me and a wall of fire knocks me down hard. Fragments of stark black and white marble erupt from the holy building in front of us and a ball of flames surges from its centre, consuming everything in its path. Its blistering fingers wash over my face, dragging fresh sweat to the surface of my skin, smearing my features with soot. Dirty smoke sits deep within my nose, making me gag.

The brightness fades. My eyes dance with vermillion stars, focusing on the trails of black smoke scarring the otherwise clear blue sky. Numbness engulfs me. Ringing consumes my mind. Gasping, I can't catch my breath. My mouth is filled with copper and salt. Something wet and hot is rolling down my face.

The world is miles away as I watch my body pick itself up from its tangle of bruised, soot-stained limbs. My grimy hands move amongst the shower of flaming amber ashes on the ground and I crawl to see what's left of the Grand Temple.

Wrathful red flames claw into the sky, writhing like a monster. They devour everything. Sickening black smoke stains the air and the white stone pillars of the Grand Temple stand like a trampled rib cage.

My soul slams back into my body.

Father. Giulia.

"No!" I scream, scrambling upright on battered limbs.

Tears blur my vision, eyes stinging with soot. I stagger towards the building, stumbling over the smouldering steps leading to the destruction.

As I navigate the blistering rubble, the heat is drowning me, stealing the air from my lungs as the skeleton of the temple starts to crumble.

Hacking coughs rip through my body as I try to move forwards, past the charred marble that used to be the aisle. Splintered, vicious fragments of stone are sprayed in every direction, the blast of the explosion having unleashed a violent wave of tiny marble knives upon those trapped inside, before crushing many with a collapsing ceiling. Everything that can is burning, wooden pews, curtains, tapestries, *people*. It's all consumed by wicked, orange tongues. Greedily the blaze devours everything in sight. Blood is sprayed over broken white stone. Blackened corpses of my colleagues and friends are crushed and marred to the point that I keel over in the flames and vomit.

"Father! Giulia!" I scream into the inferno. I spin around, searching through the smoke and flames for any sign of life.

"Please! Father! Giulia! Anyone!" My throat is raw with desperation. I plough forwards, searching for something—anything or anyone. I spy a familiar figure lying on the floor through a gauze of sweltering smoke.

Getting closer, I fall to my knees next to them.

Jacopo Patricelli. Mangled and limp, his lower half is still buried under the collapsed stone. Blood is caked over his hazel eyes, open and staring blindly into the smoke. My insides crumble, fresh tears brimming my eyes. I shake my head, catching sight of another familiar face to his side.

My heart plummets, splintering as it falls.

"No! No!" I sob, desperately scrambling for the body. I reach my father, limp and unmoving. Head caked with blood, features blackened by the fire, eyes staring endlessly into the writhing red monster around us. The scream that rips through me could split me in half. I grip hold of my father's body, as though I could physically claw him back from the afterlife. Every part of my body is shaking. I might shatter at any moment.

"Renza! Renza!"

That deep voice, thick with worry cuts through the black. Through the scorching flames and curtains of fumes I see a tall figure diving around the rapidly crumbling stone.

"Renza!" Nouis's relief crushes something inside me. He charges towards me, grabbing hold of my arms.

"We have to go," he yells over the flames.

"Giulia! We have to find her!" I gasp.

"We have to go *now*," he shouts, dragging me away. Then I see a flicker of something pink in the distance. Giulia's dress. She was wearing pink this morning.

"Giulia!" I scream, wrenching towards her. My hacking coughs tighten like a noose around my throat. Falling embers plant burning kisses on the naked skin of my face and hands as I stagger over the rubble.

I collapse next to my sister, pulling her over.

"I can't ... I can't leave her," I sob. Anguish tears through my body, catching and crushing my heart. Nouis doesn't hesitate. Reaching down, he grabs Giulia and throws her over his shoulder.

"Move! Move!" he chokes on the smoke. The world is

spinning. My limbs are refusing to obey, grief rendering them stone. Nouis drops a hand to my forearm, dragging me backwards. The world is swirling with flames and ashes and I feel my face blistering, hands scorched.

Nouis pulls me outside. All I see is a brilliant blue sky stained with cinders before everything fades to black.

CHAPTER 9

The doctor moves deftly, smearing soothing ointments across my palms. Our home has turned into something of a command centre. Nouis put the City Guard on high alert. I can't even think about Halice right now. The image of my father in the fire runs around my head again and again. It devours me, stealing all thoughts, all words, all energy.

On the brief occasion I can think about anything else, it's my sister.

My poor, dear sister.

Alive. That was the first word the doctor uttered when I came around, scrambling to her side. But his morose face and sombre tone made it clear that he wasn't optimistic. She lies in her bed in our house, eyes closed. She's so pale, vicious burns covering her left arm, shoulders and neck, red blistering vines wrap up over her jaw to mark her cheek. There are bruises caused by falling rubble coating every part of her body and a nasty, gaping head wound that makes me want to vomit. She's wrapped in so many bandages there is barely a scrap of skin to plant a kiss.

She hasn't woken up yet.

The doctor continues his ministrations, wrapping my palms in clean white linen. How they aren't marred with grime and residue, I don't know. I'll never be clean. The heat's venomous kiss will stain my skin forever.

"There," says the doctor, finishing his work. "All finished."

Nouis's head jumps up in an instant. He ends his conversations with Captain Collier, the head of the City Guard, rushing over to my side.

"Will she be okay?" he asks, his face rippling with concern.

"Physically, yes, in time. Though charging into those flames was not advisable for her health."

Fresh tears pile up along my lashes.

"She's lucky you pulled her out in time," the doctor continues. "You're a hero, Signore Rizaro."

"Hardly," Nouis dismisses. "Is there anything we should do?"

"Rest. As much as possible."

I can't hold in the scoff as I fold tighter in my chair, eyes glued to the unmoving face of my sister. My singed tunic and trousers crackle as I pull my legs tight to my chest. The stench of burning still clings to my clothes.

"Perhaps a tonic ... to help her sleep?" offers the doctor.

"Leaving it can't hurt. She can make that decision tonight." Nouis offers the doctor a thankful pat on the back.

Nouis sits on the edge of Giulia's bed to face me properly.

I swallow, daring to turn for a second to look at him. The concern rippling from his eyes floods me with gratitude. He saved Giulia. He got her out of there. My tongue falls limp in my mouth. *Fate's Fury, how on earth do I properly thank him?*

"Here." Nouis hands me a glass of water. "Drink this. You need to stay hydrated."

My hands are so bandaged I need them both to pull the drink close to my body.

"I've had the men search every inch of this house. There are no explosives here or anywhere on this street," Nouis says. "They've searched the High Chamber building as well and came up empty. It seems like the Grand Temple was the only target so far. Extra guards are posted at every important site in the city, and everything coming in and out of the gates is being searched thoroughly."

"Any clues? Any claims?"

"None so far. But we'll find the culprits. I promise."

I swallow, my throat raw with ash and grief. "Nouis ... how do I thank you?" I whisper.

Nouis frowns, shifting closer. "You don't need to thank me."

"Yes, I do." My voice crumbles in my throat. I can't bear to look into those crystal green eyes for a single second more. Instead I look at my water. Nouis reaches for me, a gentle hand squeezing in support around my wrist.

"Renza, I've ... been where you are right now," Nouis reminds me. My stomach overturns yet again. Of course he has. Both of his parents were crushed in a building collapse when he was a child. My throat tightens; my eyes well; bile builds at the back of my tongue.

"Nouis," I croak in horror, "I'm so sorry. Of course this must be awful for you. I'm so—"

"Don't you even think like that right now," Nouis cut me off in a tone that was firm yet kind. "I didn't bring it up to add to the misery. I only meant to say that I understand that you need me. I know *what* you need right now, and what's more I know I can give it to you. I can help. I more than want to; I need to. I need to help you."

My breath catches on the thick lump in my throat. My chest aches with a warmth that's somehow both sweet and sour at the same time. *Am I going crazy? How can one person wheel through all these feelings at the same time?*

"So, you can thank me by taking a drink," says Nouis, soft but serious. I nod, diligently lifting the glass to my lips.

"I'm here for you, Renza. However I'm needed," Nouis promises, then gives me a gentle smile. "Although I'd appreciate it if you didn't run into a burning building again."

"I'll do my best," I whisper, trying to smile at the joke but only tears spring to my eyes. He shuffles closer, wrapping an arm around my shoulders, pulling me closer. I settle my head on his shoulder, breathing in his addictive scent of almonds and vanilla that chases away the lingering ashes and charred hair clogging my nose.

"Right now, you're in shock. Soon it'll wear off," Nouis says calmly, rubbing soothing patterns on my back, "And when it does, I'll be here. For your tears, for your anger, for the torrent of grief that's coming. Let yourself feel it, Renza; I can weather the storm. I'm not going anywhere."

I squeeze my eyes tight, digging my fingers into the smooth fabric of his tunic. I grip him in desperation and fear, like I'm about to be swept away by a violent storm and he's my anchor keeping me in the harbour. He's the only thing making any of this remotely bearable.

I hear a commotion behind me, raised voices as feet fly over the mosaic floor of my home.

"Maineri!" comes a sharp voice, like a bolt of acid to the brain. My gut sinks, throat tightening as I freeze in Nouis's arms.

Nouis leaps up, face filled with fury as he throws a hand forwards. "Patricelli, now is not a—"

I turn, watching as Idris storms into the room. Grief blazes in those golden eyes with an intensity that could destroy the world. He looks like someone slapped him when he sets eyes on my sister. Words seem to vanish from his mind.

How dare he look at her. How dare he storm in here to gawk at her pain. I grit my teeth, heat flaring up my neck and buzzing through my mind. Every single instinct in me screams to rip him apart, shred by shred, to break through these bandages and wrap my blistered, battered fingers around his throat.

I get to my feet, baring my teeth. Nouis's arm comes down instinctively, hovering in front of my waist. A reminder not to take another step closer.

"Get out," I hiss at Idris. "There has been enough violence in this city today. Don't you dare invite more."

Idris stops, fists clenched and jaw straining. His eyes run up and down, clearly taking in my charred clothes, sooty skin and freshly tended injures.

"What happened?" he demands, visibly shaking.

What would his blood feel like on my hands? How good would it feel to break every bone in his body? I turn my eyes away, gripping at my head.

"There was an explosion, but you already knew that," snaps Nouis, putting a steadying hand on my shoulder.

"Is that the only thing you know? That an explosion happened?" Idris snarls. "You did nothing else?"

"Renza and I ran into the flames looking for survivors, and we found Giulia. Then we called the Guard, put them on alert and arranged a deep search of the city in case there were anymore explosives. What exactly have you done?" Nouis spits back.

Idris scoffs like he might punch him right then and there.

I suck in several deep breaths, the boys' bickering brewing a fresh headache.

"Who else did you find?" Idris's voice sounds unusually brittle. I open my eyes, sucking in a deep breath. He's not evil. He's not. Rationally I know that. He's in pain. Like me. He's just lost everything too.

"No one alive." Nouis answers shortly. "Leave. This isn't helpful—"

"Wait," I say, my voice feeling foreign as I choke out the words. "Idris ... in the flames I found Jacopo. He was already dead. I'm so sorry. It looked like he was crushed by part of a falling pillar ... I believe it was quick."

Idris is silent. I can feel his eyes like a drill into the back of my skull. I want to scream. I want to shriek in rage and claw out his eyes. I take a deep breath, ordering every trembling muscle to stay where I am.

"What are you going to do?" demands Idris, voice thick.

"Do?"

"You're the last living member of the High Chamber, for Fate's sake!" Idris's words are thick and teetering on the edge of rage. "*Do* something. Find those responsible and make them pay."

"What do you think is happening as we speak, Patricelli? Of course I'm going to do that." I fight to keep my tone even but I'm starting to lose. "But first, the City Guard are searching the city for other explosive devices, making sure the people are safe. Their safety has to come first."

"While the culprit could be getting away?"

"All the entrances in and out of the city are on lockdown, but safety is the priority. There could be other explosives, we need to make sure there aren't. The culprit will be found—they will face justice—but justice won't come at the expense of more lives."

Idris mutters something I can't make out.

My father would know what to say. My father would know what to do. The instinct to turn to him for guidance makes me want to scream. I'll never have it again. He would be so much better for the city. *He should've survived, not me.*

Nouis fills the silence. "Patricelli, you should leave. When there is information on the death of your family, you will be informed—"

"Screw that, Rizaro. I'm a Patricelli. My family helped lay the very foundations of this city. If you won't do anything, I will."

With that, he marches off, his expensive boots smacking against the tiled floors. Nouis wraps his arms around me, his front against my back. The whispers fade from my mind, the rage slowly slipping out of my blood.

"Hey. I've got you," whispers Nouis softly. His embrace is strong and warm. My shoulders sag, my head rolling back to rest against him.

"Thank you," I whisper.

"I won't let him come back. You need rest."

"He's right. I'm the only Electi left. I have to lead. The people need to see me, need reassurance that we're not leaderless."

"You're not the only Electi," Nouis disagrees softly, rubbing my hands. "Cardinal Bellandi is still alive; I've already sent word of what happened. I can't imagine he'll stay away in the face of a tragedy like this. He knows he's needed."

"You sent word already?" I frown, turning to look at him. Nouis's brow puckers, worry brewing behind his eyes.

"Was I wrong? I thought backup would be helpful. Another Electi to help around here."

"No, you weren't wrong. I just... Why didn't you mention it?"

"I was just trying to help; sometimes speed is helpful," Nouis says. Worry tinges his soft words. "You have a lot on your plate, but eventually you would've written ... right?"

"Of course."

"Did you want to write the letter? You're right, I should've said something." Nouis shakes his head, scolding himself more than anything. "I was just thinking about all the things that needed to be done and didn't want to waste time. Next time—"

"Fate's Fury, never let there be one." I cut him off, reaching for his chest. "It's okay. But in the future, I need a run-through. Patricelli might be … difficult, but he's right. I'm an Electi and my city is in crisis. I must lead."

"You are leading. The guard is at work already, people are being questioned. These people will be found. But you're also grieving. There is nothing wrong with that."

I drop my head to his chest. His arms are so warm and so strong. So safe. My aching eyes slip closed. I wrap my arms tighter around him.

"I know," I whisper, "I know."

CHAPTER 10

My nose stings. Humidity steals the air from my lungs, making every breath harder than the last. A gentle breeze makes the winged silk sleeves of my black and white dress flutter against my sensitive skin.

Black and white—the colours of our faith. Of mourning.

Dried tears cover my cheeks. My eyes are swollen and itchy, the skin on my face tight. My mind staggers like a drunkard between crippling grief and overwhelming numbness.

I don't know how long I've been sitting on Giulia's balcony, staring out over Halice. I can't take my eyes off the spot where the Grand Temple used to stand. That gaping, smoking hole in the skyline is a seeping wound burrowing ever deeper into my chest.

From here you can see out over the city all the way to the Argenti Straight. The rooftops of thousands of homes undulate like waves. The original city wall snakes through them, that old boundary abandoned generations ago. In the mouth of the river, an ancient fortress has been repurposed and converted into our prison, standing on a little rocky island. Closer to home, to the far left of my view, the sun glints on the domed glass ceiling of the Old Watchtower where, inside, the emergency bells lie dormant, gathering dust.

The old vestiges of war and violence hadn't been needed for centuries. They crumbled and languished because we didn't need them anymore. We had built better.

Now they're screaming at me like a swollen blister.

Behind me, Giulia lies unwaking in her bed. A nurse is by her side every minute of every day, taking her pulse and making sure she's still breathing. A tube has been placed down her throat, for water and liquid food, so she doesn't starve while she sleeps.

There's no sign of her waking yet. No flickering eyes. No reaction to anything.

Michelle holds her hand like they're welded together. She talks to Giulia constantly, telling her silly stories or reading little poems. We seem to trigger each other's tears, so an hour ago I'd decided to step out for a minute, to let us both catch our breath.

I haven't been more than thirty paces away from Giulia since this whole thing happened. I'll have to leave her with the nurse soon enough, return to the world and my city. Fate's Mercy, I hope she wakes up. Because my city is in a state of emergency and mourning, and it's my job as an Electi to fix it.

How on earth do I fix it?

Nouis approaches the balcony. He hasn't left. Not since it happened. He slept in a spare room last night, while I lay awake next to Giulia, staring at the rise and fall of her chest. I was terrified that if I closed my eyes it would stop. Nouis has put food in front of me, been a shoulder to cry on when the tears wouldn't stop. His arms have been so strong, at times they're the only thing stopping me from falling apart.

"Here." Nouis sets a glass of water on the dark wooden table.

"Thank you." I take the drink, that numbing coolness dripping through my fingers.

"Any word?" I ask, hating how coarse my voice is.

Nouis sighs, sitting down next to me. "The excavation is finished. No survivors. The blaze... There isn't much of anything. Nothing discernible."

Fresh tears well along my lash line. I nod slowly, letting them fall. "Okay," I say with a thick voice.

Nouis reaches out, his hand wraps around my arm and squeezes softly. "Focus on what is in front of you," Nouis coaches softly. "What do you want?"

"I want to catch these monsters," I hiss, pain rippling up my throat like a venom. The rage twists at the words. "I want them to pay."

"The City Guard are already on it. Idris Patricelli is personally overseeing their work."

I grit my teeth, turning my head away. Patricelli. Practically a stranger to Halice, spending the last ten years dancing from country to country in the name of education. *He was handling this?* His family may have a long history of supporting the Guard, but did he even care?

A cool breeze wriggles past my ear, bringing with it a sharp dose of reason.

Of course he cares. His parents were just murdered.

"Focus on the immediate, Renza," repeats Nouis, thumbs drawing mercifully distracting circles on the back of my hand. "Right here, right now. What do you want to do now? Little steps we can achieve today will help you feel so much better. I promise."

"I... I..."

"Think small," encourages Nouis. "Grief can make big things seem like mountains. How about you start by deciding what you want for dinner? Or perhaps we can go for a walk in the garden, hmm? A change of scenery might help."

"Giulia," I stammer in protest, twisting in my seat to glance back in her direction.

Nouis takes both of my hands in his, pulling me back to look at him. "Giulia's condition is stable. If there is a change, someone will fetch us."

I shake my head. *I can't leave her. I can't.*

Nouis nods slowly, releasing my hands. He lifts up the book resting on his knee, one of those foreign texts from Malaya.

"I started to give this a read last night. I couldn't sleep," he admits, sliding it my way. "I think you should read it. Some of the techniques in here could be useful for all kinds of situations. The breathing techniques in particular might help when the grief gets really bad. I think they would've helped me when ... I was a kid."

I slowly stretch my fingers for the green leather. I pull it closer, running my hands over the foiling of the spine. I will myself to open it, to try and begin doing something mildly useful. Fresh tears well on my lashes as I turn my gaze out over my city, squeezing my lips into a tight line. It's still. Quiet. As though the very stone itself is still reeling from the shock.

Not completely quiet.

Rhythmic thumping hovers at the edges of my ears, slowly growing. I stand up, my hands wrapping around the stone railing as I search the city for its source. "Do you hear that?" I squint against the harsh attention of the sun as I scan the city.

"The marching?" Nouis offers hesitantly.

My heart spasms. "Marching?" I snap, spinning to face him. "Why marching? Where?"

Nouis comes to stand by my side, one hand going to the small of my back as his green gaze cuts across the city. He points out. "There. Black and white, heading this way."

My stomach churns as I follow his finger. He's right, a wave of black and white is pouring through one of the gates into our walled city, heading this way.

"Fate's Fury, what is that?" I hiss in horror.

"Signora," comes a quiet voice behind me. One of the servants, Leo, stands in an all-black uniform of mourning. "Cardinal Bellandi has arrived and is waiting in the foyer," he announces before darting away.

Cardinal Bellandi? Back so soon?

I hurry inside, half running across the mosaicked floors and past the tall columns of my home. I hurry towards the staircase at the front of the house and I stop dead at the top when I see armed Church Militia. Their heavy boots track mud over my mother's mosaics, backs straight as a spear and vicious swords poised at their side. Their pristine black and white cloaks are proudly wrapped around their shoulders, the holy colours of the Church.

Cardinal Bellandi stands amongst them, sharp brown eyes examining the foyer. He is a tall, thin man—his usual uniform of heavy robes has been replaced with riding leathers and a matching Militia cloak. His bald head shines with sweat as he looks up at me, his strong features lined with the marks of time. The sun has blistered the ridge of his long nose, and sleep-deprived curtains of purple hang beneath his eyes.

"Ah, Electi Di Maineri, it's good to see you. How is your dear sister?"

"Not awake yet." My voice grates. I swallow, my eyes flickering to the men in my hallway. The cardinal turns, waving a hand in dismissal.

"I brought some extra protection. They're for you—to keep you safe. Clearly we can't be too careful."

"You think they'll come for me?" I croak, fingers digging into the wood of the banister.

We can't find these monsters, so they're either in hiding or have fled. Or what if they're biding their time? I clench my fingers to stop their trembling, hating how my pulse throbs at the back of my dry mouth.

"They might," the cardinal shrugs. "Better safe than sorry. Don't worry, the Church Militia is the best army on the continent."

And the largest. Everyone in the Holy States must serve in it at some point.

"How many did you bring?" I hate the crack in my voice at that question.

"Enough to double our City Guard. The Holy Mother sent them on loan, to help us secure the city and keep our people safe from more attacks."

"At what price?"

"Price? It's a gift. Help for a friend in distress," scoffs the cardinal.

"We haven't found any more explosives; the city has been searched top to bottom twice over," I argue, descending the steps. My knees feel weak as I come to a stop two steps above the cardinal. "There won't be any more attacks. Not like that anyway. Though the gesture is ... kind, I don't think the Militia are needed."

"I hope you're right"—the cardinal nods—"but we can't be too careful. You and I are the only Electi left. We need to stay safe ... or this city could quickly become leaderless."

He's right. From seven strong we now stand at just two; it wouldn't be hard to take us out completely, leaving Halice without a protector.

"Don't worry, Renza." I jump as Nouis's hand goes to my shoulder—I hadn't even heard him on the steps behind me. "The Church Militia are designed to help. They'll protect the people."

My stomach wriggles uncomfortably. I search for the right words, but I come up empty. We were attacked and here are trained soldiers ready to help us.

How can I refuse? Why should I?

"But Renza, dear, how are you?" asks the cardinal, placing a hand over mine on the banister.

A short, horrible laugh bursts from my lips as I pull my hand away. "Horrendous, Cardinal. Absolutely horrendous."

I step around him, walking past the statue-like soldiers and into my living room. Sunlight ploughs in through large arched windows and drowns the pale blue walls and plush sofas. The mosaic floors quietly clip underfoot as I head to my drink's cabinet and pour myself a generous glass of wine.

The cardinal follows, hands smartly linked behind his back. The riding leathers he wears groan softly as he moves to stand by one of our large windows overlooking the garden.

"I'm sorry for the careless question, Renza." Cardinal Bellandi watches me clinically as I set the decanter filled with wine back in its cupboard. "I meant more physically. You weren't hurt?"

"Nothing permanent, thank Fate's Mercy," answers Nouis for me, leaning against one of the bright bookshelves with the tips of his fingers in his trouser pockets. "A few burns and bruises, but we're both fine."

"Good, good. You said as much in your letter but … it's good to see it with my own eyes." The cardinal gives Nouis an approving pat on the back. I sit on the cool leather couch and stare at the white wine, swirling it around the patterned red glass as I think.

Bellandi and I. That's it. Only us guiding this city though such a tragedy.

We're going to need help.

"We should hold an election quickly," I announce.

Both men turn and the cardinal walks forwards to sit on the opposite couch. "Why?"

"We need our numbers back so we can make some proper decisions."

"You and I can make them," responds Bellandi.

"No. We need at least three. A minimum of an odd number to decide a split." I shake my head, feeling a sweaty curl slip free from the back of my neck. "Besides, it'll show the world we won't be cowed by underhanded, dirty tactics like this."

"I disagree." The cardinal frowns. "Yes, we should hold elections but we don't want to rush it and swear in someone who is wholly terrible at the job."

"There's one person still alive who's been preparing for the job his whole life, even if he was off in other countries." The words spring from my tongue before I realise what I'm suggesting.

Cardinal Bellandi throws a curious look to Nouis, who frowns at me. "Really?" Nouis asks, perching next to me so his knee presses against mine. "You want to support Idris Patricelli for Electi?"

"He's my Soulhate, yes. But he's also a smart man who wants what's best for this city. I shouldn't stand in his way when he can do good here. He can help reassure the people, with a name they know and respect. Then we have three Members, and the ability to make any emergency decision without a split vote."

"Well, I agree, he's the perfect candidate," says Cardinal Bellandi with a chuckle, throwing his arms over the back of the leather sofa, "but he wants to wait."

"He wants to wait?" I repeat, leaning forwards and setting my wine down on the coffee table. My brow pulls together and I narrow my eyes at Bellandi, waiting impatiently for his explanation.

"I went to see him before coming here. Since he's been

running the City Guard and I wanted to ensure the Militia are welcomed and settled," Bellandi reasons. "I brought up the idea of his election. He said he wanted to wait at least until after the public funeral—for tact. He doesn't want to be seen as a tragedy profiteer."

My lips form a line. I tap one finger to my knee, chewing on that.

Such a petty reason, particularly when we don't even have a date for the public funeral yet. Of curse, we have to have one. The people need to grieve the loss of their leaders as much as we do our families. They need to grieve and move on. But we need his help *now*, to enable our Electi to simply run and make decisions.

"Well, given you're both going to back him, why don't you make him a proxy for now? You can hold the official election after the funeral?" offers up Nouis, his hands moving to cover my restless fingers.

"Now that might work," agrees Bellandi. "Treat him as an Electi, but wait to make it official."

"That's not how the High Chamber works," I argue. "The law states that—"

"No, but we've declared a state of emergency in the midst of a tragedy. You can be forgiven for a little rule-bending, if it makes things better, right?" Nouis asks softly, squeezing my fingers.

I sigh, lifting a hand to my brow.

We need three Electi to function. If this is how we have to fudge it, because Patricelli is being difficult, then so be it.

Stupid, arrogant jerk.

"Fine," I mutter.

"Excellent. I'll write to let him know," says the cardinal, getting up.

"Let's set a date for the public funeral as soon as possible, to officiate Patricelli's position as soon as we can. I don't like bending the law, if it can be helped," I say. The cardinal doesn't answer as he sweeps from the room. I repress my sigh, picking up my wine again.

"Aren't you happy? We've made progress," asks Nouis, leaning back against the leather with me.

I glare at my red crystal glass, running my tongue across my teeth. "Trust Patricelli to make things awkward. I mean, can you imagine caring about appearances? And at a time like this?"

"He's just trying to protect his family legacy. He doesn't want to damage all the good his father, and his father before him, has done. Don't let him upset you," Nouis advises softly. He lifts a hand, gently sweeping my face to return a stray curl behind my ear. His touch ripples my skin with sparks. He pulls me closer and I rest my head against his shoulder, warm arms holding me tight.

"He does upset me, that's the problem," I whisper, breathing in Nouis's addictive scent. "It's hard to distinguish between what's truly me and what's the bond's interference."

"Don't worry. I'm here, I'll help you sort through it." Nouis's promise gently breaks against my ears, prying a grateful smile from me.

I twist my face up to his, lifting a hand to cup his jaw. "Thank you."

"Always," he barely whispers.

I decide to close the distance between us, wiping all thoughts from my mind as I wrap my lips over his. We haven't kissed since the river, neither of us has even mentioned it. And just as before, the world stills into blissful silence. Caught in this moment, something lifts off me. I sink into that quietness in my head, focusing on nothing but the glory of his fingers weaving through my hair. A shiver runs down my spine and I press my body against his, feeling the rumbling of his chest. He breaks the kiss. A ragged breath breaks across my nose and he forces some distance between us.

"Perhaps we should put a pin in things between us for now," Nouis says quietly. "Wait for when you're feeling more yourself."

"You told me to think of what I want," I argue quietly, wrapping my fingers around his tunic. Nouis smiles almost sadly, lifting his hands to wrap those warm hands over mine.

"Renza, I want you too, but I don't want it to be as a distraction from what's going on," Nouis says softly, gently stroking my hair back from my face. I swallow tightly, my cheeks rushing with blood and I look down in shame.

Because that's what I'd been doing. Grabbing a delicious distraction.

"No, don't do that," Nouis breaths softly, "Don't feel guilty, I understand more than you think. When things are less ... raw, we can see where we are. However the cards fall."

I nod, not daring to meet his eyes.

"Come on, let's try that walk and when we get back you can read that book," Nouis says, standing up and offering me his hand. My chest goes warm. My hand leaps eagerly to his as he pulls me to my feet, holding me close.

This wonderful man leads me towards our gardens, and I can't help but look up at him with a flood of gratitude. Fresh sunlight breaks over his dark face and hypnotising green eyes. A tightness in my chest begins to loosen and a small smile breaks free.

I'm feeling more like myself already.

CHAPTER 11

New College has a large circular main hall, with other circular classrooms bubbling off of it. The tall, domed ceilings are richly painted with vivid images of famous Halicians to inspire the students. All they have to do is turn their eyes to the sky to see the endless possibilities of their potential. Large, decorated archways framed by thick violet curtains lead outside to the bursting flower gardens and grassy square, allowing errant rays of sunshine to sneak inside.

The children are patiently waiting, lined up on the red and blue tiled floor, many wearing black or white. They fall quiet as I enter, Nouis's hand wrapped firmly around mine.

It's been three days since the explosion. Three days of dodging the Militia in my own house, sat at Giulia's side reading those mind-stilling books and waiting for news. Any news.

But nothing has changed. Giulia remains unconscious. The culprits are still at large.

I have duties to fulfil.

Nouis had offered to send my apologies for today. He's right, everyone would understand. Everyone except Father. These schools were his pride and joy. I won't let his legacy fall apart after just three days.

So here I am, in a fresh black and white tunic, to open the school's new library.

Thankfully my eyes fall on a set of familiar faces.

Emilia doesn't say anything, her face rippling with sadness as she sweeps forwards in a flurry of white and black silk. Her dainty arms wrap around me as I return her embrace. I grip tight, grateful for the strength of my gentlest friend.

As I pull away, Emilia wipes her eyes. Sniffing sharply, she forces a wet smile. Serra steps forwards, dark eyes tight as she pulls me into a bear hug. That familiar scent of rosemary swells like a lump in my throat.

"I... We all..." she sighs, giving up on finding the right words. "I'm just glad to see you."

"Me too," I croak, an icy lump brewing in my throat.

Serra releases me, brows pulled.

"Dare we ask?" Emilia's voice holds a slither of hope.

I shake my head. "Nothing new." I clear my throat, forcing myself to take a deep breath. Nouis's supporting hand goes to the small of my back.

"Nouis, meet the girls. This is Emilia and Serra," I introduce, grateful for anything else to do but linger on this topic. "Emilia is a brilliant architect, and Serra is the best engineer this side of the Halician Plains. They worked together to design the library."

Emilia blushes as Serra flashes a grin.

"This is mostly Emilia's work," Serra corrects, nudging our shy friend with her elbow. "I just helped with turning some theory into reality."

"It's lovely to meet you both." Nouis greets with his signature charm. "Congratulations on finishing the project."

"Thank you. We made some last-minute adjustments," Emilia admits, biting her lip, "but they seemed right."

Two of the teachers step forwards.

"Shall we head over to the library then?" asks Teacher Veletor as brightly as he dared. I nod, forcing a practised smile to my face.

"Oh absolutely. I'm so pleased it's finished already," I say warmly, completely at odds with the permanent numbness lodged in my chest. I push ahead with him over the warm tiled floors. Just as we're about to set off, I spy a familiar face at the front of the group. His wide brown eyes look up at me hopefully.

"Maso, isn't it?"

"Yes, signora!" he answers immediately, bouncing in anticipation.

"Well now, why don't you come and show me all the books you're excited to read?" I say, holding out my hand for him. He wastes no time, shooting forwards to put his small hand in mine.

"I want to look at the maps," he says excitedly, skipping up and down as he pulls me swiftly into the gardens, "so I can travel to all the places of the world! There's a book filled with them, and stories about the people there."

"That type of book has a special name. Do you know

what it is?" I ask, focusing on this child's bubbling energy. It's refreshing, faintly stinging but in a good way. To see someone so happy after all this grief.

Maso pulls me along, my feet hurrying over the bright green grass towards the new circular building. We pass a rippling blue reflection pool edged with mint and lilac. Sunshine spews glitter off its surface in every direction, dousing the world in slithers of diamond.

"No. What is it?" Maso chatters brightly.

"It's called an atlas," I explain as we approach the new building.

Emilia has outdone herself. The drawings were good but this is phenomenal.

The large circular building is surrounded by luscious open spaces, scattered with benches and lounging chairs that the kids have brightly painted in their art lessons. The outside walls are intricately carved, each external pillar a different colour as it reaches for the striped dome ceiling, tiled in blue but sporting names of famous authors written in red. The heavy doors are already open wide, showing off a white and grey swirling mosaic floor.

Maso pulls me inside and we both stand in awe for a few moments. The inside of the domed roof is completely mirrored. Forming a star pattern just beneath are running oil-fed burners. Light is tossed into every corner, giving every surface a golden glow and transforming the dust in the air into glittering spirits.

Rows and rows of tall bookshelves are brimming with books, with additional tables and chairs dotted in private locations so groups can study more openly. In the centre of the room is a large plinth, but the statue from Emilia's original drawings is gone.

Instead stands a large painting, from the hand of an all too familiar artist. The simple silver plaque underneath reads:

Tomas Di Maineri, Renza Di Maineri and Giulia Di Maineri
sponsors of this library and patrons of the future.
we will never forget.

Seeing my family's faces is a sharp blow to my gut. I crumple inwards, clamping a hand to my mouth as tears spill down my cheeks.

I stagger forwards, eyes running over Michelle's masterpiece. Father sits in the centre, an open book in his hand. Giulia stands to one side, her perfect face filled with her familiar teasing smile, and me on the other, chin high and wearing a knowing look.

I've cried so much recently, I always think I'm done. I can't possibly find more tears to shed. Yet they keep coming.

Father should be here. He would be so much better at handling this crisis. If he were leading us, no doubt the traitors would've been found by now. Instead, this city is stuck with me. I've always wanted to step out of his shadow, to shine by my own merit, but never without him there too.

Emilia's arms wrap around me from behind, pulling me close as she rests her head on my shoulder.

"Is it okay?" she whispers.

I swallow, desperately trying to blink away the waterworks.

"Yes. Yes, they should be remembered," I manage to wheeze. I grip Emilia's embrace tightly, forcing the salty lump in my throat back down to my stomach.

"Michelle was going to give this to Giulia as a birthday present," says Serra, "but she realised we should use it here."

"I was about to say"—I sniff, wiping my eyes—"when did she have the time? She's been at Giulia's side for days."

"How is Michelle?"

"Holding on to hope. Like we all are. Better at it than I am truthfully," I admit. Hurriedly I wipe my eyes again, turning to Maso.

"Show me those atlases then," I encourage, clearing my throat.

The children love this place. They all rush in, excitedly chattering about the different books on the shelves. Some sit in groups reading poems, others alone with their nose wedged between the pages of a far-off story, many gather around their teachers to listen to epic tales from history.

I sit outside with Maso and his friends amongst the grass, pouring over an atlas about the far-off world as we soak up the late afternoon sunshine.

"Coari is a country across the sea," reads Maso in staggered words, head comically tilted to one side. "It is rich with precious metals and jewels, which has caused it to be attacked many times. This had led to its people becoming very focused on war and battle, making them the experts on their continent. Now many Coari lords and ladies have formed their own private armies, and rent them to other countries."

"Excellent reading!" I encourage as Maso flashes me the

warmest smile. I look up as Teacher Veletor comes around with water for all the kids. I gladly take mine, about to take a sip when my gaze catches on the school building. I drop my water and burst to my feet.

A group of Church Militia, mingled with some members of our own City Guard, march towards the school. They trample the flowers in their path as they try to push inside the library. Headteacher Yaven stands in the doorway, arms wide, chin held high and polished silver hair gleaming.

"Stand aside!" barks a member of the Church Militia.

"What are you doing here?" Headteacher Yaven doesn't back down. Violently, they barge past, throwing her to the floor.

"Hey!" I shout, running to Yaven's side. She struggles to pick herself off the grass, blood pouring thickly from one side of her face. I crouch next to her, grabbing a handkerchief from my belt and pressing it against the side of her head.

"Hold this here."

Banging and smashing starts inside. Furniture is thrown, belongings crushed. Children are crying, while scared and arguing voices ring out from the columns.

My jaw clenches. My blood turns to fire.

I march inside. "Stop! Stop! I command you to *stop*!" I shout at them. The Church Militia make for one of the classrooms. I run forwards, throwing myself in the door frame and blocking their entrance. My fingers are fixed on the stone frame either side. I will not be moved so easily.

"ENOUGH!" I roar at the top of my lungs. "Get out of this school!"

"We have a warrant for the arrest of Serra Stacano." One

of the Militia marches forwards. His skinny nose wrinkles with disgust, fists clenched.

My gut drops as shock forces me to straighten my back.

"Warrant? Signed by whom?" I demand.

"By Order of the Electi."

"Funny, because I'm an Electi and I gave no such order," I snap right back.

"No one said it was you. But I did tell you to move." Those grey eyes blaze with violence, his thin lips puckering in a snarl.

I narrow my eyes, standing ever taller. "Stand down by Order of the Electi."

"We have the warrant. Serra Stacano will come with us, and those who get in our way will be charged with treason." The soldier launches a hand for his sword. He rips the weapon free from its scabbard, arching it high.

"No!"

Captain Collier—the Captain of the City Guard—launches forwards, a blade in hand. The slamming of metal against metal crashes through the room. Everyone freezes. Breaths tense in our lungs. My heart throbs in my throat.

Collier pushes the Militia leader back a few paces, standing at the ready in front of me. "Stand down, that's an order!"

"My orders come from the Holy States. I am a Soldier of Fate," he snarls. The City Guard congregate on one side of the hall, the Militia on the other. My mouth goes dry, eyes flickering to the children still cowering under tables or hiding behind columns.

"Not while you breathe in our walls," Captain Collier

snaps. "Here your orders come from Signora Di Maineri. Obey your orders; stand down and leave!"

"Enough!" Serra's voice cuts through the tension. Horrified, I whip around to see her standing with a congregation of onlookers. Emilia has both hands wrapped over her mouth in terror, Nouis only a pace behind them both.

I focus on Serra, pressure building in my chest as my heart sputters. Her eyes are wide, voice shaking slightly as she continues.

"Why am I being arrested?" she asks, eyes locked on Captain Collier.

"You were found to have explosives in your workshop," he explains, his tone kind but firm. He reaches into his pocket, retrieving the arrest warrant and holding it up.

"Yes, she's been working on a device with explosives for weeks," I argue. "I knew about this; it's not linked to the Grand Temple."

"But the quantity and the knowledge she possesses ... it all needs questioning."

"Questions don't require an arrest."

"Normally. But the circumstances are exceptional and no one can be too careful. I have the arrest warrant. I have to carry it out; it's my job," sighs Captain Collier walking towards me with the paper outstretched. "When I was given it earlier, I wanted to carry it out myself with just a few of our own men to aid me. But Bellandi insisted on lending ... assistance."

His discerning eyes drift to the Militia in their stark black and white armour and a tinge of distate briefly flickers across his features. I take it from his hands. I scan my eyes down the document, seeing it signed by "Order of the Electi".

Electi, huh? I think perhaps it's time to remind them exactly how many Members there are in the High Chamber.

Captain Collier takes a step towards Serra.

"No," breathes Emilia, her hands clutching Serra's forearm. For the first time I've ever seen, there isn't a shred of humour on Serra's face. Only fear.

"Serra Stacano, please come with us. There is no need to cause more of a scene today."

"Surely there is something you can do." Nouis tries to prevail. "An Electi is vouching for her, saying that this is a mistake."

Captain Collier shakes his head. "The law is the law. Serra Stacano is under arrest."

I throw the arrest warrant on the floor, pushing past him. I take Serra's forearms in mine and look into those dark eyes, talking quickly.

"Say nothing. Do nothing. I will sort this out. I promise. I will get all of this sorted out."

She swallows thickly, a nod shallow and sharp making her dark curls bounce erratically.

"No," sobs Emilia, trying to reach her. Nouis holds her back, shaking his head with a grim expression.

"Do you hear me?" I repeat as Captain Collier takes hold of Serra's upper arm, "Say nothing. Do nothing. I will sort it." Someone has tightened an invisible noose around my throat as Serra walks away with shaky steps, throwing us a terrified look over her shoulder.

"You look after her, Captain. I swear to Fate if she has so

much as a bruise, there will be hell to pay," I yell after him. It's not fair to blame him. He's right, he has to carry out his orders.

There is someone else I need to yell at for this.

"Renza?" Nouis gently ventures as I glare after the intruders.

"How dare they? How *dare* they." I'm seething. My fingers itch for action. My blood screams for it.

"I know. But they're just following orders."

"This was more than orders." I scowl. "That reprobate drew his blade in a school; he assaulted the teaching staff. This kind of mindless violence is disgusting. Who is allowing them to get away with it?"

"Patricelli and Bellandi probably." A frown puckers Nouis's handsome face. "Patricelli's been running the City Guard since the attack, right? You don't think he's encouraging violent behaviour?"

I clench my fingers, my arms shaking with the effort. Sourness spills over my tongue, tugging my lips down and wrinkling my nose.

"Patricelli," I hiss, the name poison on my tongue.

"Don't let it wind you up. It's not worth it," sighs Nouis.

"It's absolutely worth it; Serra is heading to jail!" I shout, breaths coming hard and fast. Fire itches under my skin. I turn on my heel, marching down the road.

Perhaps I was wrong. Perhaps Idris is nothing like his father. Perhaps all the time abroad taught him underhanded scheming and manipulation would push him to the top. Maybe in other countries it'd work. But not in Halice. Not today.

Not against me.

The sunshine's blinding rays can't stop my warpath away from the school. Each breath races. My jaw sets.

"Renza? Renza, where are you going?" Nouis races in front of me, putting both hands on my shoulders.

"First, I'm going to scream at Patricelli, then I'm going to scream at Bellandi. Then when they have released Serra I am going to show them how to do their damn jobs and actually find the traitors who killed my father."

"No," says Nouis sternly.

"No?" I spit. "Are you mad? I'm not letting them get away with this."

Nouis holds up both hands, taking a step back.

"I'm not saying don't say anything. I'm saying let me go to Idris instead."

"What—"

"You're angry, rightfully so," Nouis quickly reasons, "but if you go and see him like this, you'll try to kill him. The anger and the hatred, it'll be too much. You won't be able to hold back and you'll get yourself killed."

"You underestimate me."

"We can't take that chance. Sneaky and untrustworthy he might be, but we still need him alive. We still need you alive. We can't compound your city's grief with more death." Nouis's green eyes search my face, hoping his message is sinking in.

I growl with frustration. He's right.

I take several deep breaths, each exhale feeling like steam against my lips.

"I'll go. I will scream at him for you, I promise." Nouis

drops the firmness in his tone. He steps close, cupping my cheek with one of his warm hands. I lean into his touch. Somehow it pulls all the horrible thoughts away.

I sigh.

"Okay. Go. But tell me everything, and don't let him off easy. Make him sweat," I grumble. Nouis kisses the top of my head.

"I promise. I'll meet you back at the house later."

Then he jogs off down the road, in search of that monster Idris Patricelli.

Time for Bellandi to learn why you never cross a Maineri.

CHAPTER 12

The Watchtower is the oldest building in this city. Large, rectangular and several stories tall, it dominates the middle of a large open square that has since become a vibrant marketplace colloquially known as Market Square. Today it's crowded with bright stalls, the air thick with mouthwatering spices and sweet perfumes. Smoke tickles the back of my nose; loud vendors chime off in every direction. People weave amongst the ever-changing maze of bodies, carving their own path through the chaos as relentless sunshine batters down from overhead.

"Signora! Signora Di Maineri!" calls a deep voice. A familiar round, bearded face with red cheeks shares a beaming smile. He opens his thick arms wide in greeting, his broad frame standing tall amongst the throng of people. In front of him a vast stall brims over with cheeses from all over the continent.

"Signor Greco," I greet, forcing my usual political warmth

to my tongue, stopping abruptly in my path. "How's business?"

"Doing very well! It's good to see you out and about, signora. We've missed your face around the city," he chuckles. "I don't suppose you'll be opening the bank again soon?"

"It's not closed, is it?" Alarm floods my throat.

"No, no," soothes Greco quickly, "but no new loans are being authorised. Your sister approved them all you see, and I was hoping to borrow again."

"Oh! Well, I'll be sure to look into that. I've been a little preoccupied recently."

The ever-present light in Greco's hazel eyes dims a fraction.

"Ah yes. I understand. I just figured no harm in asking. The first loan I got from the Di Maineri Bank helped me start this business, back when you were just a girl."

"Now you're the best cheese importer in the city," I chuckle. "We know a good investment when we see one. I'm afraid I must be off, but I promise to look into that as soon as I have capacity."

"Of course, signora. Have a pleasant day!" Greco waves me goodbye before yelling at the bustling customers about his cheeses. I turn on my heels, shaking my head. So much to do, the list is only growing longer. How am I supposed to manage it all without Giulia and Father to help me?

I march towards the old building, ducking through the flock of people. Church Militia line up outside the creamy stone building almost shoulder to shoulder, baking in the blistering summer sun but somehow not daring to buckle. I half expect them to stop me on my journey but they don't move a muscle as I stalk through the ridiculously tall black doors of the Watchtower and out of the sun's aggressive gaze.

Inside is much cooler. Large black stone basins filled with glassy smooth water line the edges of the room. Candles lick the old stone walls at regular intervals, the dark stains of centuries of work have become backing shadows. I march across the black and white chequered floors, crossing through a wide circle of sunshine. A small glass dome sits in the centre of the ceiling several stories overhead, filled with a number of old brass emergency bells. They lie covered in dust, silent for almost a century.

This old, open space used to be the home of the Electi. That was before my grandfather built the current High Chamber over seventy years ago. Gifting it to the city, he impeccably demonstrated the endless possibilities of the Garden—securing the city funding that it so richly deserved.

I head straight for the back of the offices, passing one or two curious Church officials as I carve my warpath up the old wooden stairs. Bellandi's office is easy to find—there aren't many rooms back here. I rap my knuckles impatiently against the chipped black door.

"Enter," his deep voice floats back. I grit my teeth, steaming into the room.

Bellandi sits at a large, flat desk. A slim window strikes a curtain of sunlight over the piles of papers resting on the worn wooden surface. Low, dark bookshelves teeming with trinkets and treasures surround the edges of this room.

Bellandi lifts his head in surprise. The long sleeve of his

white cardinal robes flies wide as he runs a hand over his balding head.

"Signora Di Maineri, how may I help?"

"By explaining yourself." I march across the room and rest my hands on the other side of the desk, leaning over where he sits. Bellandi pauses, lips thinning.

"I don't understand."

"Serra Stacano was just arrested. It was quite the violent spectacle, I might add."

"She tried to run?" Bellandi sighs as if he expected this and I can see his suspicion of her crystallising in his mind. I slam my hand back down on the desk.

"Of course not! Your overzealous Church Militia started smashing furniture and assaulted teachers at a school in the name of trying to find her. The children were terrified. Serra went quietly, because she knows she's innocent. So do I. Now explain yourself."

"Well, you're absolutely right, that kind of behaviour is outrageous." Bellandi's shock is far too muted for my taste. "I'll have to remind the Militia that this isn't a hostile city but they're under Patricelli's command at the moment. He's taken command of the City Guard; he's responsible for executing the warrant."

"Oh don't worry, I'm dealing with him. But you are just as complicit, the arrest was signed by Order of the Electi. Funny seeing as how I had no notion of it."

"All we needed was a majority, and when Patricelli brought me his concerns I agreed with him."

Patricelli? Oh Fate's Fury, when I get my hands on him I'll strangle him.

I narrow my eyes at Bellandi, fighting the urge to scream. "Serra is innocent."

"Then why the explosives? We've covered every inch of this city searching for a dangerous stash and she just so happens to have a good supply and calculations about mixing chemicals all over her workshop?"

"She's working on a device so we can watch explosions safely for entertainment. She's not a traitor," I explain, rubbing a hand to my forehead in exasperation.

Bellandi sighs, shaking his head.

"Well, I hope that's true."

I lean closer, outrage dripping off my tongue. "It is. Now release her."

"I can't. Idris is right, we have to be seen to be doing something, catching these people."

"So you'll arrest the wrong person, just to be seen to be doing something?" I spit, disgust curdling behind my teeth.

"Listen"—Bellandi spreads his hands out flat on the desk, taking a deep breath—"she'll be questioned and, if you're right, she'll be cleared. Then she'll be released. So you really have nothing to worry about."

"And what if she isn't cleared? What if you find no one else to blame? Are you going to keep her then? Just to be seen to be doing something?"

"Of course not. But I won't reverse the order, Renza, I'm sorry. There is too much evidence not to investigate it properly."

I let out a huge breath, hanging my head. I glare down at the desk below me. I can't stop picturing it, Serra locked up in a cage with thieves and killers. Bright, cheerful Serra surrounded by all that darkness.

I blink, my eyes narrowing on a piece of paper on the desk. It's addressed to my bank—the Di Maineri Bank—and is officiated with the High Chamber seal. I turn it around, scanning down with a fury. Outrage boils in my throat.

"You ordered the rebuilding of the Grand Temple already?" I hiss. "Without a vote?"

Bellandi sits back in his seat, face smoothing.

"People find comfort in religion. After such a tragedy, having somewhere to grieve and recover will be a balm."

"That's what the public funeral is for." I scowl.

"Are you suggesting we seriously go without a Grand Temple?" Bellandi widens his eyes in horror.

"I'm saying let's wait until the city can actually afford it." I throw up my hands, pacing in front of the desk. "The funds for this year have already been allocated! Wait until the next budget and we can rebuild the temple to the dignity it requires without crippling our city with debt in the process."

"We won't go into debt. We're going to rework the budget—"

"Says who?"

Bellandi sighs, crossing his hands over his chest as he looks at me. That patronising smile on his lips makes me want to smack it right off. "Idris Patricelli and I agree. We need to do this."

My stomach coils, the air pulled from my lungs in a short, sharp tug. They've discussed this? They've discussed the arrest. They've been complicit with each other on everything.

All without me?

Unbridled heat rises through my blood. I grit my teeth, mouth pinching. While I've been grieving, they've been scheming in dark corners. Conspiring behind my back.

How could I have been so blind? No wonder Bellandi was so on board with considering him a Proxy Electi.

"Patricelli isn't an Electi," I spit.

"You yourself agreed to treat his vote as one of ours. You were the one who wanted to confirm his election as soon as possible. I'm simply treating him as we both agreed we should." Bellandi frowns as though I'm not making any sense.

"Except there wasn't a vote at all. There should have been a proper vote where I could've argued my point."

"Why?" Bellandi sounds as if he's scolding a child. "There are only three of us, and you two cannot be in the same room. The gods would compel you to complete your Fate and our High Chamber has seen more than enough violence. I thought you wanted to avoid that?"

"Don't pretend you wouldn't love to see it end that way," I scoff, folding my arms as I study him.

"Watch your tongue, its venom will burn what bridges you have left," Bellandi fires back. "I respect your choice, insane though I find it, because you have the right to make it. I support it. I support you! Renza, you know this. I'm your ally. We all want what's best, for Halice to recover from this horror."

Bellandi presses his hands together, studying me through narrowed eyes.

"You can't make decisions without a vote, Bellandi. That

is a founding principle of the High Chamber. It's section three in the Founding Charter. You have no right."

Bellandi slowly nods, keeping silent. That stillness grows between us thicker with each passing second.

Because I'm right. They don't have the right to do this. Spending High Chamber funds requires a vote. Did they really think that I wouldn't fight them taking complete control? That I wouldn't fight to serve this city in the way I think is right?

Did they forget themselves?

Did they forget who I am?

I'm Renza Di Maineri. I'm the daughter of Tomas Di Maineri, a great and fierce politician. Just because he isn't here, it doesn't mean his strength isn't. Because I'm still here. And I'm still fighting.

"I'm sorry the decision upsets you," Bellandi begins. I hold up a hand to stop him.

"No. I'm not upset, because I'm going to fix your mistake," I say calmly, holding my chin high. Bellandi sits forwards, eyes narrowing.

"What?"

"There was no vote, and as such, there can be no release of funds. Given the High Chamber's accounts sit with the Di Maineri Bank, and I'm now the acting head of that bank, I cannot authorise the release of funds that don't line up with a budget that has been ratified."

"You would hold this city's money hostage to get your way?" snarls Bellandi, launching to his feet. His white robes flail with the movements as he slams his hands on the desk.

"I absolutely do not. I protect the money, and the people.

I protect the High Chamber and our process. Bring a motion for a new budget to the High Chamber and let's debate. When it gets ratified via a legal vote, then I will absolutely release the money. In the meantime, funds will remain allocated as per the previous ratified budget."

Bellandi wrinkles his nose, anger thinning his lips as he glares at me. Silence passes, frustration crackling like invisible sparks around him but I hold my ground. Hands on my hips, not wavering away from the anger in his eyes, I wait. Here is the power play; here is the delicate unspoken art of politics.

The first to speak loses.

Bellandi sits down, face pinched like he's sucking a lemon.

"Of course. In my eagerness to help the city heal, I got ahead of things. A proper vote—does two weeks sound reasonable?"

"I'll be prepared," I nod, turning to leave.

"There's not enough time for an election," Bellandi calls after me, "so we'll have to allow Patricelli to vote without legally being an Electi."

"We'll pass a motion first," I respond, fixing one of the decorative pins running along my sleeves. "He'll be considered his father's proxy for a month. After that, he'll need to win an election. A month is more than long enough for him to distance himself from being a tragedy profiteer."

"Agreed." Bellandi shakes his head, turning to glare out of the window. I roll my eyes, exiting the room but leaving the door wide open. Sometimes, in politics, you have to be satisfied with the little jabs. The little power moves. A subtle reminder that he has to work with and around me, as much as I do with him.

I wind through the narrow corridors, a determined scowl playing around my lips.

I'm back, and there's work to be done.

My grief can't smother me anymore. I can't buckle under that consuming weight in my mind. I've been so irresponsible, blindly letting things slide. I won't let things fall apart around me anymore.

Halice is my city. Serra is my friend.

And it's my honour to serve.

CHAPTER 13

I haul the box of papers onto the table, setting them down with a thump. Exertion slickens my brow, my breath coming faster than I'd like.

Damn, these documents are heavy.

I'll come back for them later. Instead of diving into the work, I pull off my cloak and throw it over the back of an obliging chair. I haven't seen Giulia since I left this morning; I should go check on her, make sure nothing else has changed, even though it feels the world has.

I hurry up the stairs of our home, each step creaking softly like a welcome. Outside the sun is starting to slip into a minty blue sky. Long bright patterns of sunshine stretch over the mosaicked corridor floors, falling through large arched windows. I reach Giulia's door, pushing against the warm wood. Inside are two familiar faces.

Michelle sits in an armchair beside my sister, again holding her hand. In another sits Emilia, her hand on

Michelle's shoulder to comfort her. The two turn their heads the instant I walk in.

"Serra?" asks Emilia immediately, eyes hopeful. I shake my head, gut clenching.

"They won't reverse the arrest order. Too many explosives and calculations in her workshop for her not to be considered a suspect." I sigh, hating that I've failed, hating the light that dies in Emilia's eyes when I tell her this. She sits back in her chair, turning her gaze to Giulia.

"She wasn't involved," Michelle says quietly, reaching up to smooth back an errant strand of Giulia's hair. "The notion that Serra would hurt anyone is ridiculous."

"Agreed," I groan, sinking down on the bed next to Giulia. Her face remains totally still, no sign of consciousness under the surface. The burns are being treated with ointments every few hours, but they'll scar. Still, I don't think scars could mar her beauty.

"So that's it?" Emilia asks, "We can't help her?"

"Of course we can help her," Michelle interjects. "We can visit her. We can keep her spirits up."

I sigh.

"No, actually ... you can't. She's arrested on suspicion of treason. That means she's isolated." I get up, walking to the cabinet I know Giulia keeps her wine in. I pour myself a shallow glass. "Only Electi and City Guard will be allowed anywhere close to her."

"Then what about you? You can go."

"And I will. But..." I trail off. The words get stuck in my throat. I take a swig of the wine, hoping that'll flush the words free.

"You don't think"—Emilia's eyes widen as I turn to look at her—"she'll actually get ... blamed for this? Do you?"

Michelle's face falls with horror, eyes darting repeatedly between me and Emilia. "That's not—No! No they can't," she stammers, blood draining from her face. Emilia keeps her gaze steady, not backing down from the question.

I hesitate for a moment, hating to share that hollow feeling in my chest with anyone else. But they deserve to know what's going through my mind. We're all close friends.

"I think ... if they can't find someone else ... that Bellandi and Patricelli are not above sending an innocent person down for the crime. Just so they can put it to bed and move on." I shake my head, folding my arms in disgust.

How am I left with this? These self-serving, vain, primping peacocks running the greatest city in the world?

How low of a person can you be to just want this to be over, with little care for making sure you have the right person?

"What will happen if she's convicted?" Emilia asks, the faintness in her voice tells me she already knows the answer. The image of Serra in the dungeon floats to my mind, alone in the darkness in a locked cold cell. I think I might be sick. I drain my wine, turning around to fill it with another generous portion. I can't look at them, to see the disappointment on their faces.

I've let them down. I said I'd handle this and I've done next to nothing.

"We can't let that happen." Emilia's voice is strong now, determined. I twist around to see her face set and eyes blazing.

"I won't," I promise, leaning back against the wall. My

ponytail digs into the back of my head as I raise my eyes to the painted ceilings. How I'm going to clear her, I have no idea, but one problem at a time.

"No, Renza, *we* can't let that happen," Emilia repeats, the chair creaking as she stands up. She brushes her long hair over her shoulder as she folds her arms and gives Michelle a pointed look.

With a sombre expression, Michelle nods. She rubs her forehead, a decision hardening. "You're right. We can't."

"We?" I repeat.

"Yes. We. No matter what the law says, we know Serra is innocent. She's our friend. *We* won't let them hurt her." Emilia's words are laced with an unusual fire.

Then I get it. My eyes go wide with shock. I stand straight off the wall, mouth falling open a little. "You're not suggesting—?"

"I know you believe in the law with your whole heart Renza, but sometimes it just gets in the way. I personally have no qualms in breaking it," she says with a calmness that seems totally at odds with the words she's saying.

Timid, gentle Emilia wants to ... break Serra out of prison?

I love my friends to pieces; they are truly brilliant women. The best. But Michelle is an artist and Emilia is an architect. Neither are criminal masterminds, and Halice's prison is one of the most well-guarded places in the whole city.

"We can't let Serra go down for this," repeats Michelle, squeezing Giulia's hand. "Giulia would agree."

"Giulia is unconscious, don't speak for her," I snap, setting down my wine glass. "Do you even hear what you're saying? You want to break a suspected traitor out of prison?"

"Serra didn't do it, you know that," Emilia snaps back.

"Of course I do!"

"And what chance do you think she has? Realistically, do you trust Bellandi and Patricelli to keep her safe? Do you think they'll let her go down for this?" Emilia steps towards me, waiting pointedly for an answer.

No. I don't trust Bellandi or Patricelli to keep Serra safe. Not at all.

It's been three days since the explosion. Three days and there are no other suspects. Three whole days and we're no closer to finding the real culprits. How long before all the evidence just vanishes like a puff of smoke?

"I swear, no matter what, I won't let them hurt her." My voice feels thick like rubbed raw sandpaper. Emilia shakes her head unsatisfied. Silence echoes around my sister's bedroom.

"Any ideas, honey?" Michelle jokes softly, giving Giulia a nudge. I swallow tightly, shaking my head. Right now I need to focus on what I *can* do. The things I can fix.

Like a new budget, after all Bellandi and Patricelli want to rebuild the Grand Temple. I need to make sure that their vanity doesn't cripple the city. That I can fix.

Time to get to work.

CHAPTER 14

My hand flies across the paper in front of me. Its dryness sucks all moisture from my fingers, the inky quill scratching quickly over the soft surface. One hand supports my forehead as I bend over the pages.

I pause, assessing the words in front of me.

It's a letter to the Di Maineri Bank, requesting a reassessment of available funds for another budget. I've already sent one stopping the removal of funds that don't align with the original budget to Dorado, my sister's assistant.

I went straight to my father's study and dug up the papers he used when he was suggesting work on the current budget. They're sprawled over my desk now, as I try to make the numbers add up to allow for Bellandi's new Grand Temple.

Because if Patricelli and Bellandi want it, then we'll need to make room for it. What does that leave for the remaining money? Will there be enough for everyone else?

But my proposal also needs to be a bit outrageous. Enough to have the two of them arguing for weeks. I need to slash repairs budgets for the church, City Guard and the dock, but do it in a way that won't align the two against me. I need to get them arguing with each other.

Sitting in my study, surrounded by my books and my plans ... it's empowering. My hand flies; my mind has kicked back into gear as I start juggling the problem ahead. Inspirational words from my favourite authors, bound in bright leather cases, sit proudly on wooden shelves behind me. The furniture is painted with bright climbing vines. My large desk is made of a rich, deep wood and the stamps of my years of dedication litter its surface. A cup ring here, an ink stain there, all currently covered with a mountain of different papers.

Outside the patterned window, the sky is bleeding crimson as the sun claws the sky with bloody fingernails. It slides inelegantly behind the horizon, tossing its last half-hearted rays of marigold light over my city.

Rubbing my forehead, I reread the words of my letter, making sure I haven't missed anything important.

"Renza? Renza, where are you?"

Nouis's deep voice carries down the hallway. An involuntary smile stretches across my face at the sound of my name on his lips. He walks past the open study door, then steps back in a double take.

"Renza?" he asks surprised. He stops in the large doorway, confusion puckering his brow.

"Hi." I smile, setting my quill down.

"Is everything ... okay?" he asks, gesturing to the piles of papers.

"There's likely going to be a new budget coming to the High Chamber, and I was pulling together some ideas for it."

"Already?" Nouis walks into the room, crossing to the desk. I nod, chewing my lip as I look over the sprawling nature of my work.

"Politics never sleeps."

"How did all this happen?" Nouis frowns.

"Bellandi had already commissioned work on a new Grand Temple using the High Chamber coffers, so I reminded him he can't do that. He had no right to make those orders."

Quiet outrage simmers on my lips as I fold up my second letter to the Di Maineri Bank. This one requests a reassessment of all the High Chamber accounts.

"No right? Isn't he an Electi like you?" Nouis asks, leaning down to pick up one of the papers. The thick muscles of his arm flex with the moment, making my insides simultaneously clench and melt.

"Meaning we needed to vote on changes. There was no vote." I throw down the letter in my hand, rubbing my brow.

"Everyone is a bit frantic and on edge at the moment. I'm sure he'd have brought you in before anything serious happened," Nouis reassures, playing devil's advocate. "Besides, people find comfort in religion. I certainly do. Not to mention rebuilding the Grand Temple would be a good international symbol. We won't be afraid; we will move forwards. Halice has always been a place that looks towards the future."

I sigh, thinning my lips at that answer. Nouis is right, I suppose, but I can think of far better ways to send that message.

"Doesn't matter now." I sit up straight in my chair, surveying my evening's work ahead of me. "I've put a stop to Patricelli and Bellandi running around pretending I'm not here."

"How?"

"The High Chamber accounts need votes to authorise spending. I simply reminded them that as acting Head of the Bank, I cannot authorise a deviation from the current ratified budget without an official vote." I flash Nouis a wicked grin. His face ripples with delight.

"Sounds like you showed them." His words barely contain his mirth. He gestures to the papers over my desk. "Can I help at all?"

"You want to?" Surprise colours my tone more than it should.

"Of course." Nouis walks to my side and surveys the hectic layout. His warm hand goes to my shoulder. The silk of my tunic is barely enough to hold back the goosebumps he pulls to surface, or the breath that hitches on my throat. His touch is addictive, that easy, wonderful warmth sinking deep into my muscles. I lean into him, craving the sensation of having him near.

"I also run a bank you know. Money is something I'm good at."

"Okay!" I grin. "Bellandi and Patricelli want to fund the building of a new Grand Temple, and eventually I won't be able to stop that. We need to find the money."

Nouis walks over to a small round table in the corner of the room. He snags one of the wooden chairs and pulls it over to the desk next to me. He's so close that his arm brushes up against mine, his tall frame and dark hair outlined in candlelight. My mouth goes dry, and my heart drums so loud I'm surprised he can't hear it. He takes the pages, and leaning back, instantly gets to work.

I can't help it. I reach for him, wrapping both hands around his arm. I drop my head to his shoulder, pressing my forehead against him. I soak in his calmness, his readiness, his impossible aptitude and generosity.

How would I manage any of this without him?

His other hand comes up to rub mine in comfort, soft shivers blooming where our bare skin touches.

"How did things go with Patricelli today?" I keep my voice quiet.

"Oh ... as you'd expect," he sighs, running a hand through his silky black hair. "Denied all knowledge of what his men were doing. Got all big and blustery about his men finding the attackers."

"Jerk," I scoff.

"I don't believe him"—Nouis shakes his head—"but rather than have that argument I demanded to know how he was going to fix it. He promised he would, but said that sometimes violence was required to move forwards."

"Urgh! That's barbaric." Disgust rolls off my tongue, bitterness taking root at the back of my mouth.

"I'm going to keep a closer eye on it. And on him. If that works for you?" Nouis offers, gaze darting to me. "I don't want to step on any toes."

"No, of course. I think perhaps Idris could use the supervision," I mutter, leaning back in my seat and folding my arms.

"After that I went and found that City Guard, Captain Collier? Thanked him for saving you," says Nouis, scratching his jaw. "I wanted to empower him to report to us anything he feels isn't right. Of course, orders are orders, but there's no harm checking them."

"That's a good idea." I grin, giving his arm a grateful squeeze.

"I have a couple of those," he teases, leaning closer. My spine shivers, my heart thumping as he leans closer. His face is so close to mine, I'm awash with his scent of almond and vanilla. He reaches for my face, trailing a slow finger down the side of my cheek as he brushes a stray brown lock back behind my ear.

I lean forwards. His every touch sends sparks flying across my skin, a warmth taking root in my belly and spreading through my gut. He pulls back but not far, a grin shared across both our lips as he presses his forehead to mine.

"Come on, let's work out some of this budget. Then we can have some dinner," he whispers. I nod, pressing a quick peck against his smile before turning back to my work—for some reason struggling to focus on the numbers and not think about the tall, dark, intelligent man working by my side.

～

"Here," says Nouis, gently draping his jacket around my shoulders. I smile, standing with him on the balcony. I look out over Halice, awed by the peaceful city. Painted streetlights glow around every twist and turn, a whisper of a thousand slumbers drifting into the clear night sky. Light bounces off the various roofs of this sleeping city. Three stand out, their glass domes insides lit up like dreams. The High Chamber, the largest and most vivid with its exquisite colours, the Di Maineri Bank headquarters, and then the Watchtower, the clear glass dome showcasing the old emergency bells.

We both lean against the solid stone banister, its cool touch soaking into our skin. The calmness of a restful night bolsters the success of the day. Nouis reaches for my arm, straightening one of the white pins on my black sleeves.

"I was thinking I should get some Halician clothes," he muses quietly. That deep voice is so rich I could melt into it.

"You'd look good in them," I smile, although I will miss the tighter fit of his usual attire.

"It's more practical. Looser. Lighter. Designed for the heat," Nouis says softly. "The last few days have been blistering."

"It's High Summer. The heat will break soon."

"I should've thought about that when I packed my wardrobe."

"I know some good tailors we can visit, if you want?"

"Yes. Though I think I'll stick to wearing trousers. A lot of men here walk around without them, their tunics reaching their knees like a dress."

"What's wrong with a dress?" I frown. Nouis chuckles.

"Nothing. Just not my taste."

"Is fashion much different in the Holy States?"

"Very. Everyone here seems to wear loose tunics or dresses. In the Holy States, men wear tight doublets like this, with thick trousers. Women wear fitted corsets tops with a skirt down to their ankles. No knees out for the world to see."

"Sounds uncomfortably hot."

Nouis cracks a wicked smile. "It works for our climate," he chuckles, running his fingers lightly over the back of my neck, fingers playing with the ends of my ponytail. Delicious tingles run flying over my skin.

I lean into him, not for his warmth but craving the touch of his skin. His strong arms wrap around me, strong and secure. Is this the embrace of a friend or something more? We both want more, but will Nouis believe me when I tell him this isn't a distraction. I take a deep breath, enjoying the calmness of the night, letting it fill my insides and keep me steady.

"Would you like a drink?" offers Nouis quietly. I nod, though I'd hate to lose the embrace of his arms. He kisses the side of my head, pulling his arms away.

"I'll be right back," he promises, before slipping inside.

I take another deep breath, a smile flirting with my lips as I study my sleepy city. Suddenly I can see it, my way forwards. Together we could achieve so much. Of that I have no doubt.

This city will thrive.

Disgust coils in my stomach. The hairs on my arms jump. My breath feels hot. Sucking in a deep breath while fighting down the boiling in my blood, I search for him.

For Idris Patricelli.

He isn't behind me, or in the dimly lit corridor. Instead I follow that sensation around to just below my balcony. I search the darkness for a minute, then spy a flash of Idris's infuriating golden head marching down the road, glaring at the distance, face red with fury.

He stops where he stands, head snapping up to glare at me on the balcony.

"You!" he snarls, jabbing a finger in my direction. "What the hell are you thinking? You should be ashamed of yourself."

Bile clamps my jaw shut. My fingers dig into the railing of my balcony.

Breathe... Breathe... What did the book say?

I shut my eyes, growling to myself as I try to slow my racing heart. I force myself to take a breath in through my nose, desperately stamping down on the coiled loathing spreading like venom through my veins.

"Explain yourself, Patricelli." I snarl back.

"Have you always been this self-serving or are you just a heartless opportunist?" Idris snaps at me.

My eyes fly open as I glare at the prick. "You dare come to my home yet again, just to launch insults at me? While my sister lies unconscious in the next room? Where is your sense of honour?" I scream back. My breathing is ragged; my heart is racing; my vision is tinted red.

"*My* honour? Coming from you?" Idris slams his fist into the cypress tree on his right, the leaves shuddering with the blow. "What are you playing at with the temple? With the budget? I knew we'd disagree on some things, but I never thought you were so power hungry you'd destroy Halice to get it."

Me? Destroy Halice? Oh, that's rich!

"Listen here, tourist," I snarl, "if you want to criticise Halice and her laws, maybe live in the city longer than a fortnight. Learn how our laws work. Respect the Electi and the process of the High Chamber. All of them, not just your friends who support your own self-serving agenda."

"My agenda? *My* agenda?" Idris laughs, anger pulsating on every syllable.

"What the hell is going on?" shouts Nouis rushing out onto the balcony, slamming the two drinks on the table. "Patricelli? Go home. Now."

"You! You're no better." Idris seethes, punching a wild fist up towards him. He growls in frustration, kicking a stone. It fires off his foot, bouncing off the walls to smash through one of my windows. I flinch, faltering back a step as the crash echoes across the night.

Idris freezes, seeming to only now realise what he's done.

"THAT'S IT! GET OUT NOW OR I'LL MAKE YOU!" roars Nouis.

Idris glares at Nouis as his arm wraps supportively around my back. He spins on his heels, marching off into the night. I force my eyes away from his retreating form, digging my nails into the stone railing and forcing myself to calm down. In through my nose. Out through my mouth.

In through the nose. Out through the mouth.

"Are you alright?" Nouis asks gently, rubbing my arm supportively as Idris's nauseating presence drains from my body. I nod, rubbing my brow.

"Maybe I shouldn't back him as an Electi," I mutter. I mean, what did I really know about the man? I knew his father. Jacopo was a good man. I don't know Idris.

"Maybe that's a good idea," says Nouis quietly, "Honestly, the man is so angry ... I wonder how he'll ever hope to keep up his part of your agreement."

"Agreement? You mean ... the Soulhatred?"

"I know you'll be fine. You have composure, honour, strength," Nouis says as I take the wine from him. "But him? So much anger has to boil over eventually."

I sip on my wine thoughtfully, remembering the force of my tree trembling under his blow.

"I'll talk to him again tomorrow," Nouis sighs, "at a far more reasonable hour when there is less drink in his system."

"I should do it. He's angry at me."

"Which doesn't help the bond. Don't tempt Fate, Renza. I can do it," promises Nouis gently.

I sigh, before taking another sip of wine. It's probably best I leave wrangling Idris to Nouis. Just his presence a few feet away was enough to make me murderous. If I actually have to talk to him, with good reason for my anger, who knows what'll happen?

"While your chef is brilliant," says Nouis softly, dragging me from my thoughts, "you don't have to wear his creations."

"What?" I lift a hand to my mouth, eyes going wide. Nouis grins, that wicked mischief sparkling in his eyes as he lifts a finger to the corner of my mouth, brushing the crumbs away. Embarrassment crawls in my throat, and I groan.

"Hey, it's okay. Cake crumbs are a good look for you," Nouis teases.

"Oh really," I chuckle as Nouis steps closer. I gaze up at him, as slowly he wraps an arm around my waist, holding me tight. I smile. A real, true smile. One not tainted by the grief that has consumed me. Or the anger or the tiredness. Real and free.

Nouis has done that.

He leans down, his lips hovering over mine like at war with himself. A war between his head and his heart. I know it too well, and I'm tired of fighting it.

I press my lips to his, and my world shrinks to him and only him. The feel of his soft mouth on mine, the way his hand moves to the back of my head. Sparks fly. My pulse races. My heart gallops in my throat as I lean into this kiss. Into him.

I slide my hands up his chiselled chest, knotting my fingers in his hair. I deepen the kiss. He tastes of wine and his lips move with slow, sure confidence. He's not in a hurry. He's determined to enjoy every single second he has me.

I press myself against him, needing to get as close as I can. One arm circles around my waist, pulling me tightly to him as the other hand runs down my back slipping lower and lower.

My insides melt; my breathing is ragged. Nouis moves us both backwards, his mouth still leisurely exploring mine. My back hits the stone wall of the house. Pressed between him and the stone, Nouis's hands continue to wander. His hand ventures down to pull my leg up and over his hip, before sweeping back to take a nice, firm handful of my ass.

I moan into his mouth. Nouis breaks the kiss, planting hot kisses onto my neck.

"Renza," he breathes my name.

"Don't you dare stop," I groan, head rolling back as my legs begin to tremble.

"Are you sure?" Nouis asks, those green eyes bright with hot, heavy desire.

"Yes, I'm sure," I answer, reaching for him again. He smiles as our lips meet again.

"Thank Fate," he groans, suddenly his arm cuts downward and he knocks my legs from under me. I gasp as he effortlessly sweeps me up and swiftly marches us to my bedroom. He kicks the door shut behind us, flashing me a wicked, mischievous grin before placing me gently on the bed.

He kisses me, long and leisurely until my mind is spinning. The world narrows to only his touch, how his fingers trace the length of my hipbones and linger on the edge of my trousers before slipping beneath. I arch up, the fierceness of my response from the simple touch shocks me but it elicits a dark, proud chuckle from Nouis.

Breathlessly he breaks the kiss, yanking his tunic off. I gape at the chiselled, dark soldier, kneeling shirtless between my legs. The look in his eyes melted my core and drenched my undergarments. His muscles flex deliciously in the golden candlelight, as he leans closer claiming my mouth again. I shuffle further back on the bed, and pull off the decorative belt at my waist. I reach down, pulling my silk tunic up and over my head, throwing it to one side.

Nouis lets out a strangled breath as he climbs back over me.

"Fate's Mercy, you're perfect," he moans, running his hands over my stomach to gently knead my breasts. A gasp is pried from my lips at the pleasure of his mouth against my skin. His tongue explores the slopes of my torso, taking his sweet time to worship every inch of my sensitive skin. I tremble with anticipation, back arching off the bed as he lowers his lips to my nipples. I'm a quivering mess as he pays them his devotion, building a storm inside me that scrambles any thought or sensation that doesn't come from him. His hands play with me like a masterpiece, sweeping hard strokes up and down my body before paying attention to the small details with care. My insides are hot and clenching, desperate for release.

I can feel his thick, long length between us, and my mouth waters. I reach down for him, a sharp breath cracking through his teeth. He buckles as I stroke. Fate knows I can drive him as wild as he makes me calm. I do away with his trousers, the thin fabric gone. I look down at him, losing a breath as I drink in the large, delicious sight of him at full attention.

Nouis closes the distance between our bodies, pressing me against him without crushing me. I can feel every sculpted inch of him, every glorious muscle flexing as he positions himself. His hands firmly grip my ass as he nudges towards my entrance.

"Nouis," I moan, wrapping my legs around his hips as he fills me up with a blissful, vexing slowness. The world evaporates, and there is only him. Groans of pleasure escape from his lips as he kisses me, savouring this moment as he starts to move. He is gentle and careful, his lips moving to trace patterns along my neck.

It's not enough. I want him in his entirety. I want to be filled with him. I want to feel him utterly unleashed. I grab his firm, muscular arse hard, digging in my nails and pull him home, letting my desire ripple through my teeth.

He doesn't need to be told twice. Nouis buries his head into my shoulder, driving home, again and again. My moans are loud as he fills me up. Each time he withdraws with an agonising, breathless slowness, taunting me with the very tip of himself. Over and over, a hard delivery and languid withdrawal so pleasurable until my breathless whimpering fills the room. Stars build in my body, piling higher and higher until the mountain collapses. My body shudders and shakes with the glory of release, the world splinting around the two of us.

"Renza." Nouis claims me, finding his release at the sight of me ruined.

Panting, the two of us lie there for a long moment. I gaze up at him with his cheeky, satisfied smile. His tousled hair spread out over the pillows, his strong arms wrapped firmly around my waist. My teammate. My partner.

I could really get used to this.

And suddenly I can picture it all. Waking in the morning to his tousled hair amongst the pillows. Kisses and sweet nothings before breakfast. Coming home from High Chamber to his smile and calming nature, chasing the stresses of the day away. The two of us spending our late summer evenings just like this on the balcony, working together for this city.

"Well, I think we've thoroughly ruined our friendship," I whisper. Nouis laughs, burying his face in my hair.

"It was worth it. You are worth everything," he whispers in my ear. I smile, settling my head against his. He was right about waiting. I wouldn't trade this moment for anything. Because this wasn't about my grief. This was about us.

And the beginning of something incredible.

CHAPTER 15

The High Chamber is empty.

Far too empty.

It's the middle of the week. Voices should be bouncing from the technicolour ceiling. Citizens should fill the spectator pews, their low muttering an ever-present background noise as the future constantly evolves around us.

It lies empty, silent as a tomb.

I grip the arms of my seat, smothered in pillars of blue and pink raining from above. My cheeks are dry and crusty, my swollen eyes jump from chair to chair, remembering the faces and voices of my colleagues. But one chair I can't dare to face. One chair haunts the corner of my vision, its power trampling over my heartstrings as if to crush me. My fingers bite white as I dig into the twisted wooden arm-rests.

The funeral was the hardest thing I've ever done. All I had to do was stand there, and even that was a struggle. Every step following the memorial through the city threatened to pull me down. Every sympathetic look pulled fresh tears to the surface, every gentle word ripped fresh sobs from my lips.

The Garden had put in so much effort. It was beautiful. Perfect even.

And now it's over.

Now it's done.

How can it be done? We haven't found the attackers. We don't know who did this. We don't know why. All we have are questions, panic, and heartache.

Yet, we're supposed to press on as though nothing has changed?

I reach up, using the ends of my black and white sleeves to wipe my eyes. Nouis wanted to take me home, but I couldn't face it. Not when I knew I'd never see Father walking through those doors again.

I went for a walk by myself, and somehow my feet brought me here. The High Chamber, where I'd always felt so powerful, so hopeful, so strong. But stepping foot inside, I felt nothing but loss. I did what I always do, found my seat and sat down.

Alone.

Barely days ago, the only thing I wanted was to find a way out of my father's political shadow. To be seen as my own woman, rather than his extension. Now I'd give anything to be in his shadow again.

I wrap my arms around myself, trying to pick up the pieces of my spirit. I know grief lasts, that time chips away at the load until it gets easier to carry. When we lost my mother, I thought the pain would bury me. But it didn't.

This will pass too, though now it seems impossible.

My heart jumps. My fingers tense, biting into the wood. Revulsion writhes in my stomach as the urge to gag flies up my throat.

I bolt upright in my seat, spine twinging sharply.

It takes everything I have not to watch Idris Patricelli walk through the doors of the High Chamber. His slow footsteps move down the aisle towards me. I grit my teeth, fixing my eyes to the white central stage, focusing on keeping my breathing under control.

In through my nose. Out through my mouth. In through my nose, count to four, out through my mouth.

"Maineri," he greets softly, standing at the edge of the stage.

"Patricelli," I manage to say calmly, the breathing forcing my heart to slow a fraction. "Why are you here?"

"When I think of my father, I think of this place." Idris's voice is tense but broken. The grief is screaming. Relief makes my breath catch and the edges around my heart prickle.

"Me too," I whisper.

The silence passes between us for a moment before Patricelli steps towards his father's chair. Each step clangs like war bells in my ears. I lock my jaw, jerking my head away from him.

"I'm sorry for your loss," Idris whispers. I track his movement, hear the wood of his father's chair creaking.

His chair now.

But he doesn't sit, just stands next to it, running his fingers over the wood.

"And I for yours," I respond, linking my fingers over my

lap to stop them reaching for the knife at my waist. "Your father was a good man. I respected him greatly."

"I thought you didn't like him much," Idris muses. I swallow tightly, clenching my fingers.

"That would do both him and me a disservice. He and I differed on a few issues but we were one High Chamber, both of us devoted to the same city. We were sometimes opponents, but we were never enemies. He had great passion and skill ... and he taught me as much about this chamber as my own father, if not directly. I admired him greatly."

Idris lets out a short laugh. I wince, the noise like a punch to the gut. Whispers spiral at the back of my mind.

Kill.

Kill.

Kill.

I grit my teeth, closing my eyes and clamping my hands over them. In through the nose, count to four, out through the mouth like blowing out a candle. And again. My satin sleeves rub against my face, thick with the scent of my tears.

"I'm so sorry about the other night." Idris broaches the silence. "I was wrong; letting my control slip like that was unfair and inexcusable. I hope you can forgive me, and please allow me to pay for your window."

"Thank you for your apology." I clear my throat. "The window is already fixed."

"Then allow me to reimburse you. I will be better."

"That's all the reimbursement I need," I sigh as silence settles between us again. The air grows uncomfortably hot. My fingers bury into the wood of my chair. I should go before

Fate tempts my fury any further, but I can't move from this spot.

"I'm almost glad of it," Idris says suddenly.

"Of what?"

"The Soulhatred," Idris barks in laughter. "Being here, with you ... I can finally feel something else. Rage is so much easier than grief."

Surprise shudders down my spine because he's right. My breathing is easier, though each is blistering, and my mind feels clearer. Tears have finally retreated from my eyes. The tiredness, the numbness—they have all vanished.

"Agreed," I mutter, voice cracking.

"Still, we need to talk," Idris continues, words falling harsher as he takes Jacapo's seat. I dig my fingers into my hairline, each breath in and out of my lungs hotter than the last. I take a moment to soak in that feeling, to bathe in the absence of grief. This hatred is so much easier.

"Indeed we do," I agree sharply, Serra instantly springing to mind, "starting with—"

"Why did you stop me from running an election?"

I freeze. My shoulders pinch. My head whips around to him in surprise, but I catch myself before I let my gaze fall on him. Instead I stare at the white circular central stage, analysing every crack and corner in the pearly tiles.

"What?"

"Why did you stop me? I truly thought you were better than that. When we spoke in your garden you seemed so ready to try, and in the High Chamber the following week it worked. We worked! The two of us contributed in the same room and there were no disasters, so why block me? I thought you weren't going to let this stupid Soulhatred get in the way of our city," Idris laments, frustration barely masked behind his vile accusations. "Or are you just that obsessed with power? Our laws clearly state we need at least three people for a proper vote. I could've been that vote."

"What are you talking about? I didn't stop anything. I suggested a snap election. I wanted you in that seat officially days ago." I glare at the central stage, turning over his venomous words. "I was told you wanted to wait."

"That's ridiculous."

"You're a proxy. I didn't block you. Fate's Fury, I actually *insisted* you be your father's proxy until *you wanted* to run your election, because I know we need three votes. That's the law, one of the most basic. Bellandi agreed. It's not completely legal but in times of crisis and all." I scowl, getting to my feet and stalking a few paces left and right, walking that tight line over and over to try and quiet the storm screaming in my ears.

Breathe. Breathe. Slow my heart. Control my pulse, control my mind.

"When did you decide this? Why didn't you bother to tell me?"

Fire floods through my blood like an explosion, charring my bones and blistering my gut. "Don't. Don't you pretend with me, Patricelli," I snarl. "You and Bellandi are thick as thieves. You arrested Serra Stacano!"

"I've arrested nobody. What are you talking about?" Idris snaps back, getting to his feet. He stalks towards me, his eyes burning into the side of my face.

"Serra Stacano, the engineer. Who was arrested on

suspicion of treason at a school where soldiers started smashing furniture and terrifying children. One of them even beat a teacher. Serra isn't one of the attackers. She has explosives for a device she's been working on for months. But Bellandi made it crystal clear that you don't care if she's innocent. All you want is to be seen as making progress, but I won't let you do this. I won't let you hang an innocent woman." I seethe, my boiling breath coming fast and short as fire wriggles like worms under my skin. Idris is right there, his stupid, smug, arrogant self is right there. My hands shake as I clench them together so tight my knuckles turn white.

"What are you talking about? They've arrested somebody?"

"I told you, don't pretend with me," I growl, my breath turning to short, hot pants, "I'm not an idiot!"

"I'm not pretending." Idris seethes, low and dangerous, stepping closer his arms going wide with frustration. "How dare you insinuate that I would condemn an innocent woman for such vain self-serving reasons? I want justice, not façades."

"Justice?" I scream, finally turning to look at him and his stupid blond hair and those blistering hazel eyes. "Justice? Serra is in a dark cell terrified for her life because of you!"

I leap at him, tackling him with all my strength. We smash into the ground, my fingers gripping onto his tunic as I punch for his face. It lands and I land the second too; the warmth spreading across my knuckles is addictive. Idris bucks his hips and throws me sideways. His teeth grit in determination as I hit the tiled floor inelegantly. He clambers on top of me, pressing his tall, athletic body into mine and grabbing my wrists before I can reach for the knife at my belt.

"Get off me! Get off me you self-centred, disgusting little cockroach," I scream, writhing underneath him as he pins me securely to the floor, both of us panting furiously.

"Enough!" shouts Idris over me, "Don't push it, Renza, enough!"

"Screw you!" I scream with all my chest. My pulse echoes around my ears with the rage of a tempest.

"I need you to listen to me! I didn't arrest Serra Stacano," he roars, jolting me sharply. Somehow his words cut through, hitting me to my core. I stop struggling, the realisation crashing over me, somehow more powerful than the seething desire to crush Patricelli's skull.

"I didn't block your election," I whisper, looking at Idris. Both our faces fall. Silence lingers between us as his body hovers over me. The unquestionable truth of the situation begins to settle around our shoulders. My breath hitches, shaking in my lungs. I swallow tightly, gasping for air. Idris is panting too, the air thick between us. He's so close, I can barely think. I can just feel him, his body setting off a chain reaction of shudders along my skin. Idris slowly peels himself away, but the memory of his blistering touch lingers on my wrists. Fighting for calmer breath, we sit back-to-back on the tiled floor. He's like the sun, a roaring blistering beacon at my back, I dare not look directly at. I keep my eyes glued to a chip in one of the black floor tiles.

"We've been fools," whispers Idris. The horror of the lies that've been woven around us win out against the desire to tear out his throat.

"Why? Why would Bellandi do this?" I choke.

"To seize power? To reset the government he was losing control of?" offers Idris. "The influence of the Church has been dying in Halice for some time. Perhaps he sees this as his chance to fix that. He's been handed a perfect opportunity."

I lift a trembling hand to my lips, horror engulfing me like a wave.

"What's more likely? That he's been handed the opportunity, or that he created it?" I ask, the words shuddering in the air. Idris swears loudly, bolting to his feet as he begins to pace. I wince at the sharp movement, hurrying to get to mine too.

"It lines up too perfectly," I continue, tears of hatred springing to my eyes. Fate's Fury when will I ever stop crying? "Bellandi was away, but not so far that he couldn't be back at a day's notice. He left without telling anyone why and returned with a small army that equals the size of our City Guard, yet is better trained and more vicious, loyal only to him."

"He could've easily planted the explosions before he left. Or arranged it," Idris adds.

"Fate's Fury," I breathe, sitting in my seat again as the strength leaves my knees, gripping my head with both hands. "Why? Why do this? Why like this?"

"Desperation?" Idris offers. "He was the only Church member left in the High Chamber. Perhaps he felt like we were gunning for his seat."

"He had Member Morteselli on his side."

"An old man who couldn't have more than two or three

good years left in him," Idris counters. "When he retired, who would've been his replacement?"

"Leone Strozzi," I answer quietly. "Leone has no love for the Church, or anything really except only his own wealth and privilege." I beat Leone during my election; my seat used to belong to Leone's grandfather. He'd been my fiercest competitor and it'd been very close. He's the clear successor to Morteselli.

"So Bellandi knew he'd soon lose an ally," sums up Idris, "that the Holy States would have only him representing their interests."

"Bellandi did this. Bellandi blew up the Grand Temple."

Saying the words out loud, nausea forms a noose around my throat. Blood drains from my face. My insides are hollow.

"It's worse than that," Idris says darkly. "He's trying to take control of the city. Playing us against each other like this was convenient. He's got Church Militia everywhere. They obey his orders. If he says so, they'll kill us. Lie to the people, make it look like an accident—he'll have absolute power."

I thought I was crazy, imagining that the Militia outside my house were watching me. "Protection," Bellandi said when he dropped them off. He was telling the truth of course, but all he's protecting is himself.

"What's next?" I ask, "Why hasn't he just killed us and declared himself king? Or started installing a puppet government or whatever his plan is?"

"I don't know, that would be the play," growls Idris, rubbing his eyes. "It makes no sense. Why let us live all this time?"

"We must serve a purpose. It's the only reason to accept the risk of exactly this, us figuring him out."

"What purpose though? Scapegoats? Martyrs? Colluders?"

"Speculation does nothing; the options are endless. We're alive, and now we're on to him. He doesn't know that we've figured him out," I clear my throat. "Halice is in danger, but we have no proof and we don't know how... We need answers."

"Then we get some. Discover his plans, find the proof. We kick the Church Militia out of the city, then we can put Bellandi on trial and convict him for treason." Idris stops marching around, a plan forming between us.

"We haven't had a charge of treason in Halice since my grandfather's day," I murmur.

"Yet, here we are." Idris's words are soft and quiet. "What about Nouis?"

"What about him?" I ask with a frown.

"Do you think you can get rid of him without arousing suspicion?"

"Why in Fate's name would I do that?"

Idris rolls his eyes like it's obvious. "He's working with Bellandi! He works for the Holy States who orchestrated this whole thing. Surely you can see that."

"No. No way." The answers come to me instantly. "He almost died with me the day of the explosion."

"Almost being the key word."

"He's the only reason I'm alive, he's the only reason Giulia is alive too! Not to mention we were literally headed back inside the Grand Temple. If we had been even five paces closer or two seconds faster we would be dead too. We were going inside. There's no way Nouis would willingly walk to his death, knowing about an explosion like that. He wouldn't let me or my family do that either. There is no way he knew about this."

Idris was quiet for a long time, but the scepticism bubbles on their air like bile.

"Meet me tomorrow. There's a cafe on Tana Street, the Amica. Meet me there at sunset."

"To do what?"

"To start a plan. To work together to bring this traitor to justice."

I grit my teeth, a fresh wave of loathing crumpling me forwards.

"We can't tell anyone," Idris says eventually. "We have no idea who else might be complicit."

"Agreed."

My stomach churns, I press a hand to my mouth. I march for the door, my long black tunic slapping my legs as I stride.

"Don't tell anyone, Maineri. I mean it," shouts Idris as I exit to freedom.

CHAPTER 16

I walk home. Rage has left a vile energy inside me. I need it gone like I've never needed anything before. Blistering sweat batters my skin, soaking into the black fabric of my tunic and baking my nose. The pain is a mild punishment for my own stupidity.

Bellandi is a traitor.

It all makes too much sense. I was supposed to be in the Grand Temple when it exploded, as I normally go every week. Bellandi also had no idea that Idris would be returning to Halice, no idea that someone who could rally the people might be left.

I'm going to make him pay. I'll find a way to make sure this city is free from his clutches forever.

And apparently Idris is going to help me? With this Soul-hatred between us?

Fate really does hate me.

My arms still sting, remembering the tightness of his

grip. My shoulders ache from being pressed into the tiled floor.

Strong. Swift. He'd been trained to do that. He clearly knows how to hold his own in a fight. I want to scream, self-loathing curled up between my ribs. I'd attacked him, slipped from my self-control and attacked him like a common animal. Fausta is screaming at me from her grave for my stupidity.

How on earth are we supposed to work together with the Soulhate bond in the way? Would I have seen Bellandi's treachery sooner if I hadn't had all this revulsion and hatred distracting me? I was all too willing to believe that Idris was the bad guy, because of course he was. He was my Soulhate. I wanted it to be true.

These blinkers are too dangerous. Too new and untested. They could ruin everything.

But what choice do I have? Idris is invaluable as an ally. Someone with real influence on the other side of the chamber—people who saw Maineri as the political rival.

I reach home, my skin flushed, tunic drenched with sweat. As I step inside, I catch sight of my reflection in the window. My nose is beginning to blister, my brow resembling a tomato. Great, just what I need.

I close the front door behind me. I slide down the wood to sit on the intricate mosaic floor, letting the coolness of the stone sink in for a long moment. I let my mind drift and go blank. I close my eyes for just a second.

"Signora? Are you well?"

Giulia's nurse interrupts the numbness. I peel my eyes open to spy her pause at the base of the stairs, a glass of something in her hands. I nod, throwing myself back to reality.

"Yes," I answer, throat tight as I pull myself into a sitting position. "Yes, I walked home."

"I can see. I have a salve in my bag that might help. For the sunburn."

"Thank you." I haul myself to my feet as the two of us head towards Giulia's room. It isn't a long walk, and the nurse babbles gently about how the salve worked wonders on her nose this time last year. I don't have to say anything to keep the chatter coming. I push open the door to Giulia's room, and my stomach drops.

A man in a dark cloak is leaning over Giulia's body. A vicious knife gleams in his hands, hovering above Giulia's throat.

"No!" I scream, throwing myself at the assailant. I leap onto his back, grabbing hold of his arm with both hands as we descend to the floor, the knife clattering like a clanging bell. The nurse is screaming, the glass in her hands shatters on the ground as the assassin throws me off with an elbow to my stomach. He turns around, slamming a fist into my face. I yelp in pain, my jaw aching as I'm dazed. He snatches his knife from the floor, spinning back to face me and with both hands, he plunges the knife towards my neck.

I throw up my hands, grabbing his wrists, trying to stop the impending knife with all my strength. My arms shake, my back pressed flat to the floor. My entire body screams as he pushes down harder, starting to win as inch by inch the knife descends towards my throat.

I scream with the effort, realising I'm going to lose.

I'm going to die.

A roar erupts behind me like a beast unleashed. In a blur the assassin is wrestled off me. I'm gasping for breath. Nouis is suddenly on top of him, a knife in his own hands. He slams the short blade deep into the assassin's chest. The assailant shrieks in agony, hands scrabbling hopelessly at the wound for a few moments and then he goes completely still, his glassy eyes staring at the ceiling.

The silence is deafening. Panting furiously, Nouis staggers back, hand still slick with crimson as he stares at the lifeless body on the floor.

He rounds to see me, eyes wild.

"Are you okay? Renza, are you hurt?" he demands, dropping next to me on the floor. That dripping red knife in his grip slips and hits the stone floor as he takes me into his arms, blood still wet on his hand.

"Who is he? Who is he?" I babble frantically.

"Renza. Renza, stop!" Nouis instructs, firm but calm, "He's dead. He's not going anywhere. Answer me, are you hurt?" I shake my head, gaping at the dead man on the floor of my sister's bedroom. I can barely breathe, I can't even think.

They tried to kill Giulia.

"It's okay. I'm here now. I'm here."

"He was going to kill her," I manage to garble between my pants. Nouis frowns, crouching in front of me. He takes my face in both his hands, looking at me seriously.

"Her? Not you? He tried to hurt Giulia?"

I nod. Energy surges into my numb limbs as I scramble to my feet and throw myself to Giulia's side, scanning up and down her unconscious form for any sign of damage. I grab her wrist, pressing my fingers in tight to make sure. The wave of relief in finding her steady pulse almost makes me pass out.

"Is she okay?" asks Nouis.

I nod, sinking into the bed as new tears form in my eyes. I reach for her blonde hair, stroking it out of the way. My little sister. Lying here, she's so vulnerable. Who would ever want to hurt her? She is loved by everyone.

Why would *they* want to hurt her?

Suspicion crawls up my back like a frost. The question builds on my tongue.

What did she know?

"Good, I'll call the doctor to be sure. And we should hire some security. More security, private, not the Militia," Nouis babbles. "I'll ask around. You don't recognise him?"

I shake my head, not daring to turn back and look at the fresh corpse in my sister's bedroom.

"I'll make sure to ask the City Guard when they arrive— maybe they'll have a record or people they can ask or something," Nouis says, nodding as he formulates his plan.

I turn to look at him. His funeral tunic is slashed open and splattered with gore. His bare feet pad on the stone as he talks, hands gripping the sides of his head like he could physically force himself to think of everything.

"You saved us," I croak in gratitude. Could my debt to this man ever be repaid? He's done so much for me and he just keeps adding more to the pile.

Nouis faces me, a kind smile filling his face. "It's okay. I'm just glad I could help."

"We'd be dead. Both of us. You saved us." The words catch in my throat as I think of what this ghastly man would've done to my sister had I not arrived. Or after I had failed to protect her and died myself.

Nouis had saved us. Risked his life for us. Again.

He sits down next to me on the bed, pulling me closer. The smell of him, almonds and vanilla, washes over me like it could wipe away everything bad that's ever happened. I grip him tightly, like he's my only lifeline in this awful hurricane.

"Thank you. Thank you. Thank you," I garble into his warm chest. He holds me closer still, arms so strong they could be a fortress.

"Shhh, it's okay. I'm here now. You're safe. You're both safe."

I wrap my arms around him so tightly they're shaking with the effort. I press my head into his shoulder until my blistering nose is squished almost flat.

"I'm here for you throughout everything, Renza. I hope you know that, no matter what," Nouis whispers softly in my ear, "I just want to help."

I let out a short breath. I know that. Of course I know that. I twist my head up, pushing forwards to kiss him softly. Gentle, whisper soft. I sit back slightly, looking at him and those intense green eyes. I press my hand to the side of his face.

"What are you doing tomorrow evening?"

CHAPTER 17

Four figures walk down Tana Street after dark. We don't talk particularly, minds consumed by our task. Hooded cloaks obscure our faces, though I suppose it wouldn't be weird for me to be seen with Michelle and Emilia. Nouis's hand is wrapped around mine as we walk, the pressure of his fingers a great balm to my nervous fidgeting.

The road is lit by old and tattered burning street lights, the glass which is supposed to protect them is grimy with decades of smoke, colouring the light a murky orange. Paint peels from the posts, and many are covered in the scratched names of strangers professing undying love. The cobbled road has too many potholes for my liking, filled with dust or sand as a quick fix. This will be at the top of my list for the repair fund, when Halice is back to normal.

We arrive at the cafe, the word *Amica* painted in fresh green paint above the wide doors. Everything is closed for business, the window shutters secured and the door firmly shut. I raise my gloved hand, knocking at the door. Emilia looks around the street behind us, devoid of other travellers—a side effect of the Church Militia doing their unwelcome patrols.

There are heavy footsteps as the door opens a crack. A stocky woman narrows her eyes at me as I lift my hood to show her my face. She huffs, pinching her nose in, like she has a headache forming. Then she opens the door wider for me.

"They're in the back," she says unhappily, eyeing me like I'm about to carve out her heart. We file into the cafe space, cluttered with mismatched tables and chairs. She closes the cheap wooden door quickly, rattling through the locks and bolts with fierce movements.

"That way," she mutters, jabbing a short thumb over her shoulder. I follow her gesture to a blue door in the back corner. My heart hammers as a familiar itch takes root in my fingertips. I suck in a breath, forcing myself to calm down to little avail.

Remember the breathing. In through the nose, out through the mouth, count to four, repeat.

"Thank you," I answer, taking off my cloak completely. Emilia and Michelle do the same.

"I want no Soulhate nonsense from you," she barks, pointing a short finger at me. "You don't touch a hair on his head, you understand me? Or there will be me to answer too."

Surprised but not worried, I can't help but smile. A threat clearly made out of love. However this woman knows Idris, she must have great affection for him.

"You have my word, signora. I will control myself if he does," I swear, hoping fervently it's not a lie.

"Go on in then," she scoffs, shaking her head as she walks towards a set of stairs, leading up to what I assume are her rooms. I head for the back door. Every step is like fire ants biting at my toes. I take a moment, preparing myself for the revulsion, and push the door open.

The room inside is small and windowless. A large dented round table sits in the centre, surrounded by a smattering of wonky, painted chairs. There are two green cabinets pressed against one wall, both showing scratches, chips and clearly in need of a lick of new paint. Candles with swaying flames are clustered on their shelves.

The two men inside are already quiet.

Idris is a blister in my vision. My pulse slams in my throat, the whispers taking route in the back of my mind. He slowly forces his eyes off the table to see me. I swallow tightly, the motion like hot ashes down my throat. I force myself to look away, breathing deep. I aim for one of the chairs, sitting down and digging my nails into the wood to keep myself there. Slowly the fire begins to quell.

I keep my eyes low, focusing on taking note of everything else in the room. I keep my breathing even. Slow and purposeful.

The other man I recognise as Alfieri Barone. His family had always been staunch supporters of Jacopo. The Barones are sea merchants, and successful ones at that, with lots of business in Chalgos. We've crossed paths on occasion.

I keep my eyes on him. His chin-length mousy hair is tucked behind his ears as he leans back in his chair, nursing a large flagon of ale as he rubs his stubbled jaw line. He studies me in turn, offering a cheeky grin.

"Renza," he greets with a wink.

"Alfieri," I respond.

"How many times have I told you to call me Alfie?" he chuckles.

"Five. But it annoys you, so Alfieri you'll stay," I tease gently. He cackles in good humour, taking a swig of his ale.

"You told people?" Idris scowls, gesturing to Emilia and Michelle as they walk through the door. When Nouis appears, Idris bolts to his feet, blond hair flying.

"No. No, absolutely not. Are you insane?"

"Stop, he's on our side."

"Do you think I'd let her go anywhere near you without protection?" snaps Nouis walking to my side. He sits next to me, a hand wrapping around my arm.

"You're an idiot." Idris seethes at me. "You told him? *Him*? He's working with Bellandi."

"How dare you." Nouis's voice rolls with righteous indignation. "Of course I'm not. What he's done is disgusting and vile and totally deranged."

Idris slams his drink on the table; it shudders angrily from side to side. "You were his damn proxy," Idris hisses.

"A convenience." Nouis takes a deep breath, using a tone to imply Idris is behaving beneath himself as Nouis steadies the rocking table, "I did him a favour because he knows my aunt, but I would never be complicit in such a disgusting scheme. I spent all my summers here; Halice is a second home. I would never do anything to harm it."

"Idris, I understand why you think this, but you're

wrong. Nouis saved Giulia. He saved me. *Twice*. Not just at the temple. He saved us last night." My throat burns with his name, but I force myself to meet those golden hazel eyes. It's like staring into the sun at High Summer, the heat searing into my mind.

"Saved you?" repeats Idris grinding his teeth but his eyes narrow dangerously. "Last night?"

"An assassin broke into Giulia's room, trying to kill her. I found him before he could, and then he tried to kill me too," I say slowly, forcing the words out without screaming or sobbing. Idris helps, looking at him makes the tears dry up and my mouth go dry. "Nouis is the only reason I'm still alive."

Idris looks like he wants to murder someone. *Anyone*. Probably me.

He glares at Nouis. "Where is he now?"

"The morgue," Nouis answers.

Idris scoffs, throwing himself back into his seat to glare at his drink. "Convenient. We can't even question him."

"I did my best. Not all of us are trained killers," Nouis defends himself hotly.

"No, but you are. I've seen you wield a blade before," accuses Idris. That slaps me in the face, and not just because of the bond.

"Wait. You two have met before?" I venture, turning my whole body to look at Nouis, the chair juddering underneath me.

"In passing," Nouis growls out his distaste, wrinkling his nose. Idris scowls, draining his flagon. Neither volunteers their history.

"Well, I think perhaps we're wasting time?" offers Alfieri, clearing his throat. He smiles at Emilia warmly, gesturing to an empty orange seat.

"Would you ladies like a drink?" he asks cordially, easing to his feet.

"Thank you," Emilia answers, gracefully lowering herself into the offered seat. Alfieri goes over to the cabinet and pours a few glasses.

"I said tell no one," Idris mutters unhappily, eyes drifting to the girls. The idea of him ever setting eyes on them makes me want to burn this whole room to the ground.

"Pot and kettle, Idris," I snap back, looking over to Alfieri as he puts a glass of wine in front of me.

"Alfie can be trusted," seethes Idris.

"So can Emilia and Michelle. We all have an interest in making sure Serra isn't used as Bellandi's scapegoat."

"Why Giulia?" Alferi claps his hands, interjecting the comment rather pointedly by jumping into business. He plonks the new drinks on the rickety table and sinks into his chair.

"What?"

"Why kill Giulia?" Alfieri elaborates. He pauses a moment, a sheepish look edging around his eyes, "I mean ... is she improving?"

"She's still with us," I croak. Michelle tenses and Emilia pats her arm.

"So she could wake up?"

"Doctor says any day now," I nod, forcing myself to smile. I know it's not convincing. Alfieri turns to Idris with a pointed look. I get what he's implying.

"What does she know?" Emilia says for the room. "What don't they want getting out?"

"Exactly," Alfieri smiles at her. "I'm sorry, we haven't met. I'm Alfie, and you are?"

"Emilia," Emilia answers, her eyes cutting him up and down in quick assessment.

"Emilia," Alfieri repeats, leaning towards her, "it's a pleasure to meet you."

Idris gives him a kick under the table. I wrap my fingers around the glass of wine, desperate for something to keep me in this seat and not start a brawl.

"Giulia was looking into something at the bank." Michelle scratches her head. Her mind's eye somewhere else. "She was stressed about something, in the last few days leading up to the attack. She never said what it was, only that it was work."

"You didn't ask about it?" Emilia frowns. Michelle pulls a face at the question.

"Of course I asked, but she didn't want to share. Besides, it's not like I get the intricacies of the bank and I didn't want to make her any more uncomfortable," Michelle answers a little begrudgingly.

"You think something might be going on at the bank?" Alfieri asks.

"That would make sense," Emilia chimes in. "I mean, isn't Bellandi trying to build that ghastly new temple?"

"Ghastly?" asks Alfieri in good humour.

"Oh the designs are awful!" Emilia wrinkles her nose, leaning forwards to dig her elbows into the table as she rubs her eyes. "No ingenuity, a stupid amount of gilding and art to make it gaudy, and other than that ... it's just plain ugly." I can't suppress the grin as the artist in Emilia pokes her head to the surface.

"So you've seen them? The new plans?"

"I'm an architect and I'm nosy. I collaborate a lot with my colleagues and I see most of what gets built in this city, particularly something that big. It needs collaborators," Emilia explains, resting her head on an open palm. "But the beastly thing is an absolute money pit. I'm not surprised Bellandi has to play with money to fund it."

"Perhaps, but why 'play with money' before the explosion?" Idris ponders. "It would have been far safer to wait and not risk getting caught." I fight the urge to look at him, keeping my eyes on literally anyone else in the room.

"You don't think it's for the new temple?" Nouis asks pointedly.

"I wouldn't like to say," Idris spits, the silence following making it clear that Nouis's presence is what holds Idris's tongue. I grit my teeth, setting down my glass.

"Then I'll look into it. It's my bank after all," I answer. "It won't be strange if Bellandi finds out I'm there. He knows I'm working on a new budget." No one raises any objection, so I assume that's a set plan.

Silence fills the room for a long pause. The candles dribble beaded wax down their tall, slender stems as their tops wobble with marigold flames.

"The temple explosion, I did some digging..." Emilia sets the roll of paper she'd brought with her on the table. Alfieri helps her, weighting the corners down with empty glasses.

We all stand up, pressing hands on the table and leaning over for a good look.

The Grand Temple's blueprints.

"This must be over a hundred years old," Michelle mutters, running her hand over the old dry parchment.

"One hundred and twenty-six, to be accurate," Emilia agrees, tapping a scrawled date in the bottom corner, "but the temple itself is younger. It took five years to finish. There was an issue with—"

"What did you find?" Alfieri interrupts kindly, giving her a cheeky wink. Emilia nods, roses blooming across her cheeks as she gets back on track.

"Back when this was built, the Grand Temple had the tallest and largest domed ceiling anyone could've ever imagined—for the time that is. So big they realised they didn't know how to build it without these massive stone columns to support it." Emilia gestures towards them. "Not like we do today." I remember those white columns, seeming to sit so awkwardly amongst the rows of pews.

"Meaning?"

"Well, each column supports part of the roof, but they put in extras because people were afraid of it collapsing. Meaning that if one or two columns went, the others would still stand and the roof wouldn't completely cave in."

"How many columns would need to go to see that kind of devastation?" Alfieri connects the dots quickly. Emilia nods slowly, certain of her words.

"At least seventeen out of the twenty-one. And given they were destroyed by explosives rathern than by axe or hammer ...

my guess would be they tried to sabotage all of them. But there's more." Emilia takes a deep breath as we hang on to her every word. "These columns weren't just resting on the tiled floor. If you look here, the stones were sunk into the very foundations of the building. Metres deep. They were buried and cemented into place, immovable if you will. Meaning for one to fall down, you would need to crack the stone pillars all the way through. With an excessively powerful blow."

"Hence an explosion," Alfieri says, leaning over the page.

"I went through Serra's things and tried deciphering some of her maths," Emilia says, frowning at the memory of it. "The woman doesn't keep notes as tidy as she should, but I think I got enough: an explosion is most brutal at its centre. As it detonates outwards, it loses force. So the explosive devices would've been directly on the pillars to cause ... what happened."

"The people in that church weren't stupid. They would've seen explosives," I point out.

"Not if they were disguised? Decorations perhaps?" offers Michelle. "It's easy to disguise or conceal things with art."

Blood leaves my face. "Wasn't Terzo supposed to get married there later that day? That would explain any unusual decorations."

Terzo was one of the Garden's artists, a sculptor set to marry his Soulmate, the daughter of a wealthy wool merchant. The two were nauseatingly happy in their love, and Halician society was thrilled for them. That would've explained how no one saw anything. Terzo was rather eclectic and now very wealthy. I could only imagine how the decor must've looked.

"How did they work it out? Those at fault I mean." Alfieri frowns, rubbing his jaw.

"*We* did that quite easily," counters Emilia. "I mean the theory anyway if not the exact maths."

"You did, but you're clearly an expert," Alfieri corrects, eyes sparkling at her. "But how did *they* do it? You understand building structure, and your friend, Serra, was researching explosives. Between you, you've got the skills to put it together. What about them? Did anyone see this document before you? Maybe they're linked to the culprits?"

"No, the Court of Records had to pull this from their archives just for me. It was covered in dust." Emilia shakes her head.

"So how did they know about the columns, and where to place the explosives?" Alferi asks.

That's a very, very good point.

"Maybe the Church has a copy?" ventures Emilia. "I often give clients copies of my drawings to keep or display."

"The Church has a copy? A copy they could look at and work all this out from?" Michelle asks pointedly.

"Maybe, or maybe the family of the original architect still has it. Who knows? But to orchestrate what they did, they needed to see something like this. This wasn't spur of the moment; it was meticulously planned."

"If the architect's family did have it, it wouldn't be too hard to steal or buy it off them," adds Alfieri.

"Why steal when you can simply request documents from the Court of Records?" Nouis frowns, gesturing to the work in front of them. "It's public record."

"Because they keep a log of who requests what," Emilia answers instantly. "For security."

"Which makes sense considering everything," Michelle grumbles under her breath.

"What do you think, Renza?" Nouis asks softly.

"I think this is good. This is evidence we can use, if we can prove the Church has a copy of the plans," I answer, folding my arms. "But it doesn't tell us what Bellandi is planning next or indeed clear Serra's name."

"Well, maybe I can help with that. I can get close to Bellandi," offers Nouis.

Idris scoffs, shaking his head and lurching away from the table to glare at the nearby wall. I flinch at the sudden action, fighting the hair standing on end all over my body.

"Sure, Rizaro, you go do that." Idris's bitter sarcasm clogs up my ears. "Let us know if you find anything."

"Why would that work?" I ask Nouis, forcing myself to focus on the task and not the irritable man who sets my teeth on edge. "Do you think you can get Bellandi to trust you?"

Nouis takes my hands in his, considering his words for a minute before speaking delicately.

"I mentioned Bellandi knows my aunt right?" Nouis says with a wry smile. "Well, let's just say he's a favourite of hers. An *intimate favourite*."

I blink in shock and press my lips together. Really? Bellandi and the Holy Mother herself, an item? *Seriously*?

"Oh!" Emilia suddenly gets it, cupping a hand to her mouth to smother the shock.

"I thought your aunt was ... significantly older than Bellandi?" I clear my throat, not sure how to process that information at all. Nouis shakes his head, seeming uncomfortable.

"She is," he agrees, wrinkling his top lip with a grimace, "but I'm fairly certain the infatuation started with him."

"Old love is just as lovely as young love," Alfieri grins wickedly, chuckling to himself.

"I said infatuation, not love," scoffs Nouis "My aunt is not that type. But I think I can use it to ... talk to him. Earn his trust."

"Well, if you really think you can get him to trust you then it's worth a try." I pointedly refuse to acknowledge Idris shaking his head like an angry toddler in the corner.

"Okay, Nouis will get close to Bellandi, and Renza will look at the bank. So how are *we* going to break Serra out of jail?" Michelle asks, ticking off tasks on her fingers like a shopping list.

If Idris's head had moved any faster, he'd have snapped his neck.

"You what?" he barks. I drop my head to my hands. I thought they'd given up on this insanity.

"We need to get Serra out of prison," Michelle repeats like it's obvious. "We can't leave her to Bellandi's whims. He's trying to pin this whole thing on her. He will kill her to quiet the public."

The noise escaping Idris is delicious, like he's about to burst into flames. Even Alfieri looks surprised, though he's also enjoying Michelle's revelation far too much.

"What on earth are you thinking?" Idris demands in despair. He turns to glare at me, his gaze blistering against my brow. I grit my teeth, gripping the table so hard I might break my hands.

"Me? I told them this was mad. I thought you'd both let it go." I sigh, turning to look at Emilia and Michelle in turn. Emilia rolls her eyes and folds her arms.

"With all that we now know about Bellandi? If we fail to stop him, Serra will die if we don't get her out. We can't risk that."

"Breaking her out only makes her look more guilty," Idris snaps, hands raking through his hair. "And what damn business do any of you have trying to arrange a jailbreak? What makes you think you can do it?"

"Haven't you heard? Diamonds are made under pressure," Michelle answers, jutting out her chin.

"So is coal. It's dirty and dark and only useful when burned," Idris hisses. "You'll all get killed. Or you'll get caught, accused of treason and executed, which will have the same end result."

"We can't leave her there," says Emilia, scowling.

"We won't. When we have Bellandi out and Halice is safe, we'll free her then," promises Idris. "For now at least we know where she is and can make sure she stays safe. Renza, back me up here."

I pause, picturing Serra in that dark prison cell. I swallow tightly before speaking, my chest clenching uncomfortably.

"Do you really trust Bellandi not to use her against us?" I ask the real question on my tongue. "He knows I care about her. Serra is…"

I trail off. To say she's my friend seems like a disservice to what we once had. To say ex-lover seems like a disservice to what we have now. Idris takes a long, deep breath.

"We won't let anything happen to her," promises Nouis.

"You can't make that promise," Emilia says quietly. "No one here can."

Idris doesn't answer. He forces himself to take a deep breath, before speaking in a low, uneven voice. "Renza, listen and really hear me. The safest way to look after Serra is to do this by the book. In the prison, we know where she is. I will even go and speak to Captain Collier to make sure he keeps her safe, alright? You know this is madness."

He's right, though it pains me to admit it.

"He's right, Renza. This would be suicide," whispers Nouis, a hand going to my arm. I look between the girls. Their gaze is just as determined as before, perhaps even more so now the challenge has been laid down. I can see the question in them. Am I in?

I rub my eyes and bite my lip. All I can see is Serra, swinging from side to side before my eyes. I can't—I *won't* let Bellandi take someone else I love.

I meet Emilia's dark eyes before giving her an imperceptible nod.

It looks like we're doing this alone.

∼

We leave the little back room and start to put on our cloaks again. Idris talks quietly with the cafe owner, who keeps throwing me dirty looks. I shake my head, wondering how on earth they know each other.

I pin my cloak together, thankful for the light, breathable cotton. The High Summer sun might be resting for now but the air is sticky and clings uncomfortably to the skin.

"So, what time shall we meet tomorrow?" Idris asks. My head whips around and I regret it the instant I meet his frustratingly captivating hazel eyes. I gasp, reeling backwards two paces as I let that pulse of disgust and violence roll over me. Idris is patient, not flinching as I swallow to try and get everything under my control again. My pulse begins to slow as the wave settles back to the uncomfortable bubble in my chest.

"What are you talking about?" Nouis's tone makes it clear Idris should step back immediately. Idris pays him no mind.

"I was talking to Renza." He returns his address to me. "So, what time?"

"What are we doing tomorrow?" I frown, turning my eyes to the fastening on my cloak.

"The bank. We're going together," Idris says matter-of-factly, as though we're discussing the weather. I glare at my fingers, refusing to look up.

"What do you know about banking?"

"My family owns a slew of businesses, and I spent six months working with Bevrick Morton, the Chief Financier of Chalgos' famous Merchant Row," Idris answers. "Who knows, another pair of eyes might be helpful."

"What were you doing in Chalgos?" I ask, the question tumbling out before I can really think about it.

"Learning about business of course," Idris answers, like it's obvious. "So, tomorrow?"

"I'm coming too," Nouis insists. "I don't like the idea of

you two alone. You have no need to tempt the Soulhate bond like that."

"I thought you were cuddling up with your best pal Bellandi?" snipes Idris.

"Enough," I warn the two men. "Nouis, you're with Bellandi tomorrow. Stick to the plan. Idris, I don't think you being around tomorrow will be at all conducive to actual work."

"Perhaps. But after you were attacked by an assassin yesterday, you can't go around without someone to protect you. I don't trust the Militia or anyone outside of this group, and Alfie is busy tomorrow meeting with some of his contacts about the Militia. So you're stuck with me."

Protect me? Idris? I'd laugh if the whole situation weren't already so insane.

"You're just as likely to kill me as protect me."

"You must think so little of my self-control," Idris chuckles, voice dropping an octave, "but twice now *you've* started the altercations between us. Not me."

"Twice?" hisses Nouis, his eyes zeroing in on me. "What happened?"

I shake my head, hands going to my hairline. I'm going to be spending an entire day alone with him and not kill him?

This is going to be an unmitigated disaster.

"Renza, a word in private?" Idris gives Nouis a pointed look before beckoning me to the side. Fire itches in my throat as I sigh and follow him a few paces away. Every muscle tenses in preparation for a sudden movement or surprise attack.

Idris leans against the wall, looking at the floor. I dare to steal a moment to look at him, analysing those chiselled features, broad shoulders and the thick muscles of his arms and thighs. I drop my gaze again, noticing those expensive brown leather boots he's wearing. They're meant for action and marching rather than the sloping streets of Halice.

"We need to trust each other, and we need to understand this bond better," he says quietly. His voice is as deep and low as the oceans, yet sits uncomfortably in my ear. "This situation with Bellandi looks like it might get worse before it gets better. While I know you trust Rizaro, please understand that I don't."

"That much is obvious. But why? What has Nouis done to earn your distrust?"

"There was an incident a few years back..." Idris answers, voice dark. "I'll tell you another time, but for now I need you to take me at my word."

"He saved Giulia," I repeat in a quiet hiss.

"I'm grateful, but it doesn't change my mind. You and I need to stay alive long enough to free Halice and work out exactly what is going on here, so whatever your personal feelings towards me, put them away and know this as an absolute fact: I am going to keep you safe, Fate be damned."

My head jumps up, my eyes lock on the shadows of his angular features on the wall. That promise—that vow—held so much determination I couldn't question it. My heart skips a beat in surprise, warming a touch knowing that he loves this city as much as I do.

"I have no personal feelings of hate, Idris. This isn't me." My words are barely more than a whisper. "It's the bond. I swear it's not personal."

"Either way. I am going to keep you safe," he repeats, making to leave. My hand moves of its own accord, latching onto his forearm to stop him. He freezes on the spot.

"It matters to me that you know," I insist. "It matters to me that you know that I don't hate you, not in my rational mind anyway."

Idris seems to relax as a beat passes between us, and I remove my hand.

"I'm sorry, you're right. Of course it matters; I didn't mean to dismiss it," he says softly.

"But also, I have to know..." I shake my head, biting my lip before continuing. "Why weren't you at service that day?" I hate the accusation as it comes from my mouth.

"Because I knew you'd be there. And you deserved at least one whole day without fighting ... this," Idris answers softly. "I've really never been one for religion."

I take a deep breath and nod.

Silence lingers a moment. My eye catches on the cafe owner watching us unhappily with her arms folded.

"Okay, what is your story with her?" I ask. Idris turns to look over his shoulder, a small smile crinkling his mouth.

"That's Paula."

"Paula promised I'd have her to answer to if I slipped up this evening," I inform him. Idris laughs, real warmth lacing the sound.

"Paula was my nanny when I was little. She inherited this place from her father when he died and turned it into a cafe after I left the city," Idris says. "She's the best. If she ever offers to tell you a bedtime story, take her up on it. You won't regret it."

I snort with laughter. "I'll remember that."

"Her brother was at the Grand Temple when…" Idris trailed off, voice tight. "He was her only family."

I take a deep, shaky breath. "I swear I'll get justice," I vow.

"*We* will get justice. You're not alone in this," promises Idris. Despite the way his words taste like curdled milk, my heart does feel lighter.

I take a deep breath. "Tomorrow. Outside the bank. After lunch. We'll need a cover for why we're together; we can't look like we're getting along. Bellandi will have spies everywhere."

"Don't worry, I already have a plan for that," Idris smirks.

That sounds like trouble.

CHAPTER 18

The Di Maineri Bank oozes wealth and security. The two-storey building isn't painted with flashy colours, but instead its tall windows are framed with different carvings, and all its doors adorned in polished metals. At the top of the impressive building is a large, blue-coloured glass dome. Rumours say that my grandfather built it to test the design for the High Chamber.

I believe it.

Columns run along the outside, each of them painted blue with white figures depicting every kind of work. Fishing, building, farming, sewing—you name it, it's there in blue and white. Large lemon trees stand tall and proud at the base of the steps, with bursting purple flowers thriving around their feet. Bank tellers and citizens alike traverse up and down the huge blue and white striped steps.

I take a deep breath looking up at the huge monument, paid for and built by my family. Unlike many of the sites in the city, which fill me with pride to be a Halician, this building is one of the rare times I am proud to be part of the Di Maineri banking family.

A family that is undoubtedly more trouble than it's worth. Letters have started pouring in from all corners from the various cousins, filled with a distasteful mixture of hollow sorrows and opportunity grabs.

I'm waiting for Idris. After last night, I tossed and turned in bed. No matter how hard I tried, I couldn't get him out of my mind.

Either way, I am going to keep you safe. His words echoed through my head again and again like a vow. An oath. As did the feel of his toned forearms through his tunic shirt. Muscled, strong. The fire that had ignited in my fingertips lurked like a ghost every time I tried to close my eyes.

Now here I am waiting for him, fighting the yawns that bubble to the back of my throat.

My hair stands on end, as my pulse jumps. I'd know that sensation anywhere. "Patricelli," I greet as he comes to stand at my side.

"Ready for this?" he asks, scanning the crowd.

"Ready for what?" I demand. He laughs low, before taking a deep breath.

"All I want is to look at the account for myself," bellows Idris at the top of his voice, making me jump. My muscles tense in panic at his sudden jump in tone, but I see where he's going with this. I shake my head, chasing the smile from my lips as I force my limbs to relax.

"Well, come on then," I snap back, marching up the steps. "Take a look. But I'm right as I always am, you arrogant prat."

"You are so full of yourself, you can't imagine that you'd

possibly be wrong!" Idris snips back as we step through the doors into the great building. The crowd parts to let us through, not wanting to be anywhere near this volatile fight.

"I'm not wrong."

The central hall stretches all the way to the roof. Left and right are two storeys of offices, and some corridors leading to the great vaults buried deep below the building. One way in, one way out. They are the most secure vaults on the continent—or that's what we've always believed until now.

At the front of the hall are lots of counters where citizens handle their affairs with the banking staff. Behind them, the space is crammed with accountants at desks diligently updating log books. At the back of the grand hall is a huge, white stairway. It splits halfway up, one side reaching left and the other right, leading to the upstairs offices.

Above it is a pristine white wall, carved in which are the names. Our names.

My family history.

Right at the top, going back to the founding of this city, is my great, great- great- great-grandfather. The flowing tree trails down the walls, with names of people I've never met, their bloodlines whisked away to other cities and countries marked and dated in the stone.

"Shut up and follow me, Patricelli," I snarl, marching through the throng of people. They all look up in shock to the visceral interruption.

"You know what, Maineri, no. I won't shut up. I have a right to see the account for myself. Prove to me this isn't all one great lie." Idris flails his arms in anger.

"Happy to. I've done nothing wrong," I shriek back as we storm up the steps to the second floor.

"Signora? Signora, can I be of help?" comes an alarmed voice hurrying to my side. Dorado, my sister's assistant, stands anxiously, glancing between myself and Idris.

"Yes. I'd like to see all of the ledgers for the accounts we hold with the High Chamber, so this vile excuse for a man can crawl back into whatever cave he climbed out of," I snarl at Idris.

Those are our biggest accounts. If Bellandi wanted to steal funds, that's the best place to start and the easiest place to hide it.

"Are you sure, signora? There is a lot to sort through," he frowns. "We haven't summarised it for the month yet."

"Just go get it," scowls Idris.

"No, you will not speak to my people like that," I scold, jabbing a finger at him, "And yes, Dorado. Please fetch it. Fetch everything."

"Of course," Dorado sighs unhappily. "Should I set them up in your office?"

"My office?" I frown. I don't have an office here. He hesitates before elaborating.

"Um, the Head Office?" He clears his throat.

Oh. Of course. The office for the Head of the Bank. Giulia's office...

My office.

"Oh, yes. Please," I nod.

I turn away, walking the familiar turns towards Giulia's office. I push the heavy wooden door, heart hammering as I look around her empty room. A large window looks out over the city below, the framing blue and pink striped curtains pulled back and held by silver ties. The floor under our feet is a tiled marble, mostly white cut with blue diamonds. A large fireplace sits empty by two low sofas. A large table is pushed against one wall, over which hangs one of Michelle's masterpieces. A depiction of the two of them walking together through the Garden.

On the back wall is another tapestry of our family tree, simpler this time. Starting with my great-grandfather, who started the bank, leading to his five surviving children, all of whom married and established branches of the bank in other independent cities when they left. I follow the line down to my grandfather, where it shows both his first and second wives. My grandmother died giving birth to my father. When Grandfather remarried, his second wife gave him three daughters—my half-aunts who have since married various wealthy men around the continent, taking Di Maineri Bank branches with them. None remain in Halice.

All the branches of our bank still report to us though, as the head of them all. We oversee the entire family business, much to the disgust of some of my cousins.

"You good?" Patricelli asks, pushing the door shut. I nod sharply, breaking out of my stupor and sucking in a deep breath to steady my nerves.

I stare at Giulia's empty desk, the edges of my heart tugging. I walk towards it, forcing myself to sit down in her seat, making my fingers open the drawers in search of paper and ink. Idris says nothing, but I can feel his fierce gaze blazing on my face.

"Don't look," I snap. I loathe to think what he sees.

Dorado returns with boxes and boxes of ledgers. Some of the other assistants help to carry them, and in and in they come. The boxes keep coming. When I think they'll stop, they just keep stacking them in front of the fireplace.

Eventually they do stop, and with a dry mouth I look up at the towering pile of ledgers.

"What have I got here, Dorado?" I swallow, looking at the number of thickly bound books.

"Everything we've found so far," Dorado answers briefly as though this was my own fault. He sweeps the door shut behind him and I'm alone with Patricelli and a mountain of numbers.

Patricelli stands there, staring at the boxes for a moment. He rakes a hand through his blond hair, muttering something under his breath. The noise wriggles like ants in my brain. I close my eyes.

In through my nose. One, two, three, four. Out through my mouth.

First, a drink. A strong, strong drink.

Knowing my sister, I go to the bottom drawer and pull it open. Inside is half a bottle of wine and a set of glasses. I smirk, pulling them both free and setting them on the desk.

"Now that is a good idea," Idris mutters, walking over expectantly. I pour quickly as Idris's shadow falls over the drinks. I stopper the bottle again.

"What are we drinking to? To Halice?" Idris snags the glass and I wince at the swift movement.

"To not killing each other today?"

"That works," he snorts, throwing his head back. I drain my glass quickly, breathing in deep through my nose to soothe my pulse. I pour myself another, turning to look at Giulia's portrait, a gentle lump forming in my throat when I think of her lying still and unconscious at home.

"You'd be so much better at this than me," I tell her quietly. I set the bottle down with a soft thump.

I drink deeply one more time before turning to face the mountain of paperwork we need to get through. As I catch sight of Idris, the awful whispers start to spiral in my mind.

Fate have mercy, this is going to be a long day.

~

The sun has started sliding from the sky which ripples with rose and violet hues. The mottled windows dapple the pages of the ledgers with swirls of blush as I pore through them. The floor is strewn with books. Piles and piles of them, open at the most recent entries.

All day, Idris has been hovering like a blinding sun in my vision. I can feel him when he moves. Each time he shifts, each turn of the page, each deep breath sticks in my mind like a growing itch. I'm going crazy, my hands turning to claws in my head as I force my eyes to scan the pages below me over and over.

A yawn hovers at the back of my throat as I rub my eyes in frustration. Numbers start to blur together, my own calculations littering the large table in front of me. I grab the most recent ledger for one of the school accounts, walking over to the sofa and sinking among the plush, velvet cushions, desperately trying to ease the sore muscles in my neck.

This is pointless.

The account withdrawals are all consistent with previous histories. Nothing abnormal whatsoever.

But, if not from the High Chamber accounts—the largest in the city—then where? What was Giulia concerned about?

"I'm calling it," scowls Idris, throwing his ledger to one side. I flinch at the sound of his voice and the slap of leather on the table, letting out a low growl of irritation. All day I have wanted to jump out of my skin and strangle him. All day I have fought clawing out his eyes with my bare hands.

The least he could do was not make sudden movements for Fate's sake.

I rub my eyes. Perhaps a nap would help? Or trying again tomorrow? I drop my hands down again. I blink, staring at a small mark at the edge of one entry.

That shape ... I've seen it before.

"Renza, did you hear me?" asks Idris shortly. I ignore him, getting to my feet and crossing to the other ledgers. I set the book down, and scan down the list for anything else. There it is again for the City Guard fund—a withdrawal made today for salaries. A squiggled diamond. Exactly the same mark.

"You have something?" Idris asks. As he gets closer my skin crawls. His body radiates heat, it strokes my skin like fiery, ghostly waves and sends shudders racing up my spine.

"Maybe," I grunt. I search around the floor for another ledger, grabbing one labelled for the City Repair Fund. I flip all the way to the last few pages, scanning down the entries.

There it is again. A scribbled diamond.

"What is it?" Idris pushes. I point to the squiggle.

"Some entries have these," I say. Idris leans down next to me, so close I can smell him. Lavender and mint set my teeth on edge. Yet the smell hits at that itch in my head, daring me to remember any other smells exist.

"A mark?" scoffs Idris. "That's it?"

I grab as many of the books as I can, dragging them all closer and flipping across to the most recent pages. Again and again, there it is. A scribble. A mark. A quick flick of the wrist, messiness around the edges.

I step back, shaking my head.

"Maybe I'm crazy. It could just be someone testing the ink on their quill before committing to the page—it certainly looks that way. This is certainly not proof. The scribble could mean nothing. But … it's only in the last few pages. Nowhere else is there a mark like that, going back months, the pages are completely pristine," I say quietly. Idris doesn't look convinced.

"What if it's just a new bookkeeper with a new way of doing things? They all have the same handwriting."

"I know that hand, Dorado made these entries," I answer. That's unsurprising. He often takes responsibility for the High Chamber accounts with my sister. During her … unavailability, he would've wanted to keep the wheels turning.

I bite my tongue, narrowing my eyes for a moment.

Dorado made all these scribbles? He's always so neat and precise.

I flip back a few pages, scanning for Dorado's name against the authorisation for withdrawals. I switch to other books, flipping the pages back. Again and again, going back weeks.

None of Dorado's other entries have these marks. Every

entry is precise and clean.

And these scribbles, tiny little marks at the edges of the pages—that could be nothing ... except they only started appearing five weeks before the Electi died. And then almost regularly.

I snap my fingers.

"Michelle!" Realisation hits me like a hammer. "We need to go to her place."

"What? Why?"

"My sister often kept files at her house. If she suspected Dorado of being dirty, she wouldn't keep the evidence here where Dorado could find it. We need to go to the Garden."

"Okay," Idris nods, frowning, "but these could still just be scribbles."

Were this the other way around, were Idris the one proposing this to me, I would've laughed the suggestion out of the room. Some squiggles as the only evidence? It's too easily explained away.

But also, far too convenient. Not enough to condemn, but enough for me to be sure I'm right. This makes sense too, why Dorado came up to me in the bank. And why he overwhelmed me with so many ledgers. Trying to scare me off, to stop me from piecing together what little evidence there was.

"If I'm right ... how much has he stolen from our city?" I mutter to myself.

I hurry over to the desk, grabbing a fresh piece of paper. I return to the ledgers, flipping to the messy entries. Idris reads out the numbers and I start scribbling them down, trying to tally them up into a reasonable figure. Giulia was the numbers girl. She would've done this so much quicker, yet here I am with sheet after sheet of calculations, trying to total the various different numbers.

"And the final result is?" Idris asks.

"Sixty thousand Hali-Pounds," I breathe, heart pounding in my chest, "but twenty thousand of that was before the explosion."

"Exactly? Both times an exact figure?" frowns Idris. He's thinking what I'm thinking.

A round, precise number? That sounds like a price tag. Bellandi is buying something. But what?

Suspicion crawls into Idris's voice. "I think we need to visit your friend Michelle to see what Giulia was looking into."

I nod, closing up all the ledgers. My eyes catch on one entry in particular. The one from today, marked to be moved immediately. That means tonight, since the bank makes most of its large transfers at night when the streets are emptier. I shake my head in frustration and close up the ledgers. I shove the paper with our calculations into the fireplace, making sure to get rid of the evidence.

"Ready to get out of here?" I ask.

"Yep," Idris laughs, stretching his neck. "Showtime."

CHAPTER 19

Idris and I take separate routes to the Garden. We don't want to be seen together more than is necessary in case we rouse suspicion with Bellandi that we're getting on.

Being free of him, even for one short walk is ... immaculate. Euphoric. I can breathe again without the fire, move without acid eating away at my fingertips. There is no monster at the edge of my vision, no fire thrumming through my blood.

Yet, even with him gone, Idris lurks like a spectre in my mind. His voice replays again and again. The scalding hazel of his gaze. That irritating, unforgiving, devastating smell of lavender and mint.

But I managed it. I survived. Idris survived. And neither of us has so much as taken a swing for the other ... by some miracle. Who knows how this decision will age. The few, rare stories I've heard of Soulhates refusing to duel, such as terrible pairings between family members, always result in at least one party moving far, *far* away to try and avoid the eye of Fate. I've never heard of anyone refusing to duel their Soul-hate and then sticking around to see the end result.

As I walk down the wonky path to Michelle's house however, my hairs begin to stand on end. My blood runs hot, my skin is riddled with goosebumps. The feeling is back.

"Fancy seeing you here," I say sarcastically as Idris steps out from one side of a sweet blossom tree. He hovers on the edge of my vision like a black, blistering aura threatening to swallow me whole. He's not alone; Alfieri is there too, grinning as he watches events unfold.

"Missed me already?" Alfieri asks brightly. "It's only been a day."

"Did you do anything useful today?" I retort sceptically.

"Define *useful*," he says vaguely. "Idris says you might've found something but you need the papers at your friend's house to confirm it?"

"Indeed," Idris says, "but when we got here I realised I don't know which house is Michelle's."

"Follow me, and watch yourself in Michelle's home." I sigh, heading down the track with as much speed I can muster. The sooner we do this the sooner he can go, and I'll be free to breathe in peace again.

"With a warning like that, what must you think of me?" Idris muses darkly.

"Nothing, Patricelli," I bite out with fake sweetness, "I don't think of you at all." It's a lie, he occupied my mind far, far more than I'd like. But he doesn't get to know that.

Idris doesn't answer, but Alfieri lets out a low whistle, a smirk pulling at his lips.

The trees rustle in quiet trepidation. Their leaves carry

whispered gossip from branch to branch. I refuse to let my gaze wander, to risk glancing at Idris. I stick firmly to the path. Soon we come to a mark on the ground, a dead patch of grass where Serra's machine stood only a few days ago. My throat goes dry and coarse.

Right now she's in a prison. A dark, dank prison filled with all kinds of thieves and murderers, wondering when I'll rescue her. The guilt rises in my throat and spills bitterness on my tongue. We move as a group in silence down the winding path till we reach a familiar little house. I don't hesitate, pushing through the front door.

"Only me," I call, entering the room. Michelle and Emilia bolt up from her kitchen table, both plastered with guilty expressions. Rather than the casual, warm welcome I'm used to, the air is oddly stiff.

"Renza, hey!" Michelle's beaming smile is so fake I cringe. Eyeing Idris nervously, Emilia hurriedly wraps up the paper on the table. Idris doesn't waste time with greetings and marches over, snagging the paper out of her hands.

"It's rude to snatch," Emilia tries to scold. Alfieri chuckles, peering over Idris's shoulder as they both inspect the unrolled document. Alfieri's face stretches into a naughty grin as he turns to Emilia.

"Now how did you get your hands on these?" Alfieri barks with delighted surprise.

"What are they?" I dare ask as Michelle stands sheepishly to one side, arms folded with one hand covering her mouth.

"Schematics." Some storms are calmer than Idris's voice. "For the prison."

I close my eyes, fighting the smile that comes to my lips.

Damn, the girls move fast. I turn to look at Michelle who just points at Emilia.

"It was all her. Or mostly her, I was told to bring paper and charcoal and then she did this."

"What did you do?" Alfieri's dark eyes sparkle like this is the best day of his life. He sits next to Emilia at the table who sits up straighter, raising her chin defiantly at Idris.

"A friend of a friend knows that the prison is in desperate need of repairs. Obviously it's on an island, and the tides and waves and a few storms have ... left their mark, shall we say. Captain Collier really wants the whole thing repaired and updated; he's campaigned for it a few times. So I went over there and told him that Idris has asked me to come up with a proposal. He showed me the weak spots that worry him. Then I said I couldn't come up with something properly without seeing the original plans. It took some persuasion but he showed me his copy of the schematics briefly. I memorised it ... and copied what I could when I walked out."

I can't stop the laugh that bubbles from my teeth. Emilia is amazing. Utterly and unashamedly amazing.

"Is this ... right?" Idris asks Alfieri, grinding out the words like they're poison. Alfieri looks over the documents and nods.

"Yeah, from what I can tell. Damn, you got this from a brief look?" Alfieri doesn't bother to hide his awe. Emilia blushes and sweeps her hair behind both ears at the same time.

"Wow, beauty, brains, and bravery to boot. Is there something you can't do?" Alfieri only half teases, nudging Emilia with his elbow.

"What were you thinking?" Idris snarls in rage. "We agreed you weren't doing this."

"No, you barked out orders and expected us to listen, like you were somehow in charge of us. But in case you've forgotten, Halice is a democracy," Michelle answers harshly without flinching. "And we aren't letting Serra fester in prison just because you're a coward."

Oh, low blow.

"Coward? Me?" hisses Idris.

"Okay, okay. I think we need to wind our necks in," Alfieri says firmly. "Idris, calm down. Michelle, back off. No one is a coward. Idris is trying to protect us."

"It's not his job to protect us," Emilia answers softly.

"Who else is going to do it? How many battles have any of you faced?"

"Battles?" I snap, suddenly finding words leaping to my mouth. "You've been in battles?"

Idris takes a deep breath, stalking away from the table and towards the back window. He doesn't say anything, clearly done with this conversation. I look at Alfieri who pointedly shakes his head slowly.

Alright. I won't push it. Instead I turn to Michelle.

"So, you have the schematics... Do you have a plan?"

"We were just getting to it. Come see," Emilia perks up, grabbing the papers back from Alfieri and rolling them out. The four of us lean over the table as Emilia talks us around the prison. Alfieri adds some colour to Emilia's descriptions, but doesn't offer up how he knows any of it.

"Okay, so Serra is probably there," Emilia says after a while, pointing to a section of cells. "Given she's wanted for treason, she'll be separated from the others for her own protection and extra security." I nod, scanning over the plans.

"This is the best spot. If we can get her here she can walk to the beach and we can wait with a boat," Alfieri says pointing.

"Don't help them!" hisses Idris. "I won't have you get swept up in this idiocy too."

"It's too far," I say, ignoring Idris's outburst and shaking my head. "Too far from Serra's prison cell. She'd have to break out of her cell, walk miles and a set of stairs and then break out of the building, to then walk to the beach? What if she's injured? Besides, how is she supposed to get all the way over there without getting caught?"

"What's your plan?" Alfieri asks.

I press my lips together. I press my finger to the nearest weak spot that Emilia mentioned earlier. The prison backed right up onto the ocean, the land slowly crumbling like a cliff under the stonework. "If we can get her there, and have a boat waiting underneath, she can jump into the water. We can fish her out and get her home."

"But how? The wall is at risk of subsidence, yes, but it's still a solid wall," frowns Emilia, folding her arms and straightening up.

"So let's trigger the subsidence," I grin.

"How? You can't just snap your fingers and make a wall fall down." Alfieri frowns.

"It's almost like we need someone who can understand explosives?" I chuckle.

Emilia's eyes go wide. "I can't do those calculations. I can't make an explosive."

"No, but Serra can. All we need to do is tell her where to put it."

"This is madness. She was arrested for having explosives. Now you want her to escape using explosives?" snaps Idris from the corner, his sudden unwelcome input flaring the flames that had gone quiet.

"Subsidence," I snap back. "Weren't you listening? Best to get your story straight now."

"How many other prisoners do we risk letting out—and that's if you can get Serra out of her prison cell in the first place," Idris hisses.

"Serra can pick a lock," I snort confidently.

"Oh yeah, Serra is the lock whisperer," Michelle nods, snapping her fingers. "Very useful when I lose my keys." Emilia nods with a small smile, having witnessed it too.

"As for other prisoners that might escape? None. That part of the prison is empty because of how fragile it is. If we can get Serra out of her own cage and to this wall ... she can do the rest," Emilia says quietly, eyes glued to the paper in front of her.

"Emilia, work out our weak point and where best to place the explosives. You'll also need to gather the things we need to get to Serra."

Emilia nods.

"Michelle, can you make everything look ... harmless? We'll need to make sure they pass inspection."

Michelle nods, mind's eye already on the problem. "I can make some things."

"Excellent, and you can sail right?" I push. She nods

again. "Great, then you'll man the getaway boat while I get Serra everything she needs."

"You what?" Idris snaps. "You are staying far, far away from this."

"Serra is suspected of treason. Only an Electi could get in to see her now, and it won't be weird that I'm there. Captain Collier knows I am trying to help Serra. If we do it right, it won't look like I've had a chance to leave anything with her. I won't be a suspect."

"No. It's too risky. Halice needs you. You are the only other Electi that can go against Bellandi, given I doubt he'll acknowledge my fake proxy status without you there to hold him accountable. You can't get caught up in this or Bellandi will brand you as a traitor. You'll swing right next to Serra and hand Bellandi the city on a silver platter."

"Then I won't get caught."

"It's not as simple as that." Idris stalks towards me. I spin, forcing myself to glare into those burning, golden eyes. I refuse to blink, twisting my face into a mask of pure determination, and fold my arms.

"I'm not leaving Serra to rot. I'm not letting my friends risk their lives when I can make things easier and safer," I answer with finality. "This is happening. So either get on board or get out of the way."

The silent challenge hovers on my tone. Idris's face contorts, his face dropping inches from mine. My pulse sprints; my throat goes thick.

"This is madness. Absolute madness." Idris scowls. He yanks himself backwards roughly, as though it took all his strength to tear himself away. He storms towards the door of

Michelle's house and stalks into the dark. Alfieri sighs, staring at the creaking door as it swings on its hinges.

"Don't worry about him. He just needs to cool off a bit. Well, it sounds like you ladies have a plan. But, this isn't what we came for ... is it?" Alfieri turns to look at me, round face pulled with a question.

No. He's right. The girls have very successfully buried the lead.

"Did Giulia leave any papers around, Michelle?" I ask.

Michelle nods, walking towards the cabinet by the table and opening a drawer. She pulls out a few thick files, handing them over. "Enjoy."

I slowly sink into my chair, sorting through the pile of information in front of me.

"I'll make us all some tea," offers Alfieri, hopping up and leaving me to it. I flick through Giulia's files. Letters from our various cousins are thrown to one side as I pull a few of her sheets together. There are letters from Captain Collier, merchants and schools to name a few, asking for their money and wondering why payment was late.

Then on a small piece of paper, a single number is circled.

Twenty thousand Hali-Pounds. Exactly the same amount that had been missing before the explosion. Before Giulia ... became unavailable.

"Looks like we're both right, Giulia," I mutter. My sister knew. She had been on to this for weeks now. She just didn't know what she was on to.

I lean back in my seat, eyes lost to the familiar room as I turn over everything in my mind again. One of those entries is for today right? Marked as an immediate move? So the money will be moving tonight. Perhaps I can follow it. Perhaps I can work out where all of this is going.

"I'm going back to the bank," I announce, jumping up from my chair.

"What, now? It's very late?" frowns Michelle pointing to the encroaching darkness outside her window.

"This can't wait. They're moving the money tonight. If we're right we'll be able to find out who is complicit in all this—finally we'll have some witnesses, some evidence," I promise, leaping forwards to give her a quick hug. I give Emilia a quick squeeze too, as she sits with Alfieri.

"Wait for Idris to get back," Emilia argues softly. "Or go find Nouis. Don't go alone."

"Who knows where Idris has stormed off to, and there's no time to find him or Nouis. I'll be fine."

"You can't go alone," Alfieri insists, setting the kettle down.

"My bank, my money," I scoff, rolling my eyes. "Try and stop me."

"I wasn't going to stop you; I'm coming with you. Idris would gut me if I let you wander off by yourself given we know someone out there wants you dead," Alfieri answers, setting the tea aside. "I'm fairly useful you know, particularly in a sticky situation."

"Fine. But don't slow me down."

"I wouldn't dare."

CHAPTER 20

The moon doesn't show her face. The stars have been banished from the sky and the breeze has died, rendering the world silent and still, as if holding its breath and waiting for death herself to finish stalking our painted columns.

Further proof the gods have turned their backs on Halice. Fine. Let us be godless.

Watch how heathens fight back.

Alfieri and I don't wait immediately outside the bank. I'm not that stupid. The Church Militia will be on the lookout for anyone spotting what they're up to.

Instead we wait down the street, around a building corner with my ears open and eyes flickering back to the bank building. The heat of the day is winding down now, thank Fate's Mercy. Breathing is easier, the cool shadows a welcome embrace. Wrapped in a black cloak and smothered in shadows, I'm all but invisible to any prying eyes.

Nouis wasn't home when I got back, so I didn't need to do an awkward dance with him about why I was leaving in such simple clothing. Plain trousers, boots, and a simple dark tunic were much more practical for this. If uncomfortably warm for this time of year.

My pulse thunders in my ears. My fingers itching and tingling to do something. My very blood has taken a chill, sending nervous shivers up and down my limbs.

This is *not* my thing. I'm not trained to skulk in shadows and trail armed and experienced soldiers when they commit crimes. Alfieri, though, is a natural. So at ease in the dark and not at all uncomfortable in this role of a spy. Part of me wonders exactly how many times he's done something similar.

Fate's Fury, I'm glad to have Serra's dagger at my waist. Its wooden handle presses into my soft flesh as I wait, its security sometimes the only threadbare reason I don't give up and go home.

A faint clipping of hooves and the rattling of a vaulted wagon pierce the stillness, each second growing louder and louder. I dare to peek around the corner again, looking down to see almost twenty Church Militia swarming a small black wagon.

It stops outside the bank. Three men march up the steps into the bank foyer, and reappear moments later hauling large, locked boxes. I swallow, aiming to release the tightness in my throat but finding no relief. They load the boxes into the back of the wagon, securing it tight.

That's when Dorado stands in the doorway, talking

intently with one of the Militia. Their leader—the one that swung for me back at the New College school—he's coordinating this.

He'll rot. I'll see to it personally.

Dorado suddenly doubles over, gasping as he collapses to the floor. I flinch, realising what's just happened as the Militia leader just walks away barking orders. The wagon sets off, its rhythmic beat swaying side to side on the cobbled floors. I ready myself to run for Dorado but Alfieri holds me back.

"No, they'll see you," he hisses frantically.

"We can't let Dorado die," I argue quietly but firmly. "He's our witness. Evidence. He's in on this whole thing."

"Fine, I'll go. You just ... stay here." Alfieri whispers the command uneasily, appearing to melt into the shadows. I hold back, bouncing on my toes as the carriage disappears down the street, the noise of the horses hooves getting fainter and fainter.

That's it. I can't just let the carriage leave.

I set off making sure no one sees me as I trail behind. Thank Fate they make so much noise. I'm hardly heavy footed but I can follow at least one or two turns behind them without being spotted or losing them. I keep to the side of the road, flitting from shadow to shadow as best I can. Alfieri would certainly be better at this than me.

This is our main road through the centre of Halice. The city is washed with navy, but illuminated by tall columns holding bowls of slow-burning oil. They'll keep burning through the whole night until they are put out in the morning. They flicker the world with streaks of crimson and amber, trying to wash away the safety of the ebony shadows.

As my pulse throbs in my ears and tingles in my fingertips, a sinking feeling starts to settle in my gut. I hesitate at the next corner, knowing the western gate will appear around the next turn. I slip closer to the corner, daring to edge just one eye around the stone.

Yes, as I suspected. Church Militia all over that entrance. Not a single City Guard to be seen.

In the distance, the vaulted wagon is now far outside the city, disappearing into the luscious green hills of the horizon with my city's money in its belly.

So, the money *is* leaving the city.

That still doesn't tell me where it's going.

Disgust pools in my gut. Bitterness coats my tongue as the urge to scream and rip my way through each of the guards scratches at the tips of my fingers.

Wait, no. It's not the guards.

Every hair on my arm snaps to attention. My stomach coils, my breath curdling on my tongue. I spin around, as someone leaps forwards. My enemy's hands are strong as I'm shoved back against the wall. My head hits the stone hard and my assailant's elbow goes to my throat. The dark silk of my hood falls around my shoulders as I stare up into the hazel eyes of an enraged Idris Patricelli.

"You!" I hiss throwing my chin to the side, desperate to break from his gaze. As I fight back against his grip, he only digs his hands in harder, his muscled body flush with mine against the hard stone.

"You," he retorts, his voice low and brimming with dark

anger. He leans closer and pushes his elbow deeper into my throat. "Do you have any idea how dangerous this is?"

Blood crashes like thunder in my ears. My vision is tinted red, and my limbs throb with rage and revulsion.

"Get off me." I try to push back but he doesn't give me any room. He leans in closer, his warm breath breaks across my nose. My pulse races under my skin, as I stare up at him once more. He looks so furious he might rip my head off with his teeth. I scrabble against his marble grip, hissing with rage.

He takes a deep breath, forcing himself to breathe through his nose as he closes his eyes.

"Close. Your. Eyes," he commands, voice like scalding nails to my mind. My entire being rages against the gall he has to attempt to control me.

"Up yours," I snap back, loathing boiling over as I thrash against his grip. His other hand leaps for my mouth, slamming my lips shut and my head back against the wall. My protesting growls are pathetic as he squeezes our bodies even closer together. The heat of his grip sinks its claws through my flesh and sends shivers running across my bones.

"Shut. Up," he snarls, head dropping next to mine as he tries to slow his breathing. "Just shut up. Don't look at me."

My world is tinted red. Disgust writhes around my throat and my fingers itch with the urge to claw out his eyes. All my limbs tremble as I force my eyes away from his face. The fire begins to ebb away, but far too slowly. It aches in my bones. In through my nose—like I have any other choice with his large, calloused hands wrapped firmly around my lips. I close my eyes, in through my nose, count for four, release. In, count to four, release. Next to me, Idris is unbearably still. His shoulders and chest move slowly, and I realise, he's mind-stilling too.

He's the one who sent the books.

I throw my head side to side, ripping my lips free from his hand.

"You're the one who left me those books?" I spit at him. Idris takes a deep breath, nodding sharply once before opening his eyes.

"Obviously, who else do you think sent them?"

"I had no clue, dimwit. You didn't leave a note! Fate's Fury, you went to Malaya?"

"Yes. Nouis didn't mention it?" Idris snipes back, lip curling in disgust. I blink in shock, filing that away to discuss with Nouis at a later date.

"Surprisingly you're not a topic of mine and Nouis's conversations. What are you even doing here?" I hiss, realising he's pressing so hard against my chest that it's hard to breathe properly. My nose fills with his scent, aromatic mint and delicate lavender. It burns at the back of my throat. "How did you know about this?"

"Michelle told me that you went back to the bank with Alfieri. Who seems to have vanished." Idris's tone makes it clear Alfieri will be in trouble at their next meeting.

"He's trying to save Dorado. He's most definitely an accomplice but was stabbed by the Militia. We need him as a witness," I argue.

"Alfieri shouldn't have left you alone," Idris growls.

"Well, now you're here, would you kindly *get off me*."

"What the hell were you thinking going after these

people on your own?" he growls, not moving. There's no space between us, only the thin silk of our tunics between me and his heaving, muscled body. I swear I can feel his pulse, his arms pressing so firmly against mine. "Do you have any idea—"

The night shatters in a second.

"Over there! Spies!"

Idris and I spin around. Church Militia are tearing our way, vicious blades already in their hands. My heart drops and my mind empties. Fear snakes a clawed grip around my throat. My mouth fills with ash. Idris swears loudly.

"Run!" Idris grabs my hand and pulls. I sprint with him down the road. The Church Militia aren't far behind, yelling and screaming for us to stop, for their companions to join the hunt. I pant, lungs aching, legs screaming with the effort to put as much space between us as Fate will allow. Every nerve comes alive, sparking as fear shoots through me cold and sharp.

I don't know where we're going, but I follow Idris's lead. Without looking, I know exactly where he is. His dark, hot aura shifts around the edges of my vision. His footsteps are quieter on the cobbles than mine. His breathing steadier.

He's holding back to run with me.

"Go," I pant, tearing my hand free of his. "If we split—"

"You'll die. Not an option. Just move faster!" snaps Idris. Gasping for breath I race down the hills towards the docks. Salt fills my nose and the sound of creaking boats floats softly in the air. Idris pushes around a corner, and we skid to a stop. The old city wall blocks off the end of the small alleyway, the abandoned stonework stretching like a prison.

Dead end.

My heart drops.

Behind us two of the Church Militia cut off our exit.

A trembling gasp escapes my lips. I shrink back against the wall, clenching my fingers to keep them steady.

"Climb," instructs Idris, reaching for something at his hip. The flash of a sword passes through my vision as he turns around.

"What?"

"Climb!" he commands again, swinging the sword with expert precision. I gape at the man instantly transforming into a soldier I don't recognise.

"But you—"

"I'll be fine. I studied for three years in Coari with the Princess of War herself. I can handle some Church Militia."

Wow, that's a name and a half. Okay then.

Deciding to process *that* later, I tear towards the old stone wall and grab hold of the ruined brickwork. The ancient cement turns to dust beneath my fingers as I pull myself up. I move quickly, scaling inelegantly up the wall. My boots scrabble against the weathered stone, my fingers screaming as they support my weight. Centuries-old dust falls in my eyes as the swords crash behind me.

Someone yelps, not Idris, before suddenly being cut silent and dropping to the floor.

"You'll pay for that!"

"No, I won't," Idris snarks behind me. My stomach rolls.

My heart thunders as I get to the top of the wall. I straddle it, a leg on both sides. I should drop to the other side, leave Idris to his fight and keep running.

Guilt knots through my stomach.

I can't leave him.

I turn my head slightly, watching the two inky shadows wobble against the cobbled ground. I might not be able to look at him, but his shadow doesn't seem to stoke the rage in our bond.

The two people circle each other, poised to strike.

"He's buying time," I hiss at Idris. "He's waiting for backup."

"I know," snaps Idris launching into movement. Their foggy black shadows ripple over the old stones, the street light turning their theatre into a world of flickering orange and yellow streaks as they slash violently at each other with whistling blades.

Idris ducks and parries, putting his opponent on the back foot. With one more sure swing, the soldier's blood sprays over the cobbles and his corpse collapses to the floor.

"Come on," I hiss, relief battling with rage in my gut. I reach down with one hand, turning my head away as Idris's warm palm fits in mine. I pull hard, slipping over the other side of the wall and using my weight to pull him up.

The two of us drop down on the other side, landing with short breaths. We crouch, the two of us pressed together for a long moment as we assess this new scene. Empty, dark, quiet. Idris adjusts the sword in his grip, his hand brushing against the small of my back as he steps around me and out into the alleyway.

"This way," Idris pants, his head tilt suggesting I follow, "quietly."

We hurry down the dark streets. We round a corner and skid to a stop, more Church Militia right down the other end.

We silently backtrack the safety of our dark alleyway. The air is thick with salt. Sweat coating my neck and arm, we press our backs against the building wall. My hands drop down the wall, the sound of our breath taints the air. My little finger brushes his hand, red-hot fire racing up my arm like a river.

"What now?" I gasp.

"Working on it," Idris growls, eyes cutting around for something.

"Pst. Pst." A man leans out of a low window. He gestures to us frantically, eyes darting down the road where the Militia are searching.

"In here," he calls, then disappears into his dark house.

Idris takes off after him. Seeing him, no matter how brief, slaps me with an urge to leap at him. To drive my dagger into his stupid blond head.

But I can't. I need him.

I hurl myself through the open window, landing inelegantly on the floor. I close my eyes, lying there panting for a moment, not prepared to face whatever is inside. The strange man shuts the window tightly, before putting up boards to cut off the outside world completely.

"You can both hide here while the Militia are searching," the man says, moving to light a candle in the darkness. Now he's illuminated, I can see his balding salt and pepper hair and large frame.

"Thank you, Franco," says Idris, setting his sword on the

table. My eyes catch on its vicious silver edges, spattered with fresh scarlet.

"Of course, signore. Anything for the Patricellis. Now I don't want no bodies on my hands. Particularly not yours. Are you two really able not to kill each other?"

"I don't think I'd stand much of a chance, signore," I admit dryly, shifting to a seated position on the floor, my eyes still fixed on Idris's weapon.

"Renza, this is Franco. He works in our shipping yard." Idris explains, raking a hand through his blond hair. I meet the man's gaze with a grateful nod.

"I'm in your debt, signore."

"And yes, Franco, we'll both be alive come dawn," Idris answers. He sounds so sure.

I'm certainly not.

"Fine. This way."

The man leads us up the stairs to a small bedroom. The narrow double bed swamps the room. A dirty window overlooks a narrow alleyway right down to the end of the docks. The man sets the candle down on a thin dresser.

"Hide here until morning if you like. There's water in the bedside cabinet." He nods at Patricelli before closing the wonky door with a clatter.

The air in the rooms gets heavy and tense. Sweat turns my silk tunic into a clingy second skin. My hairline feels damp; my feet hurt; my legs protest from the frantic chase.

Alone, with Idris, everything rushes back. Hot, thick revulsion grinds my teeth together, welding my feet to the floor. Idris walks to the bedside. I force myself to turn away, facing the chipped wooden wall with my back to him. He clatters two wooden cups onto the surface. The water he pours gurgles on its short slide down.

"Let's ... stick to our sides," I suggest, letting out a slow, calming breath. Breathe. Just breathe. Control your pulse, control your mind.

"Yes," agrees Idris. "And don't look."

"Don't look. Yes. Good idea."

"Reach behind you," Idris says quietly. I frown and then hold out my hand. Idris places a wooden cup in my sweaty fingers.

"Drink. That was a long run."

"Thank you," I mutter, perching on the edge of the bed. My skin jumps; my lips itch; my fingers and toes won't stop clenching. "And thank you ... for saving me back there. You could've left me to die."

"Thank you for waiting and pulling me over."

The awkward silence passes between us. I sip on my water, clearing my throat only for bile to pool at the back of my mouth. I suck it back down.

"How are you so good at this?" I groan, gripping my head. "How are you so calm?"

"Trust me, I'm not," Idris barks dryly.

"Better than me."

"As you know, I spent some time in Malaya, far to the West. They don't believe in the gods there. Instead they practise spirituality and presence of mind through a practice called mind-stilling. I got to study with Eshin Shakya, their spiritual leader, for about six months. It helps ... to keep me centred."

I roll my eyes, rubbing my brow. "Well, I'm rather new to it. Got any tips?"

Idris rasps a short, surprised laugh. "Try searching for a distraction. Something to focus your whole attention on, a sound to listen to. A conversation even, that will take up your whole mind."

I rock back on the bed, the creaking of the springs crackling like static between us.

I imagine spinning around, wrapping my fingers around his throat and dragging him back against these patchy blankets.

No, don't be stupid. He's an expert fighter. You saw him earlier, taking down those Militia soldiers with confidence and ease.

I could surprise him. I still have my knife, and he left his sword downstairs. One blow is all it would take. His blood would be so soothing against my clammy fingers.

No.

I desperately throw my mind back to something else, retracing what I've learnt this evening. Dorado collapsing to the ground replays in my mind. That traitor makes my blood boil. Hopefully Alfieri will keep him alive long enough to be questioned, even if he did leave me. I should try and warn him about Idris's ire before those two meet next.

The memory of Idris's hand radiates sparks across my lips. How his unforgiving, marble-like arms had held me against the hard stone of that wall.

No. Something other than Idris. Why do my thoughts always come back to him?

I fix my eyes on a particularly large chip in the wooden

floor. My throat feels tight, my breath shallow and trapped. I reach up, deftly unlatching the cloak binding around my throat. It falls to the itchy bed sheets with a short plop. Something to focus on, that's what Idris had said. Like a problem, like the one facing us right now.

"What's the money for? Why are they stealing it?" I croak, desperately trying to work what we now know into an answer. Yet all I have is more questions.

Idris lets out a sharp sigh. "It's leaving the city," he grumbles.

"Yes. What do you think it's for?"

Irritation licks at my teeth as I tap my foot on the floor. Idris walks to the window, looking out over the dank alleyway.

"Your guess is as good as mine. Nothing good, that's for certain."

What a useless answer!

I grit my teeth, tapping my fingers against the wooden cup in my hands.

"Are you okay? You didn't get hurt?" I ask, clearing my throat.

"I'm fine," Idris answers. "Takes a lot more than two soldiers to get the better of me."

"Good." The silence stretches, until I blurt out whatever is waiting on my tongue. "I never learnt to fight. I wasn't interested in it. It always seemed so pointless ... until now."

"I know," snorts Idris. I hear the sound of another drink being poured as he talks.

"You know?"

"You really think I came back to Halice without doing my

research? You're a key political player in this city, and if history holds, my biggest opposition."

"You think you know me?"

"No, but I know a lot of facts about you."

"Go on then. Where did I go to school?"

"Trick question. You and your sister were tutored privately. Both of you had a thorough education in languages, the arts, philosophy, ethics, mathematics, and the law. As a young girl you showed promise as an orator, and it was apparent by age ten that you'd be your father's political successor. You enjoy all forms of art and engineering but prefer to admire rather than partake. You enjoy being outdoors and have a penchant for clever, comedic writers. You started shadowing your father in the High Chamber at thirteen, you started speaking at fifteen. You were elected to your chair a week after your sixteenth birthday and in the five and a half years since that day, you've only five times voted in a way that differs from your father."

Only five times, like it was all I dared to do? I voted how I believed was right, not because my father told me to. I grit my teeth, my heart thumping in my chest so loud I'm surprised he can't hear it. My blood boils inside me.

"Believe me yet?" The grubby smugness that radiates off his voice is acid to the brain.

"You think I didn't keep tabs on you? I can recite your history too. The only child to your parents, you were sent away at eleven for your education. You jumped from one expensive school to the next, moving every few years in the name of 'cultural education'. You haven't been back to the city in years. It's almost as if you were..."

I trail off as one thought explodes in my head.

It's as if you were avoiding Halice.

I've loathed every minute I've spent with this man, but I don't question that he loves this city. He can't fake it. That kind of passion and resolve, the willpower to put up with this Soulhatred ... it can't be fake. Yet he never came back here. Not even for a day. Not once since he left.

He wasn't avoiding Halice. He was avoiding something in Halice.

It isn't hard to piece together what that was.

He had spent time studying mind-stilling in Malaya. Why go all that way for something so obscure? Why bring the books back with him? Why surrender them just when he might need them most? Unless he didn't bring them back for himself, but for someone else.

Meeting on the temple steps wasn't an accident. It wasn't luck. It was by design—his design. No one can carry weapons into the temple, meaning I wouldn't be armed when I finally saw him, when I finally learnt what he already knew. I thought it was luck, but look at us. Look at all of this. When has luck ever been on my side?

I bolt off the bed. I turn slowly, my eyes locking on the back of his golden head. He sits facing the dusty window, the shallow wooden cup in his hands. Fire throbs in my brain, my fingers itching for the blade at my waist. My breaths come short and hard as I grit my teeth together.

"You knew," I accuse, venom dripping off my tongue. Idris's shoulders pinch together, lips thinning in his reflection.

"Don't look," he says quietly, taking a large swig of his water.

"You knew!" I'm so furious spittle flies from my lips. "All these years away—it was to avoid me. You knew I was your Soulhate!"

"Yes." He glares at the drink in his hands, closing his free fingers into a fist. "I knew."

He knew.

He always knew.

My blood is screaming. My mind is raging. Every fibre of my being feels like it's being ripped apart, splinter by splinter, by boiling hot pokers. It takes every ounce of self-control I ever possessed not to tear him limb from limb. Instead, I spit my words like poison.

"You should've said something. To someone. To anyone."

"My parents knew."

"Why didn't they—"

"Because we were children!" He slams his drink on the windowsill. "Because back then the Church still had huge political sway in this city. They would've forced us to obey tradition. I would've been forced to kill you. You weren't even nine years old. Now, do us both a favour and turn around."

My jaw aches with the force of holding myself back. My teeth feel like they're welded together. I force my eyes back to the wall, my heart slapping in my ears like a war drum. I slam a fist into the wall.

"This explains so much. Why Jacopo tried so hard to tear the Church out of the city—"

"It was for us."

"For you!" I snarl, slamming my fist against the wall again in rage.

"For you too. You also benefit." Idris's self-righteous anger cuts across the room. "Don't pretend if this ever came to blows it wouldn't be a hard fight."

A hard fight? He'd slaughter me in seconds. He knew and spent years studying the art of the blade, studying mind-stilling, getting to process what that meant for the future. That fact blisters in my skull. I kick the wall, hands on my hips. I shake my head, heart throbbing in my throat.

"I deserved to know." My voice is thick and shaking. "I deserved to know I had a Fated. This is *my* life, *my* decision to make."

A moment of quiet passes, the only sound is my racing, gasping breaths.

"I wanted to tell you." Idris's deep voice is low and soft. "I drafted the letter so many times…"

"What stopped you?"

"If you demanded to duel, which is your right, I wanted to wait until you were an adult and stood a chance. I couldn't have the murder of a child on my hands, Soulhate or not."

Oh so noble, robbing me of the chance to arm myself with skills while he gallivanted off to study swordsmanship and meditation and everything he needed to master this. He left me in the dark, utterly clueless and without any preparation.

Silence reigns between us. Thick and heavy. My eyes fill with tears as I struggle to work out which demand he answer first.

"When?" I hate that my voice croaks in that one syllable. Idris sighs. I hear him scratching his stubbled jaw.

"Your mother's funeral. I was in the carriage. You were outside the Grand Temple, sitting on the steps with Giulia, comforting her as she cried. You gave her a giant sunflower and wiped away her tears with a small white hanky, ignoring your own. You wore a black satin dress and had your hair in a low ponytail, like you prefer to wear now..."

He trails off.

I'm not surprised that day is burned into his mind. The first time I saw him lives like an infectious mould in mine, no matter how hard I try to wash it away. It replays over and over again, the golden sheen of his hair, the light gleaming off his pearly skin. His warm hazel eyes filled with loathing. I remember it all, down to every minute detail.

"That's why your family missed the funeral."

"My parents held me back and took me home."

I pant, desperately trying to suck enough air into my lungs. I can't. I can't be here with him. I just can't. I march for the door, Idris darts for me. He grabs hold of my arm, pulling me back.

"Renza—" he starts but I slam my hands hard against his chest, trying to pry him off me.

"How dare you keep it from me!" I seethe at him, hating how my voice shakes and cracks. "Don't tell the Church. Don't tell anyone. Fine, I get it. But me? I deserved to know."

"No, you didn't want to." Idris's voice takes on a rueful jealousy, his hands tightening on my forearms and the gap between us shrinks. "I grew up wondering my entire life if one day I'm going to kill you. You, a little girl crying at her mother's funeral. You, who's devoted to this city, who's good and kind and passionate, whose only crime is being Fated to me. I spent the best part of a decade hanging on to every story of you like a prayer, and all I heard about you made me hate myself. That self-loathing and horror was a lead weight around my neck for years. Trust me, ignorance is bliss."

"Ignorance is risk. I could've prepared better. Searched for coping mechanisms, like you did. Planned with you on how to handle things. We could've been a team. But no, instead you left me in the dark. You left me vulnerable and weak."

"I left this city. I left my family for you." Idris's voice splits with pain. "I spent years away from my parents, all of it for *you*. And now they're dead, and I'll never get that time back with them. Never."

My eyes fill with hot tears, my voice quaking at the rage and grief churning inside me.

"I never asked."

"You didn't have to."

I grip my head, the feeling of my nails pushing into my skull provides relief from the dizzying weight of this reality that threatens to crush me. My lungs can't get enough air. My eyes are lined with blistering silver tears.

"I need air."

"Renza—"

"Don't!" I shove against him as hard as I can, throwing all my weight behind it to rip myself free. I tear through the door, marching down the stairs.

"Renza, stop! It's not safe! Renza!"

I ignore him and race for the front door, yanking it open. I have to get away. Away from him. Away from the deceit and the treachery. If I stay with that traitor a moment longer my restraint will shatter. I'll kill him, and perhaps now he deserves it.

I race into the cold night air, the pounding in my veins so desperately needed. I run. Lungs aching, blood pumping, legs throbbing. I follow my feet, avoiding the Guard's detection by staying in the shadows. For once in my life, luck appears to be on my side. I take a path I could walk blindfolded all the way home.

Back to the people I love and trust, who would never betray me like this.

CHAPTER 21

The air is sweet with dew. Crowns of sunshine dust the tops of buildings as I slip quietly through my front door. Closing it with a soft click, I press my forehead to the wood, letting that numbing cold drip slowly into my brain.

I left this city. I left my family. For you.

I deserved to know.

I don't care about his reasons. That he was protecting me is the kindest argument I can fathom—but it's not the only one. Perhaps he truly believed that was why he was doing it.

But he's had ten years to prepare! He's had ten years to search the world for coping mechanisms. Fate's Fury, he's had ten years to become an excellent swordsman. He knew one day he might use those skills on me.

As children, in a duel, I had an outside chance.

Now? It'd be a slaughter.

He's built his life so that no matter which way the cards

fell, he'd be on top. I don't blame him. I resent the chance not to have been able to do the same.

He's had a decade head start.

I kneel down, my tunic bunching around my thighs as I tug on my boot laces. Tossing them into the corner, they clatter softly over the brightly mosaicked floor. My toes drink in the chill seeping through my socks as I cross the bumpy tiles. Candles have burned nearly to their stumps, sat in little pools of their own wax, filling my home with delicate wisps of lavender. It smells like Idris. The memory of us pressed together rolls through my mind, his ghostly palm over my mouth, his firm grip on my hip. I bite down hard on the inside of my cheek, letting a short frustrating breath race through my nose.

I make for the stairs, my hand dropping to the banister as I slowly climb. My eyes are heavy. My shoulders droop. Motivation for each trudging step is the thought of my bed. My nice clean sheets and piles of soft pillows. Somewhere I can roll up and forget about Bellandi, Idris, and this horrible coup. Just for a few hours, I might pretend the world is safe.

"Where were you?"

I jump a mile. Heart in my throat as I spin to see Nouis. He marches out of his room, dark hair tousled, and still in his day clothes. His shoulders are pinched, and his steps hold too much purpose.

"What?" I blink.

"Where were you? You didn't come home and didn't leave a note. What was I supposed to think?" Nouis takes my forearms, his fingers digging in a touch too hard. His eyes are stormy. "Renza, I was worried sick. I thought something bad had happened to you!"

"Nouis, I'm so sorry. I'm fine," I say with a tight smile. "Just—"

"What happened?" Nouis follows, his words insistent. I stop, a shaky breath bringing tears to my eyes.

"Renza?" Alarm rings like warning bells in Nouis's voice.

"Idris knew," I sniff, wiping my eyes. "He knew."

"Knew what?"

"For years. Since we were children. He knew."

Nouis goes still for a moment, processing. He takes a deep breath and pulls me into a hug. He holds me close as I rest my head against his strong, muscular chest. He holds me together as I let myself wallow in my self-pity.

"Selfish prat," sighs Nouis under his breath. "He didn't tell anyone?"

"His parents."

"Then they're selfish too. They should've told you," Nouis says softly. "You had a right to know."

"We were just kids. Children... What if we had to duel?"

"But it didn't happen." Nouis rubs my arm. "Lingering on what-ifs never helped anyone. You deserved to know, and deserved not to be ambushed like that. To have been given the chance to prepare yourself."

It's so validating to hear Nouis say all the things that have been doing laps in my head all night. So good to hear and realise I'm not overreacting for feeling betrayed. That it *was* a betrayal.

"You don't think ... it was malicious?" Nouis asks quietly. My head jumps up as I frown at him.

"What do you mean?"

"That he used the time to ... swing things in his favour?"

"He's certainly done that. He went to Malaya to study mind-stilling. He's studied with the *Princess of War in Coari*," I mimic bitterly. Nouis shakes his head, lips thinning as he sits down next to me.

"So that's why he was there. You know, he never answered that question," Nouis wrinkles his nose in distaste.

"What happened in Malaya?" I ask. Nouis takes a deep breath but doesn't speak, his mind slipping back into old memories.

"It's not ... pretty. I didn't tell you before because I didn't want you to make up your mind about Idris based on my interactions with him," Nouis answers finally, mouth twisting uncomfortably as he turns back to look at me.

"Idris did something?" I surmise. Nouis takes a deep breath, weighing his response.

"I saw the kind of man he is," Nouis answers diplomatically, "but that was years ago, history that didn't feel worth repeating."

He takes my hands in his, rubbing gentle circles on them with his thumbs. I lean forwards.

"Tell me. I can handle it."

Nouis nods, pausing to choose his words before he starts.

"It was three years ago. My uncle sent me to Malaya for bank business. We were looking for new merchandise, techniques or new revenue streams..."

I nod slowly. Malaya is far to the West, across a vicious and unpredictable ocean. It isn't really a serious trading ally for the continent, given how long the voyage takes and the number of the ships that stretch of stormy ocean has doomed to lurk eternally on the seabed. But a few commodities have been brought from that continent to this over the years.

"Malaya has three distinct provinces, and we went to one called Pasadi. It's filled with huge mountains covered with thick green forests that the Malayan people have populated with the most magnificent temples. Their beliefs and values are so different from ours, it's strange." Nouis shrugs. "But their architecture and country are beautiful."

"Sounds lovely. Maybe we'll go sometime," I chuckle, leaning closer. Nouis shakes his head and wrinkles his nose.

"Anyway, we went around all the villages in our search, and we came across Idris and his friends in a village near a temple called Sadhu. It's the biggest temple in the province, so I asked their spiritual leader if I could take a look around. I was curious and it was so pretty, yet really old. My best friend Orsino was with me at the time and he met his Soulmate there. It was a beautiful moment. We were thrilled, but the locals were furious. They tried to imprison him."

"What?" My mouth falls open. Nouis nods, face pulling, holding up his hands as though helpless.

"Right? It makes no sense. So obviously we fought back. It got ugly. Idris and his gang sided with the Malayans in the fight."

"What? Why?"

"To this day I still don't understand it." Nouis swallows tightly. "The fight was... It got really nasty and I saw Idris ... kill Orsino."

Nouis's voice cracked over those last two words. My

stomach turns over as he continued. "I had to take my crew and flee that same night just to escape the violence."

I have no words. My brain empties at the horrible pictures floating through my head. My stomach upturns. My mouth goes dry. This is the man that's my Soulhate? This man has a thousand secrets. I don't know him. I might think I know a few facts, but clearly I don't know him at all. He's a stranger to me, a violent stranger.

My throat goes thick. My lips tremble. I get to my feet, hands going to my hair. "That's awful. Nouis, I'm so sorry. If I'd known—"

"It's history now," Nouis answers, green eyes tracking my movements, "but I'm glad you know. I'm glad you have some insight into this guy, and his time away. That sword he carries isn't just for show. He will use it."

That I know for myself. That bloody sword on Franco's table fills my mind, as a cold dread soaks into my bones.

"He's a master swordsman and I can barely hold a dagger correctly," I swallow, in a futile attempt to move this lump lodged in my throat. I move to my bedroom window.

Nouis walks up behind me, putting a calming hand on my back. "Well then... Why don't I teach you?" He takes the dagger from my belt with his other hand and holds it out to me, taking my hand.

"Hold it like this," he says, moving my fingers and thumbs. I nod, moving the dagger around slightly to test the grip. Dawn pours through my bedroom window and glints in minty blue off the simple polished blade.

"Good. You need to think smart in a fight, Renza. You

don't have strength or skill. But you're fast. Being fast is good," says Nouis.

"Why are you teaching me this?"

"Because it might save your life," Nouis says softly, lifting his fingers to fall under my chin, "I never want to lose you, for any reason."

He dips down, his lips so soft and sweet. I could melt into him for days. I lean into his embrace, resting my head on his shoulder. Warm and strong, his touch magically wipes all the stress away. Tonight's exhaustion feels like lead weights on my eyelids.

We both lean back against my bed, and I rest my cheek on his warm chest. His steady heartbeat pulses softly in my ears.

Soothing. Predictable. Calm.

His strong arms around me feel so safe. So secure. Nouis rubs slow, lazy circles at the tip of my spine until I drift off into a deep but troubled sleep.

CHAPTER 22

Sunlight leaks through the spindly bones of a dead tree outside the prison window. It creaks pitifully in the light wind. Skittering shadows flee across the table before me as I stand opposite Captain Collier in this small stone room. Somehow the natural creamy stone has taken on a blueish quality, and it seems a stern look might crumble it in some spots. As much as this fact is rather useful right now, Captain Collier is right. This place needs a serious upgrade.

Collier's jaw is set as he roots around in the basket of things I've brought for Serra. He leafs through the books, opens the food and wine to give it a sniff, turns over all the clothes to run his fingers through it. He dutifully searches everything.

"Much longer, Captain?" I ask, trying to keep my voice sweet and inflection-free. Collier nods, putting the book back in the basket.

"Fine. This is clear," he nods, standing and putting his hands on his hips. His eyes scan me for a moment.

"Any more trouble with the Church Militia?" he asks suddenly. I frown.

"Not personally, though I'd hardly call them warm and friendly."

"That bruise, you didn't have it the other day at the school," he gestures pointing to the fading bruise the assassin left on my hairline.

I nod dismissively. "You may have heard we had a break in? A robber?" I sigh, tapping the dark inspection table as he walks around it towards the door.

"I did. I'm sorry to hear it got that close."

"Seems the Church Militia aren't fabulous security after all," I scoff, grabbing the basket off the table before being escorted out the door. "So much for the continent's most deadly army."

The corridors of the prison are narrow and windowless. Torches of writhing, orange fire burn in old holders dotted down the halls, the stench of centuries-old smoke and stale urine mangle together with salty sea air to form a pungent aroma that brings tears to even the strongest of eyes.

"Could've stopped after the word fabulous," Collier mutters unhappily.

"They aren't ... in the prison are they?" I ask sceptically.

Captain Collier's horrified face says it all.

"Absolutely not!" Captain Collier answers instantly.

"I don't like them in the city. I don't like them anywhere close to our people," I say, feeding into the obvious malcontent in his tone.

"You and me both," he mutters, his footsteps banging over the uneven floors. It's tough to keep up the conversation and go over the map in my mind. To make sure I get to that weak point that Emilia repeated to me over and over again. *Ten paces, right, up the stairs, thirty paces, left*—the long sequence of moves burns in my head over and over again with every step.

It's time. We're at the spot. Time for a show.

My knees buckle and I go sprawling to the dirty stone floor.

"Signora!" Captain Collier immediately comes to my side, checking I'm okay.

"Oh, I'm fine," I groan, running a hand over my hair. I'm wearing a giant ornamental ring which is unusual for me. Not that the Captain knows me well enough to know that. Because the white stone in the ring isn't any old stone.

It's white pharolite. Once I rub it on the weak spot on the wall, it'll react with the old stonework over the next hour to turn bright red. It'll show Serra exactly where to put her device.

"My things," I sigh, gesturing to the widely scattered array of props. Captain Collier stoops to help me gather them up. I lean towards the base of the wall, walking my fingers up to the right space and scraping the ring as quietly as possible against the crumbling wall in a large spot.

Okay. That should do it.

Captain Collier helps me put everything back into the basket, before offering me a hand up.

"Thank you, Captain, I really appreciate this," I say, offering him a small smile. He nods quietly.

"Of course, signora."

"You weren't kidding when you said this place needed

repairs. I should've come sooner, to see it for myself," I say conversationally, "I hear Patricelli is looking to make a proposal in the High Chamber."

"I heard that too. Will you support it?" asks Captain Collier instantly. "Don't dismiss it just because he's a Patricelli."

"I wouldn't do that—dismiss it just because Patricelli brought it forwards I mean. And clearly the two of you are right," I answer, winkling my nose as we go deeper into this behemoth prison. The stench only gets worse and worse the deeper we venture. Surely we can offer even our worst prisoners better than this.

"I have a lot of ideas. It would be great to speak to you about them actually. To list the key things we need," Captain Collier continues.

"Make a meeting with me sometime next week," I tell him, mentally crossing my fingers this will all be over by then. "We'll discuss it in more detail and see what we can do."

Collier stops outside a passage barely wide enough for one person, gesturing that I venture into the dark alone. There is a cell down the far end, a blurry smudge of orange interrupting the unending dark stone. I walk down slowly in the dark, coming to Serra's cell.

Oh my god. Serra.

She bolts to her feet the minute she sees me, surprised delight radiating across her face. There are faint violet smudges under her eyes, and her face is a touch pale but other than that... *Fate's Fury, it's good to see she's alright.*

"Renza!" Her voice is giddy with relief. Captain Collier unlocks the cell door. I wink at Serra, as I push the door in.

"I brought you some things, my dear," I say, stepping inside the cell. I pull Serra into a big hug, holding her tight. Oh Fate's Mercy, I didn't expect seeing her would sucker punch me like this. I turn to face Collier, pulling my brows together.

"A moment, Captain?"

"I'm not supposed to leave..." he trails off, guilt flirting with his face. I sigh, tilting my head to the side.

"Captain, you checked everything. Please? Just one moment of privacy?"

He nods. "I'll just be down here," he mutters, taking a few paces away.

Serra turns to me, talking frantically. "They used my explosives. I think I was drugged the night before. They were going through quantities of what they found and there is far less than there out to be in my supplies—"

"Enough, we don't have time," I interrupt in a hushed whisper. I reach down for my shoes, pulling off the heel on my boots. I extract the small parcels, handing them to Serra. I reach into my brassiere, taking out small vials of other things. Then I turn to the basket, unwinding some of the weaving to pry out a set of lock picks I'd pilfered from Serra's cupboard.

"What the—?" Serra hisses.

"No time to explain," I say, pulling the instructions out of my sleeve and pressing them into her hands tightly. "You need to do everything on this list. Read it the moment I leave. You only have two hours. Do you hear me?"

"Renza, what the—"

"Do you trust me?" I ask her seriously, looking up into those dark eyes. She swallows tightly, and nods. Her dark curls bounce like a halo as she presses her lips together.

"Good. We'll explain everything when you get there."

"Get where?"

"Trust me," I hiss, finishing putting everything back where it was. I take a deep breath and wink at Serra.

"How can you say that to me!" I howl at the top of my lungs, "You're my friend! My best friend!"

The look of utter confusion on Serra's face is the pinnacle of comedy. Man, I wish Michelle could've seen it to capture it forever. I grab my basket back, as Captain Collier hurries to the door to soothe the commotion.

"I was doing this for you!" I shout. "I came for you. I won't do it again!"

I turn on my heels and march out the door, basket in tow. I sniff, pressing a hand across my nose like tears might come to my eyes. Captain Collier says nothing, but the keys rattle in the lock as he shuts Serra away again.

I sweep down the corridor to wait for him, shaking my head as though torn between anger and sadness. I spy the two guards Alfieri said would be there, and I march towards them. I thrust the basket into their hands with a huff.

"Here, you might as well enjoy these!" I sulk dramatically before marching away. Captain Collier hurries to keep up with me.

"Is everything alright, signora? What happened?"

"It doesn't matter!" I force my voice to break like I was on the brink of tears. "This place, heck, everything has just been terrible for so long."

"Agreed," sighs Captain Collier. "Come, let's get you back to your boat. I'm sure everything will look better soon."

As I leave I offer Captain Collier a grateful smile, taking several deep breaths as though trying to steady myself. When he closes the door behind me, I force myself not to sprint for the boat where Michelle and Emilia are waiting. I force myself not to act suspicious and give away everything at the last minute as I head for the dingy. Now it's time to wait in the cave Alfieri told us about. Wait for Serra to find us, and pray everything goes to plan.

~

"Wait, so Idris just killed the guy? That's it?" Michelle asks. The boat rocks softly on the undulating salty water beneath us. We're waiting in our little boat in a tiny hidden cave in the rocks, barely feet from where an explosion should rain down any minute. If things go to plan.

"No, Nouis said he sided with the Malayans and the fighting got ugly. He didn't provide more details and I didn't really want to push it," I answer, deciding the best way to distract ourselves from the endless waiting was to fill the girls in on everything that happened last night.

Emilia frowns.

"Have you asked Idris?" Emilia ventures quietly, dark eyes serious.

I shake my head. "I haven't seen him. I don't know what to say to him about ... everything."

"That's understandable. Lots of big revelations to wrap your head around. But now you're calmer, you should talk to him. Hear his side. I'm sure he has one."

"Yeah," Michelle adds. "He's not a bad guy, and he doesn't strike me as someone who'd just kill someone, even if the fighting is ugly."

"But he lied to me." I keep going back to that. "He kept the truth secret all these years."

"Yeah, and that sucks," Michelle agrees, "but he also had good reasons. I'm not saying that means he made the right decision, or that it comes without consequences, but remembering he made it from a place of good intentions is important."

"And what if they weren't wholly from a place of good intentions?" I ask.

"If that were the case, he would've challenged you to a duel the instant he got back, and been done with this whole thing," Emilia answers. "Now you've had time to calm down, go back and talk to him."

I nod, slumping back in the boat. I know they're right. My eye slips to Michelle as the water licks the side of the boat in tiny gasping breaths.

"Are you sure the timer is right?" I ask Michelle, only to earn a withering look.

"I'm sure," Michelle retorts, holding up the flask of sand as it slowly trails from top to bottom. Every second feels like an hour; every minute feels like a year.

"She has the items. The guards have the Red Root. It's up to her now," says Emilia.

The plan is certainly aided by the drink and food in the

basket given to the guards. Because it's been laced with Red Root, a herb that can make people drowsy. If we're lucky it'll get them to go to sleep entirely.

Part of me is racked with guilt for tricking these men; after all, they're only trying to protect us. They're doing their job. But at the same time, I'm not sorry enough to regret it. Not for Serra.

The boat rocks listlessly in the languid water, which peppers the side of this narrow cave with a steady stream of lazy, salty kisses. In the dark, we wait, looking out through the opening towards the horizon, hoping for a sign that anything is about to kick off. Anything at all.

We fade back to silence, our hearts in our mouths, our insides jumping and twirling like acrobats.

What if Serra can't make what she needs? What if she's been caught? What if she refuses to go through with it? I mean it's a crazy plan at best.

My heart throbs in my throat. Swallowing does nothing to banish it back down to my chest.

CRACK!

A rain of creamy debris falls into the sea, throwing plumes of salty water into the air. The boat is thrown violently left and right as the carnage rains down from above. I grip the edge tightly with both hands, desperate not to make myself an idiot and fall into the sea.

Following quickly afterwards is a figure, dropping into the water like a dark arrow.

"There!" I shout, pointing. The girls rush to my side, peering into the water. We wait anxiously, waiting for her to come back to the surface. I hold my breath, my lungs feel like bursting.

Then a dark head comes to the surface. Gasping for breath, Serra spins on the spot.

"Here! Here!" shouts Emilia with a wave, as Michelle hurries to get the boat ready to go as fast as possible. Serra races towards us, swimming with all her strength. Emilia and I reach over the boat, hauling Serra into the dinghy as Michelle gets us moving.

Panting furiously, Serra sags onto all fours in the basin of the boat.

"Stay down, we don't want people seeing you if they spot us," I explain hurriedly as Emilia wraps Serra in a large, fluffy towel. Coughing, Serra nods, lying down and out of sight as Michelle masterfully picks up speed on the boat.

I turn back to the prison, my mouth falling open in shock. The gaping gash in the side of our prison is far worse than I'd been expecting. But just as I'd hoped, it looks like subsidence.

"You came for me," Serra manages when she finally catches her breath. She looks at all of us, the sun shining like gold dust on her damp skin as she turns to each of us.

"Of course we did," says Emilia, rubbing our friend's back to warm her up. "We couldn't leave you there."

"Why all this? Why not clear my name?" Serra asks, looking around the group till her dark eyes fall on me.

"Serra, it's a long story," I start, sitting down to keep out of Michelle's way as she races back to the mainland, "but we know who set the explosives in the Grand Temple."

CHAPTER 23

I'm Renza Di Maineri, and today I was part of a successful jailbreak.

Fate's Fury, I never thought I'd say that!

Emilia whisked Serra away the instant we got back on solid land, stating that Alfieri had somewhere the two of them could hide. In any case, I need to be far away and somewhere public. Somewhere out of suspicion thanks to my earlier visit. We don't need people to have good reason to question my involvement.

They'd be right of course, but we don't want anything to stick.

It was so hard to let Serra go, but at least she is out of that disgusting, dank cell. I shudder at the mere memory of the smell. I would have to get Serra a plethora of scented candles, anything to cover up the memory of that stench.

I walk through the front door of my house, slipping off my shoes.

"Nouis? Nouis, you home?" I call up the stairs. I can't wait to tell him everything. He's going to be so relieved Serra is safe. This is going to be amazing. Finally a win for us! For our team! When I'm met with silence I realise it's still the middle of the afternoon. Nouis is supposed to be working on Bellandi for information, trying to get something we can use.

Oh well, this will be a fabulous surprise this evening. Or perhaps not much of a surprise—I'm sure word will spread pretty quickly that there is a gaping hole in the side of Halice's prison. I hurry to the stairs, hopping up the steps with a bounce in my gait.

I can't believe it. I pulled off a jailbreak. *We* did it. Serra is safe, and Alfieri's confirmed Dorado survived his injuries so we have a witness who can give evidence against Bellandi too. Things are far from over but they are looking up. *We can do this*.

I pause at the top of the stairs. It feels a piece is missing... Something big, but I can't put my finger on it. I try to shake off the feeling as I sweep down the hall. I hum a little tune as I reach Giulia's room.

"Just me, Giulia," I call as I push the door open.

My heart drops and shatters in my chest.

The bed is completely empty. The sheets are strewn wildly over the floor, her feeding tube and a large, glass pot shattered and scattered across the room.

A bloody handprint is pressed against the pink-painted walls.

"No. No. No!" I scream at the top of my lungs, falling to the stone floors. Everything shakes and tilts. My hands tremble; my vision blurs; my breath feels rotten in my lungs.

"Giulia! Giulia!" I scream at the top of my lungs. The

physical pain of her absence is agony. I stagger to my feet, racing out into the halls.

"Help, someone help!" I sob, but nobody comes. There isn't a soul in the house. I grip at my stomach, the aching unbearable as I turn to see the empty room again. That bloody handprint glows like a vicious, demonic smile.

Giulia is missing. The pain in that short sentence makes me double over again.

Gasping for breath and with fresh tears streaming down my face, I race down the stairs. I shove my feet into the nearest pair of boots, yanking them on. I only have one thought.

Find her. I have to find her.

Nouis.

Nouis has helped us so much before, he can do it again now. I need him. I scramble to my feet, sprinting out the door as fast as I can. My breath echoes in my ears, my pulse turning to thunder and stars. I barely see anyone else, the water on my face and the burning in my lungs separated by a thousand degrees of numbness.

I move as fast as my sputtering lungs will allow, tearing off into the city towards Market Square, where I know Nouis will be. He'll be occupied with Bellandi but I can pull him away. I have to.

The sky is sliding from mango to violet, streaked with vicious white gashes. People gape as I tear past, caring not for anything except moving faster over the creamy white streets.

The memory of that handprint taunts me, pushes me on when my feet feel as though they might drop off my legs.

Nouis. I need to find him. I have to find him.

I charge towards Market Square, pushing through the throng of bodies as I look up at that hideous square building. I stop, panting for breath as I begin to carve my way up the stairs towards the main door. Four men from the City Guard sweep forwards, locking their swords to bar my way.

"Let me through! Let me in, it's an emergency," I sob.

"No one in. Orders of the cardinal."

Screw the cardinal. He did this. He knows what happened to her. I know it—who else would do it?

I scream with frustration as I turn back to the throng of people in the square. I scan for someone, anyone, an opportunity.

I march off through the crowd, circling the building for any other way in. I bite my lip, breath still bursting through my lips. I scan the crowd again and then I see it, two men approaching the back door with a huge crate of something. Then they disappear straight inside.

An idea forms in my mind. My eyes catch on a large crate brimming with shiny, red apples by one of the vendor's stalls. An idea ticks over my mind.

Now or never.

I approach the vendor, pulling out my purse.

"Hello, signora, how can I help?" he asks readily.

"I'd like to buy this crate of apples."

"The whole crate?"

"Yes. How much?"

"Well, that's a lot of apples there. How about ... thirty-four Hali-Pounds?"

"No more than twenty."

"Twenty-five."

"Done," I say, fishing through my purse to free the money, "but I'll need your help to move them."

"Signora, I have a business to run. I can't just—"

"It's only for the Watchtower," I point over there. "I just need some help getting them all inside."

"Oh, in which case. Paolo! Paolo!" He turns around, looking for someone. A young man with floppy brown hair appears by his side, rubbing his long nose.

"Yes, Father?"

"Help the signora carry the apples into the church building, will ya?"

"Of course, Father," says Paolo, hurrying to grab the crate.

"Thank you," I say, grabbing one side of the box. The two of us lift together, the weight uncomfortable on my arms. We start waddling awkwardly through the crowd towards the back of the building.

Paolo narrows his eyes at me over the bundle of fruit, then a look of realisation dawns across his face. "Wait, you're—"

"Play along and you'll get twenty Hali-Pounds for your silence," I hiss at him. His grey eyes go wide but he nods, mouth snapping shut. My heart hammers. My pulse rushes around my fingers and toes. My breath is shallow and sharp. Together we toddle for the back door where two Church Militia are standing guard.

"Stop! Who are you?"

"Just making a delivery," Paolo says brightly before I even have the chance. "Apples for the kitchen."

"Apples? Let me see."

The guards come closer, and I drop my head, hoping my ratty hair will cover most of my face. Light bounces off their polished weapons like a razor flare. They start pulling apples off the crate, inspecting the inside to see if there is anything hidden.

"Fine. But don't linger," scowls the soldier.

"Absolutely," says Paolo, leading the way forwards. The relief of the building's shade is instantaneous. My hair clings to my sweat-gripped face. My clothes are damp with perspiration.

Okay, I'm in. Now what?

"Go," whispers Paolo. "Do what you need. I'll wait."

"Wait? How?"

"I'll strike up a conversation in the kitchen," Paolo explains. "Try to sell them on the business. That'll give you a good twenty minutes. Then we can leave together, no one the wiser."

"How— Why—" I stumble for words, taken aback by his generosity.

"You're a Maineri," he chuckles. "There's a reason you don't want to be seen."

My throat closes as I try to come up with a good answer.

"Whatever you're doing, I trust it. You're an Electi after all," Paolo whispers. "Now go, before people spot you."

"You're a good man, Paolo," I whisper, shuffling my end of the crate to him so he holds all the weight. I stretch my fingers, flexing out the stress of the load.

"A Maineri loan saved our family business." Paolo shrugs. "I've got your back."

I smile at him, heart bursting with pride. This is it. This is the spirit of Halice that I love. "You ever want another, let me know. Directly."

"I'll remember that," he snorts as I dart down the narrow hallway and up the servants' stairs. My boots set off a flurry of whispered creaks with each chipped step. At the top, I look around, trying to work out where I've appeared.

I keep my steps as silent as possible as I move down the empty corridor towards the cardinal's office. My heart crashes in my ears. My breath seems louder all of a sudden, louder than thunder.

I pause, my hand about to reach up and knock on the dark wood.

"I'm telling you I didn't do it," Bellandi says with derision. "I didn't take the girl." I pause before the door, leaning closer to listen against the tall, dark wood.

"Then who did? Because I get home and she's gone. Gone!" Nouis roars. A massive bang makes me jump away from the door for a second before leaning closer again.

"Why don't you look a little closer to home?" hisses Bellandi. "After all, the sister was attacked by an assassin while unconscious. Maybe Renza moved her to protect her."

"No, Renza would've told me. She trusts me."

"So you think the assassin did the trick? You got to play white knight for the lady and have now secured her undying loyalty and confidence for all eternity?" Disgust crawls around Bellandi's words. "Be smarter, Nouis. And really, did you have to kill him? He was so useful."

"And leave him alive to spill our secrets?" Nouis scoffs in

derision. "I'm the one with the plan, Bellandi. You do as I say, remember?"

Ice rips through my entire body. Stinging radiates across my eyes. My breath catches in my throat. I tremble in place.

Nouis.

Idris was right. Nouis is playing me. All this time… This is just some sick game. Through every touch, every kiss, every stolen laugh. He's been part of the planning this whole time. He's robbed us. He's slaughtered our Electi.

He killed Father and probably Giulia too.

Wait, no, he doesn't know where she is. He didn't do this; he didn't take Giulia. That's why they're fighting.

If he didn't take Giulia, and I didn't take her either…

Fate's Fury, who has my sister?

My stomach turns. I might be sick on this very floor.

I grit my teeth, ice replaced with fresh, blistering fire in my every fibre. My nails bite into my fists as I try to keep the screams inside. I feel dirty, like I need to peel off my skin and shred it.

That monster. That sick, disgusting monster. I've known him my whole life. We've been friends since we were small children. He's been part of the family for decades. And yet, he did this to us? He wrought this devastation on my city, my home, my family?

I'm such a fool. I'm so stupid for falling for his lies.

I take a deep breath, fighting to steady my frayed nerves. They're talking, planning their next steps. I need to know what they are.

Determined, I wipe the tears from my eyes. Steel tightens in my core as I force my breathing to slow.

Nouis scoffs. A creaking sound makes me think he's sitting in one of the chairs, "There's a reason the Holy Mother sent me here to babysit you."

His voice is so harsh and sharp. Gone are the gentle tones and warm lilts. Every word has an angle meant to slice at his opponent.

"You're here to help me," Bellandi snaps. "Not run things."

"No," Nouis smirks, "I'm here to make sure you don't ruin things. Again."

Bellandi slams his hand down on the table. "Watch your tone."

"Watch yours!" Nouis snaps back. "Because only one of us has lost control of an entire city. Only one of us has let the Holy Mother down. And it's not me."

The silence between them is thick and crackling. At any moment Bellandi could launch across the desk and try to batter Nouis's head in on the worn wood.

Instead Bellandi sighs as he searches for words. "We need to be rid of Patricelli and Maineri—sooner rather than later."

My heart goes cold. My mouth runs dry.

I shouldn't be surprised; they slaughtered an entire church filled with people after all. But hearing him actually say it, so cold and calculated—a man I've known all my life—my stomach flips.

"What if we make it look like they lost control?" Bellandi continues. "Bludgeoned each other to death? Soulhatred and grief mixed together."

"No. We just get rid of Patricelli. Accident or illness or robbery gone wrong. I'll go tonight, after sundown. Make it look convincing," Nouis says so matter-of-factly. My brow pulls together, nausea sweeping over my tongue.

If Nouis doesn't plan to kill me ... then what *are* his plans for me?

"What?" the shock in Bellandi's voice is more obvious than the sun in the sky. "Leave Maineri alive? Are you *mad*?"

"I can control her." Nouis is so certain.

Now I'm definitely going to be sick.

"Now, perhaps," retorts Bellandi. "She's crippled by grief but soon she'll throw off that shadow and the warrior will return—with a vengeance. We need her gone."

"I can control her," Nouis hisses again.

"She's Renza Di Maineri," Bellandi argues. "If you truly think that, you're an idiot."

"Watch yourself, Bellandi!" Nouis barks, poison thick on his words. "Renza Di Maineri is my job—touch her and I will kill you for the mere principle of daring to undermine me."

Bellandi goes quiet for a minute. "You fool. You've fallen for the girl and now you underestimate her," whispers Bellandi.

"Why should I listen to a washed up, failing cardinal?" answers Nouis, lethal anger rippling through his words.

Why? Why would Nouis keep me alive?

As a sick game? As a trophy of his slaughter?

"Either way, we're all paid up now. Whether Maineri is dead or alive, the mercenary army will be here soon," says Bellandi.

Army? What army? That's who they were paying?

"Agreed," Nouis grinds out reluctantly. "When the

Askerler Company arrives, we need to be ready. Do you have somewhere prepared to safely sit out the invasion?"

The Askerler Company? Soldiers? My head goes light as my entire body goes numb. The war of icy horror and fiery rage running through me might make me pass out or vomit, or both.

"I do. I take it you do as well?"

"Yes."

"And Maineri?"

"She'll be with me," Nouis says. I fight the bile flooding the back of my throat and the way my skin crawls in disgust.

Bellandi scoffs, shaking his head. "There is no way that woman will sit out an assault on this city."

"She won't have a choice. I have everything in hand."

I jolt back from the door in shock. The stolen money was to pay an army. To sack this city. Shaking, I back away. Every bone under my skin judders; my pulse gallops as my eyes water.

I need to find Idris.

He might be a liar. He might have secrets. But he doesn't deserve to die at the hands of a monster like Nouis Rizaro.

Nouis said he'd kill Idris after sundown, so I don't have long. Where would he be? I have no idea how he spends his days. Nouis will know. Nouis will be using the Militia to keep track of him. They're all over this city now.

Well, one thing is certain: Idris isn't here.

I tiptoe away from the cardinal's door, making it to the servants' steps. I hurry back down to the kitchen where Paolo is chatting up a pretty kitchen maid. I wave at him frantically to catch his eyes. He doesn't waste a second, winking at the kitchen maid before walking to my side.

I want to run. To sprint as fast as I can till my lungs explode. But I can't. That'll get me caught, so I force my legs to move slowly. I force myself to stop shaking as we walk out the servants' door. We're not troubled by the Church soldiers on our exit.

"Signora, you look pale. Are you okay?" Paolo queries once we're a few steps away, keeping his voice low.

"Do you know where I could find Idris Patricelli?" I ask, gripping his arm.

Paolo frowns. "Uh, he has business offices down by the docks?" he suggests. "Even if he isn't there, the dockworkers might know where to find him."

"Brilliant. Thank you. Thank you for everything." I yank open my coin purse and pull out a fistful of coins. I shove them into his hand, head snapping around towards the docks. I don't waste another second, jostling through the crowd. Their bodies are like a wall of heat as I push my way past by any means.

My heart slams in my ears. My breath races through my lips.

The sun sinks by the second from the sky. The world twists to stretching shadows and columns of amber. I break through the throng of bodies, sprinting down the creamy cobbled street. My hood falls down, my hair flapping against my back as sweat forms a ring around my hairline.

I fly over the cobbled road. Blood rushes to my face, the air somehow thin. Stabbing fills my side, but I don't have time for a stitch now. *Don't stop. Don't think. Don't worry.*

Move.

Salt fills my nose. I stagger out into wide, open docks. Rows and rows of large commercial ships sit on bleached wooden platforms. Creaking gently, they teeter from side to side, their watery bed rippling shades of peach in the dying sunset. I spin around, searching for a sign of where to go. I grip my head, pulse crashing in my head like war drums.

I sprint to the closest dockworker, stopping him dead in his tracks.

"Patricelli offices. Where?" I pant, gripping my stomach as though I could fight back the agonising stitch building in my ribs.

The man frowns. "Ain't you his Soulhate?"

"Yes. Not going to kill him. Where's the office?"

"Well, over there but—"

"Thank you!" I sprint off towards the building. My legs protest. My lungs scream with the effort as I push through the main doors and into the office space below.

Everyone turns their head in shock to see me.

"Idris? Where?" I gasp, gripping the door frame for support.

"Not here, signora. He's visiting one of our warehouses," answers one of the clerks quietly.

Fate's Fury, of course he is. "Which one?" I groan.

"Number eleven."

"Where?"

"Is everything alright, signora? You don't look well."

"Where?" I repeat insistently. The clerk points to the wall behind me. I spin around and see a map of the docks, all labelled out perfectly. Panting I stare up at the large drawing, sweat clamping stray hairs to my face and my tunic to my damp skin.

"Eleven," I breathe.

Of course, it's on the other side of the docks.

Seriously, Idris?

Seriously?

Clenching my fists, I propel myself through the office doors and sprint down the long length of the docks. I weave in and out of the straggling dockers on their way home, jumping a stray rope pile on my journey. My lungs scream. My legs ache. Sweat coats every inch of my skin.

Fading sunshine blazes into my eyes, sending dancing stars around my vision. The water giggles softly. The boats creak and their flags flop limply around the mast overhead.

The sun slips further and further down the horizon.

Every muscle in my body is screaming by the time I get to the other side of the docks. Spinning on my feet, I desperately search through the big red-painted numbers on the side of the old wooden buildings.

Eleven. Eleven. Eleven.

Got it!

I burst through the door, searching through the dark piles of goods. My heart hammers, my tongue dry as sandpaper as I haul heavy air into my lungs.

He's not here.

No hot loathing. No revulsion at our proximity. No goosebumps or nausea or a desire to set the world on fire.

There's no one here. Dropping my hands to my knees, I desperately try to think. Nouis's betrayal hits me like an avalanche. Giulia's kidnapping and Father's death. All his fault. Alone in the dark, frustration, desperation, and anger all boil out of me.

"Idris!" I scream at the top of my lungs. "Idris, where are you?"

My voice echoes around the large, empty building. I hiccup a few deep breaths, trying to pull myself back together. With tears in my eyes, I dig my fingers into the ground. Desperately trying to catch my breath, I search every corner of my mind for something resembling a plan. *Where else might he be?*

My stomach convulses. Goosebumps run down my arm. My mouth gets slick with a sour sensation.

Yet the relief is so potent, I could sing.

CHAPTER 24

"Renza?"

I've never been so pleased to feel my brain blistering.

Idris walks in. Every step he takes over the dirty floorboards is both a slap and a balm. The relief is so strong, I'm drunk on it. I ease back to my feet, the memory of his hands on my arms, my wrists, my lips, surges through me, stealing all thoughts, words, and reason. I close my eyes. The darkness helps. I can still feel him as he turns his back to me, fighting to control his breathing.

"Nouis," I pant, oddly my breathing feels easier now he's here, even if each lungful is scalding hot. "He's coming. He's coming to kill you."

"When?" Idris doesn't hesitate, doesn't even sound scared.

"Sunset."

"So now," Idris swears. "Fine. I'll put him down. I need my sword and you need somewhere to hide."

Could he put Nouis down? Nouis is strong. A few scars on his arms tell me he's been around blades before. He wouldn't come to put down Idris by himself if he wasn't confident with a sword.

Fate's Fury, what if he kills Idris?

"You ran all the way here?" Idris asks, "To warn me?" His voice quiet and deep. My eyes shoot open when I realise: he's right in front of me. I gasp, slammed with the reality that he's barely a few inches away from me, his molten, hazel eyes scanning me from head to toe. He reaches for me, running his hands over my arms as if checking for himself. Those fingers weave a trail of exploding stars across my flesh that strangle any other sensation fighting for acknowledgement.

"Are you hurt?" he asks quietly.

My entire being pounds and throbs, my vision blurring out everything that isn't him. I shake my head, my breath shallow and sharp, throat so thick I might never swallow properly again.

"Come on." Idris grabs my hand. He guides me along the darkening docks. I keep my eyes on the water and the teetering boats as I try to fight my racing heart.

Idris is like a dark magnet just outside of my vision. A dark, pushing sensation that makes me want to turn away but at the same time drags me closer like an undercurrent.

The sun has all but vanished behind the skyline. The navy shadows encroach closer and closer. Stars start to pop out of their burrows in the sky. Stray dockworkers seem to have vanished, abandoning us amongst the ships. Idris guides me into another warehouse, searching for a threat.

I pause by the door as he makes a beeline for some

boxes. I scan the empty street for signs of movement, waiting with bated breath for the danger that can't be far away.

"Anything?" asks Idris, buckles jingling softly as he straps a sword around his hips.

"No," I breathe, the air in my lungs suddenly cold.

"How did you find out about this?"

"I overheard them in Bellandi's office."

"You went there? Are you insane? After the jailbreak?" Idris's outrage explodes from his lips like an attack. Every nerve singes and bristles.

"Giulia is missing. I was panicking." I fight back the swollen sob in my words. "All reason left my body... I just acted."

"How could you be so reckless?" Idris walks back towards the door, checking left and right down the street. "They could've caught you—they would've killed you."

"Do you want to argue about what's been done or talk about what I discovered?" I snap, glaring at the chipped floorboards.

"Fine what did you— Shh!" Idris stops dead. I freeze, breath turning to ice in my lungs.

Ships creak. Water babbles.

Idris slowly moves back towards the dock entrance. Treading as quietly as possible, listening keenly, I follow him down the outside of the warehouse. Flags flap. Our breaths whisper. Then, there it is.

Marching.

Idris grabs my hand and bolts.

"Faster. Faster!" Idris hisses.

"I'm trying!" I growl back, yanking my hand free. "I ran all the way here."

When this is over, I'm going to exercise every day. I swear it.

Idris skids to a stop by one of the warehouses, throwing himself against its stone wall. I press myself flat against the crumbling stonework, fighting for air. Stamping boots and barking orders crack through the air as the Church Militia pour into the docks.

Looking for Idris.

Kicking down doors, they enter the warehouses. Slamming and crashing leaks through the stone between us and them.

Idris doesn't flinch. I wish I could say the same. I close my eyes and clamp a hand over my mouth to quiet any rushed breaths as I fight to control my breathing. For once, Idris wasn't the source of this.

"Hey, Renza, it's alright," Idris whispers quietly, his hand coming down to mine, still hanging at my side. His warm fingers wrap firmly around mine and goosebumps run up my arm like tiny bursting stars, "I'll get you out of this. Just stick with me, alright?"

I pry my eyes open to meet his. The golden hazel might destroy me but right now sure as Fate I need the certainty lurking in them.

Idris slips towards the back of the warehouse, keeping his back against the brickwork. He moves smoothly and with confidence. I follow, trembling fingers running along the rough stone surface an inch behind him. My throat is thick. My breaths are shaky.

Around the back is a narrow alley, winding chaotically

between warehouses. Barely one person wide, it's disgusting. Coated with decades of grime and cluttered with rotting crates and grimy old fish traps. I clamp a hand over my mouth to keep myself from retching.

Taking care to step exactly where Idris does, we move quietly down to the end of the docks. Banging and smashing continues to echo through the warehouses, roaring voices demanding answers as they stamp over the wooden pontoons and walkways.

We reach the last warehouse and Idris pauses before stepping out into the street. I hurry after him, wanting to be free from the gunk and grime of that alleyway. The Church Militia are still busy in the docks behind us, their savage search still clattering through the night.

"Where now?" I croak.

"I know somewhere we can go. Then we can talk about—"

Idris's words die, the silence cracking like lightning. I spin around, spying a dark figure who's just rounded a warehouse by the water's edge. A short sword brandished in hand. A familiar man with dark hair, green eyes and a fitted fighting tunic in the style of the Holy States.

Idris's hand leaps for his sword. The metal flashes in the moonlight as it springs free. I jump at the movement, heart throbbing in my throat.

Nouis's malicious grin falters, green eyes locked on me. "Renza?" his face crinkles. "What are you doing here?"

My mind kicks into overdrive, the lie spilling forward so naturally.

"Patricelli asked to talk to me. Said it was urgent. I just

got here. What is all this? Why are they destroying the docks?" I fold confusion into my words as I walk towards him. Fate's Fury, I hope the desire to keep his charade with me will be enough.

"Quickly, Renza, come here!" Nouis commands, holding out his free hand for me. His eyes are beseeching. Sick to my core, I hurry over to keep my cover. Nouis's warm touch is now revolting against my fingers. He pushes me behind him, facing Idris with a raised blade.

"Nouis?" I insist. "What is going on?"

"He did this. He blew up the city," Nouis says quickly. "Think about it, he comes back and suddenly everything goes up in smoke? It's too convenient. He wants it all—all the power for himself."

Convincing. A few days ago I would've believed it.

Today I know better.

"The same could be said for you, Rizaro." Idris seethes. "Suspicious, no?"

"Nouis saved me. He's helped us. He pulled me from the fire." I babble the same spiel I've been foolishly telling myself for days. The words feel rotten on my tongue.

Nouis stalks towards Idris. "Why else would the gods have made him your Soulhate, Renza? You love this city. Of course they made the man who wants to destroy it your enemy. They were trying to stop this. All of this."

That's low. Anger boils up my throat. I glare hatefully at the back of Nouis's dark head.

"But we can fix it now." Nouis smirks, before swinging at Idris. Their swords clash, again and again. Idris grunts; Nouis snarls. Their blades scream into the night as they grapple for the other's death.

My breathing is fast and sharp. Every inch of my body wants to intervene. I need to stop this! *What can I do? What should I do?*

Frantically I look around, searching for something. Anything. For an answer to appear.

Idris forces Nouis back towards the water, every step of retreat making him growl in frustration. Every slam of metal sends a frozen bolt through my gut. Horror pools in my lungs. Idris ducks, and swings to catch Nouis's leg. At the same time Nouis shallowly slices Idris's arm.

"No!" I scream. That catches Idris off guard, head snapping to look at me. Nouis swings, and Idris only just manages to catch it and sweep the blow high.

Both their swords are locked high above their heads, arms straining with the effort. Nouis growls, barging forward to body shove Idris hard against the stone warehouse wall. The slam of Idris's head on the large bricks turns my stomach, and vomit surges up my throat.

Idris drops to the floor, sword clanging as it kisses the stone.

Nouis raises his blade to finish the job.

No.

Every touch. Every word. Every kiss.

It was all poison.

My brain goes blank. My hand wraps around the dagger on my hip, holding it exactly like he showed me.

The blade flashes with teeth of silver as I drive it into Nouis's back. I yank it out, gasping, panting, crying, as rage chokes around my throat. I slam it back down. Then again. Tears stream down my face as I stab and keep stabbing, hoping I'll hit his heart. Blood sprays across my face, soaking through my trembling fingertips.

Nouis roars in pain and drops to his knees, the sword slipping from his grip.

Gasping, I step back. My fingers are shaking and sticky with hot crimson flecks. My childhood friend and confidante. My family welcomed him into our home freely and warmly. Tearfully, I glare at the traitor at my feet.

Betrayal washes over Nouis's face.

"Renza?" he whispers before toppling sideways. His body flops over the wooden edge, slipping between the ships to be swallowed by the tumbling black waters.

He was there. Then he wasn't.

Gone.

Dead.

My hand is still raised. My eyes are still fixed on Nouis's cold, dark, watery grave.

He's dead.

I killed him.

I did this.

The crashing of the Church Militia in the warehouses cracks like a whip.

"Fate's Fury, what have I done? Bellandi will know we're on to him now," I stammer to the empty air, hiccups crawling up my throat. My breaths come short and fast. Shaking on the spot, I can't work out what to do next. Blood coats my palms and is speckled across my face.

We need to run. We need to get away.

I turn, gritting my teeth to see Idris crumpled against the base of the wall. A trail of blood pours down the side of his golden face.

I freeze, staring at his unconscious form. Half his angular face is smeared with scarlet, his floppy blond hair dripping into little puddles. His chest rises and falls.

I could do it. Crawl on top, wrap my fingers around. He's unconscious; it would be so damn easy...

I snap my eyes away gasping. I raise a hand to my face, giving myself a sharp slap. No. I need him.

Marching heavy boots start coming this way. *Fate really does hate me.*

I grit my teeth, making the snap decision to grab him. Damn it, why did he have to be so tall? Grabbing his wrists, I yank as hard as I can, dragging a mass of muscles backwards down the dark alley we just left. Gasping for breath, my body straining with effort, I desperately search for a hiding spot. Somewhere they wouldn't dream to look for us.

My pulse rings in my ears. My hands are sweating. Sucking deep breaths, I look anywhere—anywhere but the person I'm dragging with me. Panting, I search for cover, then I see it. The gutters. Shallow gutters run across all the streets in Halice, but this is a big one—a main one. More than large enough for us both! I run over, grabbing hold of the barred metal covering, I haul it to one side, opening up the narrow passage down to the sewers.

I take a steadying breath, turning to grab Idris. I shove him with all my strength, pushing his well-built body into the smelly hole in the ground.

"Look a sword, and blood! Someone's close. Who's there?

Come out now!" The Militia are barely paces away. Ten more seconds and they'll see me. I dive for the metal covering, my pulse screaming in my ears as I dive down the hole, feet slipping over the cold, steel ladder. I grip on tightly, pulling the metal grate back into place over my head. I freeze, as the orange of their torches highlights the metal bars.

My breath comes shallow and sharp. I'm all but hugging the ladder rungs as I hear their heavy boots marching around upstairs. My heart spasms in my throat. My blood turns to ice.

They pass.

Fate's Mercy, the relief is so strong I almost lose grip on the ladder.

I drop the three rungs to the bottom.

Patricelli lies unceremoniously in the pale light from above. He's at such an angle, he could be dead. His face is slack, blood slowly spreading over his perfect features. I shudder. My skin crawls.

Kill him. Kill him.

My fingers would slide so easily around his neck. It'll be easy, and it would be over. I could leave him here. No one would know. No one would ever suspect.

He deserves it.

"No!" I sob. I grip my head, throwing myself against the grimy, dirty sewer wall. I slide down it, my nails digging into my skull.

Why? Why am I thinking these awful things?

Because you want it.

"No! No! I won't," I sob, gasping for breath as I war with myself. I'm a monster. I killed Nouis. Now I want to kill Idris.

I'm a murderer. I'm a killer.

"Renza?"

That voice is so soft. So kind. So familiar.

My head darts up, locking with a familiar set of brown eyes. Tears spill down my face in relief at my rescuer. Serra crouches in front of me, a glass covered candle in hand. She wraps her arms around and pulls me close.

"Help me," I beg.

CHAPTER 25

"He'll live," says Serra. I don't turn. It's so much easier if I can't see him. I can breathe. I can think. The whispers are beaten into silence.

"Not lethal?" I ask again.

"No, but he'll have one hell of a headache. And a scar I imagine. You didn't do this?" Scepticism drips off her words, her eyes darting to my bloody fingers.

"No. Nouis did," I say searching down the sewer line for trouble. The tunnel echoes with drips, wave after wave of ammonia fills the air and smothers my nose. The light from Serra's candle bounces off the old, arched brickwork, creating a wobbling flaxen bubble around us.

Serra sighs. "I did wonder if he was part of this." Of course she did. Serra's one of the smartest women in this city.

Nouis's face floods my mind. The betrayal torn across his features.

"Serra," I begin, "there's something you should know."

"It's okay. I know."

"You know?"

Serra walks towards me, dropping a hand to my wrist and pulling up my bloody palm.

"It's not Idris's and it's not yours. You ran into Nouis. The leather sheath on your hip is empty, and the knife is gone. It's easy to put it all together."

My eyes sting as water lines my lashes. "I... I killed..."

"It's okay." Serra raises a soft hand to cup my face, a calloused thumb gently brushing my cheek. "It's okay. You did the right thing."

"I killed him," I breathe. "I'm a killer."

"He was going to kill you. He was going to hurt our city. He killed your father," Serra reasons steadily. Her eyes glitter with buttery candlelight. "It's okay."

She pulls me close. Instinctively I wrap my arms around her body, burying my face in her shoulders and neck. Her dark curls press against my face, gentle with the fragrance of rosemary.

She pats my head, releasing me. "You good?" she asks.

I nod, blinking desperately as I try to pull myself together. "Yes. Yes, of course." I clear my throat and brush off my clock and tunic.

"That's my girl." A proud smile ripples across Serra's face. "Come on, let's get back, hmm. Help me with him."

"Back? Back where, and what are you doing out here?" I ask, gritting my teeth. I take several deep breaths, keeping my eyes fixed away from Idris as we each grab one of his bulky arms.

"Okay, lift." We stand up at the same time, an arm

around each of us, his feet still dragging on the floor. His weight is uncomfortable, draped over my shoulders, dragging me down like an anchor. He reeks of mint and lavender, their blend bringing bile to my tongue.

"Okay, this way," says Serra confidently, holding the lantern out in front of us. The glass glints softly, the handle rattling with each step. The jittery flame wriggles over the grimy, stained stone. The circular tunnel has a river of skanky water to one side. Our steps seem to bounce down these narrow bends.

"What are you doing down here? And where are we going?" The question springs from my lips as I turn to look at the engineer.

Serra smiles wryly, flashing me a beautiful smile. "After being in ... that place"—her tone pulls in disgust at the memory—"I've needed to move and walk. Being down here, without any walls ... it helps."

"And the sewer doesn't remind you of it?" I ask, confused.

"It might stink to the gods, but it's a different stink. It's the only way I can move anywhere without being seen at the moment, the only way I can have even a semblance of freedom and peace from the others."

"The others?"

"You'll see," she smiles knowingly.

"How did you find us?"

"I didn't mean to," Serra muses, shifting Idris's weight slightly on her shoulder with a small grunt, "but I started wondering if this was how they moved the explosives for the Grand Temple, given they took such a large amount, and that if they had, maybe there were traces of it left. Some kind of evidence."

"We're too late for evidence. After tonight, Bellandi will know we're on to him. He'll be out to kill me and Idris before we can do anything."

Serra scowls, but doesn't seem surprised. "After what I've seen this evening, I figured something had changed."

"What did you see?"

"Nothing useful. Good old fashioned terror tactics and abuse of power by the Militia."

"Oh great, so they're hitting the coup classics." I scowl sarcastically, as we stagger around another bend in the sewers.

Serra nods. "They've established power. The city is theirs. We didn't fight back—heck we didn't even know we needed to fight back." Serra's anger strikes a chord with me. One that hums in harmony.

"We'll get it back."

"With what weapons? What army?"

"Working on that."

"Well, I hope you work quickly," she chuckles, the humour bouncing off the curved walls. My grip on Patricelli's arm is slipping some.

"Damn, he's heavy!" I groan.

"Almost there," promises Serra, panting, sweat beginning to bead along her hairline.

"At least we know the best way to move around the city undetected now," I mutter. "How do you know your way around so well?"

"Map," says Serra. "Borrowed it from Alfieri. Interesting character that one. Ah, here we are."

Thank Fate, I could drop at any moment. Serra drops Idris, coming to a small ladder. She hops up the few steps, pushing on the grate to move it to one side.

She disappears up, then hangs down, offering one beautiful dark arm highlighted in silver moonlight.

"Pass him."

I shuffle closer, gritting my teeth. I have to look at him, pushing his limp body up the small gap. My breath runs hot. I shove his gangly limbs aggressively upwards, caring little when he lands inelegantly at the top. I follow Serra up, looking around a strange, tiny neglected garden.

Cast in hues of navy and onyx, some candlelight dares to leak from shuttered windows. The threadbare grass lies like errant strands of spun silver. A building is about ten paces away, with tiny windows shuttered tightly. Serra walks to the door, rapping sharply with her knuckles in a strange, precise pattern.

A moment later a slender bolt of gold appears between the door and the stone. Alfieri's unusually worried face appears, sees Serra and relaxes. He opens the door, face catching when he sees Idris on the ground.

He swears loudly, hurrying outside to grab him. "What happened?"

"Nouis," I say, the name the only explanation I can offer as Serra and Alfieri begin to drag him into the house. Serra adds more colour to the story as I exhaustedly trudge across the threshold of the run- down building.

I'm met with three familiar faces smiling at me. Emilia. Michelle.

Giulia.

She looks tired and pale, but her blue eyes are open as she lies across a dishevelled couch, a knitted blue blanket tucked over her legs.

The relief hits me like a ton of stone. Fate have mercy, I could've collapsed into an ocean of sobs right then and there. I stagger across the tiny room towards her, exhaustion forgotten. My heart might erupt as I throw myself on my sister, holding her tight as delighted tears roll down my cheeks.

"Hey, hey, I'm okay," Giulia whispers softly. Her melodic voice is music to my ears, a voice I worried I'd never hear again.

"You were gone, and I didn't know where you were. I thought Bellandi..." I trail off, gripping her tighter for a few more seconds before eventually daring to let her go.

"I went to get her," says Alfieri. I whip around, wincing a step back when I catch sight of Idris still slung over his shoulders. "While you orchestrated the prison break. Idris didn't trust Bellandi or Nouis not to do something nasty. Turns out he was right."

"What?" I hiss in horror, head snapping to my sister. "What happened to her?"

"Her fingernails," Alfieri continues. I grab my sister's hand. "The discolouration."

Discolouration? Perhaps they were a bit darker than normal, a slight orange tinge right at the base of the nail.

"Apparently my prolonged coma was thanks to long term

use of Red Root," Giulia says, disgust rolling around her tongue.

Nouis, he ordered that. I want to vomit. I want to scream. He'd been drugging my sister for days while sleeping with me in his arms? I need a whole body scrub. I need to scour my skin and my mind until I'm raw and boiled.

"The colour will fade," promises Alfieri as Michelle crouches over an unconscious Idris.

"Get my things," says Michelle quietly, and Emilia hops to a chipped sideboard. With the seven of us in this small room, the space is entirely too cramped. The faded blue on the walls cracks away, showering the worn stone floor with dust and scraps. One sofa holds the recovering Giulia, the other the massive and unconscious Idris. At the other end of the room is a narrow wooden door.

"What is this place?" I turn to Alfieri who stands guard over Idris while Michelle works on sewing up his head.

Alfieri shrugs, his eyes tight. "Old family property. Off the books."

He doesn't offer up any more information. I throw a quizzical look at Emilia who shrugs, eyes wide. Then she gives Alfieri a pointed look, and rocks a flat hand from side to side.

Is Alfieri's family ... dodgy?

I press my lips together, saying no more. Right now that's the absolute least of my problems. I sit next to my sister, perching on the slip of couch her knees have left spare. Right now, I'm grateful for having a roof over my head, crooked or not.

"So, what happened?" Emilia asks. I sigh, rubbing my

eyes. Giulia gently strokes my arm, trying to pull away the stress.

"Nouis is dead," I say, forcing myself not to stare at my own blood-coated fingers. "Bellandi has an army coming for the city soon."

Heads snap around to me in an instant.

"An army?" hisses Serra. She folds herself onto the floor—the only available sitting room in this box—right next to Giulia's head.

I nod. "Mercenaries. The money missing from the bank." I meet Giulia's eyes. "That's what they were paying for. I overhead Bellandi and Nouis talking about it."

Giulia wrinkles her top lip, loathing radiating from her blue eyes. "Dorado is going to pay for everything," she hisses.

"Where is Dorado?" I turn to Alfieri. He taps his foot on the ground, tilting his head downwards.

"Retained for ... questioning," he says, a lilt to his words as he looks pointedly towards the closed door at the back of the room. "As is that crooked nurse who fed your sister the Red Root."

"The bloody handprint on the wall?" I venture.

Alfieri waves it off. "Neither your sister or I bled today" is all he says in reassurance. I'm not a big enough person to feel sorry for the injured person—whoever they are.

"Okay, that should do it. He'll have a scar though, but hopefully his hair will cover it," says Michelle straightening up.

"We should get him upstairs," says Serra.

"There's an upstairs to this place?" I gape.

"One level below, one level above. Upstairs are two rooms

and some bunks; he'll get some proper rest there," says Alfieri. "You should go too. You look like you need it."

To say today has been eventful is the understatement of the decade.

It takes longer than I'd like to admit for us to manoeuvre Idris up the winding stairs. We squeeze him around the cramped bends and corridors and then drop the man on the narrow bed. My jaw feels one wrong move from cracking as I stagger back. I lean against the wall, clenching my eyes.

"Come on, the other room is waiting," promises Emilia.

"All the girls together." Serra throws her arms over my shoulder as we make towards the tiny box space. "Cramped, but it works."

I open the door to a slightly larger room than the other, complete with two bunk beds, a makeshift cot and a cracked, boarded window.

"Take your pick," Serra says.

"So ... what do we do now? With the army coming?" asks Emilia quietly. "Do we have a plan?" I sink down on the closest bunk, the springs creaking in protest. I rub my forehead.

What's the plan? Good question.

I have an engineer, an artist, an architect, a dodgy trader, and my unconscious Soulhate.

Bellandi has control of the City Guard, a Militia, and another army coming soon. No idea how soon of course. It could be hours, it could be weeks.

A plan would be really great.

"The plan ... will be formed in the morning," I sigh, hoping inspiration will strike. Halice depends on it.

I can't sleep.

I tried. Michelle snores and Giulia seems to be making up for all that time stationary by tossing and turning like a wriggling octopus. But even when Michelle rolls over and Giulia goes still ... sleep evades me.

I've washed, but the blood is a permanent, invisible stain on my hands. The memory of the handle still digs into my palm, the vicious blade dripping in dark scarlet is burned into my retinas.

I've gone to the sofa downstairs, pinched a pillow for my head and pulled that blue knitted blanket across my legs. But I can't find sleep. I can barely find rest. I close my eyes and I see the bloody knife protruding from Nouis's back, his body disappearing into the darkness.

I can't escape the truth, I am what I'd never in a million years thought I could be.

I'm a killer.

Killer. Killer. The word races around my head as though Nouis's ghost is already haunting me. Worse of all, I have no rebuttal.

Anything is better than this. The grief, the fear, the self-loathing. *All of it.* All-consuming hatred is so much better than this.

I'm so exhausted I find myself drifting back upstairs, that red-hot rage like a siren call I can't refuse. I tiptoe across the creaky floors, quietly slipping open the wonky wooden door to the boys' room. I'm stunned to find one bed empty. Alfieri must be ... somewhere else. Where? I don't know.

Unable to look at the man currently occupying the other bed, I curl up on the available bunk. My mouth goes dry and bitter. My fingers itch. My heart picks up its pace and throbs steadily at the base of my throat.

But my mind is consumed. Focused.

This is better. I can't sleep, but it's a powerful relief.

I give up on sleep pretty quickly. Instead, I scramble around for some paper and charcoal pencils. I light a candle, and wrap myself in a blanket. I start planning, recording everything I know so far. Any edge. Any information. Any possible ideas.

Who knows what would spark a moment of genius? Or madness? Both seem to be avoiding me so far.

A deep groan pulls me out of my downward spiral.

In my peripheral vision, Idris begins to move.

"Careful," I warn, daring to toss him a look. I clench the charcoal in my fingers with tight knuckles.

Idris bolts upright, blanket falling from his shirtless body, gasping for breath. My eyes zero in on the flash of colour across his sculpted abs. A crimson tattoo of a scorpion's tale sits just below his left shoulder. When did he get that? It's beautiful. *He*'s beautiful.

Confused, Idris screws up his face to see me gawking at his half-naked form. Colour floods to my cheeks.

"Renza!"

"I love how you state the obvious with such a sense of discovery," I tease, rolling my eyes. I turn back to the paper in front of me. I underline the word "sewer" more fiercely than I need to. "Don't think too hard, you'll rip your stitches."

"My— You—" he stumbles.

"My, you. What?" I raise an eyebrow expectantly without looking up.

A frustrated growl escapes his gritted teeth, as he scrabbles to put more distance between us. Panting, he scans the room confused. "Where are we?"

"Alfieri's safe house. Apparently it's 'off the books', whatever that means. Don't elaborate, I don't think I want to know any more."

"You don't," Idris promises.

"Quite some friend you have."

"There's no one better."

"How do you know him?"

"My time in Chalgos. He has a large, extended family over there. He and I got into some trouble together, and then we got out of it together."

"Are you going to elaborate?"

"If you don't like the idea of an off-the-books safe house, you don't want to hear it," snorts Idris, rubbing the back of his neck ruefully.

Illegal. *Of course.*

"How did we get here? Nouis—" His name makes me flinch. Idris stops dead, seeing my reaction in his peripheral vision.

I force myself to swallow the mouthful of sawdust, spitting out the truth. "Dead."

The silence kicks like a mule.

"How?" Disbelief explodes from his tongue. Idris twitches, fighting the urge to look at me. His shadow crawls along the floor slightly, wobbling on the bed he just vacated.

"I killed him." I manage to force out the words.

I killed him. Me. The killer.
The murderer.
Idris falls silent, shock stealing his ability to speak.

"I'm sorry," he manages eventually.

"No, you're not. You were right. He's a traitor."

"You deserve better than him, I always knew that. But still... You shouldn't have had to be the one— Fate's Fury, I should never have let it be you who had to—"

"Oh please," I scoff, rolling my eyes.

"Don't do that!" snaps Idris. "You trusted me to get you out of there and I failed."

"Don't be ridiculous, you didn't get hit on purpose. I was stupid enough to distract you. It was my fault."

"It wasn't your fault and you weren't stupid."

"I was scared and brainless and it almost cost us our lives." I seethe quietly, glaring at the paper in my hands but not seeing my scrawls. Idris is quiet for a long moment before shifting to sit on the bed opposite me. He reaches forwards, pulling the pages from my hands and discarding them to one side.

"There is no shame in fear. Without fear there is no bravery," Idris says quietly but insistently, his deep voice taking a softer edge. "And you, Renza, are one of the bravest women I know."

I shake my head, hating the words he directs at me. Undeserved, untrue words.

"I killed him. I killed Nouis while his back was turned. I'm a ... killer." I force the words out, unsure why I'm divulging this to Idris of all people. But he doesn't flinch. His hand slips over mine, tightly squeezing. Seering heat leaps up my arm but I drink it in, focusing on the sensation of him and nothing else.

"You are not defined by one action. You are so many things, defining you at all is an impossible task. You have done so much before this and will do a thousand things in the future. Do not let one moment of survival overshadow how you see yourself. No one will see you any differently. I certainly don't."

I fight to keep my eyes from snapping to his face.

"Rest up," I interrupt him, not wanting to talk about this anymore. *That's why I came here, to get away from that. To feel other things.*

I get to my feet. "I'll go get you some water—you took quite the blow."

"I hit my head. Why do my arms hurt?" Idris's deep voice boils. I scowl, fighting the urge to look at his face as I make for the door.

"I had to drag your heavy, unconscious body through half the city. What else should I have grabbed?"

"So, why do I smell like urine?"

"I had to haul you through the sewers."

"Urgh," he mutters, voice thick with disgust.

I fold my arms, snapping off my words. "Most people say thank you after having their life saved. Next time I'll just leave you."

Idris falls silent for a moment, like he's trying to swallow something massive. "Thank you."

"Pulling teeth would be easier," I mutter, marching towards the door. Idris darts towards me, catching my elbow.

I whip around to look at him, catching myself just in time to squeeze my eyes shut.

I suck in several breaths and I let that hot wave wash over me. This feeling is so familiar now. It's like an echo of him. I let it rush through, not letting a single drop take root.

"Seriously Renza," says Idris quietly, that deep voice soft and serious. "I don't— That trip— You must..." He sighs before continuing. "You're strong. Stronger than me."

My heart gallops in my throat. "Yeah well, you left this city for a decade because of me. This was the least I could do."

Idris frowns, leaning closer so his head is mere inches from mine. I can feel his breath brush against the tip of my nose. His hands come back to my arms, fingers warm through the thin fabric of my silk tunic.

"I left Halice as much for myself as I did for you. I thought about you every day, wondering who you might be, wondering if you were worth fighting Fate. Now I know you and I regret nothing. You owe me nothing, Renza." Idris's voice is so low. He says my name almost like a prayer.

"You're wrong. We owe each other everything."

Idris's grip tightens for a moment, tingles rippling up my arms.

He leans closer still, the barest slither of air between our faces.

"Why are you here, Renza?" His voice is so impossibly soft. I swallow before answering.

"I brought you here—"

"No, why are you *here*?" he says. I know he means this bedroom.

I hitch a breath and the honest whisper tingles as it leaves my lips. "The rage is easier."

"Easier than what?"

"The guilt," I admit, pressing my lips together to hold back any more. I'm unable to look at him. But not for rage, for shame. I take a deep breath, focusing on my galloping heart and the fireworks of his fingers against my body.

Idris lets out a deep breath, a hand sweeps upwards to the side of my head as he lowers his forehead to rest against mine. My heart hammers. His skin against mine wipes all other thoughts away.

There is only him.

"If I am to be your distraction, Renza, then I will do it properly."

Idris's mouth crashes upon mine, swallowing my shocked gasp. His lips are simultaneously soft and firm as they move like a man starved. Searching and hungry. I am devoured.

He pushes his body up against mine and suddenly we're welded. His touch blisters like hot coals. The roaring pain dances with the pleasure in a delirious mind-melting madness that steals all control and reason and thought. My entire body contorts with sparks, sizzling and wild as they start fires in my flesh. His talented hands sweep over my body, consuming me with a burning that chars my bones. He knots his fingers into my hair, angling my head to gain better access to me. The devastating, agonising pleasure of his tongue starts an all-enthralling war between our mouths, one I refuse to lose. Idris's other hand sweeps down my waist, taking a few moments to explore my arse before sweeping down to my knee. He hitches my leg up and over his hip, that firm grip searing the small of my back like a fresh brand. He pulls me closer, the strong muscles of his arms tightening as I'm somehow pressed even more tightly against his shirtless, chiselled chest.

His lips on mine are a sinfully delicious fire. I drink in the cursed, divine mixture of pleasure and pain like a fine, poisonous wine. I let my anger swell, my rage for everyone and everything that has happened, unleashing the fury upon him. My hands tangle and tug sharply at his hair, returning the passion of his mouth with my own, my tongue darting forwards to punish his mouth. I can feel him, every impressively large, thick inch of his manhood straining against the cage of his thin trousers between us. Dark, hot wetness begins to form between my legs, the battle between us reaching new desperate, hungry heights.

His fingers sweep down to memorise the curve of my waist, trailing rivers of lava over the soft flesh. His lips pry themselves from mine only to find a new target of attack along my neck. The blissful, tormented sigh ekes out from my throat as I tilt my chin to the sky, baring it all to him and his dark, devouring heat.

I'm ablaze for him.

Fate's Mercy, has it ever felt like this before? Lords, not that I could think of. Not even with Nouis.

Nouis.

The name slams my head into a wall.

I gasp, forcing my eyes open. *What am I doing?* This is madness. A divine, voracious kind of madness, but madness all the same. He's my Soulhate.

Kill him. He's at your mercy. Strike now.

The loathing returns so thick I'm drowning. A revulsion so sharp I want to vomit takes control of my limbs. Reflexively, I shove hard against Idris's shoulder, prying us apart. Idris stops at the silent command, no question of bemoaning in his demeanour. I force him further back, covering my face with my hands as I fight to control my breathing. Both our breaths are ragged for a moment. I grip my head, leaning back against the cool wall as I struggle to rein in the Hate coursing undiluted through my blood. After a moment or two, I manage to force my pulse to slow and I push that disgust and loathing to the back of my mind.

"I should go," I whisper, worried how paper-thin my control is right now. Idris nods as I turn towards the door.

His fingers brush my wrist, stopping me a moment. "Thank you for saving my life."

I chuckle softly, turning back. I take his chin in my hands, forcing him to look at me. "Your life belongs to me, Patricelli. Fate decreed it so. Never forget that."

I spin on my heels, stride swiftly out of the room and close the door behind me. I stare at the ancient floorboards beneath my feet, breathing deeply for a few seconds to calm my stampeding heart. What was Idris thinking? Did he want to push the limits of my already threadbare control?

He'll be the death of me.

But if that's the price to save Halice? Then so be it.

CHAPTER 26

Pancakes.

    The sweet, mouthwatering aroma peels my eyes open, the world feeling like cotton wool around me. Blinking and scrambling for my bearings, I ease upright.

I'm alone in the abandoned upstairs bedroom of Alfieri's safe house.

My stomach whimpers, demanding some of the delicious breakfast, the scent of which is currently wafting through the door. I breathe in that heavenly, sweet smell and stagger to my feet. Fate's Fury, my back aches! That's what I get for lugging a man through the sewers. I hurry through the doors, making the mistake of looking through the open door to Idris's room.

Rubbing the sleep from my eyes I catch sight of the bed. I flinch, expecting to be hit with a now familiar wave of disgust and nausea. It doesn't come. Instead I'm surprised to see the bed empty and perfectly made. You could bounce a coin off those crisp edges.

Where's he gone now?

I hurry down the stairs towards the tiny, cramped living area. The promise of pancakes makes my stomach impatient as I stop on the bottom step. Everyone is sitting with plates on their laps, laughing and chatting. In the centre of the floor sits a stack of gorgeous, fluffy, golden discs. Right there waiting. Just for me.

"Morning!" calls Michelle from her seat next to Giulia.

"How? Is there a kitchen in this place I don't know about?" I ask, hurrying over to Serra's side as she holds up the plate for me. Emilia laughs, shaking her head. She sits with her legs curled up on the couch next to Alfieri.

"Nope. This is all Idris," she says, waving her fork at the food.

"He went out for it?" I ask, before devouring my first forkful of food. This is heaven.

"He knows a lady up the street who let him borrow her kitchen," says Alfieri.

"Wait, Idris made all this?" I repeat, shock colouring my words more strongly than they should.

"Right!" Michelle says. "Who knew?"

I pause mid-bite, the mix of flour and sugar suddenly feeling lumpy in my mouth. I swallow, eyes beginning to water.

"Just something I picked up in Nava Gao. I spent some time with a celebrated chef called Darwish Saeed," comes that deep voice. I turn my head, catching sight of his golden head. He stands in the doorway to the courtyard, like he just materialised there. I force my eyes back to my plate, fighting the rising lump in my throat.

His gaze on my face feels hot, and not just in the way I've come to find familiar.

"Well, you picked the right breakfast! Pancakes are Renza's favourite," chuckles Serra. Her dark eyes lock with mine, raising an eyebrow expectantly. I throw her a withering look, stabbing my meal with more force than necessary. Michelle sets down my coffee for me.

"So. Plan. Surely you geniuses have one," Michelle says.

"We don't have long," I say. "We might need a miracle." Idris walks into the room, folding himself onto the floor far away from me. I stretch, trying to get used to the burning sensation in my eyes and fingers to let it settle. I take quiet, long controlled breaths. It works. My pulse starts to ease up.

"Well, I don't think we can count on the gods after all this," Idris says in good humour. "Besides, we're Halicians. We don't need miracles. Just hard work."

I struggle to swallow, the pancakes turn to ash in my mouth. If the gods wanted to help us out right now, I certainly wouldn't say no. I set down my fork.

"The army," says Serra, staring down the silent bull in the room. Idris swears.

"Yeah, it does help things make sense. The stealing. The delay in taking power. I see the plan now," Idris all but growls.

"Idris?" I push, waiting for his answer.

"Think about it this way. If we didn't know everything we know now, how would it look? The Electi are murdered in a vicious explosion. Merely days later an army attacks the city—"

"Wait, if Bellandi hired them, won't the hired army tell people that?" asks Alfieri.

"No. It would be part of the plan for them to 'loose'. They'll probably be paid a fee for it. And even more to keep quiet," Idris answers quickly. "Many will die but the army will be repelled, and thanks to Bellandi's leadership and the brave Church Militia—on loan from a benevolent Holy Mother—they'll manage to fight them off. They'll even capture the insider who helped them do it, or they'll paint Serra's escape as proof that she was in on it." Idris poses the all too believable story. "On the international stage, it'll explain the massacre and paint the Church as the hero."

"The rest is obvious," I breathe. "More Militia will come to 'protect us' while Halice gets its High Chamber up and running again. The new Electi will be mere puppets of the Holy States and Halice will essentially become an extension of it."

"Until, in a year or two, Bellandi will present a bill suggesting we join it formally, and the puppet government will vote in favour," Idris finishes. "And how can the rest of the world argue when its own people voted for it?"

"It's devious," breathes Serra.

"It's international politics," I grumble.

"Wait? How does that explain the stealing?" asks Michelle.

"Private armies won't fight without a deposit," answers Idris matter-of-factly.

"Private armies?" Michelle quizzes as Emilia starts to gather the dirty cutlery together.

"Groups of mercenaries that come together and fight for gold," Idris explains.

"But why take our money?" asks Emilia, frowning. "Stealing from us is surely more risky."

"To keep it off the Holy State's accounts. To keep it hidden. The Holy States can't be seen to be invading another country, let alone buying an army to attack an ally. The international community would go into uproar," I explain.

"Enough to help us retake the city?" ventures Serra hopefully.

I shake my head. "Not enough to start a war over an already lost cause, but probably enough that things could get very uncomfortable. Trade embargos, broken military alliances, lost trust and faith in the Holy Mother. They might even remove her and select a new Holy Sovereign."

"All of which would be sour consolation prizes," Idris sighs. "When will the army get here?"

"I don't know," I answer.

The silence is so thick, the barest whisper would shatter it. Emilia raises a trembling hand to her face as Alfieri leans over to comfort her. Serra leans back in her seat, eyes wide and mind far away. Michelle and Giulia link their hands together and squeeze tightly.

My heart could crack open. My friends, my family—terrified for their futures. In our city.

"I do know their name though," I offer. "The Askerler Company."

"Askerler," repeats Idris like a shot. "Are you sure?"

"Yes, why?"

"I've fought with them before," Idris breathes. "I know their leader."

"Will your friendship turn him away?"

"No, they've accepted the contract. They have to fight, otherwise who else would ever hire them again? But if we can shut the city gates and get rid of Bellandi before they get here..." Idris trails off.

"Wanna share with the group, bud?" teases Alfieri, giving Idris a nudge.

Idris takes a deep breath. "If Bellandi is dead and the city ours again before the army gets here, I can argue that their contract is with our city and not Bellandi. I can argue that they have fulfilled their obligations and their contract is over. Essentially, I can try to convince them to go away without a fight," Idris explains. "I know their leader, that'll buy me an audience. But we need Bellandi gone before they arrive. If he's still breathing, they are honour-bound to fight for him and they will."

"How do you know this guy?" I ask without looking at him.

"We fought on the same side before, when I was in Coari."

"Oh right, your time studying with the Princess of War," I snort. Alfieri barks a short laugh, before immediately trying to smother it.

"Studying, was it?" he mutters as Emilia gives him a gentle elbow to the gut.

"We still don't know when the mercenaries are going to arrive," Serra says. "Closing the gates won't matter if we're too late."

"Would any of our guests know?" Alfieri says, gesturing his thumb at the closed door. Idris shrugs.

"They might."

"I see. So perhaps you and I need to ... get to work?" offers Alfieri, clearing his throat and avoiding Emilia's eyes as his hand falls to the dagger on his belt. I go still, examining the look on his face and the dark suggestive lilt of his tone.

Work on them he means.

I discard what's left of my pancakes, stomach tightening. No, no, this is not who we are. Not who I am! There has to be a better way than ... that.

"Wait, does Dorado or the nurse know you're working with us?" I ask. Alfieri shakes his head.

"No, of course not."

"Why?" frowns Idris.

"Well, what if we try something less messy first? A trick?" I suggest, getting to my feet. I brush off my hands and try to neaten up my hair.

"What kind of trick?"

"Can you create noise like stomping around and moving furniture? Like soldiers doing a search?"

"Why?" repeats Idris.

"Just ... let me try something. Go, go on!" I gesture for them to hurry up. I walk towards the door. Alfieri lets out a surprised shout as the girls get into stomping on the floor. Serra gets really into it, barking orders like a drill sergeant.

I rattle the door loudly before opening it.

"Are you here?" I shout down, descending the dark, uneven steps. I grip the hard metal railing.

"Dorado? Dorado?" I shout. "Are you here!"

A crash comes from upstairs, the stomping seems to work as I get to the base of the stairs. Three doors face me.

"Dorado?" I shout, rattling one of the doors.

"Signora?" comes a weak voice from the other door. I race over, hammering on it.

"Dorado, are you in there?"

"Yes! Yes, signora, Fate's Mercy, I'm in here!" he yells, relief giddy in his voice. I look around for a key.

"Stay there, I'm coming. We've found you alright."

I see a set of keys hanging on the wall, and grab them. The second one I try turns in the lock and I push in to see Dorado...

Oh. Fate's. Fury.

He looks terrible.

He lies on a bare cot, and an empty plate of food lingers in the corner along with a pot for his "waste". His bandages are slick with old blood—probably from the medical treatment for that stab wound he got. He looks so pale and is covered in dirt. He crawls up from his position on the floor.

"Oh thank Fate's Mercy," he cries.

"Dorado, it's okay. It's okay—I found him!" I yell up the stairs as if reporting back. I turn back to Dorado, gripping his shoulders. "This is serious, Dorado. We've been looking for you since you went missing. Patricelli is on to us, he knows about the Askerler Company."

"He does?" Dorado gasps in horror.

"Tell me you didn't tell him anything. Did you give us away?" I demand, giving him a shake.

"No, no, no! I swear it!" Dorado babbles. "I didn't tell him anything!"

"Are you sure? Because only a few people know the date. You didn't tell him the date that they'll get here?"

"No! No I swear it! I didn't say anything!"

"Good," I sigh, running a hand through my hair. "Maybe we can still pull this off in time then. What do you think, Dorado? Today is the fifth."

"The fifth? I mean the army gets here tomorrow," Dorado babbles. "How much damage can he do in that time?"

"Tomorrow. They get here tomorrow," I repeat, my insides turning to ice. I straighten up, backing away from the disgusting traitor in front of me.

Dorado's face falls.

"You're not— You're working with Patricelli ... aren't you?" he realises. I look at his pathetic face, the traitorous letch who knew about the explosion, the army, who betrayed my sister. And for what?

"What did they promise you?" I ask darkly, fist shaking at my side.

Dorado wrinkles his face with as much pride as he can. "The bank," he answers. "I've run that place for decades for your ungrateful father, and then he has the gall to put his daughter as my boss?"

My fist flies, landing square on his nose. A sickening crack echoes around the tiny hovel, and he crumples to the floor.

"My father was a great man, and my sister is one of the most brilliant women this city has ever seen. We are Maineri and that bank is ours, by blood and birth. You? You're nothing but a disgusting, dirty traitor who's going to die in this cell."

With that I walk out of the room, slamming the door behind me. The keys jangle as I turn it in the rickety lock. I slow down, taking a deep breath. I hope he rots.

Slow claps pull me out of my dark stupor. I look up, sucking in a breath when I see Idris at the top of the stairs.

"That was genius," Idris chuckles. I force myself to look up at his face. Those hazel eyes burn but also ... sparkle with a bit of pride? I roll my eyes, scratching at the goosebumps running up and down my arms.

"Tomorrow."

"I heard everything," Idris says, the corner of his mouth twitching upwards. "No wonder you're so formidable in the High Chamber if you can play games that convincing at the drop of a hat."

"Unfortunately, there is almost no one left of any real challenge to play with me," I answer, voice low and serious as I climb towards where he stands, hands slowly sliding up the wrought iron railing.

I come level with him, forcing my breathing to remain even. My heart picks up, my throat closes. The corner of his mouth twitches up as he takes a step closer to me, golden eyes narrowing with something I can't quite place.

Idris steps closer, the air between us gets tense and hot. Everything is burning; my breath is hot; my heart hammers against my ribs. I turn my eyes away. But Idris lifts a hand to my chin, using a single finger to force my gaze to meet his blistering golden eyes.

"If you want a game, I'll play with you," Idris whispers softly. "My divine nemesis."

Then he whisks away, disappearing through the door like he was never here. The memory of his finger on my chin still ripples with tiny exploding stars.

I let out a shuddering breath, steeling my nerve as I follow after him, to face what comes next.

CHAPTER 27

Goosebumps rise up my arms. Bile pools at the back of my tongue as the cheap door between the inside room and the courtyard opens.

"Here." Idris sets a wooden cup on the stone floor where I'm sitting. This little courtyard is protected from the breeze by large crumbling walls that box out pretty much everything but the sun. The sky is a brilliant blue as sweet birds call to each other from the undulating rooftops.

For a moment I forget the bloodshed. Forget the horror and the death.

But not for long.

Alfieri, Emilia and Serra left an hour ago via the sewers to scout for more information, whatever that means. Michelle is taking care of Giulia, who has returned upstairs for another nap. There is still a lot of healing for her body to do, though thankfully some colour is returning to her cheeks as the Red Root leaves her system.

I've spent that time resting—on strict orders from my friends. Apparently I'm to try and recover while coming up with a plan, as though such a thing is easy. I cross one leg over the other, the stone biting uncomfortably into my butt as a wave of goosebumps crawls over my arms. Tilting my head down, I watch Idris's shadow sink to the ground on the other side of the doorway. His back rests against the opposite side of this wall. With only a wall between us, he leaves the door open so we can speak.

I pick the wooden cup off the ugly stone patio. "Thank you," I say, sipping on the water much to the delight of my dry lips.

"No worries. So, you got anything good?"

I sigh, running a finger around the rim of the cup. "Lots of bad ideas. You?"

"Lots of bad ideas," he agrees.

I snort. "Shame. I thought you might've spent time with some master coup strategist during your world tour," I tease.

"No. Eight months in Rhone with the Sarpong family. But ... nothing we can use here."

"You're such a name-dropper," I groan half-heartedly, tilting my head back against the cold wall. Its gentle chill soaks into my shoulders, providing a moment of relief against the brewing headache.

"Had to do something with my travels," he chuckles, completely unabashed.

"What really happened in Malaya?" the questions spills forwards. Idris is quiet for a minute.

"What did Nouis tell you?"

"That you killed his best friend," I summarise quickly, deciding not to breathe any more life into the potential lies I've fallen for. Idris pauses for a long time before telling his version of events

"I went to Malaya with some friends I'd made in Coari, to learn the art of mind-stilling. We'd been there for about six months, studying with their spiritual guides, helping amongst the community, befriending the locals, when Nouis's expedition turned up," Idris says, a sigh lurking in his voice. "Instantly they started to rub people up the wrong way. They were so disparaging of the local people, their culture, and above all their religious practices. The Church Militia, with their black and white garbs, called themselves defenders of the Holy Faith—but they were just insulting and disrespectful of their hosts. It was appalling to even think I shared a faith with these people. Their conduct made me question a lot of my beliefs in the Father Fate and his Daughters, Sister Love and Sister Hate." Idris sighs again before continuing, "Still, they demanded they be allowed to look around. They demanded entrance everywhere, including a great spiritual temple called Sadhu. Sadhu is a temple reserved for Spiritual Vestals—holy women, their versions of nuns. Many live their lives in isolation there, for a variety of reasons. Others train up in skills like midwifery or other service skills. It's also a refuge for any woman in strife. Anyway, they forced their way into this sacred sanctuary."

I close my eyes to the horror of what comes next. Nouis's crooked words and half-truths change their footing and make me want to vomit.

"While looking around, as they called it, Nouis's commander Orsino found his Soulmate. A girl called Ananda. She was a Vestal, a midwife—one of the most talented in the region. Ananda refused to leave with him, so he tried to take her by force. But no one would let him. It wasn't just the other Vestals; everyone in the village was alerted and came to try and help her. We of course rushed with them. Ananda had delivered many of the babies in not only this village but many of the surrounding provinces. Every man and woman knew someone she'd saved. She's beloved and the people were ready to leap to her defence without hesitation. But by the time we got there, the fight had already broken out. So many were dead, including many of the Vestals. Unarmed."

Idris's voice gets thick. He pauses, clearly skipping parts of a story that aren't relevant or are too painful to voice aloud.

"I managed to find Orsino, in the chaos. Then I saw him, in a fit of rage, shove his Soulmate into a bonfire."

The gasp had my mouth hanging open in horror. My eyes burn with how wide they are; my stomach pushes bile up my throat until I almost gag. How could someone do something so awful?

"So yes, I killed him," Idris said, voice low, lethal and filled with regret, not for his actions but for not feeding an altogether darker instinct, "And chased Nouis and his company all the way back to their ships and off that continent. After everything, we didn't stay long. The locals weren't too fond of violent outsiders anymore—and I couldn't blame them."

"Did she survive, Ananda?"

"Fate's Mercy, she did. But covered in burns from head to toe."

I sit there for a long moment, trying desperately to understand how on earth I could ever have believed Nouis's version of events. My stomach curdles. My mouth fills with something sour.

We soak in the silence for a long time, breathing slowly.

Idris clears his throat, clearly aiming to lighten the mood. "So let's hear your bad ideas. Because we don't have long to get even a bad idea into motion."

I take a deep breath, blinking to clear my head and bring my thoughts back to the problem at hand. "If we can close the gates, the army will pause. Because having open gates will be part of the plan?"

"I would've thought so. Bellandi wouldn't make this harder for the Askerler Company, given it's all a ploy anyway. Besides, closed gates means someone in the city knows they're coming, and this is supposed to be a surprise attack from foreign enemies. No one inside the city is 'supposed' to know it's coming."

"Okay. And you think if Bellandi is dead and the gates are closed, you can use your connection to the Askerler Company leaders to convince the army to turn around?" I reaffirm.

"That sums it up."

I set my cup down, dragging my feet up the stone until I can hug my knees. "So, first issue," I state out loud, "we need to close the gates. We need to ring the warning bells which are in the Watchtower."

"Which is in the Market Square ... which will be absolutely crawling with Militia because that's where the cardinal is."

"The positive being that hopefully it'll be mostly City Guard manning the gates. Meaning if we ring the bells, they'll actually close them."

"'Hopefully' and 'if' are not great planning words," Idris groans, "but I agree."

Silence passes between us for a second, both of us aware of the increasingly dwindling chance of this happening. I rub my eyes, taking a deep breath.

"Okay. So, we need a distraction so you can get inside the Watchtower," I start again.

"Yes, it should be me," Idris agrees as though he was expecting to fight me on this. "Undoubtedly they'll be guarding the bells, meaning there'll be violence."

"If we get the distractions right, you won't face too much."

"That's fine. I'm used to dangerous situations."

My heart spasms. I bite my lip, looking down at my knees. Guilt flickers up my gut—his educational world tour had brought him this much danger? A world tour he took because of me.

"That doesn't handle the Guard in the city," Idris pushes forwards.

"No, but if we can convince the City Guard to fight with us, that we are the ones to trust, then maybe we could win. Particularly if the Militia aren't expecting a fight within our walls."

"It'll be bloody ... but we stand a chance," Idris muses

unhappily. "I suppose this could work. But it all hinges on those damn bells. So, distraction ideas. What have you got?"

"Well ... I'm thinking we'll actually need at least two. Bellandi will be expecting something. But the more we have ... the more we confuse him."

"Smart. Two distractions then. One big and obvious. One more subtle?"

"Exactly. Get him chasing his tail."

"What could we do?"

"Serra has an explosion throwing machine," I begin.

Idris barks with laughter. "What is it with your friends and explosions?"

"Hey, we didn't start this," I point out.

"Bunch of pyros," he teases. "Still, I owe you an apology about Serra. You were right to rescue her. The more time I spend with her, the more I like her."

"Yeah, she's like that." I don't fight the wry smile spilling over my face.

"Okay, so explosion distraction. Alright, that's big and obvious sorted. Any other ideas?"

The best idea is the one he'll like the least. I hesitate before speaking, tensing for his backlash. "Me."

The air instantly chills. All warmth drops from Idris's voice. "What?"

"If I turn up, Bellandi will be preoccupied. I can be the distraction."

"That's suicide," hisses Idris.

"It would work."

"This is a sick joke. Tell me you're not serious," Idris snaps at me.

"It could work."

"Bellandi will kill you." Idris's voice shakes the door. "You'll die regardless of whether the City Guard fight or not, of whether we win or not!"

"Then I'll die saving my city. Saving my home," I shout back, hating the way my voice rings off the wall. Idris pants furiously, the shadow of his fist shakes on the floor.

"Selfish," he hisses. "We need you—the people need you—and you're going to give up? After everything?"

Selfish? After everything I've lost. After everything I've been through?

That bolt stole the air from my lungs.

"This isn't giving up," I gasp incredulously. "This is a strategic sacrifice."

"No, it's a loud and messy suicide. A spectacle of martyrdom." His fist slams into the door, and it swings back to slam against the wall. I flinch backwards, knocking the cup on the floor and pooling water over the stone between us.

Silence hovers between us, brittle and thick.

"I can't..." His whisper barely limps to my ear. "I can't lose you too."

Blinking, words flee from my tongue as my lungs swell painfully. "Idris—"

"I have lost everything. Everyone." Idris's voice cracks at his confession. "You are all I have. You are all that's left of my world. I can't lose that. I can't lose you. I cannot watch you die. Please don't make me."

I sniff, wiping the water bleeding from my swollen eyes. He's right. He's become a constant in my life, an important strength I can't let go. Someone I can rely on in a way I didn't realise I needed.

I reach out, wrapping my fingers softly over the fist he slammed into the ground. I soak into the fiery warmth of his touch, drawing strength from the sensation that is entirely Idris.

"Isn't it funny? Two weeks ago I thought I'd be lucky if I never saw you again. If you died some other way. But now? When Nouis was going to hurt you, all I felt was horror and pain. I couldn't bear to watch you die," I admit softly.

"What's all this about dying?"

Michelle appears in the room behind us, Giulia at her side. Giulia squeezes through the open door towards the courtyard, taking a deep breath of the fresh air. Sunshine traces a crown through her blonde curls and dusts her skin with gold. Behind her walks Michelle wearing a quizzical expression.

"Renza has a suicide plan," scowls Idris. Giulia sighs, as though not surprised.

"It would work," I argue indignantly, hurriedly getting to my feet.

"We like you breathing, Renza." Michelle rolls her eyes and folds her arms. "So any plan where you die is a non-starter."

"We need distractions for the Militia so I can get into the Watchtower and ring the emergency bells to close the gates. Something other than Renza turning herself over," Idris says, catching them up quickly.

"Distraction you say? Spectacle?" Michelle asks, a wicked grin springing to her face. "I think we might be able to muster some of those. Spectacle is something we Garden professionals are rather known for."

"There's a massive crowd in Market Square—we should be able to use that. What about actors pretending to see you? Even be you?" suggests Giulia, "They could even dress up like Church Militia and lead them marching in the wrong direction and barking the wrong orders."

"I love it!" grins Michelle. "Break them into groups chasing down fakes."

"Even if we could find people stupid enough to do this, what happens after that?" I argue. "When the Militia work the trick out, they'll kill the actors."

"Not if the actors get away," points out Giulia.

"Or, hear me out on this ... what if we lead them into traps," Michelle says excitedly. "There are loads of little corners in Halice, ones the Church Militia won't know about. We could design some traps around the city to take them out."

"What kind of traps?" Idris moves to stand with us in the courtyard.

"Prisons, explosions, collapsing walls," Michelle begins to list, eyes lighting up with ideas. "We can use the sewers to move around and set them all up tonight."

"How? How are we meant to do all this?" I argue hotly. "We are only seven people."

"We'll get the whole Garden in on this," grins Michelle. "They love you and will absolutely believe us. You can bet everyone will be begging to get their own back on the Militia."

"They're the best and brightest. If any set of people can pull this off, it's The Garden," says Giulia.

"This could work," Idris mutters softly. "If we can thin out the Militia numbers, when the City Guard fight back they'll have the numbers and a home-field advantage. We could win that fight if enough of the traps work."

Horrified, my heart thunders in my chest. My mouth goes dry. My throat closes up.

"The City Guard need a leader," says Idris. "They need Captain Collier to rally them quickly."

"That could be your job, Renza. Get to Captain Collier and persuade him to fight," Giulia suggests. "You're so good with people."

"He'll be in Market Square. Bellandi will keep him close, just to be safe," Idris adds. "You'll have to find a way to get his attention to talk to him privately."

"The crowds in Market Square should make it possible," says Giulia. "You could blend in with them."

"So this is the plan? Actors tricking one of the deadliest armies on the continent into setting off last- minute traps crafted in the dead of night that were transported through sewers? All in the hope that we can convince the City Guard to rally together and fight off what's left of the Church Militia —if enough of the traps work? In that time, Idris will sneak into the church building and ring some bells to close the gates to an approaching army. That's what we've got?" I repeat.

This is going to be a *disaster*.

"It's not a guaranteed plan," Idris admits. "But it could work."

"This is going to be fun. I'll go gather the others," says Michelle, planting a kiss on Giulia's cheek as she hurries over to the hatch leading to the sewers and drops down. I stare at the hole in the stone as she vanishes from view. Giulia comes to my side, wrapping a hand around my arm.

"This will work," she promises. "We can do this."

I grip her hand tightly, heart spasming in my chest.

"If we pull this off, it'll be a miracle."

CHAPTER 28

Market Square is a roasting tray. The heat is so thick it clings to your fingers and clogs your nose. My tunic is plastered to my back. The hood of my cloak is melted into my hair. A bead of sweat runs from my hairline, dribbling across my cheek to balance on the very edge of my dry lips.

Market Square is busy as usual, but something is wrong. The stall owners aren't yelling. People move with their heads down, not looking anyone in the eye. Everyone avoids the three large rings of Church Militia stationed around that Watchtower, giving them as much room as possible.

The Militia stand with their backs to the awful building, their black and white cloaks pooling lifelessly to the ground at their feet. Their polished weapons glint in the light blinding all who dare to sneak a glance. They glare at the crowd, unfriendly grimaces etched into their features.

I lick my lips, the sweat instantly dissolving on my parched tongue. I'm buried deep into the crowd, having been here for a few hours now. Watching. Waiting. Making sure we haven't missed too much. I have no doubt Bellandi is in that building—why else would all these soldiers be outside?

I take a steadying breath, waiting for the signal. For it all to begin.

My pulse flies beneath my clammy palms. My heart throbs against my lungs. Around the city, my people—my friends—are lying in wait with a bunch of homemade traps waiting to set them off. Ready to fight back.

I hope they work.

There she is.

Michelle runs into Market Square, slipping to an uneasy stop. Her chin held high, dark hair shining in the relentless sunshine, she searches for me. Her eyes skip past the throng of other civilians before she winks, flashing me the signal.

Time to get to work.

Michelle taps one of her actor colleagues on the shoulder before disappearing amongst the crowd in search of the next one.

"Hey! Maineri! Over there! Don't run! Maineri! Maineri!" A voice rings out—the actor giving it his all before he goes racing down the street. Ahead of him is a girl in a short tunic and wig, sprinting away as fast as she can.

Instantly the Church Militia react, a group breaking off from their large position and chasing after the actors.

"Hey, look, it's Patricelli!" cheers another actor. "How are you here? No, don't run! Patricelli, wait!"

Two more actors run, and another large group of Militia charge after them.

The commotion of the crowd gets louder. The Militia

Captain starts barking orders, dragging Bellandi out of his slimy burrow inside the building. He walks purposefully down the steps, teeth gritted as he scans through the crowd.

By his side is my target, Captain Collier.

I take a deep breath, praying to whomever cares to listen. Let me find the right words.

BANG! BANG! BANG!

Colourful explosions fly over the heads of the buildings. People gasp, some scream and everyone starts moving. People push up against the Church Militia, mingling them with the crowd and allowing actors to reveal their Militia disguises.

"Come on, this way!" shouts one fake Militia actor encouraging a breakaway group of Militia to go after the explosions.

"This way! Come on, quick, they're over here!" shouts another actor.

The layers of the Militia peel away like an onion, sprinting down the roads after fakes. My eyes flicker to the servants' door, a sharp wave of relief hitting me as I catch Idris's shadow slipping inside.

My turn.

I move forwards, weaving through the throng of confused people. Captain Collier marches through the crowd, trying to make sense of what's going on around him.

I duck and weave desperately past the bustling people, trying to reach him in time.

"Captain!" I gasp, my hand closing around his forearm. His head snaps to me, hazel eyes narrowing.

"Maineri," he hisses with venom. My heart shatters. Ice stakes through my lungs. Mistake. This is a terrible mistake.

He sweeps close, pressing his sword against my throat. "You traitor!"

"No. No, Captain, I swear," I breathe, the edges of his blade cutting the soft flesh of my throat.

"You blew up my prison."

For Fate's sake! How had we not thought of that? Idiots!

"How could you?" Collier's face is torn with loathing. "I trusted you. You're Electi."

"Captain, I will explain everything, I swear—"

"You betrayed Halice. You stole from us. Bellandi showed me everything."

"No, Captain, I swear. It's him—it's all him," I plead. "Bellandi is the thief. Serra is his scapegoat. I know the truth—you have to believe me."

"Why should I?"

"Why else would I be stupid enough to come here? To try to talk to you—"

"ENOUGH!" roars Bellandi, "EVERYONE, STOP MOVING THIS INSTANT! DRAW YOUR SWORDS!" The Militia do as commanded, standing their ground and brandishing polished weapons. The entire crowd gasps in horror, before terrified screams erupt as some people scramble to leave.

No.

No, no no.

I need more time. Collier doesn't believe me yet.

"NO ONE LEAVE! EVERYONE QUIET!" Bellandi stalks in front of the building, glaring at the people.

"This is a trick. A dirty trick," Bellandi mutters to

himself, eyes manic as they bounce around the faces of the people in the crowd. A psychotic smile stretches over his lips when he sees Captain Collier with a sword to my throat.

"Well, well. You found her."

People shuffle nervously, parting the crowd between me and him. They whisper to each other, confused and afraid. Bellandi's smirk says it all as he spreads his arms wide.

"Good people of Halice! You have been lied to!" Bellandi starts. My heart sinks. "Renza Di Maineri has stolen from you. She has robbed this city in its time of grief!"

"You dirty little—" I start shouting.

"Enough," snarls Captain Collier pushing the blade closer to my throat and forcing me silent. I glare at Bellandi, standing tall with my chin held high. I will not show fear. I will not let him shake me.

I've been caught. I'm a dead girl walking—it's only a matter of minutes now. But I still have a job to do.

I have to convince Collier.

"Renza Di Maineri killed Nouis Rizaro, the hero in our hour of need, in a fit of violent rage. Because he uncovered the truth of her treason. Thankfully, before he died, he told me what she's been doing. The crimes she's committed against you, good people. And now, she will pay for her actions. Captain, bring her here."

"No! You're the traitor! You betrayed the people!" I scream, fighting against Collier's grip as he starts to drag me towards Bellandi. I dig my heels into the dusty stone pavement, thrashing against his marble grip.

"Citizens of Halice, let this be a lesson. See this as the

punishment for all those who go against the will of Fate," Bellandi sneers.

"Halicians, I beg of you, don't fall for his lies," I scream at the top of my lungs, fighting with every step as they drag me up onto the steps. "Cardinal Bellandi blew up the Grand Temple. Why else was he not there for service? Why else would he return with a Militia he's used to beat us down, to scare us in our own homes. To stop you asking questions. To stop you working out the truth."

"Enough of this—"

I'm dragged next to Bellandi, Collier forcing me to my knees in front of him. My knees sting against the stone floor, but I keep shouting, keep screaming to anyone who would listen.

"An army is on its way here right now. An army that will slaughter and destroy. Murder our children, rip away our freedom once and for all."

"Enough drama." Bellandi sighs dramatically like it's all beneath him. "Captain, do your job. Execute her."

"Why else would he want me quiet?" I scream, turning desperately to Captain Collier, "Why else would he want me dead? He stole from my bank to pay the army. He killed the Electi to have an excuse to bring his men inside the city, to take it from us. Bellandi is the traitor."

"Captain, I already explained to you—"

I turn back to Bellandi, screaming so loudly my throat might be shredded. "You lied. You used my Soulhatred to turn Idris Patricelli and I against each other. But we figured you out. Idris and I worked out the truth. We defy you. For the people of Halice, we defy the gods themselves! You're a traitor! A dirty, bloodthirsty traitor!"

"Your wicked lies won't save you now," barks Bellandi, face pulling tight with a sneer. "Captain."

Silence reigns over the square. Collier glances between us both, mouth thinned and eyes wide.

"Captain," Bellandi snarls. "You know your orders—execute her."

"Please. Believe me," I plead with Collier, staring into his brown eyes. "Even if you kill me, please, please, believe me. The army is coming. You need the City Guard together. You need to fight back."

"If this were real, then where is Idris Patricelli?" smirks Bellandi. "You say you worked together, so where is he?"

Captain Collier hesitates. The sword in his hand quivers as he stares at me with narrow eyes. My pulse mimics a landslide, crashing and rumbling and tumbling chaotically through my body. My breath rushes in and out of my lungs. My fingers tingle.

The bells ring. Tears of fear and joy slide down my face, a frantic laugh slipping from parched lips. I close my eyes in relief. Everyone turns their head up to the clear, glass domed roof to see him there, Idris Patricelli yanking on the bell ropes with all his strength.

Idris did it. The gates will close.

"We can keep the army out. We can fight them off," I gasp, unable to hold back the smile.

"You and Idris ... really are working together," Captain Collier realises loudly. The questions on his face make his hands tremble.

"They're traitors together. Can't you see that—" Bellandi starts.

"Then why ring the bells? Why come here, and risk all this just to close the gates?" demands Collier sharply. "Unless they really, truly believe an army is coming."

Bellandi scrambles for an answer. His grey eyes fly around the square, searching for an answer to spring from anywhere.

Heads snap to movement.

A child climbs onto one of the tables. I know him. Maso, from the school. His dark hair barely pops above the crowd. Determination mingles with nerves as he starts shouting.

"The Di Maineri gave me books. Gave all the kids books. Where else in the world can all the kids learn? Nowhere—I checked my atlas! But that didn't stop them. The Di Maineris did better, they gave us better, so I believe them. I believe Renza Di Maineri!"

I could cry. Maso is so brave. Gratitude and tears swell like a noose around my throat. But relief wins out pulling the foot off my lungs, finally letting me breathe properly for the first time today.

Another man starts talking, Franco. The sun bouncing off his soft mousy hair as he looks around at the people next to him.

"The Patricellis have brought industry to our city, and provided strong, steady jobs. They have kept my family in work for generations. If Patricelli says it's so, then I believe him. I believe Idris Patricelli."

"The Di Maineri sponsor the Garden," shouts Michelle, and I can feel the laugh and love bubbling up inside me as a stray tear rolls down my cheek. "Our city is an international beacon of science and art. I believe Renza Di Maineri."

"The Patricelli have fought crime," says Captain Collier far more quietly, turning to face Bellandi as his hand goes to his sword. "They've always ensured that the City Guard is well funded and well trained. They've always ensured fair and considered punishment. Halice is a safe city, and that's down to them. I believe Idris Patricelli."

Cries ring out from around the square. Some with stories. Some with just gratitude. It all blends together. But those words stand out.

"I believe Renza Di Maineri."

"I believe Idris Patricelli."

Honour, gratitude, relief, determination. It all mingles into a sensation both suffocating and empowering. My heart throbs; my blood sings with energy. Every muscle in my body wants to run and scream and fight and sing. Tears of joy jerk from my eyes, seeing them.

Them. My people. Their power is breathtaking. This is the beautiful, fighting spirit in the Halician people. The heart of our community.

"Don't let them take our city. Don't let them take our homes. For our futures, for our freedom. For Halice!" I shout at the top of my lungs, punching towards the sky. The crowd erupts with cheers, the noise all but deafening.

"Get her. Kill them! Kill them all!" snaps Bellandi. His face has lost any semblance of colour.

Collier spins to face the Church Militia in their black and white cloaks. They're quicker. The vicious silver metal slashes through his shoulder and into his heart. Collier drops to the stone stairs as his blood sprays over my face. My screams of horror melt into the roars of anger from the crowd as I try to fight for him. Two Militia grab my arms, hauling me towards the Watchtower behind Bellandi. Collier lies, eyes staring unblinkingly at the Halician sun, as he's suddenly swallowed by the advancing angry mob.

"No. Get off me." I resist, throwing my weight as much as I can but it's useless. They're so much stronger, I'm dragged out of the baking sunshine. Around me the people overwhelm the Militia, knocking them down. Hitting, kicking, fighting back however they can. A swarm of Halicians climbs the steps towards the building. Towards us.

But the large black doors are slammed shut. A large plank of wood comes down locking it in place.

Leaving me at the mercy of Bellandi.

CHAPTER 29

"Maineri! Patricelli! Halice!"

The chant is deafening. It bounces from every surface. It echoes in every corner. The city is shaking with the strength of its people. They refuse to be conquered. They refuse to surrender.

Their defiance and strength is true divinity. The most incredible privilege to experience, an honour to witness.

I've done all I can now. The rest is up to them.

I have little doubt of the outcome.

Bellandi is pale as stone, marching across the tiled floors. His ridiculous black and white robes flail around him, the hems still spattered with Collier's blood. He grips his head, spinning on the spot as if the answer might magically appear.

The Militia gripping me are not kind. Their fingers bite into my arms like teeth, yet the pain doesn't stop the smirk painted across my lips. Seeing Bellandi's distress is a savage kind of nectar.

Bellandi spots me, fear fleeing from his face. With teeth bared and eyes narrowed, he stalks towards me. His skin slowly turns red.

"You think you've won? You think you've done something? The army will be here soon. I just have to wait it out." Spittle flies from his lips, eyes bulging from their sockets.

"Even if you can, your Militia can't," I chuckle. "When that army arrives to see closed gates, then receives word that you are dead, that the city chewed up your zealots and spat them back to the gutter ... do you really think they'll continue? They aren't expecting a real fight. You didn't pay them for it."

Bellandi's back hand comes with such force I'd have been swept off my feet if it weren't for the Militia's painful grip on my arms. The slap ricochets around the hall. My head is flung sideways, my jaw straining under the jarring motion.

Pain floods my face, my cheek raw and stinging. My lips split open and copper coats my tongue.

I turn back, a laugh spilling from my broken lips and swirling with the blood.

"Isn't it funny how facing the truth can bring out the violence in weaker men? They rarely react so viscerally to lies. But the truth? Even if they're afraid to admit it? Oh how they erupt," I muse softly. "Violence is the mark of a weak man's truth."

I look him in the eye. If this is my last moment, I'll make it strong. If this is it, I shall die on my feet. Fighting till the very end.

I dig deep into the adrenalin flying around my body. My heart hammers like a stampede.

Banging starts at the doors. Dust falls from the ceiling. Windows start to smash as projectiles are launched inside. Diamond fragments fall in a river of gushing sunshine. Violent screams ring around this hallowed chamber. Bellandi grabs my face with one hand, digging his nails into the soft flesh of my cheeks. Metal, sharp as a razor, is pushed against the base of my throat and a trail of hot, sticky blood slowly starts to leak down my front.

"You think you're better than me?" Bellandi snarls. "Huh? You're going to die here, just like me. You're going to bleed out on this cold, unforgiving stone. I'm going to kill you, just like I killed your father. You'll die here, alone and in agony."

Disgust itches at my fingertips. Bile slowly crawls up my throat. My breath turns blistering and sharp.

I smile, embracing that familiar fire. "I'm not alone."

Bellandi wrinkles his nose. "Well, there's some good in this. At least I can finally shut you up."

Bellandi pulls his blade back, ready to strike.

Idris leaps down from the balcony around the bells, crashing on top of Bellandi as he falls. Bellandi slashes the knife wildly at me as they tumble. Agony explodes from my thigh and a shrill scream leaks from my lip. Crimson runs from the wound, the handle of the knife still protruding from the deep gash. I collapse to the floor, barely able to stand the pain tearing up and down my body. Bellandi kicks Idris off him. Two Militia grapple with Idris as Bellandi sprints off towards the stairs.

I grit my teeth and wrap my hand around the knife handle. I suck in a breath and yank hard, a roar escaping my lips as I spin and drive the dripping red blade into one of the

Militia's back. I tear it free, wrapping my arm around and slicing at his neck. The solider stops fighting, clawing at his throat as fresh, dark blood explodes forwards. A weaponless Idris quickly manages the last one, slamming his opponents head into the ground over and over.

Bile claws up my throat. My leg screams. My fingers itch with rage.

What's a little more? It would be so easy. No one would ever have to know.

Just some more blood.

More. More.

Idris gets to his feet, and I roll over, clenching my eyes shut.

"Get him! He ran to the stairs!" I pant, hand clamping over the wound on my leg.

"Together. Come on! We *need* to finish this together."

"I can't—" I gasp.

Idris stalks towards me, collapsing to his knees. He grabs my face with both hands, slamming his mouth down against mine. A bonfire surges through my blood. The rage, the fight sinking its teeth into every fibre of my being as he rips his punishing mouth from mine.

"You are stronger than any gods-cursed bond. Fate's Fury I would know," Idris says, gently shaking my head as he speaks. "Now get up and finish this!"

Finish this. For my father. For my friends.

For Halice.

I lock my gaze on the stairs Bellandi ran for. A surge of energy floods through my limbs. Fresh tears well in my eyes, frustration, loathing, grief, all brimming over. Above them all is rage. Fierce and brutal.

Idris grips my arm, hauling me to my feet. Gasping for breath, fresh pain splinters up my body. I take a step. My heart hammers in my ears. My skin ripples with sparks. My pulse itches at the tips of my fingers.

Half running, half lurching, we hunt down Bellandi. Idris is in step beside me, that familiar dark magnet always hovering at the edge of my vision. I know he's holding back, making sure I'm with him every inch of the way. But for once, I can't hear the whispers. That itching has faded into the background. Instead, I'm consumed with a visceral urge to avenge my city. The need to find justice for my family thrums in every step.

In tandem we march up the spiral wood staircase towards the roof, Bellandi's only possible path. Gasping for breath, my lungs ache as my feet hobble over the wooden stairs. Blood slips down my leg, leaving a bloody footprint trail in my wake.

"Come on. Come on," encourages Idris, as I use the banister to haul myself faster and faster up the steps. Teeth gritted, my face slick with tears and sweat, I scream with effort and leap for the door to the roof.

Nothing.

I turn the handle.

Locked. Bellandi locked it.

"Together," shouts Idris, launching his full body weight at the wood. Nodding, twisting my head away from him. I summon my strength and drive my shoulder into the door, the hinges cracking.

The hinges.

Behind me, Idris slams his body into the door again as I reach for the hinges with my blood-coated fingers, yanking out the pins. I shove it ajar. Idris does the rest, forcing the door away as in tandem we strike across the roof.

The sunshine is blinding. Above us is nothing but raw blue sky. In the centre, the glass dome of this building towers over us, our small section of roof overlooking the technicolour square.

At the far end of the building is Bellandi, still as a statue and staring over the crowd. They're raging against him, booing and hurling slurs. Calling for his blood. Trying to launch objects at him but he's too high.

Idris and I stalk towards him. The second we're in sight of the crowd, they go wild. It's deafening. Their voices crash over us like a tsunami, thrumming with my galloping pulse. We ready ourselves facing Bellandi, who slowly turns to see us.

He trembles, swallowing softly. He raises his hands to us, each digit shaking.

"You can't kill me. The Holy Mother will never forgive you."

"I can live with that," Idris answers, cold steel etched into his tone.

"Halice will be excommunicated," Bellandi breathes.

"Then we'll handle that too," I rebuff. How, I have no earthly idea. We'll have to cross that bridge later. But when I do, I have no doubt Idris will be there, like he is now, fighting right beside me.

"Alive, I'm a bargaining piece. You could trade me back to the Holy Mother in exchange for leniency."

Idris steps closer to him, and Bellandi falls silent, eyes wide with fear.

"You slaughtered our families. Our friends. Do you think you get to walk away from that?" Idris's calm tone portrays the inevitability of the outcome. Bellandi shakes his head, face twisting as he launches for us. Idris tenses and tackles him to the floor. I dive left, grabbing hold of a discarded maintenance rope from one side. Idris wrestles Bellandi onto his front, flat against the roof. The whispers run rampant in my mind as the shadows of my Soulhate and my nemesis grapple. I tighten my fingers around the dry rope, before marching closer.

"No! No, please!" shouts Bellandi as I tie one end of the rope to a hooked anchor driven into the roof. Typically they're meant to support decorative banners. Today, it will be my gallows.

The other end, I deftly fashion into a noose. Idris wrestles Bellandi to his feet, and walks him towards the edge of the building. I march forwards, slipping the rope around Bellandi's neck.

"I, Member Renza Di Maineri, last standing Electi of Halice, sentence you to death for treason. May Fate grant you mercy, for I have none."

I step back.

"No! No, you can't! No!"

Idris boots Bellandi over the edge of the roof.

Bellandi screams all the way down.

Then snaps silent.

The crowd erupts, cheering and waving.

"Maineri! Patricelli! Halice!"

"Maineri! Patricelli! Halice!"

Panting, my chest swells and my eyes sting. Tears blur the edges of the world as I fight the urge to double over and sob.

It's done. We did it.

Halice fought back.

With Idris to my left, we both stare out over the people. Our people. Their love. Their strength. It's more than I could ever have imagined.

"The people ... they fought. For us," Idris whispers in awe.

"We're Halicians. We look after each other."

I wrap my fingers around his hand. I launch our linked hands into the sky, fingers interlocked tight.

Because we did this together. No gods in heaven, nor monsters on earth were strong enough to break us. They did their best.

We did better.

And the whole world will know it.

CHAPTER 30

Patchy grey and white clouds swirl across the gentle sky. Market Square is thick with artists and engineers. I stand amongst their creations, watching their mastery unfold.

Could it only be four days ago that this square was the site of such bloodshed? The grime has been scraped from the perfect pale stone, the bodies collected, the damage repaired. Not a trace of the gratuitous violence remains.

Spotless.

Yet the city is different. Changed. Its gentle soul forever marred by bloody handprints.

I run a finger over the tight bandage on my thigh and the scar that's neatly forming there.

Scars, in all their forms, are beautiful. The marks of wars won. Of battles survived.

Scaffolding wraps around the ugly square Watchtower as the repairs are carried out. Repairs and improvements, of course. Because this spotless space chews away at my mind.

Because we can't sweep this under the rug and forget. We can't ever forget what we almost lost.

Or what we did to take it all back.

Some people didn't make it of course. The Holy Militia are a highly trained force. The Di Maineri family are sponsoring a monument to the lost heroes of Halice to sit in this square. They should never be forgotten—their sacrifice gave our city exactly what it needed.

Every single member of the Garden is contributing something to make it astonishing. All the colours of the rainbow I'm told. But it's not enough. People need to remember it all. The heroes.

And the villains.

So up on that scaffolding, amongst the builders and stonemasons are several artists, painting a rendition of what people have been calling the Great Rebellion. Of the people rising up to save their city, of Idris and me standing on the roof, hands joined in victory. But also of Bellandi, hanging from the roof, meeting his untimely end.

"That's a public building you're defacing. Spectacularly, I might add."

I smirk, not turning to the sound of that deep voice. Itching crawls up my fingers and my throat goes tight. It'll always be there, this physical reaction to his presence. It'll never leave. But now somehow ... it's become so familiar. Not easier, not better, nowhere even close to comfortable. But familiar. Likable.

Because when he's here, I have an ally.

And somehow that makes it all a fraction more bearable.

He turns, us both standing back-to-back as we look

around the square. Inches apart, goosebumps race up and down my arms. I close my eyes and let out a shaky breath, taking a moment to let the sensation of Idris's presence rush over me.

"So, why the grim painting?" Idris's voice is soft, his words meant only for me. I open my eyes, gaze turning back to the half-finished art.

"People need the reminder of what we do to traitors in Halice."

"Well, it's certainly a message. As is the wagon sent to the Holy Mother. Filled with art depicting the rebellion ... along with the rotting, beheaded corpse of Bellandi."

"She needs to know what happened here. She needs to see the results of her work."

"It's not de-escalating conflict."

"I don't care." Those words rip at my throat as they leave my tongue. "Just so long as she knows better than to try again. So long as everyone knows better."

"Everyone?" frowns Idris.

"Why do you think the Garden is so busy?" I shift, straightening my tunic. "I'm sending depictions and stories to every country you can name. Sending some of our best storytellers on commission to spread the truth amongst the people."

"That could appear aggressive."

"In their next sermon, every preacher on the continent will be talking about the horrendous slaughter of the Church inside Halice. They'll carve a false narrative about us being vicious heathens, painting the Holy States as innocent victims and scapegoats. I won't have that. People need to know the truth. Even if they don't acknowledge it, they'll have heard it and unconsciously be aware of what the Holy States is willing to try."

"Which could bring us allies. Particularly if they think they could be next on the Holy States' chopping block."

"We're going to need allies to fight off the Holy States. They were our best trading partner. Obviously we need to diversify. To fight a war we need money; to get money we need trade. To get trade, we need allies."

Idris chuckles, shifting behind me. My heart jumps as I feel the tips of his warm fingers brush against the outside of my hand. Hot sparks streak through my bones as my breath hitches.

"Playing politics already. You're clearly feeling better."

"Everything is politics, Idris. Don't you know that by now?"

"I'll consider you a master to learn from."

"Going to name-drop me in the future?"

"Are you kidding? When I was in Halice I fought in a revolution alongside the great and powerful Renza Di Maineri."

I snort. "And don't you forget it."

"Never," he promises. His fingers wrap more securely around mine, the warmth of his touch sets my pulse throbbing in my ears. A smile flirts with the corners of my mouth. The bustling square keeps moving. No one bothers to stare at us anymore. No one is worried that we'll leap at each other's throats. They believe we can do this, and finally so do I.

"I do have one question. Why'd it take so long for you to ring the bells?"

"Ah that."

"You had ages!"

"Bellandi removed the ropes," Idris snorts. "I had to run around trying to link them all up again."

I laugh, pressing my free hand to my face. Of course he did.

"How's the leg?" Idris asks carefully, joined hands reaching softly for it. The loose red dress hides the thick bandages quite nicely. The moment my fingers press against the muscles, aching shoots up to my stomach. "Sore."

"It was a nasty gash. How are the stitches?"

"I'll live. You?"

"Nothing lasting."

"Good." I mean it.

Fate might disagree.

"Why are you really here, Idris?" I push. He clearly isn't going to spit it out without a little nudge.

"I hear you're working on a new budget," he says. "Reallocating funds."

"You don't think it's valid? Our city has just been robbed blind. Don't you think a reassessment and redistribution has merit?"

"I didn't say that!" Idris laughs. "But you're being sneaky, trying to put extra money into the Garden's Fund."

"It's hardly sneaky. It's right there in the paperwork."

"We just started a war with the Holy States. We need to fully fund the Guard—we can't be weak for the next attack."

"Agreed. But we also need weapons. We don't have numbers. We don't have land. So we need another advantage. We need a surprise, just like our traps. That money is for weapons research."

"Tricks and traps need the element of surprise. Next time we won't have that."

I pause, turning that over for a minute. "So I can't count on your vote?"

Idris laughs, his back presses deeply against mine and he tightly squeezes our joined fingers. Goosebumps race up my arms and bitterness strokes the length of my tongue. I lean into that feeling, those fiery waves that come when I lean my head back, pressing into the warmth of his back.

"I guess I'll have to defeat your bill in the High Chamber, Di Maineri."

"Bring it on, Patricelli."

A moment passes between us. I swallow, forcing out the words I know need to be said.

"Halice has a long way to go, to become safe again..." I start, trailing off.

Idris pauses for a moment before answering. "I know."

"So we should be focused, on Halice. Focused on our work." I clear my throat, before continuing, "No distractions."

Idris doesn't answer for a moment, but I know he understands my meaning. Then I hear a small, amused scoff. He turns to look at me. I take a deep breath to slow my pulse as I turn around. He reaches forwards, tracing the tips of his fingers slowly from my elbow to my wrist. Stars fly in their path, my heart throbbing in my throat.

Idris gives a small smirk.

"As you wish," Idris answers, a quiet, patient challenge thick in his words. Without another word, he turns and walks away. I watch him retreat for a moment before turning back to the work happening around me. I barely see the people though, the ghost of Idris's fingers still bringing goosebumps to my arm.

I'm in trouble. In more ways than one. But I'm Renza Di Maneri. I can handle a bit of trouble.

Acknowledgments

I've wanted to be an author ever since I was five and realised that people could actually write stories for a living. Achieving my lifelong dream wouldn't have been possible without the amazing team of people who have supported me on this journey.

To my wonderful, brilliant husband, to whom I am eternally grateful, thank you for everything. For talking about topics varying from plot to prose, to calming my nerves when on query or sub, and supporting me and celebrating every success no matter how small.

To my mum, who introduced me to the first love of my life: books (sorry husband), thank you for encouraging me, pushing me, and believing that this dream could be a reality. Without you, I wouldn't have had the gumption to find my agent and none of this would be happening. Thank you.

To the rest of my family, thank you for your never-ending support. A particular shout out to my father who doesn't really get books, or reading, but has been a non-stop cheerleader during the writing and editing process. He has taught himself all about the publishing industry just so that he can support me. He's incredible.

To Georgia Gamble, one of my nearest and dearest friends in the whole world, thank you. Somehow you found time in your incredibly busy PHD schedule to read my drafts, articles and submission packets. I appreciate every single second of your support, and I can't wait to celebrate both of our achievements with a well-deserved girls' trip.

To Bethany Lucas, thank you so much for taking a chance on the girl babbling on about *The Hunger Games* and *Game of Thrones* at a writing festival.

To my brilliant agent Saskia Leach, of the Kate Nash Literary Agency, thank you for absolutely everything you do. Thank you for supporting my every query or question, and believing in me and my work. I couldn't ask for a better agent in the whole wide world.

Thank you to my amazing editor, Bonnie, and the fabulous team at One More Chapter. Talking about romantasy, soulmates/soulhates and all things fantastical has just been amazing. Thank you for answering all my questions and helping make this book the absolute best it can be.

Thank you to Emma Haynes at the Blue Pencil Agency, and also Elane Retford and Sarah Snook from I Am In Print Ltd for all your workshops, advice, writing festivals and more, not to mention all the wonderful in person support. The resources you provide are absolutely invaluable to any writer looking to hone and polish their craft. Thank you from the bottom of my heart.

Also thank you to everyone who has ever supported my small business Kingdom Book Designs. I love books in all their forms, particularly those with sprayed edges. To be able to create luxury, limited edition sprayed edges is beyond amazing, and the support I've received for all my bookish endeavours is awesome. Thank you to everyone for making that possible too!

And finally, but certainly not least, to my cat, Billy. Somehow, I completed this book despite your constant demand for attention and your countless attempts to sleep on my keyboard. Thank you for every midnight cuddle, biscuit making session and for listening to all my plot and character dilemmas with an utterly unamused expression.

ONE MORE CHAPTER
YOUR NUMBER ONE STOP FOR PAGETURNING BOOKS

The author and One More Chapter would like to thank everyone who contributed to the publication of this story...

Analytics
James Brackin
Abigail Fryer

Audio
Fionnuala Barrett
Ciara Briggs

Contracts
Laura Amos
Laura Evans

Design
Lucy Bennett
Fiona Greenway
Liane Payne
Dean Russell

Digital Sales
Lydia Grainge
Hannah Lismore
Emily Scorer

Editorial
Janet Marie Adkins
Kara Daniel
Charlotte Ledger
Federica Leonardis
Ajebowale Roberts
Jennie Rothwell

Harper360
Emily Gerbner
Jean Marie Kelly
emma sullivan
Sophia Wilhelm

International Sales
Peter Borcsok
Ruth Burrow
Colleen Simpson

Inventory
Sarah Callaghan
Kirsty Norman

Marketing & Publicity
Chloe Cummings
Grace Edwards
Emma Petfield

Operations
Melissa Okusanya
Hannah Stamp

Production
Denis Manson
Simon Moore
Francesca Tuzzeo

Rights
Helena Font Brillas
Ashton Mucha
Zoe Shine
Aisling Smythe

Trade Marketing
Ben Hurd
Eleanor Slater

The HarperCollins Distribution Team

The HarperCollins Finance & Royalties Team

The HarperCollins Legal Team

The HarperCollins Technology Team

UK Sales
Isabel Coburn
Jay Cochrane
Sabina Lewis
Holly Martin
Harriet Williams
Leah Woods

eCommerce
Laura Carpenter
Madeline ODonovan
Charlotte Stevens
Christina Storey
Jo Surman
Rachel Ward

And every other essential link in the chain from delivery drivers to booksellers to librarians and beyond!

ONE MORE CHAPTER

YOUR NUMBER ONE STOP FOR PAGETURNING BOOKS

One More Chapter is an award-winning global division of HarperCollins.

Subscribe to our newsletter to get our latest eBook deals and stay up to date with all our new releases!

signup.harpercollins.co.uk/join/signup-omc

Meet the team at
www.onemorechapter.com

Follow us!
- @OneMoreChapter_
- @OneMoreChapter
- @onemorechapterhc
- @onemorechapterhc

Do you write unputdownable fiction?
We love to hear from new voices.
Find out how to submit your novel at
www.onemorechapter.com/submissions